ARABESQUES 2

EDITED BY
SUSAN SHWARTZ

AVON BOOKS  NEW YORK

ARABESQUES 2 is an original publication of Avon Books. This work has never before appeared in book form. This is a work of fiction. Any similarity to actual persons or events is purely coincidental.

AVON BOOKS
A division of
The Hearst Corporation
105 Madison Avenue
New York, New York 10016

Copyright © 1989 by Susan Shwartz
Cover illustration by James Warhola
Published by arrangement with the author
Library of Congress Catalog Card Number: 88-92960
ISBN: 0-380-75570-X

First Avon Books Printing: July 1989

Other Avon Books Edited by
Susan Shwartz

ARABESQUES:
MORE TALES OF THE ARABIAN NIGHTS

To Alexander Borodin,
with a little help from his friends
Hajj the Beggar, Lalume, Marsinah,
and the Caliph

Special thanks to Janet Kagan

Acknowledgments

Framing material: "On Wings of Storm," "The Tale of the First Djinni," "Tests of Wit and Law," "The Tale of the Second Djinna," "Tests of Illusion," "Tests of Trust," "The Ruse That Failed," "The Tale of the Third Djinni," "Tests of Love," and "Dawn Songs" by Susan Shwartz. Copyright © 1989 by Susan Shwartz. Used by permission of the author.

"The Djinn Who Watches Over the Accursed" by Stephen R. Donaldson. Copyright © 1989 by Stephen R. Donaldson. An original story used by permission of the author.

"The Wishing Game" by Larry Niven. Copyright © 1989 by Larry Niven. An original story used by permission of the author.

"Curse of the Three Demons" by Harry Turtledove. Copyright © 1989 by Harry Turtledove. An original story used by permission of the author.

"The Tale of the Four Accused" by Gene Wolfe. Copyright © 1989 by Gene Wolfe. An original story used by permission of the author.

"The Three Brides of Hamid-Dar" by Tanith Lee. Copyright © 1989 by Tanith Lee. An original story used by permission of the author.

"The Houri's Mirror" by Esther M. Friesner. Copyright © 1989 by Esther M. Friesner. An original story used by permission of the author.

"Ali Achman and the City of Illusion" by Ru Emerson. Copyright © 1989 by Ru Emerson. An original story used by permission of the author.

"Al-Ghazalah" by Judith Tarr. Copyright © 1989 by Judith Tarr. An original story used by permission of the author.

Contents

ON WINGS OF STORM

Peter of Wraysbury lay like a dead man, staring up at an incomprehensible sky. At times, it was almost translucent, as if he stared through thick, greenish glass at the true sky beyond; in the next moment, though, it took on the appearance of brass, neglected and pitted by sand as harsh as that on which he had found himself lying. Around him, he could hear the groans and curses of the other members of his caravan, sounds curiously detached from those other noises that must accompany them: the screams of frightened horses and the hoarse imprecations of camels.

He forced attention away from the enigma of the sky and to the men around him. Weeks ago, he and the merchant prince who had been his master and was now his partner had ridden out of Kashgar at the head of a veritable army of horse dealers, silk merchants, warriors, jewelers, and even a healer and a storyteller or two—not to mention their servants, their animals, and their baggage. Now, but a few of those men drew near him. And like him, they glanced up at the strange, brazen sky.

Praise God, he thought, *at least the storm has vanished.* Fortune's wheel had come round again. At one moment, he had ridden at the head of a caravan laden with wares that would be the envy of the Holy Roman Emperor. Around him were the men whom—inexplicably—God had made his friends, his rescuers from slavery, and, yes, his brothers. *Not* around him, praise God again, were the men who had brought his ransom from Edward of England; they might be his brothers in Christ and in knighthood, but beyond that, he wanted nothing more of them, nor they of

1

him. He had wealth, he had work, he had friends on whom he had wagered his freedom—and he rode toward the fulfillment of his vow to seek the mystic kingdom of Prester John, that priest and ruler.

To the north lay the mountains called Tien Shan, or Heavenly Mountains: cloud-capped, fading into the trackless depths of the sky in what clearly must be a vision of Heaven Itself, dwarfing man, beast, and the titanic dunes that wound like dragons. Beneath mountains and dunes, his mighty caravan dwindled to the size of chessmen, and the sand whispered at them as they passed. *Ming sha*, the old Ch'in healer called it: the singing sand.

Then the song had turned savage. Scarcely had the master merchant pointed at what, only an instant before, had looked like a blotch—a flaw in the otherwise perfect gem of a sky—when the wind started to howl, the sky to darken with sand, grit, and pebbles. Veteran of many of the *kuraburan*, the black, goblin storms of the deep desert, Peter muffled his face and eyes, leapt from his mount, and raced with the others of the caravan to wrap beasts and goods in thick felt.

Piercing the howl of the storm, which had not yet built to its full frenzy, came the panicked shrieks of horses and the calls of their handlers, desperate to prevent the beasts from bolting into the storm that could flense flesh from bodies and leave the sand-etched bones whitening in the desert whose very name—Takla Makan Shamo—meant "if you enter here, you do not come out."

Shameful as it was for a knight to admit fear, Peter of Wraysbury feared the *kuraburan*. One such storm had cost him all that he possessed; had all but cost him his life, were it not for the charity of the merchant prince who had rescued him.

And with the roar of the wind, the hiss of the sand, and the shouts and screams of men and beast, came yet another sound, so quiet that it must surely be the work of demons that he heard it at all: the laughter and gossip, only half-understood, of beings that suddenly appeared in the struggling wreckage of what had been an orderly train of men and animals. Unlike the mortal creatures, these beings stood erect, untroubled by the whipping, sand-laden gusts that prevented Peter from seeing them clearly.

The one that was closest . . . it turned toward him, and winked. Surely that was a third eye in the center of its forehead. Then it laughed, a sound so hideous that Peter's knees weakened. "Free!" shrieked a voice.

The last thing he felt, though, was appallingly, ironically familiar: as a boy, he had often dived into the river by his father's keep. Now, he had the same sensation of leaving earth, committing himself to air. But instead of a cool plunge into the depths of a river, surely he felt himself falling through hot, turbulent air—and, at that, falling *upward*. He heard triumphant laughter, a few shrieked prayers, and then the wind snatched breath and consciousness away from him.

THE TALE OF THE FIRST DJINNI

Peter felt a callused hand on his shoulder. "We are out of my reckoning, friend," said the merchant prince hoarsely, his speech stripped of its usual elaborate compliments. "You too are a traveled man. Can you tell me if aught in your journeyings has resembled this?"

He gestured up at the mysterious sky, which looked like opaque glass now, of a weight so heavy that an alchemist might choose it to hold proscribed liquids. Or, Peter thought, a mage or caliph might use it to hold . . .

"Sweet Christ," he whispered, and his hand dropped from his brow to cross himself.

You do not understand the nature of the bottle." He recalled a line from a story that he had heard in Kashgar in what seemed like an infinitely better life and infinitely long ago.

The story's hero had been a sailor and a slave; and he had been slain after rescuing a djinna, only to wake and find himself pent with his love in her bottle until such time as they should be freed.

Had he and the handful of men about him been separated from the caravan only to be shut up in a bottle like djinn? Peter shuddered though the air was far from cool. Instantly, a breeze caressed his forehead, and the sand on which he stood stirred softly. He thought of thirst, and a delicate spring bubbling up by his feet.

When he saw the merchant's face pale he realized that he had spoken his fear aloud. What was more, the merchant was staring down at the spring that had appeared where no water had ever flowed before.

5

"Allah," he whispered. The Name faded into a moan.

"Excellent, most sapient Son of Adam!" a voice hailed him. Only the merchant's hand, its fingers clutching his shoulder, saved him from turning a stagger into a fall.

He had always thought that the voices of the djinn were loud and hideous. But *this* djinni was possessed of a voice as sweet and persuasive as a squire with his lady: cultivated, insinuating, and altogether terrifying.

"Show yourself!" His challenge came out as a caw, a bray, after that polished, sonorous greeting.

"I salute you, and all the rest of you, Sons of the Prophet," said the djinni. Taloned fingers materialized and flicked from breast to lips and eyes. What assumed more and more substance until, finally, it stood fully fleshed upon the sand a safe distance away, appeared to be a man, splendidly and conservatively robed in saffron and sapphire brocades, of later than middle age. His hair and beard were whitening; and he had a thin, aquiline nose, a mouth made even thinner by what seemed a habit of self-command, and eyes that caught and held the gaze of every man of the caravan.

Though they were deeply embedded in the down-turning furrows that the sun ploughs into the faces of those desert-born, they were by far the most arresting feature of the djinni's countenance: intense, black, with pinpricks of what seemed like flame in their depths. That in itself might have been fearful. But the djinni's eyes were immeasurably old and sad.

He bowed with the grace of the desert-born. Peter tried to match the perfection of that bow and achieved only the formal stiffness that, throughout Muslim lands, made men and the occasional veiled woman smile, as this veritable Emir among djinn now did.

Carefully, Peter drew a cross before him, but the djinni simply smiled more widely.

"No doubt you will tell us why you brought us here," he stated. "Wherever *here* is."

"Here?" inquired the djinni, who might have been talking of a bazaar stall. "We are in the heart of the desert here." He raised a brow in ostentatious revelation. "Ah! It is that you cannot see what lies about you. Will this remedy your care?"

He clapped his hands, and light flashed on the talons that were his most obvious difference from the humanity he aped so convincingly. Peter glanced away...

And found himself staring at an amphitheatre much like the Roman ruins he had seen once in the south of France. Its archways were curtained by the same lavish, gilt-shot silks that cushioned the pale stone seats—and clad the djinn who sat watching what they clearly expected to be a most boring entertainment. Tusked, dis- or multicolored, bearing multiple eyes, feathers, or claws, they all wore the same expression that Peter had felt on his own face during particularly boring sermons. More confusing yet were those faces, those bodies that shifted from a semblance of fair humanity to monstrosity and back again. They watched with a kind of longing, even hope.

"By the Beard of the Prophet"—the merchant prince turned and stood toe to toe with the djinn before them—"and by the seal of Suleiman ibn Daoud, I conjure you not to harm us and to release us at once."

The djinni's eyes flickered, revealing a wholly different semblance beneath the human mask he wore. Then he recovered and made another sweeping obeisance, hand flicking again from breast to lips and brow. "We honor the Prophet and Suleiman the Wise. Consider yourselves our honored guests."

Again, the imperious hand-clap and flash of light. When "normal" light was restored, the sand about the caravanners was strewn with rugs and cushions as rich as those in the amphitheatre; maidens decently veiled but otherwise scantily clad in rainbow gauzes walked among them, light picking out the aching harmonies of breast, upheld arm, and outstretched hands on which finely chased trays, goblets, and bowls lay balanced.

"It were well not to taste that," warned the storyteller at Peter's back. "The Greeks have a tale of a maid who but nibbled at a pomegranate and was confined to hell for her hunger."

"We have our own food," muttered a voice at Peter's back, truculent with fear. "He is no host but a captor!"

"Hush!" whispered the physician. "Offend the djinn, and they may make food of us!"

The merchant bent and spoke quickly in Peter's ear: "He obeys the laws of hospitality and can bear the name of Allah. In the name of Allah, let us take the adventure that befalls us."

"In the name of God," Peter agreed.

Bowing at the djinni, he and the merchant seated themselves, beckoned to the nearest maid, who brought rosewater for washing and soft cloths. Refreshed, they sank back, goblets of sherbet near to trembling hands.

"You do not join us, my lord?" Peter ventured.

"Ah no; a thousand pardons," said the djinni. "I have a condition that restricts my diet. Boredom. Ultimate, total, and terrible boredom." His dark eyes lit then, and followed the houris as they undulated by. "Though it may be that that condition will improve along with our acquaintance."

"That is why you brought us here?" The storyteller moved forward, his eyes alight with curiosity.

The djinni kindled at his presence. "Yes!" he said. "To know life once again! To feel hope and fear and desire. None of us who live in the deep desert have felt such things since Suleiman ibn Daoud set his seal upon us and made us his servants."

"So you brought us here to entertain you."

The djinni stretched out his hands to the men. "I beg you . . . *we* beg you, do we not, my brothers and sisters? Do not think of my deed as kidnapping. Say, rather, that we rescued you from a storm."

"We have survived demon storms before," said one of the men, a dealer in horses.

"Ah, but this is a storm from the very heart of the desert, such as you have never before encountered. No need for you to think, though, of your stay here as imprisonment. Think of it as a trip into wonders, wealth, and freedom such as you have never known. We can show you marvels . . . cliffs wrought of diamonds, measureless caverns holding seas that have never felt the touch of sunlight, wise serpents, flying horses, oases in which live the fair-haired descendants of Iskandar himself"—the magnificent voice turned imploring—"if you but pledge to stay with us!"

Again, the wave of longing, hope, and ancient sorrow washed out from the assembled djinn.

"Knowledge," whispered the healer; "Such stories!" marveled the teller of tales; and "Wealth!" husked from a number of the merchants.

Compared with what the djinni offered, what were the attractions of wife and family for the merchant prince, or the splendors of Prester John's court for Peter of Wraysbury?

Only the sacredness of their obligations and their vows.

"Should we accept your inestimable offer, we would be traitors to those we left behind," said the merchant. "A thousand thousand regrets, but we must beg to be returned."

"And he will refuse!" the storyteller hissed urgently, kneeling between the two caravan leaders. "He will refuse; you will call upon Allah; and those of us, man *or* djinn, who die swiftly shall be the lucky ones."

"Well, wise one," whispered Peter, with a notable absence of compliments. "What do you suggest?"

"Let me ply my trade," cried the teller of tales. He rose from his knees and assumed the grandeur that he could put on and take off for each story. "Rhymes, fine rhymes have I; tales aplenty of love, of blood, of sorrow and sweetness."

Like Scheherezade, did the man propose to *talk* them free? To the end of his life, Peter would never understand this fondness for tales and the power they held. Nor, he thought, if this worked, would he cease to be grateful to it. He would have masses said when he reached the court of Prester John; he would build a chapel . . . but what else he would do was drowned out in the roar of assent from the assemblage of djinn.

"A game! a game!" they cried, reminding Peter unpleasantly of the Romans and their habit of turning thumbs down upon victims—or unleashing lions upon Christians like himself. He dropped hand to sword hilt, and jerked fingers away from the uncomfortable heat of the leather wrapping the tensile metal.

The storyteller stood, head bowed, as if accepting an ovation.

"Aye," breathed the Emir of the Djinn (for such he was). "A game we shall have. Here are the rules by which you may win your freedom, your passage back to your caravan, and to the beauty of the open skies:

"You shall not be overpowered or overawed by the djinn. You shall tell us tales that hold our interest for as long as you may, or until you acknowledge yourself vanquished. You shall delight, divert, and entertain us utterly..."

"A moment, mighty Emir," cried the physician. "We have only your word that you are entertained. What surety have we..."

"That we shall keep our word? You trespass too far!" roared the djinni. His eyes blazed and the force of his rage and his voice battered the caravanners like the force of a *kuraburan*.

"Nevertheless," said the storyteller, "good rules make for good contests. How shall we know if we have won?"

"Why," said the Emir, "that is simple. Look at us now, as we are. If you prove the victors, we shall become young again.

"Now," he said, "for the terms of the contest. You must hear three stories, told by those among us who, during thousands of years, have been acknowledged as masters of the art. You must reply to them without hesitation. If you cower in fear of us, or confess yourself baffled or silenced ... you are ours. If we sleep ... you are ours. But if you conquer, we restore you to your people, to all that is yours, and to more besides.

"Will that content you?"

"It must," muttered Peter, though all about him, the sons (and daughters) of a tradition that esteemed taletelling as it did water in the desert, roared assent.

"Very well," said the Emir of the Djinn. "Dispose yourself to listen to me. For I shall tell the first tale."

The Djinn Who Watches
Over the Accursed

Stephen R. Donaldson

Fetim of the al-Hetal made a serious mistake when he allowed himself to be caught in the bed of Selmet Abulbul's youngest and most delectable wife. The mistake was not instantly obvious, however. Selmet was old and infirm: there was nothing physical that he could do to Fetim, who was at least as strong as he was handsome. Furthermore, Selmet was unpopular, being a usurer: he had no friends he could call on to fight for him. Public opinion, in fact, would have applauded Fetim's choice of cuckolds. And, sadly, the Abulbul clan was in decline. Selmet had no relations or children who might be persuaded to view Fetim's action as a matter of honor. In short, he did not appear to be a man who could avenge insults.

But Selmet Abulbul the usurer knew how to curse.

While Fetim preened himself beside the bed, lacking even sufficient decency to be frightened, and the young wife pretended to cower among the sheets, Selmet called upon a few names which I am not permitted to record. He uttered several phrases which it would be sacrilege for me to repeat. Then, his voice quaking with rage, he explained what he wished the powers whose attention he had invoked to do to Fetim of the al-Hetal.

"In the name of the great father of djinn, let all those he loves be killed. Let him be readily loved—and let all those who love him die in anguish. Let all his seed and all his blood be brought to ruin. Let horror cover the heads of all who befriend him. Let his friendship be a surer sign of death than any plague-spot.

11

"And let the djinn who watches over the accursed protect him, so that his sufferings cannot end."

From such a curse, Selmet's youngest wife was safe: she loved no one but herself. But the clan of the al-Hetal was prosperous in that town. Hearing his doom, Fetim should have found it in his heart to be frightened.

He did not. "Are you done?" he asked politely. "We are taught that it is rude to leave a room while our elders are speaking."

Selmet's youngest wife also did not understand curses. A snicker at her husband's expense escaped from the sheets.

"Go!" Selmet shouted as well as he was able. "From this day forward, you will never forget that you would be happier dead."

Bowing with sardonic grace, Fetim left the house of Selmet Abulbul. Although his sport with the woman had been interrupted, his spirits were gay. It was gratifying that others knew of his successes. And the vengeance which Selmet might take upon his youngest wife was amusing to contemplate. In such benign good humor, Fetim turned his steps toward the high mansion where he lived with his mother, who thought him flawless, his father, who doted upon him, and his brothers, who worked harder than he did.

To his vast astonishment, he saw over the intervening rooftops that the mansion was in flames.

Fetim of the al-Hetal was not a notably selfless young man. Nevertheless, he had a warm place in his heart for anyone who loved him as much as he loved himself. In a frenzy which resembled concern for his parents and family —and which indeed did include some concern among its other considerations—he tore his hair and ran to see what was happening to his home.

Turmoil gripped the neighborhood. Men, women, and children raced in all directions, wailing. For some reason, the thought of water did not enter their heads, despite the fact that a history of fires had taught the town to respond promptly and efficiently. No one fought the blaze which tore at the walls and flailed from the windows of the fine mansion.

The destruction of Fetim's home was not a pleasant sight; but it was more pleasant than some of its details. He heard his mother scream and saw her in flames on the rooftop. Two of his nephews fell like stones to the street when one of his brothers' wives in desperation threw them out a window. A favorite servant who had cared for Fetim and taught him a great deal of fun as a boy died trying to descend the outer wall.

"Where is the fire brigade?" roared Fetim. But no one answered him. Everyone in the street was too busy running and yelling.

Then Akbar of the al-Hetal, Fetim's father, appeared before him. Akbar's clothes were still afire, and his eyes were mad. Inspired by the curse, he cried, "This is your doing!"

Fetim was so surprised that he did not defend himself when his father swung a cudgel at his head.

I deflected the blow, and he was no more than stunned. He recovered his wits in time to see Akbar die in front of him.

On this signal, the neighborhood commenced shouting:

"There he is!"

"He started the fire!"

"He killed his own family!"

"Stone him!"

Stones began to fly. None of them struck him seriously —although I was confident that he would not soon forget the bruises they left on his body—but they were enough to make him flee.

Led only by a desire to get away from the stones, he left the neighborhood and soon found himself at the gates of the town with a howling mob on his heels. The gates were open, as was customary on occasions of fire, in case the flames spread. The mob needed only a moment to drive Fetim out of the town where he had lived all his life—out onto the bare road which led into the desert.

There it became clear to me that he would not be able to run much farther. His life of self-indulgence had not prepared him for these exertions. And the mob would surely tear him limb from limb when he faltered. Therefore I caused his pursuers to lose sight of him. Shortly, they retraced their steps and set to work quelling the fire.

In the aftermath of the blaze, the neighborhood discovered that the damage had been confined to the clan of the al-Hetal, its dependents and friends. But of that sizable group of people, Fetim was the only survivor.

Because he did not know what else to do, he continued trudging along the road until nightfall. Then he threw himself down in order to bemoan his lot.

"It is unjust," he protested. "I am blameless. Any man would have accepted the invitation that woman gave me. Am I to be punished because she gave the invitation to me rather than to another? Selmet should not have married that heartless trollop. Yet his folly is inflicted upon me.

"Has there ever been a man as unfortunate as I am?"

"Actually," I replied, "it seems to me your family and friends are considerably more unfortunate." I spoke thus to provoke him. "You're merely accursed. They're all dead."

Apparently, he had believed himself alone. He gaped foolishly about him, as though I might be visible. "Who are you?" he asked.

"Think about it. You'll figure it out."

Who I was did not yet interest him, however. "You are wrong," he said. "Their deaths were painful, perhaps, but swift. And I will be blamed for it, although I am blameless. Also, they are free from misery. I must die slowly, alone and lost. I have neither food nor water. I have no camel. I know not where to go. I am entirely pitiable, and my sorrows are greater than any man has ever suffered."

"If you keep talking like that," I said, "I'm going to get bored in a real hurry."

"You cannot fault me! It was not I who pronounced the curse. It was Selmet Abulbul, punishing me for his own errors."

"'His own errors,' indeed. Do you want me to believe he forced you into his wife's bed against your will?"

"She invited me!"

"You accepted."

"It is not my fault!"

"So you keep saying."

Pretending to ignore me, Fetim of the now-defunct al-

Hetal wept for a while to prove how miserable he was. Then, instead of dying, he slept.

The next day, he continued down the road. After all, he was young and handsome. Surely the world loved him too well to prolong his travail. And, in fact, this seemed to be true. Before midmorning, an entire caravan caught up with him. By that time, he was dirty and tired, in no good humor; but the caravan-master chanced to like handsome young men with a thick sweat on them, and he offered Fetim a ride to the city of Niswan.

If Fetim had bothered to think about his circumstances, he might have believed that I had arranged this fortuitous offer for him. He would have been mistaken, however.

He did not find the caravan-master's attentions especially pleasant, but he endured them. On the one hand, he preferred women personally. On the other, he could not be surprised by the fact that he had been found attractive. And he had no money—as well as no taste for work. How else was he to travel in comfort? It was only a journey of some few days to Niswan, he had been assured. Then the unpleasantness would be over, and he would have the whole city before him in which to make his fortune. The prospect excited him boyishly.

Unfortunately, some few days were all the caravan-master required to conceive intentions of his own concerning Fetim. His name, when he chose to use it, was Rashid, and a number of years had passed since he had last shared a bed with a young man whom he considered as succulent as Fetim. Being neither shortsighted nor weak-minded, he grew jealous well in advance of Fetim's opportunities to merit such a reaction. First he began to plot ways to keep the young man with him when Niswan was reached. Then he began to consider how he might keep other men away.

The outcome was that, after the caravan had wound its dusty way past the gates and the guards of Niswan deep into the city's teeming bazaar, and the camels were at last stopped for unloading and profit, Rashid knocked Fetim on the head and sequestered him.

At first, this was a highly successful arrangement from Rashid's point of view—less so from Fetim's. The caravan-master now had at his whim a handsome young

man made even more tasty by the occasional savors of
truculent resistance and abject beggary. Nevertheless,
Fetim's sequestration was not long. The multitudes who
thronged the bazaar naturally included many men and
women of dubious virtue, individuals who reflexively coveted anything which anyone else kept hidden. One night,
Rashid leaped out of bed and grabbed at his knives too late
to prevent himself from being gutted like an ox in an abat-
toir. A remarkable amount of the blood splashed onto
Fetim. Then he was dragged away.

Before dawn, he found himself sold into slavery as a
desirable—if temporarily blood-sotted and noxious—catamite.

His purchasers tolerated no resistance. In any case, he
had little to offer, being accustomed to seek his own pleasure rather than to willingly undergo pain. Therefore he
submitted. It seemed conceivable that with the right degree
of complaisance and cunning his life could still be quite
pleasurable. Perhaps freedom was not too high a price to
pay for homage to his desirability. A few baths, a few
perfumes, a few hints, and he was set to work at love in a
luxurious stable of young men resembling himself.

The resemblance was only superficial, of course: the
other young men had not been cursed by such a proficient
as Selmet Abulbul. Rich merchants, minor sheiks, and occasional grandes dames discovered in Fetim an attractiveness which plucked at their hearts. They were less aware of
the fact that after a night or two with Fetim they were
prone to die horribly.

For some time, this caused him no difficulty. He was
more conscious that as an object of lust he found lust to be
less and less interesting. He was constrained to humble
himself: the practices which brought him love took on the
flavor of degradation. This, he thought, was the true
meaning of the old usurer's curse.

He was mistaken, however. In the same irrational way
that Akbar of the al-Hetal had pronounced his son responsi-
ble for the ruin of the clan, the family, friends, supporters,
and adherents of Fetim's butchered patrons concluded that
the stable which owned him was to blame for the deaths.
One night when he was especially miserable, a throng of

sheiks, swordsmen, and rabble burst into the richly ap-
pointed establishment and began slaughtering everyone
present.

This was naturally not an action which the owners of the
stable could permit to pass unchallenged. In the bazaars of
Niswan, no man or woman dared make a shekel's profit
without guarding it in some way. At once, forces which
had been retained for precisely this sort of emergency were
called out. The conflict quickly escalated, and in a short
time the gauze-curtained cubicle where Fetim had pleased
his patrons became the effective center of a fervid and
bloody battle.

Maimed and dying boys and women and bystanders
screamed. And Fetim screamed as well, although he was
unhurt. He knew almost nothing about defending himself.
In any case, he was unarmed. I was forced to work quickly
to keep him from being cut apart at any moment.

When I opened a corridor for him through the bloodshed, he found his legs and ran.

As he did so, both sides of the battle turned their enmity
in his direction and followed.

By this time, the entire city had been roused. The
King's forces marched to suppress the uprising—and
joined Fetim's pursuit. Brigands and looters sought to take
advantage of the chaos—and found themselves chasing a
young man they had never seen. In self-defense, good men
and respectable families armed their servants—who immediately snatched up torches and plunged into the tumult.

The great father of djinn himself must have been listening when Selmet Abulbul had cursed Fetim of the al-Hetal.
I was hard pressed to keep my charge alive.

I accomplished it by driving him into the sewer which
an enlightened king of a previous generation had caused to
be dug under the length of the city.

The stench and density of Niswan's effluvium eventually proved to be stronger than the curse. While I dragged
Fetim through the sewage—keeping his head above the
surface largely without his assistance—his pursuers one by
one lost interest in what they were doing and retreated.
Before we passed under the wall and emerged into the fetid

swamp which Niswan used as a cesspit, we had left behind everyone who wanted him dead.

Unceremoniously, I dredged him from the far end of the swamp. Then, because he still did not wish to make an effort on his own behalf, I let him fall to the dirt.

Once again, he sobbed like a girl. This time, however, his emotion was composed of revulsion and fear: his grief was for himself. After a while, he raised his head and said, "They deserved what happened to them. I wish I could have stayed to watch them die."

"Deserved it?" I asked. "What makes you say that?"

He blinked his eyes stupidly for a moment. "You are the djinn who watches over the accursed."

"Good for you. I knew you would figure it out eventually."

"I wish that you had rescued me sooner."

I ignored this inane remark. "Now that you know who I am, why don't you explain how all those dead and damaged people back there came to deserve what happened to them?"

"They enslaved me. They forced the most disgusting acts upon me. They took advantage of my loneliness and my helplessness to sate their foul lusts. Do not accuse *me*, djinn. I know my innocence."

"Good for you again. Did you resist them?"

"How could I resist them? They were many and strong. I am alone and weak."

"It's easy," I insisted. "You just say no. Then you keep saying no until they give up."

"Easy!" He snorted derision.

"All right. For you it wouldn't have been easy. You're too weak and helpless. What about Rashid?"

"Rashid?" Fetim had already forgotten the caravanmaster.

"Did you tell him you didn't want to be his catamite? Did you offer to work for your ride to Niswan? You did not. You saw that gleam in his eyes, and you thought, 'Here is another who will do all I wish and ask nothing because I am adorable in his sight.' He would've treated you honestly if you'd done anything to deserve honesty from him. And then all those poor people in Niswan would still be alive."

"Go away," he replied, cutting to the heart of the matter. "Go away and let me die. Then you will have no more cause to reproach me."

He did indeed appear pitiable as he huddled upon the verge of the swamp. Though I knew it to be a false kindness, I granted him silence.

In fact, he could have died. He was ignorant of any roads—and little able to care for himself. After a long and rancid night, he took to his feet with the dawn and walked out into the desert as though intending to exhaust himself and thereby hasten the end of his sufferings. Soon he was thirsty. And soon thereafter he was hungry. He had come away from Niswan without sandals, and the pressure of the sand began to wear sores on his feet. The sun blistered him. His needs took on the strength of rage. They expanded until they filled the horizons. Under the weight of the desert sun, his misery increased until it became as great as his self-pity. Then he collapsed into the sand.

Nevertheless a great journey lay ahead of him, which he must not shirk. It was not my task to make him comfortable. I did not permit his thirst to kill him, however. I kept his hunger within limits his flesh could bear. I did not allow the sores on his feet to become infected enough to threaten his life. And when he laid himself down with the avowed intention of not arising again, I reached into his mind and found enough fears to goad him back to his feet.

Gradually, his physical distress ground his self-pity and his revulsion and even his pride away: he had no strength for them. He had only his pain, his fear of death, and me.

After a number of days which he could not have counted—and which I had no interest in counting for him—he came to the River Kalabras. Falling on his face among the reeds at the riverbank he drank enough of the muddy water to ensure himself a fever.

While he drank, I observed a large felucca riding the current nearby. Confident that he would be rescued, I permitted him to lose consciousness.

The craft, called *Horizon's Daughter* by its master, proved to be a vessel of commerce which plied the River

Kalabras, carrying trade and passengers wherever they wished to go. As soon as the felucca's master, Mohan Gopal, saw Fetim fall among the reeds, he put about, anchored *Horizon's Daughter* against the current, and commanded two of his men into the River to bring Fetim aboard.

By this time, Fetim's condition would have aroused pity in a heart of stone. Far from having a heart of stone, however, Mohan Gopal was a man of such kindness that he would willingly have accepted a diminution of his profits in exchange for an opportunity to do a good deed. And on this voyage he was accompanied by his only child, Saliandra, a woman whose instincts of compassion exceeded his own. When Fetim had been dragged from the River Kalabras, Mohan and Saliandra were so struck by his tattered garments and mangled feet, his emaciation, and his look of madness, that they at once vacated their cabin under the felucca's stern for his use and devoted all the resources of *Horizon's Daughter* to his care.

As it chanced, Saliandra was not a beautiful woman. For that reason—and because her father loved her extremely—she was unwed. On the other hand, she was not ill-favored. Though her features were plain, her form was comely. When Fetim first opened his eyes and turned on Saliandra a gaze bright with illness, he believed that he had at last been lifted out of perdition into the realm of the houris.

"Be at rest," she cautioned him gently. "You are among friends."

Prostrate and feverish, he replied, "You are the only friend I will ever desire."

Had I been mortal, I would have gnashed my teeth and torn my hair.

Unable to do otherwise, however, I watched as *Horizon's Daughter* slid down the River Kalabras, and Saliandra tended the young man's broken health, and Mohan Gopal and his men made Fetim of the lost al-Hetal welcome among them as though he were an honored comrade.

The felucca was on its way downriver to great Qatiis, the storied and corrupt city of the Padisha, bearing a nearly priceless cargo of saffron—a cargo which had been entrusted to Mohan Gopal rather than to a flotilla of defenders by reason of his honesty, and also in hopes that *Horizon's Daughter* would not attract the notice of the river pirates.

Of this Fetim knew nothing, of course. To do him justice, it must be admitted that he had never felt an unreasonable interest in wealth. And now he was simply an invalid, scarcely able to hold his head up unassisted—deaf and blind to other considerations. His experiences in Niswan had taught him a deferential manner: his days in the desert had taught him gratitude. These qualities made him a satisfying invalid for which to care. By the time he became able to sit up on his pallet and sip a bit of soup, he was so well regarded aboard the felucca that Mohan Gopal had begun to consider offering him a share of the cargo's profits to help set him on his feet when *Horizon's Daughter* reached Qatiis.

The master's regard was reciprocated. The comradely feelings of the crew were shared—a bit shyly, perhaps, but not insincerely. And Saliandra's attentive concern was welcomed. To all appearances, Fetim was not the man he had been.

Now he noticed that Saliandra was not indeed a houri. Recovering enough strength to stand on his legs and converse, he also recovered enough clarity of vision to perceive that she was plain. But, oddly, this did not disconcert him. For the first time in his life, he considered that a woman's virtues might be of more importance than her face. And he was flattered by the fact that she was unmistakably smitten with him. Because of her great kindness, she thought highly of all things that needed her. Additionally, his sufferings had given his handsomeness a pensive and poetic cast which she found impossible to resist. She would willingly have laid down her life for him. This was not lust: it was love.

It was not surprising that she soon went to his bed. The surprise lay in the tenderness with which he accepted the sweets of her body.

Yet even that was not as surprising as his approach to Mohan Gopal the next morning, asking for permission to wed Saliandra.

The felucca's master considered that his daughter's acquaintance with Fetim was too brief to support a decision of marriage. And he went further: he ousted Fetim from the cabin, so that he and Saliandra could resume their normal sleeping arrangements—in other words, so that Saliandra's nights would be properly chaperoned. Nevertheless, he did these things with such obvious benevolence, with such a distinct intention to relent in a reasonable time, that his decrees caused no offense. Having once slept with Fetim, Saliandra was secretly amused by her father's unnecessary protectiveness. And Fetim only looked on his prospective father-in-law with more respect.

My task was unchanged, however. I prepared myself for battle.

When it came, the attack of the pirates was perplexing. On the one hand, it appeared to be founded on general principles, rather than on any specific awareness of *Horizon's Daughter*'s cargo. On the other, it lacked the usual ferocity of the curse. Indeed, it was beaten off with relative ease. Fetim himself flailed a cutlass, drew some blood, and suffered a minor cut. And Mohan Gopal's men were sturdy and determined, familiar with the perils and exigencies of trade: they defended their vessel with both stubbornness and skill. The pirates were soon daunted and withdrew.

In consequence, Fetim raised his estimation of himself. He also dismissed any lingering qualms he may have felt concerning his fate.

To celebrate the victory, Mohan Gopal exercised a master's prerogative by commanding his men to broach a consignment of wine destined for a merchant in Qatiis— Haroon el-Temud, a man of great wealth and unsavory reputation. "Let his count be short a cask or two," pronounced Mohan Gopal with a certain unworthy satisfaction: he had accepted el-Temud's consignment to disguise his more serious cargo; but he disliked carrying goods for a man whose honesty he did not trust. "If he complains, I will pay for the difference."

The crew cheered heartily and obeyed.

During the afternoon and the early evening, the mood aboard *Horizon's Daughter* became convivial. Having sampled good wines in Niswan, Fetim was not impressed by Haroon el-Temud's taste. Nevertheless, he drank a comfortable excess among his comrades. Mohan Gopal did not refuse a glass or two. Accustomed to the company of men, Saliandra also enjoyed a modest libation.

But as night closed over the River Kalabras, and the stars shone coldly from the heavens, first one and then another of the felucca's men began to scream.

For numerous excellent reasons, Haroon el-Temud had enemies; and his enemies had poisoned his wine. A slow acid ate at the vitals of all who consumed it. Clutching his stomach, the first victim fell overboard. The River seemed to swallow him without a sound. Howling in agony, the second flung himself at Fetim.

Taken by surprise, and inspired by his elevated opinion of himself—as well as by wine—Fetim snatched up his cutlass and cleft his shipmate from shoulder to breastbone. Then he heard Saliandra's wail and realized what he had done.

No one reproached him, however. Instead, his companions sought to kill him. *Horizon's Daughter*'s people were being driven mad with pain. Blades flashed: screams beat against the darkness. Having drunk less than his men, Mohan Gopal remained himself long enough to be horrified, to struggle for order, at last to defend Fetim as well as he could. Then he too fell prey to the poison. Turning, he knotted his fingers around Fetim's throat and attacked the young man's handsomeness with his teeth.

Saliandra hung from her father's back, trying to pull him away from her lover. I kept Fetim alive, but did not feel compelled to preserve him from injury. He was bleeding from several wounds when Mohan Gopal finally stumbled into convulsions and died.

Everyone died. More from malice than from any wish to spare him pain, I did not let the poison touch Fetim: I wanted him to watch the way his friends were taken.

Saliandra was the last, of course. The wine let her live long enough to experience the ruin of her life and everything she had loved. Although her suffering was extravagant, however, it could not turn her against her lover. She expired in his arms, with his name on her lips.

For that reason, he felt the loss of her all the more severely.

Alone on the River Kalabras, covered by darkness, in a vessel peopled by corpses, he rose to his feet and cried out at the stars, "The fault is mine!"

I peered at him more closely. "Say what?"

"They were my friends. She would have married me. He would have been proud to call me his son-in-law. I am the cause of their deaths. There is no one more despicable. Knowing what would befall them, I allowed them to make me the object of their goodness. Truly, I deserve to be accursed."

"Well." This was gratifying. "I was wondering when you were going to see the truth."

Instead of answering, he took a fallen dagger from the deck and plunged it toward his breast.

I turned the blade. He bruised himself, but did not pierce the skin.

"You are the worst of the curse," he said brokenly, "the most malefic of all djinn. If you had permitted me to die, only the clan of the al-Hetal would have paid the price of my folly. Because of you, the graveyards of Niswan are crowded with my victims, and the honest and loving people of *Horizon's Daughter* have been slaughtered. By preserving my life, you wreak abominable evil."

Recognizing the justice of what he said, I demanded nonetheless, "Whose fault is that? It wasn't me who tried to take advantage of Rashid. It wasn't me who preferred slavery to resistance. I'm not the one who said, 'You are the only friend I will ever desire,' when what he should've done was jump ship as soon as he could stand."

Again he did not answer. Rather, he took a length of line and climbed to one of the felucca's yards. There he bound the line to the yard and also to his neck, then cast himself down.

I caused one of the knots to fail. Additionally, I adjusted his impact on the deck so that he was not seriously harmed.

"Help me," he beseeched. "I must put an end to myself, or I will cover the world with ruin wherever I go."

"You know who I am," I replied. "I'm part of the curse. I can't help you. If I tried, the great father of djinn would tear me apart and scatter every portion of my being to the four winds." After a moment, I added foolishly, "You've got to stop thinking like a normal man. You've got to start thinking like one of the accursed."

He drank a large flagon of the tainted wine while he considered what I had said. His bitten features seemed to undergo a number of changes, passing from self-pity and anger to emotions which were more obscure. Then he commanded peremptorily, "Repeat the curse."

I complied. " 'In the name of the great father of djinn, let all those he loves be killed. Let him be readily loved— and let all those who love him die in anguish. Let all his seed and all his blood—' "

"Enough. I have heard enough." He consumed more of the wine. Now it seemed to have no effect upon him. "I have received both decency and love aboard this vessel, and those who gave it to me have been poisoned. I must 'start thinking like one of the accursed.' Very well. Do your work, djinn. I will do mine."

He did not speak again that night. The River Kalabras bore the ship of the dead through the dark, and he rode the vessel alone, as though he were its rightful master.

Two days later, the current carried *Horizon's Daughter* past the teeming waterfront of Qatiis, the crystal city where the Padisha devoted himself alternately to civic virtue and imaginative perversion. Hailing assistance in the name of Haroon el-Temud, Fetim achieved a berth for his felucca among the wharves of the great merchants. The state of the vessel's crew—by then as rank as the waters of the city— aroused considerable comment, and there was talk of summoning the Padisha's civil guard; but Fetim deflected that outcome by invoking Haroon el-Temud's name with alarming freedom. This in turn incurred the rancor of the merchant's adherents. They made Fetim their prisoner and hauled him up into the rich city, where they threw him at Haroon el-Temud's feet as a suspected murderer.

Piqued by Fetim's fearless manner and his air of knowledge, the merchant allowed the young man to speak. At once, Fetim revealed that Mohan Gopal and his crew had been killed by wine intended for Haroon el-Temud himself.

"Yet you survive," the merchant observed. "It might be

reasonable to assume, therefore, that the wine was poisoned by none other than yourself."

"That assumption would be understandable, but faulty,"
replied Fetim. "Your men will tell you that the felucca's
crew has been dead long enough to permit me an easy
escape, which would have freed me forever from suspicion. I have risked your distrust because the name of Haroon el-Temud is known as far away as Niswan, and I have
that to offer you which can profit us both."

"What is it?"

With an eloquent shrug, Fetim indicated his bonds.

Haroon el-Temud considered. Surely it would be madness for a poisoner of wine to remain in the company of his
victims as Fetim had done. And if Fetim were innocent, he
had done the merchant a great service by making him
aware of the death his enemies plotted for him. To this
service Fetim added an offer of profit. And he was a
remarkably handsome young man. The rapidly healing
scars on his face, far from marring his features, served to
give his appearance piquancy. Even the Padisha, in one of
his lascivious phases, might be interested in such a man.

Nodding approval of his thoughts, Haroon el-Temud
commanded Fetim's release. Then he and Fetim reached a
bargain favorable to them both: Fetim was granted a well-
remunerated place in the merchant's service; the merchant
was made aware that *Horizon's Daughter* carried unpro-
tected saffron which had not yet been delivered to its rightful buyer.

The profits which accrued to Haroon el-Temud from so
much stolen saffron greatly increased his goodwill toward
his new protégé.

Fetim had no particular aptitude for his work: he had no
aptitude for any work. But he was pleasing in manner, at
once unafraid and certain, deferential and modest. And
he plied his attractiveness to great effect. He soon found
himself accepted and busy among the merchant's many
adherents—accountants, clerks, couriers, and guards; oda-
lisques, assassins, opium peddlers, and spies—whose lives
were devoted to taking advantage of the Padisha's out-
breaks of virtue and vice.

He was watched with suspicion, of course: Haroon el-

Temud had not achieved such wealth through a lack of caution. But what was in Fetim's heart was more convoluted than the malice which the merchant knew and understood. Haroon el-Temud's spies remarked on the ease with which Fetim accumulated lovers; but neither the spies nor their master feared it.

Fetim, however, found the opportunity when his lovers were sated and happy to ask them interesting questions. And as more and more people chose to make him the repository of their secrets, he gained more and more knowledge. With a celerity which would have frightened the merchant—had he been aware of it—Fetim learned the names of Haroon el-Temud's principal enemies, the locations and characters of their strengths, the parts they played in the balance of conflict which preserved the Padisha's bizarre rule. Then, almost without discernible effort, he began to extend his amorous sphere beyond the circle of Haroon el-Temud's adherents.

In fact, he began to extend his amorous sphere into the domains of his patron's enemies. The knowledge he sought with such diligence was simple: he wished to know who had poisoned Haroon el-Temud's wine.

Initially, he was baffled to learn that the merchant knew the name of this particular foe—and declined to act on the information. This seemed improbable to Fetim: Haroon el-Temud was neither forgiving nor forbearant. Nevertheless, persistence brought the young man better understanding.

In cycles of both virtue and vice, the Padisha enjoyed games of power. He played the strong men of Qatiis against each other, setting one merchant at another, shifting favor between traders, hatching treacheries back and forth. Thus he deflected challenges to the manner in which he reigned over his city.

Haroon el-Temud's wine had been poisoned by a trader who by that gambit rose high in the Padisha's munificence.

Fetim's expression became increasingly difficult to interpret. Armed with his knowledge, he formed a resolution. Then he approached his master and offered to put the extensive network of his lovers at the merchant's service.

Haroon el-Temud greeted the suggestion with relish.

After only a moment's consideration, he asked the young man to glean a certain piece of information.

For the first time since he had joined the merchant's adherents, Fetim showed a spark of passion. It was unsettling to witness because it seemed to arise from a wildness which Haroon el-Temud had not expected and did not know how to read. Nevertheless, the young man did or said nothing wild. Instead, with his strange blend of boldness and modesty, he began to bargain. In exchange for using his bed to his patron's advantage, he desired neither money nor position. Rather, he desired Haroon el-Temud himself in that same bed.

Accustomed to buying love instead of receiving it, the merchant was at once flattered by and suspicious of Fetim's proposition. He let himself be persuaded, however, by the spice of Fetim's handsomeness and desire—and by that hint of wildness, which augured well for Haroon el-Temud's particular lusts. He and Fetim kissed to seal their bargain. Then the young man went away.

That night, after the call to prayers had echoed over the gilt minaret and crystal domes of great Qatiis, the merchant went to Fetim's bed. There, after a bout of love which left Haroon el-Temud nearly insensible, he was roused by the arrival of one of the men on whom he had wished Fetim to spy.

"We had an assignation," this man cried to Fetim in jealous chagrin.

"You arranged this?" demanded Haroon el-Temud.

"Yes," Fetim replied. "Your wine killed the woman I would have married."

In a rage, the merchant struck at Fetim. The new arrival drew a blade to defend his lover. Haroon el-Temud only had time to shout for his waiting guards before his blood was spilled on the bed.

The guards charged into Fetim's quarters. The jealous lover in turn called out for help. More men came to the fray. Qatiis was a city in which no man or woman dared pass out of earshot of assistance. Cries echoed into the streets. Realizing the location of the struggle, Fetim's loves converged on each other, each bringing strength for battle.

Shortly Haroon el-Temud's house and the houses of his enemies were engaged in full-scale war.

Amid this war sat Fetim, contemplating havoc. Because of the curse, much of the violence turned toward him; but he made no effort to defend himself or flee. While blades flashed at him from all sides, and blood gushed everywhere, he murmured only, "Do your work, djinn," and remained where he was.

My work was not easy. It would have been simplified if he had been willing to move. Or—since I must speak honestly—if I had been willing to coerce him to move. I chose, however, to let him be. I covered him with myself and turned every blade and blow aside.

Before the night was over, Qatiis had been cleansed of several powerful merchants who had traded upon the vices of the rich and the flesh of the weak. When at last the Padisha's civil guard was able to beat back the turmoil, they found Fetim still seated on his bed. From that vantage, he surveyed the bloodshed as though he had become accustomed to it.

Naturally, the guards raised their scimitars to strike him down. But it was not his intention to destroy civil rule in Qatiis: his plans were more insidious. He spared the guard by raising his hands and saying in a voice of command, "Hold. What I did, I did at the command of Babera, the Padisha's vizier."

Because the Vizier Babera had a hand in suggesting and effecting many of the Padisha's treacheries and countertreacheries, Fetim's assertion was plausible enough to be dangerous. The men drew back their swords. Instead of attempting to butcher the cause of so much death and damage, they took him prisoner. While conflicting forces sought to find a new balance by defeating each other, and most of the city's strength concentrated on protecting Qatiis itself from riot and ravage, and beggars and pickthieves scurried to loot the undefended warehouses, Fetim was dragged ungently through the streets toward the gold palace of the Padisha.

His ploy succeeded: he was hailed before the Vizier Babera rather than the Vizier Meyd.

The Padisha was served by two viziers, whose fortunes

rose and fell as his phases alternated. The function and protection of the city, the command of the civil guard, the regulation of the marketplace to preserve at least a semblance of honesty, all were the province of the Vizier Meyd, whose loyalty and probity were the qualities which kept the Padisha on his throne. Conversely, the Vizier Babera was the master of the Padisha's revels and plots. He it was who conceived the vices and debaucheries, the extravagances and perversions, which gave the Padisha's life its exotic flavor.

Presented to the Vizier Babera, Fetim acted swiftly: he spat in the Vizier's face.

Babera's instant reaction was to order Fetim's head lopped from his shoulders. A moment's reflection, however, suggested a better fate. In recent days, the Padisha had developed a taste which was difficult to satisfy, even for the cunning vizier: the Padisha desired fornication with someone—man or woman, as occasion supplied—while that individual's neck was being broken. The snapping of the spine and the spasm of death brought him to climaxes which were greatly coveted. Seeing that Fetim was handsome, Babera concluded that he would make an appropriate victim for the Padisha's concupiscence.

Therefore Fetim's death was not attempted. Instead, he was drugged into a state of languor and acquiescence, and presented to the Padisha.

The Padisha met the Vizier Babera's offering with intense approval. At once, he called women to arouse him, boys to toy with him. He consumed aphrodisiacs to make him manly. He inhaled incenses which heightened the senses: he drank herbs which sensitized the skin. At the same time, Fetim was bound hand and foot into an upright frame designed so that the Padisha might penetrate from one side while his body servant, a hugely muscular eunuch, clasped the victim's neck from the other.

Drugged, Fetim suffered this indignity without alarm. He only murmured at intervals, "Do your work, djinni. I will do mine."

When the Padisha was ready, he began to exercise himself upon Fetim's body. Swiftly, the moment of climax approached. The eunuch wrapped his great hands around Fetim's throat.

But when the Padisha was engorged and aching, and the signal was given, the eunuch's hands unaccountably jerked from one neck to the other. It was the Padisha himself who met death in the moment of bliss.

Horrified by the consequences of what had just happened, the eunuch fled for his life, rampaging like a maddened bull through the palace. The Vizier Meyd entered the Padisha's disporting chamber, took one look at his master's body, and commanded his men to arrest the Vizier Babera.

Babera's supporters resisted: the civil guard was called into action. While violence echoed in the halls of the palace, propelling the Vizier Meyd to the rule of Qatiis whether he desired it or not, I released Fetim from his bonds, swept the drugs from his mind, and guided him to a safe egress.

As we journeyed together away from the changed city, I said, "You learn well."

"Learn?"

"You learn to think like one of the accursed."

"Thank you," he said. He did not sound notably happy. Yet he faced the desert ahead of us without quailing.

"You fill me with pride," I said. "You have exceeded all my expectations."

"Give me time," he returned. His tone suggested mockery of my former manner of speaking. "I might have some more surprises for you. The world has a lot of opportunities."

Had I been mortal, I would have laughed. If he continued to learn at this pace, he would eventually become one of the djinn.

TESTS OF WIT AND LAW

The Emir bowed to his assembled subjects, then held out a hand to his human "guests." They sat in consternation and more than a little fear. For, if a man might become a djinni, might they be likewise translated?

"May we have time to confer?" asked the storyteller.

"You should have stipulated such time when we made our agreement," reproved the Emir of the Djinn.

Peter rose. He was taller than the Emir, who promptly remedied that condition by growing until he stood roughly ten feet tall.

"Most impressive," said the knight. "I was ever taught to abide by the spirit, rather than the letter of the law."

"You, with your flame hair, surely are not one of the Faithful, then," said the Emir. "I thought you a noble mamluk to the merchant prince."

"So I might well have been," said Peter, "had it not been for his charity. For had I not been ransomed, I had pledged to be sold as a slave to repay him for saving my life and for harboring me for the space of three Ramadans."

The Emir of the Djinn sank to his earlier stature. "I should be diminished in spirit before my honored infidel guest, were I to forbid you to confer among yourselves. We of the djinn have had centuries to polish our tales. You may proceed."

Bowing, he made great and gracious play of leaving them to their privacy; then he vanished politely to reappear in the amphitheatre among his friends and subjects.

Formality was shattered as the men huddled together,

leaning on one another's shoulders, whispering, interrupting, and, above all, worrying that their stories might falter before the assembled djinn or, just as bad, put them to sleep.

"No, no, no!" cried the tale-teller after the anxious whispers had all but turned to quarrels. "Disagree now, and we are lost. It is not enough to tell tales to the djinn; we must also reply to the tale that has been told.

"Think you!" he commanded. "Of what does the Emir speak?"

The men were silent.

"He speaks," said the storyteller triumphantly, "of the power of djinn over men."

"Then we must speak of how men have gained power over djinn!" cried the frail Ch'in healer. "There is an ancient tale . . ."

"And I," the merchant spoke up, "know a true story— or at least my wife's third cousin swears that it happened to him—of a curse turned upon him who uttered it."

"I too will speak," said the storyteller. "You shall divert the djinn with your tales; I shall seek to impress them with law."

He rose, and the two men who would fight with words at his side rose with him. Immediately, the Emir appeared to face them.

"We are ready," said the storyteller, "and may Allah smile upon our efforts."

The Wishing Game

Larry Niven

Crunching and grinding sounds brought him half-awake. He was being pulled upward through gritty sand, in jerks. Then the stopper jerked free, sudden sunlight flamed into his refuge, and the highly compressed substance that was Kreezerast the Frightener exploded into the open air.

Kreezerast attempted to gather his senses and his thoughts. He had slept for a long time...

A long time. A human male, an older man not in the best of shape, was standing above the bottle. There was desert all about. Kreezerast, tall as the tallest of trees and still expanding, had a good view of scores of miles of yellow sand blazing with heat and light. Far south he saw a lone pond ringed by stunted trees, the only sign of life. And this had been forest when he entered his refuge!

What of the man? He was looking up at Kreezerast, probably perceiving him as a cloud of thinning smoke. His aura was that of a magic user, though much faded from disuse. At his feet, beside Kreezerast's bottle, was a block of gold wrapped in ropes.

Gold? Gold was wild magic. It would take no spells. It drove some species mad; it made humans mad enough to value the soft, useless metal. Was that why the man had carried this heavy thing into a desert? Or had its magic somehow pointed the way to Kreezerast's refuge?

Men often wished for gold. Once upon a time Kreezerast had given three men too much gold to carry or to hide, and watched them try to move it all, until bandits put the cap to his jest.

Loose white cloth covered most of the man's body.

35

Knobby hands showed, and part of a sun-darkened face. Deep wrinkles surrounded the eyes. The nose was prominent, curved and sharp-edged like an eagle's beak, and sunburnt. The mouth was calm as he watched the cloud grow.

Kreezerast pulled himself together: the cloud congealed into a tremendous man. He shaped a face that was a cartoon of the other's features, wide mouth, nose like a great ax, red-brown skin, disproportionately large eyes and ears. He bellowed genially, "Make yourself known to me, my rescuer!"

"I am Clubfoot," the man said. "And you are an afright, I think."

"Indeed! I am Kreezerast the Frightener, but you need not fear me, my rescuer. How may I reward you?"

"What I—"

"Three wishes!" Kreezerast boomed. He had always enjoyed the wishing game. "You shall have three wishes if I have the power to grant them."

"I want to be healthy," Clubfoot said.

The answer had come quickly. This was no wandering yokel. Good: brighter minds made for better entertainment. "What disease do you suffer from?"

"Nothing too serious. Nothing you cannot see, Kreezerast, with your senses more powerful than human. I suffer from sunburn, from too little water, and from various symptoms of age. And there's this." The man sat; he took the slipper off his left foot. The foot was twisted inward. Callus was thick along the outer edge and side. "I was born this way."

"You could have healed yourself. There is magic, and you are a magician."

Clubfoot smiled. "There was magic."

Kreezerast nodded. His own kind were creatures of magic. Over tens of thousands of years the world's *manna*, the power that worked spells, had dwindled almost to nothing. The most powerful of magical creatures had gone mythical first. The afrights had outlived the gods. They had watched the dragons sickening, the merpeople becoming handless creatures of the sea; and they had survived that. They had watched men spread across the land, and change.

"There was magic," Kreezerast affirmed. "Why didn't you heal your foot?"

"It would have cost me half my power. That mattered, when I had power. Now I can't heal myself."

"But now you have me. So! What is your wish?"

"I wish to be healthy."

Did this Clubfoot intend to be entirely healed from all the ills of mankind on the strength of one wish? The question answered itself: he did. Kreezerast said, "There are things I can't do for you—"

"Don't do them."

Was there no way to force Clubfoot to make his wish more specific, more detailed? "Total health is impossible for your kind."

"Fortunate it is, that I have not wished for total health."

The wish was well chosen. It was comprehensive. It was unambiguous. The Frightener could not claim that he could not fulfill the conditions; they were too general.

Magic was still relatively strong in this place. Kreezerast knew that he had the power to search Clubfoot's structure and heal every ill he found.

To lose the first wish was no disaster. One did like to play the game to the end. Still, Kreezerast preferred that the first wish come out a bit wrong, to give the victim warning.

Pause a bit. Think. They stood in a barren waste. What was a man doing here? His magic must have led him to Kreezerast's refuge, but—

Footprints led north: parallel lines of sandal-marks and shapeless splotches. They led to the corpse of a starved beast, not long dead, half a mile away. Here was more life: scavengers had set to work.

Saddlebags lay near the dead beast. They held (Kreezerast adjusted his eyes) only water skins. Three were quite dry; the fourth held five or six mouthfuls.

The prints blurred as he followed them farther. Dunes, more dunes . . . the prints faded, but Kreezerast's gaze followed the pathless path . . . a fleck of scarlet at the peak of a crescent dune, twelve miles north . . . and beyond that his eyes still saw, but his other senses did not. The *manna* level dropped to nothing, as if cut by a sword. The desert continued for scores of miles.

It tickled Kreezerast's fancy. Clubfoot would be obscenely healthy when he died of thirst. He would suffer no ill save for fatigue and water loss and sunstroke. Of course he still had two wishes . . . but such was the nature of the game.

"You shall be healthy," Kreezerast roared jovially. "This will hurt."

He looked deep within Clubfoot. Spells had eased some of the stresses that were the human lot, and other stresses due to a twisted walk, but those spells were long gone.

First: brain and nerves had lost some sensitivity. Inert matter had accumulated in the cells. Kreezerast removed that, carefully. The wrinkles deepened around Clubfoot's eyes. The nerves of youth now sensed the aches and pains of an aged half-cripple.

Next: bones. Here were arthritis, swollen joints. Kreezerast reshaped them. He softened the cartilage. The bones of the left foot he straightened. The man howled and flailed aimlessly.

The callus on that foot was now wrong. Kreezerast burned it away.

Age had dimmed the man's eyes. Kreezerast took the opacity from the humor, tightened the irises. He was enjoying himself, for this task challenged his skills. Arteries and veins were half-clogged with goo, particularly around and through the heart. Kreezerast removed it. Digestive organs were losing their function; Kreezerast repaired them, grinning in anticipation.

In a few hours Clubfoot would be as hungry as an adolescent boy. He'd want a banquet and he'd want it *now*. It would be salty. There would be wine, no water.

Reproductive organs had lost function; the prostate gland was ready to clamp shut on the urethra. Kreezerast made repairs. Perhaps the man would ask for an houri too, when glandular juices commenced bubbling within his veins.

A few hours of pain, a few hours of pleasure. For Kreezerast to win the game, his three wishes must leave a man (or an afright, for they played the game among themselves) with nothing he hadn't started with. To leave him injured or dead was acceptable but inferior.

The man writhed with pain. His face was in the sand and he was choking. His lungs, for that matter, had collected sixty years of dust. Kreezerast swept them clean. He burned four skin tumors away in tiny flashes.

The sunburn would heal itself. Wrinkled skin was not ill health, nor were dead hair follicles.

Anything else?

Nothing that could be done by an afright working with insufficient *manna*.

Clubfoot sat up gasping. His breathing eased. A slow smile spread across his face. "No pain. Wait—" The smile died.

"You have lost your sense of magic," the afright said. "Of course."

"I expected that. Ugh. It's like going deaf." The man got up.

"Were you powerful?"

"I was in the Guild. I was part of the group that tried to restore magic to the world by bringing down the Moon."

"The Moon!" Kreezerast guffawed; the sand danced to the sound. He had never heard the like. "It was well you didn't succeed!"

"In the end some of us had to die to stop it. Yes, I was powerful. All things end and so will I, but you've given me a little more time, and I thank you." The man picked up his golden cube by two leather straps and settled it on his back. "My next wish is that you take me to Xyloshan Village without leaving the ground."

Kreezerast laughed a booming laugh. "Do you fear that I will drop you on Xyloshan Village from a height?" It would make a neat finale.

"Not anymore," Clubfoot said.

Here the magic was relatively strong, perhaps because the desert would not support men. Men were not powerful in magic, but there were so many! Where men were, magic disappeared rapidly. That would explain the sharp drop-off to the north. Wars did that. Opposing spells burned the *manna* out locally in a few hours, and then it was down to blades and murder.

To east and west and south, the level of power dwindled gradually. "Where is this Xyloshan Village?"

"Almost straight north." Clubfoot pointed. "Rise a mile and you'll see it easily. There are low hills around it, a big bell tower and two good roads—"

The man's level of confidence was an irritant. Struck suddenly young again, free of the ever-present pains that came with age in men, he must be feeling like the king of the world. How pleasant it would be, to puncture the man's balloon of conceit!

"Take me to Xyloshan Village without leaving the ground." Very well, Kreezerast would not leave the ground.

The Frightener didn't rise into the air; he *grew*. At a mile tall he could scan everything to the north. Xyloshan was a village of fifteen or sixteen hundred with a tall, crude bell tower, two hundred miles distant. If he hurled Clubfoot through the air in a parabola...

He couldn't. It was too far and he didn't have sufficient magic. Just as well. It would have ended the game early.

He still had two choices.

Clubfoot had made the wrong wish. It could not be fulfilled. The afright could simply say so. Or...

He laughed. He shrank to twenty feet or so. He picked up Clubfoot, tucked him under his arm and ran. He covered twelve miles in ten minutes (weak!) and stopped with a jar. He set Clubfoot down in the sand. The man lay gasping. His hands had a deathgrip on the ropes that bound the gold cube.

"Here I must stop," Kreezerast said. "I must not venture where there is no *manna*."

The man's breathing gradually eased. He rolled to his knees. In a moment he'd realize that his minuscule water supply lay twelve miles behind him.

Kreezerast needled him. "And your third wish, my rescuer?"

"Whoof! That was quite a ride. Are you sure *rescuer* is the word you want?" Clubfoot stood and looked about him.

He spoke as if to himself. "All right, where's the smoke? Mirandee!"

"Why should I not say *rescuer?*"

"Your kind can't tolerate boredom. You built those little bottles as refuges. When you're highly compressed and there's no light or sound, you go to sleep. You sleep until something wakes you up."

"You know us very well, do you?"

"I've read a great deal."

"What are you looking for?"

"Smoke. It isn't here. Something must have happened to Mirandee. *Mirandee!*"

"You have a companion? I can find her, if such is your wish." He had already found her. There was a patch of scarlet cloth at the top of a dune, and a small canopy pitched on the north side, two hundred paces west.

Clubfoot played the game well. He had a companion waiting just this side of the border between magic and no magic, on a line between Xyloshan Village and Kreezerast's refuge. The afright had taken him almost straight to her. And to their camp, where waited two more loadbeasts and their water supply.

A puff of wind could cover that scarlet blanket with sand . . .

An afright would have gloated over his two victories. The man merely picked up his gold and walked. In a moment he was jogging, then running flat out, testing his symmetrical feet and newly youthful legs. He bellowed, "Mirandee!" half in the joy of new youth, half in desperation. He ran straight up the side of a tall dune, spraying sand. At the top he looked about him, and favored Kreezerast with a poisonous glare. Then he was running again.

Kreezerast's little whirlwind had buried the scarlet marker. But of course: the man had failed to find it, but he'd seen a dying whirlwind.

Kreezerast followed, taking his time.

The man was in the shade of the canopy, bending over a woman. Kreezerast stopped as his highly sensitive ears picked up Clubfoot's near-whisper. "I came as quick as I could. Oh, Mirandee! Hang on, Mirandee, stay with me, we're almost there."

The Frightener could study her more thoroughly now: a very old woman, tall and still straight. An aura of magic, nearly gone. She was unconscious and days from death. The golden cube lay beside her, pushed up against her ribs. Wild magic . . . it might reinforce some old spell.

Once upon a time, a man had wished for a woman who didn't want him. Kreezerast found her and brought her to him, but he made no effort to hide where she had gone. He'd watched her relatives take their vengeance. Humans took their lusts seriously . . . but this woman did not seem a proper object for lust. She'd be thirty or forty years older than he.

The man must have thought the Frightener was out of earshot. He rubbed her knobby hand. "We got this far. The bottle was there. The afright was there. The magic was there. The first spell worked. Look at me, can you see? It worked!"

Her eyes opened. She stirred.

"Don't mind the wrinkles. I don't *hurt* anywhere. Here, feel!" He wrapped the woman's fingers around his left foot. "The second spell, he did just as we thought. I don't think we'll even need—" The man looked up. He raised his voice. "Frightener, this is Mirandee."

Kreezerast approached. "Your mate?"

"Close enough. My companion. My final wish is that Mirandee be healthy."

This was too much. "You know we hate boredom. It is discourteous of you to make two wishes that are the same."

Clubfoot picked up the gold, turned his back and walked away. "I'll remain as courteous as possible," he snarled over his shoulder. "I remind you that you carried me facing backward. Was that discourteous, or did you consider it a joke?"

"A joke. Here's another. Your . . . companion must be nearly one hundred years old. A healthy woman of that age would be dead."

"Hah hah. Nobody dead is healthy. I already know that you can fulfill my wish."

Kreezerast wondered if the man would use the gold to bribe him. *That* would be amusing. "I point out also that you are not truly my rescuer—"

"Am I not? Haven't I rescued you from boredom? Aren't you enjoying the wishing game?" Clubfoot was shouting over his shoulder across a gap of twenty paces. In fact he had walked beyond the region where magic lived, while Kreezerast was still looking for ways to twist his third wish.

That easily, he was beyond Kreezerast's vengeance. "You have bested me. I admit it, but I can limit your satisfaction. One more word from you and I kill the woman."

Clubfoot nodded. He spread a robe from the saddlebags against the side of a dune and made himself comfortable on it.

No curses, no pleading, no bribe? Kreezerast said, "Speak your one word."

"Wait."

What? "I won't hurt her. Speak."

The man's voice now showed no anger. "Our biggest danger was that we would find you to be stupid."

"Well?"

"I think we've been lucky. A stupid afright would have been very dangerous."

The man spoke riddles. Kreezerast turned to black smoke and drifted south, beaten and humiliated.

Once upon a time a man had wished to be taller. Kreezerast had lengthened his bones and left the muscles and tendons alone. Over time he'd healed. A woman had wished for beauty; Kreezerast had given her an afright's beauty. Afterward men admired her eerie, abstract loveliness, but never wished her favors . . . and she was one who had shied from men.

But no man had ever bested him like this!

What did the magician expect? Kreezerast had watched men evolve over the thousands of years. He had watched magicians strip the land of magic, until better species died or changed. He had no reason to love men, nor to keep his promises to a lesser breed.

The bottle beckoned . . . but Kreezerast rose into the air. High, higher; three miles, ten. Was there any sign of his own kind? None at all. Patches where *manna* still glowed strong? None. Here and here were encampments, muffled men and women attended by strange misshapen beasts. Men had taken the world.

The world had changed. It would change again. Kreezerast the Frightener would wait in his refuge until something or someone dug him up. A companion would come . . . and would hear the tale. Afrights didn't lie to each other.

So be it. At least he need not confess to killing the woman out of mere spite. Let her man watch her die over the next few days. Let him tend her while his water dwindled.

The key to survival was to live only through interesting times.

Here was the bottle. Now, where . . .

Where was the stopper?

The stopper bore afright's magic. Sand would not hide it.

Gold would. Wild magic would hide the magic in the stopper. It was a box, a box!

The camp was untouched. The woman had not moved. Her breathing was labored.

Clubfoot lay against the next dune. He had gone for the beasts and the supplies in their saddlebags. He said nothing. The golden cube glowed at his feet.

Kreezerast said, "Very well. You can reach Xyloshan Village and I cannot stop you, if you are willing to abandon the woman. So. You win."

Clubfoot said, "Why do I want to talk to a liar?"

The answer was obvious enough. "For the woman."

"And why will you stoop to bargaining with a mere man?"

"For the stopper. But I can make another."

"Can you? I could never make another Mirandee." The man sat up. "We feared you would twist the third wish somehow. We never dreamed you'd refuse to grant it at all."

He would have to remake stopper *and* bottle, for they were linked. And he could do that, but not here, nor anywhere on this *manna*-poor desert. Perhaps nowhere.

He said, "Give me the stopper and I will grant your third wish, or any other you care to make."

"But I don't trust you."

"Trust this, then. I can repair this Mirandee's nerves. In fact . . . yes." He looked deep into her body, deep into her fine structure. This one had never been crippled. She'd never born children either. Odd. It was humankind's only form of immortality.

Clear out the capillaries, clean the jugulars and carotids, repair the heart. Now she cannot die inconveniently. More blood flows to the brain. Myelin sheaths are becoming inert. Fix it.

She stirred, flung out an arm. Her breathing was faster now.

Kreezerast called, "So sensation has returned—"

She whispered, "Clubfoot?" She rolled over, and squeaked with pain. She saw the tremendous man-shape above her; studied it without blinking, then rolled to her knees and faced north. "Clubfoot. Stay there," she croaked. "Well done!" He couldn't have heard her.

"So her sensation has returned and her mind is active, too," the Frightener called. "Now she can feel and understand pain. I will give her pain. Do you trust my word?"

"Let us see if you trust mine," the man called. "I will never give the stopper to you. Never. Mirandee must do that for me. You must persuade her to do that."

Persuade? Torture! Until she begged to do him any service he asked. But then she must go and get the stopper, where magic failed . . . fool. Fool!

The Frightener shrank until he stood some seven feet tall. He said, "Woman, your paramour has wished you to be healthy. If I make you healthy, will you give me that which he holds in ransom?"

She blinked. "Yes."

"Will you also keep me company for a day?" Postpone. Delay. Wait. "Tell me stories. The world is not familiar to me anymore."

Her thoughts were slow . . . and careful. "I will do that, if you will give me food and water. As for keeping you company—"

"I speak of social intercourse," he said quickly. To show

Clubfoot's woman that an afright was a better mate would have been entertaining. *If* they were lovers. She was far older than he was...but there were spells to keep a woman young. Had been spells. She had been a powerful magician, he saw that. In fact (that unwinking gaze, as if he were being judged by an equal!), this whole plan might have been hers.

He had lost. He was even losing his anger. They had *known* the danger. What a gamble they had taken! And Kreezerast must even be polite to this woman, and persuade her not to break her promise after she had walked beyond his reach.

He said, "Then tell me how you almost brought the Moon to Earth. But first I will heal you. This will hurt." He set to work. She screamed a good deal; and so he kept that promise too.

Bones, joints, tendons: he healed them all. Ovaries were shrunken, but not all eggs were gone; they could be brought to life. Glands. Stomach. Gut. Kreezerast continued until she was a young woman writhing and gasping, new inside and withered outside.

Clubfoot did not run to his lady to help her in her pain.

They might still make a mistake. If nothing else thwarted them, perhaps he had one last joke to play.

She'd feel the wrinkles when she touched her face! But wrinkles do not constitute ill health. But she *must* give him the stopper. Kreezerast pulled her skin smooth, face and hands and forearms (but not where cloth covers her. Hah! She'll never notice until it's too late!), legs, belly, breasts, pectoral muscles too. (She might.)

The sun had gone. He set sand afire for warmth and summoned up a king's banquet. Clubfoot stayed in his place of safety and chewed dried meat. She didn't touch the wine. Mirandee and the Frightener ate together, and talked long, while Clubfoot listened at a distance.

He told her of the tinker and his family who had wished for jewels, once upon a time. He'd given them eighty pounds of jewels. They had one horse and a travois. A hundred curious villagers were swarming to where they had seen the looming, smoky form of an afright.

But the tinker and his wife had thrown handfuls of

jewels about the road and into the low bushes, and fled for a day before they stopped to hide what they kept. Forty years later their grandchildren were wealthy merchants.

Mirandee had seen the last god die, and it was a harrowing tale. She spoke of a changed world, where powerless sorcerers were becoming artists and artisans and musicians, where men learned to fish for themselves because the merpeople were gone, where war was fought with bloody blades and no magic at all.

Almost he was tempted to see more of it. But what would he see? If he ventured where the *manna* was gone, he would go mythical.

Presently he watched her sleep. Boring.

They talked the morning and afternoon away. At evening Mirandee folded the canopy and gathered the blankets and bedding and walked away with it all on her shoulders. She had been strong; she was strong again. She crossed the barrier between magic and no magic. Kreezerast could do nothing. She came back to collect food and wine left over from the banquet, and crossed again.

She and her man set up their camp. Kreezerast heard them talking and laughing. He saw Clubfoot's hands wander beneath the woman's robes, and was relieved: he had not fooled *himself*, at least. *What of the stopper?*

Neither had mentioned it at all.

He waited. He would not beg.

Mirandee took Clubfoot's golden cube. She carried it to the margin of magic. Her magical sense was gone; would she cross? No, they'd marked it. She swung the cube by the straps and hurled it several feet.

Kreezerast picked it up. The wild magic hurt his hands. There was no lid. He pulled the soft metal apart and had the stopper.

Time to sleep.

He let himself become smoke, and let the smoke thin. The humans ignored him. Perhaps they thought he had gone away; perhaps they didn't care. He hovered.

The canopy and the darkness hid their lovemaking, but it couldn't hide their surging, flashing auras. Magic was being made in that dead region. They were lovers indeed, if they had not been before. And Kreezerast grinned and turned toward his bottle.

In her youth she had chosen not to bear children.

Kreezerast had given them their health in meticulous detail. The ex-sorceress's natural lust to mate had already set their auras blazing again. She'd have a dozen children before time caught up with her, unless she chose abstinence, and abstinence would be a hardship on her.

Some human cultures considered many children a blessing. Some did not. Certainly their traveling days were over; they'd never get past that little village. And Kreezerast the Frightener crawled into his bottle and pulled the stopper after him.

Curse of the Three Demons

Harry Turtledove

Sa'id ibn Hawqal bowed very low. "If the esteemed governor of the great city of Kaifeng would honor me by deigning to examine my humble merchandise—" The flowery phrases would have sounded better in Arabic, of course, but Sa'id knew enough of the Mongols' harsh, barking speech to get by. And a significant pause, he thought, was the same in any language.

The esteemed governor of the great city of Kaifeng punctuated the pause by breaking wind. "You may as well show me," he grunted, and reached inside his brocaded silk robe to scratch himself.

Sa'id ibn Hawqal did not let the contempt he felt show on his long, lean face. Bagadan was a barbarian; his father had counted himself lucky to have cockroaches to eat during the freezing steppe winter. But the Mongols were monstrously good at war. And so Bagadan was a rich, powerful barbarian, an important man in a domain larger than the Caliphs, the Commanders of the Faithful, had ever ruled.

Bowing again, the Arab merchant undid the mouths of the sacks that held his goods, let them fall open. "I have three strong locks of iron here, from Constantinople in the land of Rum; he who owns them will keep safe whatsoever he wishes. And look here, and smell: frankincense from the Yemen, and turmeric as well. Here too are preserved capers from Bushanj, and balsam oil from Egypt."

"I think you make up the names of some of these place," Bagadan said. Suspicion filled his narrow, slanted eyes.

"By the prophet Muhammad, by Allah the one God, the

Compassionate, the Merciful, I do not," Sa'id exclaimed. "Why on earth would I do that?" Surprise startled him into brusqueness.

But Bagadan had an answer ready for the question the merchant had intended to be rhetorical: "So you could more easily impress me with how rare your goods are, and so get a better price." That made sense, enough so for Sa'id to file away the trick for future use. Then Bagadan broke wind again, even louder than before. "As for your prophet and the god he prates of, this to both of them. The least spirit of the steppe is more than a match for their kind."

"Your excellency will believe as he believes," Sa'id said in his politest voice, all the while thinking lovingly of the eternal torment that awaited Bagadan after the demon-worshiper met the final judgment.

"You doubt me," Bagadan said with an unpleasant chuckle. He chopped down with his right hand to cut short the insincere protest Sa'id ibn Hawqal began for form's sake. "But think on this: if your precious god is so mighty, how have we Mongols and our fierce *tngri* slaughtered every army that followed him?"

"That is as God wills," Sa'id said. Bagadan laughed out loud. The merchant wished he had a better answer to give, but knew none. The Muslim's duty was to submit himself to God's will. Sa'id sometimes wondered, though, why He had to show it through the Mongols. He knew the question was blasphemous, but could not help asking it.

Still laughing, Bagadan reached out and tried to pull open one of the locks Sa'id had displayed. Muscles bunched under the wide sleeves of the governor's robe; he was not yet fifty, and still strong and vigorous. Sweat sprang forth on his broad, high-cheekboned face; his gold-brown skin went dark with effort. The lock held. Laughing no longer, he threw it down. "There are worse," he said grudgingly. "How much?"

The haggling began then and went on, intermittently, over the next several days. Bagadan started out wanting to buy everything Sa'id had. The Arab did not want to sell it all at once, not least because he was sure he could get better prices for some things from bargainers less canny than the Mongol official. Then again, after one taste Bagadan abruptly lost interest in preserved capers.

"Esteemed sir, I believe we may have a bargain," Sa'id said at last. He was exhausted, mentally and physically both; he could smell the sour sweat that soaked his robe. Bagadan did not seem to notice—what with the way he smelled, Sa'id was hardly surprised. But the sneers and flared nostrils of the governor's Chinese aides irked the merchant.

"I think we do," Bagadan agreed. "For two of your locks, for your turmeric, for one bottle of balsam oil, and for a fourth part of the frankincense, I will pay you paper money to the value of two and five-sixths ounces of gold."

"Agreed," Sa'id said. The paper money, of course, was worthless outside the dominions of the Great Khan, but within them was legal tender, with the usual bloodthirsty Mongol threats backing it even more securely than the countless ingots in Kubilai's treasury. Sa'id was sure he could buy enough local products with the paper money to turn a handsome profit when he took them back to his home in Syria.

"Bring all the goods to me tomorrow, then," Bagadan said, "and I will pay you what you deserve." As it had several times in the course of the dicker, his smile reminded Sa'id of the tongue-lolling grin of a wolf. Bagadan was as much a predator as any that went on four legs, deck himself in shining silks though he might.

The merchant bowed his way out of Bagadan's presence, headed for the caravanserai where he was staying. The interior of the governor's palace never left a great impression on Sa'id, no matter how rich and strange it was: when he was there, he was too intent on dickering with Bagadan to pay attention to his surroundings. But the moment he went outside, he was conscious once more of being in an alien land.

Even the dry, clear air of his homeland was missing here. Everything in this province of Honan seemed somehow faintly misty, so that things at no great distance, things that would have been easily visible near Damascus, blurred against an even more indistinct background. When he first came to the distant east, Sa'id had wondered if his eyes were failing. Only slowly did he realize everyone else saw as he did.

And if the air was moist, the land, by his austere standards, was the next thing to a swamp. The Yellow River ran not far north of the city, a river not much less immense than the Nile. Other, smaller streams flowed by Kaifeng itself. Green cloaked everything even now in high summer, a time of year when Sa'id would have expected his surroundings to be baked bare and brown.

Things inside the city were as strange to the Arab merchant as those without. He was used to pointed arches, to domes, to minarets leaping to the skies. These curious buildings with their roof-ends upswung as if smiling, with every beam carved into uncountable fantastic shapes, made him feel sometimes as if the djinn had swept him off into their fairyland.

The ways of the people did little to dispel that wonder. The Mongols he could deal with, apart from their ferocity. But the Chinese! At times he thought them filthy savages. They did not wash after stool, contenting themselves with paper. And by now Sa'id was resigned to performing his ablutions alone after he bought a wench—no one here, man or woman, had that custom. Nor had he found Muslims among them; save for his fellow traders, he had to pray alone.

Yet the country was richer even than Iraq—or rather than Iraq had been, before Hulagu's sack and massacre at great Baghdad a few years before. The Chinese had countless walled cities, and most of their inhabitants were prosperous enough. Sa'id hardly ever saw here a blind man or one with only a single eye; such were all too common in Syria.

And the Chinese were clever. Paper and silk sprang from China. The Chinese were also polite, almost always smiling. Even with his merchant's cunning, Sa'id had trouble figuring out what went on behind those smiling masks. At times, though, he suspected the natives found him even more barbarous than he thought them.

Well, that was their problem. Like Bagadan, they would have an unpleasant eternity to repent of their pagan ways.

The caravanserai was in the southern part of Kaifeng,

not far from the city wall. The ruins of two larger circuits lay outside the present fortifications; not so long ago, Kaifeng had been even larger than it was today. Sa'id found that hard to imagine. Even now it was bigger than any city of Syria or Iraq—any save Baghdad, Sa'id thought, but only the dead lived in Baghdad now.

The serai-keeper was a fat Chinese named Chao. He spoke the Mongol tongue, not so well as Sa'id. Bowing to the Arab, he said, "Went good?"

"Well enough," Sa'id answered. He gave no more detail; traders who bragged in serais soon regretted it.

Chao knew that too. "Rice beer to celebrate your 'well enough'?" he asked with a sly grin. Sa'id shook his head. In his travels he had eaten forbidden food now and again, when it was that or starve, but he did not touch liquor. Chao grinned again, this time perhaps at the foreigner's foolishness.

For once, Sa'id missed the conviviality wine or beer would have brought to a gathering of strangers, for he did want to celebrate. The more he thought about it, the more he reckoned up what he had paid for the locks, the turmeric, the balsam oil, and what he could buy here for two and five-sixths ounces of gold, the better his deal looked. Bagadan was no mean bargainer, aye, but Sa'id grew increasingly sure he had outdone the Mongol.

He contented himself with buying wine for a couple of travelers who were sharing the caravanserai with him. They were, he gathered, from farther south in China; he and they had only a few words in common. A grin and a slap on the back, though, meant the same thing in any language. Both Chinese were dozing with their heads on the table when Sa'id went up to bed. He felt almost as good as if he had got drunk himself.

He felt even better the next morning, because he had no headache. He was eating rice and drinking a bowl of broth made from beef stock and egg yolks when the two merchants he'd treated the night before came down to join him. They looked much the worse for wear, he thought smugly. Abstaining had its points. He was just surprised the two of them had been able to find their rooms.

He put the locks, the spice, and the aromatic oil in a

leather sack and headed for the governor's palace once more. Bagadan's Chinese underlings greeted him with their usual smooth politeness, or even a bit more. They bowed so low, in fact, that he almost wondered if he was being mocked.

He had to wait a while before a functionary ushered him in to see the governor. That only left him resigned; Bagadan had not given him a set time at which to come. If the governor needed to finish other business first, Sa'id had to accept it.

He did raise an eyebrow at Bagadan's companions: two Mongol troopers, fierce-looking in boiled-leather breastplates, stood behind the governor. But Bagadan greeted the merchant affably enough. "I see you have brought your commodities," he said. "Very good. I will pay you now."

"Excellent, esteemed sir," Sa'id said, bowing. At the end of the bow, he set down his leather sack.

Bagadan, meanwhile, was setting pieces of paper money one on top of the other. Sa'id was used to the sweet clink of gold coins against each other, but found that watching a pile of paper grow taller had a charm of its own. The little rectangular sheets would spend as well as precious metal.

Little . . . those sheets were *too* little! Bagadan finished counting them out. Smiling at Sa'id, he said, "Two and five-sixths ounces, just as we agreed."

"Ounces, aye, but in dinars, not dirhams!" In his fury, Sa'id howled out the Arabic names for gold and silver coins, not their Mongol equivalents. "I want the large pieces of paper, the ones good for gold, not these small arse-wipes, worth only silver. *That* was our bargain!"

"Not as I remember it," Bagadan said blandly. "Now kindly hand over the goods and head on your way. You may spend the money or wipe yourself with it, just as you please, but you will see no more from me."

"Thief! Son of a camel!" Sa'id snatched up his sack and started to storm out.

"Dolugan!" Bagadan snapped, adding a moment later, "Look behind you, merchant."

Sa'id did. One of the Mongol soldiers, presumably Dolugan, held a drawn bow, the shaft aimed at the small of

Sa'id's back. Ice replaced the fire in the Arab's belly. The double-curved, sinew-backed Mongol bows could send an arrow through a man wearing a mail shirt at fifty paces. What one would do to him, armored only in wool and at a tenth of that range, did not bear thinking about.

"Now," Bagadan said cheerfully, "you will put down the bag, collect your price, and leave." He chuckled—he was enjoying himself, enjoying Sa'id's utterly impotent outrage.

"Curse you for the pagan pig you are!" the merchant cried. "May Allah curse you for ever and ever and ever. May you die soon, and in great pain. May Allah Himself, the Compassionate, the Merciful, turn His countenance from you. May the djinn drag you down to hell, piercing you with their fangs and talons as they do, and may you spend all eternity there, with nothing but filth to eat and boiling water to drink."

As he ranted on, he watched the smiles fade from the soldiers' faces. The one who was not Dolugan twisted his fingers in a sign to avert evil. Even Bagadan's grin slipped. But anger replaced it, not fear.

"Curse your worthless curses," the governor said. "I will curse you in return, and we will see whose curse is mightier. I will call down on you the *kölčin*, the frightful ghosts; the *eliye*, the bird-devils; and the *ada*, the sky-demons."

Sa'id saw the Mongol troopers shudder in horror at the names Bagadan invoked. They were both making the apotropaic sign now; Dolugan lowered his bow to do so. Bagadan finished, "Take your money and go. Enjoy it while you may. You will not have long."

"This for your money!" Sa'id shouted. He spat on the pile of paper sheets. "And this for your curse!" He spat again, this time between Bagadan's shoes. "Allah the one God will protect me from your stinking demons." He stalked off.

Bagadan's voice pursued him. "No Arab wizard will ward you from the *kölčin*, from the *eliye*, from the *ada*. Nor will any Mongol shaman, for I am stronger than all those hereabouts."

"Bugger yourself," Sa'id said, and kept walking. Behind him, Bagadan laughed and laughed. The governor's Chinese aides averted their eyes from the Arab merchant. He wished they would have laughed with their master. This exquisite politeness was more wounding than open scorn.

Chao saw the expression on Sa'id's face when the merchant stormed into the caravanserai. This time, the seraikeeper did not ask him how things had gone.

Back in his room, Sa'id turned to face west. There was no mosque in Kaifeng, no *qiblah* to point him toward Mecca, but he knew in which direction the holy city lay. He went to his knees, touched his forehead to the floor. "I testify that there is no God but Allah, and that Muhammad is the prophet of God! God is great, God is good . . ."

The prayer soothed him. By the time he was done, Bagadan seemed hardly more than a nuisance. Let the thieving son of a pimp curse away, Sa'id thought. Allah would keep him safe.

Behind him, someone laughed. His heart leaped into his throat—he was alone in the chamber. He whirled. The *kölčin* laughed again. Sa'id could see the back wall of the room through the ghost, but he could see it too, all too well. Its face was like that of a man—an ugly man who had been badly battered before he died. An ugly man with long, sharp teeth, Sa'id saw when the apparition opened its mouth to cry out yet again.

"I—in the holy name of Allah the one God, be-be-gone!" the Arab quavered. He wished he knew the handsign the Mongol soldiers had made. He would have used it, pagan charm or no. "Begone!" he cried again, louder this time.

The *kölčin* showed no signs of disappearing. It slid closer, though its misshapen feet took no steps. Heavenly aid having failed, Sa'id snatched out his dagger. He slashed at the ghost. His hand might have passed through a freezing mist. The knife did the *kölčin* no harm. It laughed once more.

"Back to the pit of hell that spawned you!" Sa'id said, standing his ground—what good to flee from a ghost? "In the name of Allah I command it, in the name of the angel Gabriel, in the name of Suleiman who bound demons with his seal!"

"Those names have no power over me," the *kölčin* said. Sa'id did not think he heard it with his ears, but rather directly with his mind. It went on, "But I am not bidden to eat you now, only to give you the first and barest taste of my master's wrath. So."

It reached for Sa'id. He flinched away, crying, "Begone!" yet again. The *kölčin* paid no heed. Its hands were large and clawed. He felt it touch his cheek. Then, with a final dreadful laugh, it sank through the floor of his room and was gone.

Sa'id waited for screams to start in the hall below. None came. Could the ghost make itself invisible so quickly, or had he perhaps just imagined it? Despite his pounding heart, the latter seemed more likely.

Of itself, his hand went to his face. It came away wet. He looked down at his fingers. They were red with blood.

Sa'id went about his business for the next several days waiting for something new and dreadful to happen. Nothing did. His spirits rose and fell wildly. He understood the game Bagadan was playing. Arabs played it too, toying with a victim so his anticipation of horror became a horror in itself. Understanding did not help.

Still, life had to go on. Sa'id had to eat and sleep and move his bowels, no matter what evil spirit lurked around the corner. Eating, at the moment, was of particular concern: how long would the merchant be able to keep on doing it, now that Bagadan had stolen the best part of his goods? He almost found himself wishing he had taken the paper money Bagadan had mockingly offered him. It was not the paper worth gold, as it should have been, but it was not nothing, either.

No! If Sa'id could not get his due from Bagadan, he wanted nothing. Accepting the governor's false payment would have been like acquiescing to his own rape.

Then he met the *eliye,* or rather it him. He was on his way to the house of a Chinese noble in the southern part of Kaifeng, hoping to sell the man the one lock Bagadan had left him. Living in the city Bagadan ruled, Sa'id thought, the noble could no doubt use a stout lock.

"Watch where you put your feet!" someone shouted at

the merchant. He thought he heard someone, anyhow, but when he whipped his head around, he failed to see anybody taking any notice of him. He also failed to see the large puddle two steps ahead, and a moment later was soaked to the waist.

Cursing and splashing, he floundered free. He leaned against a building, trying to wring as much muddy water as he could from his robe. A bird was sitting on the puddle from which he had just escaped. No, not a bird, not quite —the *eliye's* shape shifted as Sa'id watched, so that it resembled now a hawk, now a goose, now a dove. Only its eyes, large and red and not at all of this world, stayed the same.

They watched Sa'id. He thought he could still see them when a local man stepped between him and the puddle. Gritting his teeth, the Arab merchant fiercely demanded, "Did you make me fall in the puddle, or did you just know I would?" The demon was already out to get him, he thought fatalistically; what point in taking a soft line with it?

Both his vehemence and his question seemed to startle the *eliye*. It blinked, which was like briefly dropping a curtain over the fires of hell. Then it answered, "I can cause ill-luck in men, or I can merely announce it. Why should the difference matter to you?"

Why indeed? Sa'id wondered. He cursed the *eliye* in the name of Allah, a name to which it, like the *kölčin*, proved disappointingly immune. "I might have known," the merchant muttered. Gathering his dignity, he pressed on to the home of the Chinese nobleman.

The noble, punctiliously polite like most of his countrymen, appeared to take no notice of Sa'id's bedraggled state. They dickered for the next couple of hours with few distractions: the noble knew hardly more of the Mongol tongue than numbers and the words for gold and silver, while Sa'id had almost no Chinese.

They managed, though, as people will who both want to come to an agreement. An ounce and a sixth of gold, Sa'id thought, while it would not redeem his losses at Bagadan's hands, would at least keep him eating a good while longer.

The lock lay on the table between the two men. The

noble was just reaching for it when Sa'id heard the *eliye* say, "What a pity the merchandise got wet." A rusty tear oozed out of the keyhole. The noble saw it. His hand froze in midair. Still polite, he sadly shook his head. He scooped back the money he had been about to pay.

Sa'id picked up the lock and left. The *kölčin*, he suspected, would have laughed at him as he made his glum way down the street. The *eliye* kept quiet. In a way, that was worse. The *eliye* did not mock for the sake of mocking. When it spoke up, trouble immediately followed.

More and more, the merchant regretted the sinful life he had led, although in fact he was no more sinful than the ordinary run of mankind. But if he had been purer, surely the demons would have had to obey when he banished them in the name of Allah. Since they would not, though, his next thought was to find someone who could bind them: in other words, a shaman.

How to go about it? As a Muslim, he had never thought he would need a shaman. Being without any better ideas, he went into a tavern, stood a couple of Mongol soldiers a drink or three, and told them most of his troubles—he did not mention who had set the demons on him. He did not say why, either; the memory of Bagadan's treachery still hurt too much to mention.

One of the Mongols thought the notion of a foreigner afflicted by the devils of his own people the funniest thing he had ever heard. He laughed and laughed, an empty-headed guffaw that reminded Sa'id why Muslims were forbidden strong drink.

The other soldier, whose name was Kisaga, proved more sympathetic. "Oh, be still, Etügen," he said when his companion would not stop giggling, and stuck an elbow in Etügen's ribs that almost knocked the laughing fool off his bench. Kisaga turned back to Sa'id. "An *eliye* once tormented my brother," he said. "The bird-demons are hard to bear, and hard to be rid of, too."

Hope, painfully strong, surged in Sa'id. "But your brother *did* rid himself of the *eliye?*" he demanded eagerly. "How?"

"A shaman, how else?" Kisaga replied. He drank again, while Sa'id waited in an agony of suspense. The Mongol belched, good manners among his people and Arabs both. Then he said, "The fellow lives in a shack out beyond the city wall, not far from the north gate. His name is Sülde—tell him you heard of him from Ulaghan's brother."

"Sülde. From Ulaghan's brother," Sa'id repeated. He wrung the Mongol's hand. "May Allah bless you and keep you and be gracious unto you!" He threw coins—Chinese style, with a square hole in the center so they could be strung—onto the table in front of Kisaga. "Drink deep, since your religion allows it." Then he hurried away, muttering, "Sülde. From Ulaghan's brother." Behind him, the two Mongols were already shouting for more beer.

A great many shacks stood not far outside Kaifeng's north gate. What had been the two outer walls were now low, ruinous mounds half-covered by grass and bushes. The buildings they had warded were most of them ruins too. That did not keep people from living in them. Some folk raised gardens in the vacant spaces that had once held adjoining houses. Others looked more likely to be interested in harvesting the gardeners. Sa'id was glad his knife hung prominently from his belt.

Few dwellers in the shantytown spoke the Mongol tongue, and the merchant could not make much sense of Chinese. He managed even so, repeating Sülde's name with an exaggerated questioning note and doling out an occasional copper when he thought he saw a spark of recognition. Some, he knew, would be wasted money, but perhaps not all.

And so it proved. The path he took through the tumble-down buildings twisted back on itself several times, as if it were one of the horde of contorted characters the Chinese used to write their language. But in the end it led him to the shaman.

Sülde stood outside a shack even more decrepit than most, watching four goats as they mowed down shrubs and clumps of grass much more efficiently than any man with a scythe. The shaman was dressed in a costume Sa'id had seen on others of his kind: a fringed coat and the apron known as the "brown-spotted tiger"—brown and orange strips of cotton cloth cunningly sewn together to resemble the pelt of the great hunting cat.

Sa'id bowed very low, as he might have before a *qadi* in a mosque. "Excellent Sülde?" he asked, wanting to be sure. The shaman nodded. Encouraged, the merchant went on, "Excellent Sülde, I am sent to you by Ulaghan's brother. He tells me you drove off an *eliye* that had been tormenting Ulaghan. One of these spirits afflicts me now. If you free me of it, I will pay you well."

Sülde did not reply for some moments. He was studying Sa'id as the Arab studied him. Sa'id saw a middle-aged man whose face, though wide, high-cheekboned, and narrow-eyed like those of most Mongols, was not the impassive mask so many of his countrymen affected. Sülde, Sa'id thought, had suffered a good deal. His face bore no physical scars, but the harsh lines around his mouth, between his eyes, and on his cheeks were as daunting as any wounds.

"An *eliye*," the shaman said. He sighed, long and slow. When he did, Sa'id saw how those lines had come to be. Unease prickled through the Arab. He did not like to think of a pagan as a holy man, but with Sülde found he had no choice. The shaman sighed again, repeated, "An *eliye*. Well, come inside. We shall see."

He *was* a holy man, Sa'id decided as he followed him in: he had not made sure of the price before he set to work. The inside of the house smelled strongly of goat. Sülde rummaged in what looked like—what was—a pile of junk. He pulled out a rod and a round mirror of polished bronze. Nine dragons coiled round its back.

"My mount to the spirit world," he said to Sa'id. Then he began to chant, "O my mirror, O my mirror, red and decorated with dragons, oppressor of infant demons." He held the mirror in his left hand, the rod in his right. It was, Sa'id saw, loosely covered with snakeskin. The skin rustled as he shook it.

Sa'id somehow sensed the *eliye* coming into the room. It hovered in the air in front of Sülde. "Begone, bird-demon, begone!" the shaman cried. He shook the rod again. "Begone, lest this serpent swallow thee down."

Sa'id rubbed his eyes. Was the wood twisting hungrily, as if alive? After being the target of Bagadan's malignant magic, the merchant was not ready to deny anything.

And the *eliye* was not ready to leave. Its laugh was high and thin and horrible. "One fiercer than you set me on this wretch, shaman. With him I stay. This for your serpent!" It darted forward. There was a dry crack as Sülde's rod snapped in two. The shaman wailed. The *eliye* laughed again. "And all your goats have run away as well," it said. Then it did vanish, but all too plainly of its own volition rather than Sülde's.

The shaman rushed outside. His second wail was not so anguished as the first, but even more dismayed. Sa'id blinked in the sunlight after the shade of the shack, but long before his eyes had fully recovered, he saw the *eliye* was right—all the goats were gone.

"My last herd," Sülde moaned. He slowly turned to Sa'id. "May the ninety-nine *tngri* and the seventy-seven earth-mothers aid you, stranger. I have not the strength."

"Would some other shaman?" Sa'id asked. How quickly he had come to accept that the pagan sorcerers had power.

But Sülde only shrugged. "I thought I did. Since I have failed, how can I say what someone else might or might not do? I will say, though, that I have never been reckoned the least of shamans."

"Wonderful," Sa'id muttered in Arabic. With an effort, he switched back to the Mongol speech: "Let me pay you for your goats, at least. Had it not been for me, you would not have lost them." He reached for his belt-pouch.

"You are a man of honor," Sülde said, bowing.

"I keep bargains," Sa'id said—unlike Bagadan, he thought. And what did it get him? Here he was, giving too much of his scant remaining money to a man who had not helped him, while the accursed governor, after cheating Sa'id who had dealt fairly with him, sent demons out against him for protest, and despite all that still prospered. Truly Allah's ways were not for mankind to understand.

Shoulders sagging, the Arab merchant walked slowly back toward Kaifeng's surviving wall. He passed through the north gate and into the city.

Something breathed in his left ear. He jumped and whipped his head around. A small grinning demon was sitting on his left shoulder. It breathed straight into his face. Its breath was unspeakably foul.

It looked familiar. After a moment, he realized why: its nasty little face was a grotesque caricature of Bagadan's. "Allah curse you and your master both," Sa'id growled, not because he thought it would do any good but because he had nothing whatever to lose anymore. "Allah curse you"—he paused, trying to remember the name Bagadan had given to the third kind of demon with which the governor had threatened him—"filthy *ada*." Maybe recalling the name would make his curse strike home.

And maybe not. The *ada* breathed in his face again. It laughed while he choked and gagged. "You should not bespeak me so, when I am here to give you the last of my master's gifts," it said. "My breath brings fever, fever for which there is no cure. Your remaining days will be short, and filled with pain. As you live them, think on the folly of insulting one mightier than you."

The *ada* rose straight into the air. Sa'id stood watching it until it vanished. Then, having nothing better to do, he started toward the caravanserai. He felt an ache in his bones—his imagination, or the first bite of the fever? He would find out soon enough. He wished he thought the demon was lying.

The glance up into the sky had surprised him. The heavens were the deep blue of twilight. Linkbearers lit torches at street corners. Kaifeng's streets were so bright at night, few footpads prowled them. Sa'id would almost have welcomed one: the bludgeon or the knife gave a quicker, cleaner end than fever.

But no footpads found him. Perhaps, he thought gloomily, Bagadan's sorceries left him immune to such, so the governor could be sure of enjoying to the fullest his own revenge.

For the first time, self-pity threatened to drown the merchant. What a hard thing it was to be dying unjustly so far from home! Every man died, aye, but better by far in one's own town and among kin than here in this alien land, surrounded by pagans and the works of pagans.

The Chinese, indeed, cared not at all about Sa'id or his troubles. The sound of joyous singing came loud from a brightly lit, brightly painted building as the Arab merchant trudged past. He hesitated, frowning. Somewhere he had heard this song before—somewhere not in China.

The memory would not come. He started to walk on down the street. Yes, it was getting late, he thought—the evening star burned brilliantly in the western sky.

He stopped. The sight of the star brought recollection flooding back to him. He had been home in Damascus five—no, six—years ago, walking through the streets when he'd heard singing like this. The evening star had blazed then too.

"L'kha dodi, l'kras kalo, p'nay shabbas—"

No, the words were not Chinese. They were not Arabic either. Sa'id shook his head in bemused wonder. He had never expected to find a synagogue full of Jews in Kaifeng. They went everywhere, it seemed. He laughed. Why, for all he knew, there were Jews in chilly Frank-land.

He took a couple of more steps in the direction of the caravanserai, then stopped again. Jews, of course, were not Muslims, and would not acknowledge the truth Allah had given the world through Muhammad. Yet Jews were not pagans, either. They were *dhimmi*s, people of the Book, for they too had a scripture revealed to them by God. And in their insistence on God's unity, in many ways they came closer to Islam than Christians did.

And Sa'id was a desperate man, now more than ever. The evening was growing cool, but unpleasant sweat ran down his face. When he touched his forehead, he found it hot. Sure enough, the *ada* had given him its evil gift.

He turned around and hurried toward the synagogue. Jews were not Muslims, but in their own way they worshiped the same God he did. And if these Jews had been in China long enough to set up this house of worship, then likely they had also made the acquaintance of the local evil spirits. Maybe too, just maybe, they knew what to do about them.

The sight of the big man standing in the doorway gave the Arab merchant pause. The fellow looked as Chinese as everyone else in Kaifeng. The man frowned at seeing Sa'id, too. He said something in Chinese. "I do not understand," Sa'id said, using the Mongol tongue.

The door guard switched to that language. "I have not seen you before. What do you want here?"

"To pray to the one God," Sa'id answered.

The big man stepped aside, a broad smile kindling on his face. "Enter, then, stranger, and pray."

Bowing his thanks, Sa'id went in and found a seat on one of the benches on the men's side of the synagogue. He sat quietly—he did not know or understand the prayers the congregation was sending toward heaven. Every so often, though, he would catch a word that seemed familiar: Arabic and Hebrew were cousins, like Islam and Judaism.

Unable to follow along, the merchant passed time studying the worshipers. What struck him hardest was how few of the people looked like him. Most seemed as Chinese as anyone else in Kaifeng; only a few had heavier beards or more aquiline features that suggested western ancestry.

When the last incomprehensible hymn had been sung, the people rose from their seats and began chattering not in Hebrew but in Chinese, which meant no more to Sa'id than had the prayers. He made his way through the crowd toward the men who stood by the altar. If anyone could help him, it would be one of them.

The rabbi wore an embroidered robe that one of Bagadan's chief aides would have been proud to own. His face might also have passed unremarked in the governor's palace. And as the door guard had, he greeted Sa'id in Chinese.

"Holy sir, do you understand the Mongol speech?" the merchant asked.

"Yes." The rabbi switched languages without effort. "This unworthy person, sir, is called Yen Hui." He eyed Sa'id with keen interest. "Can it be that you are a traveler from the distant western land of which our holy books speak?"

"Yes," said Sa'id, and gave his own name and trade. Rabbi Yen Hui bowed again. The merchant bowed too, saying, "I had not known any Jews made their homes in Kaifeng."

Yen Hui smiled. "The community has been here a hundred years and more. The first Jews in this land were merchants like yourself, sir, but since their time many here have come to accept their ways. This is a good home for us; no one in Kaifeng mistreats us on account of our faith, as the holy books and the tales of our ancestors tell us happens elsewhere."

"May you continue to prosper, then," Sa'id said. He bowed once more to the Chinese rabbi, which gave him time to think. When he straightened, though, a wave of dizziness washed over him. He shifted his weight to keep his balance.

"Are you well, excellent sir?" Yen Hui looked concerned.

"No," the merchant answered. Yen Hui looked more concerned—as well he might, Sa'id thought: illness spread all too easily, especially in a crowded city. The Arab went on to explain his predicament, ending, "And so I thought —I hoped—that you, who worship the same one God as I, yet who know the ways of this land, may also know the way to rid me of its evil spirits. I hoped . . ." His voice trailed away.

The rabbi's frown had deepened as Sa'id spoke. Yen Hui muttered to himself, first in Hebrew and then in Chinese, neither of which the Arab could follow. "As the holy psalm says, 'Guard thy tongue from evil, and thy lips from speaking guile. Depart from evil and do good," Yen Hui explained. "The Master agrees: 'Without an acquaintance with the rules of propriety, it is impossible for the character to be established.'"

"The Master?" Sa'id echoed. Having dealt with Christians and Jews in Damascus and elsewhere, he knew of the psalms and of other parts of the holy books the *dhimmi*s revered, but he had never heard any of their prophets or sages styled the Master.

"Master Kung Fu-dze, of course," Yen Hui said. "A sage who lived long ago here in China. His words may not be divine, but they are very wise, and always worth considering."

"Hmm," Sa'id said, thinking that living in the midst of the pagan Chinese and intermarrying with them was giving a pagan cast to these people's Judaism. Having already consorted with a Mongol shaman, however, he was in no position to sneer at anyone's doctrinal purity. And suddenly he felt so hot and weak that he had to sink down onto a bench. "Can you help me?" he gasped.

"Not now," the rabbi answered, and Sa'id's heart sank. But Yen Hui went on, "The Sabbath, the day of rest, began at sunset; for as long as it lasts I may undertake no great labor, and certainly no magic. But if you return after the sun goes down tomorrow, I will do for you what I can."

"Thank you, holy sir, thank you." Sa'id struggled to his feet, bowed to Yen Hui.

The rabbi raised a hand. "Do not thank me yet, man from the land where our holy men lived. God willing, I hope I will be able to free you from these demons, but I am less sure I can persuade the governor to pay you what he owes."

"Oh. That." Since the *ada*'s fever began sinking into his bones, Sa'id had stopped worrying about whether he would ever see the price Bagadan had lyingly promised him for his goods. Surviving was more urgent. "The money is of small consequence—"

Yen Hui cut him off again. "Still, I do have hope. As the Master says, 'When a man's knowledge is sufficient to attain but his virtue is not sufficient to let him hold, he will lose again whatever he has gained.'"

The Arab merchant thought that through, then slowly nodded. Yen Hui had a point: this Master Kung Fu-dze was no one's fool. And however much evil knowledge Bagadan had, if all his virture were rolled together into a ball, it would not be enough to match one of the preserved capers the governor had loathed.

"Sleep, rest, preserve your strength," the rabbi urged. "Return tomorrow evening, and I will do for you what I may."

"I will pay you well," Sa'id promised.

"'Labor not to be rich,' says the Book of Proverbs," Yen Hui said, "and the Master agrees: 'With coarse rice to eat, with water to drink, and only my arm for a pillow—I still have joy among these things. Riches and honors got by unrighteousness are to me as a floating cloud.'"

"As may be," Sa'id said. "Free me and I will pay you well, if not for your sake then for my own honor."

"Ah." Yen Hui bowed low. "'Length of days is in her right hand, and in her left riches and honor.' But remember also, 'Before honor is humility.'"

Of humility Sa'id had made a closer acquaintance these past few days than he really wanted: being beset by a magic one is powerless to resist will do that to a man. He bowed too, and made his slow, painful way to the door. He was already out in the street before he thought to wonder whether Yen Hui had been quoting from the Jews' holy book or the ancient Chinese sage.

He was not curious enough to go back and ask.

Master Chao exclaimed in dismay when the Arab merchant stumbled exhausted into the caravanserai taproom. So did the handful of men still sitting around drinking and talking. A couple of them hastily got up and left, circling round to stay as far from Sa'id as possible while they did.

I must look as bad as I feel, Sa'id thought. "Don't worry, Chao," he said. "I won't stay down here frightening your customers. I'm going straight up to bed."

"Here." The serai-keeper opened a brass box, gave Sa'id a spoonful of finely chopped black-brown aromatic herbs. "Pour boiling water over these, then drink," Chao said. "You feel better then."

The merchant doubted it but, touched, took the herbs regardless. He had to rest twice on the stairs before he made it up to his room. Though he was sure his was not the sort of fever drugs would cure, he brewed up the herb-water anyway. He drank it down. It was fragrant and soothing, and perhaps did more good than he had expected. He merely felt elderly as he slid beneath his blankets.

When he woke up the next morning, he was a great deal worse than elderly. Greasy sweat poured from him; he could not stop shivering, even under the pile of furs and silks. Yet despite his pangs of chill, his forehead burned his hand when he touched it.

He brewed more herb-steeped water. If it helped this time, that help was barely noticeable. And the effort of making the brew cost him much of his slender reserve of strength. The room was spinning when he half dove, half collapsed into bed.

He was never sure afterwards how much of what he saw that day was real, how much the product of his delirium. Did the *kölčin*, the *eliye*, and the *ada* come into his chamber and dance round him in sprightly circles? He accepted it calmly enough at the time. It seemed hardly more marvelous than the way sunbeams crawled across the floor.

In a lucid moment, he realized he would have been dead already had Bagadan not wanted him to suffer first. "Well," he said out loud, as if the governor were there with his demonic creatures, "I'm not through with you, either."

Those intervals of clarity came more often as afternoon slid toward evening. Sa'id made himself get up, sensing that if he did not do it now he might never have another chance. Each step he took was a separate, deliberate act of will. The triumph he felt on reaching the bottom of the stairs was hardly less than he had known after first making it to China.

Chao's expression told the merchant everything he needed to know about how he looked. "You go back up to bed," the serai-keeper said. "You be better come morning."

Sa'id, who knew he would *not* be better come morning, walked out into the twilight.

Where much of the day had gone by in a fever-induced blur, he remembered every painful step of the walk to the synagogue. It was a journey he always wished he could forget, not least on account of the moment of panic when he could not remember whether to go right or left at an intersection.

He stood shivering, as much from fear as from fever. If he chose wrong, weakness would surely overcome him before he could correct the mistake. He could not remember. "Let it be as Allah pleases," he muttered, and chose the left-hand fork.

Two blocks farther along, he came to a particularly ornate building that he recognized. He had made the proper choice. No wonder, he thought: instead of putting demands to God, he had submitted himself to His will. And what was Islam but submission to God?

Seeing Sa'id, the door guard waved him into the synagogue. "Rabbi Yen Hui awaits you," the fellow said.

Await him the rabbi did, along with a boy of seven or eight dressed in white robes. The boy was beautiful enough to stir longing even in Sa'id, who normally cared only for women. Perhaps the gauzy white veil the boy wore made him seem more feminine to the Arab. A symbol, presumably magical, was painted in gold on the veil.

Rabbi Yen Hui also wore white. His black veil bore the same symbol as the boy's. "Sit," he urged Sa'id. "I see the evildoer's spell has advanced in you. Rest now, as you must. Soon, God willing, your health will be restored."

The Arab merchant sank onto a bench, then struggled to rise once more. "Will you not need me for your sorcery?" he asked.

Yen Hui shook his head. "No. I shall conjure in the Holy of Holies, which only I and this child who is my assistant may enter. As well as linking me to the pure and innocent angels, he will also serve as intermediary between the two of us."

"As you wish, of course." Sa'id dipped his head.

"Fear not," the rabbi said. "As the sacred book tells us, 'Treasures of wickedness profit nothing, but righteousness delivereth from death.'"

"May it be so," Sa'id murmured.

"May it indeed." Yen Hui turned to the boy, spoke to him in Chinese. Graceful as a dancer, the boy bowed low. From back of the altar, he picked up a censer, several sticks of incense, and a lighted lamp. He carried them through a doorway set into the wall beyond the altar. When he returned, he brought with him the sweet smell of burning incense. "Now it is my turn," the rabbi told Sa'id. Yen Hui prostrated himself in the doorway, then went in. Darkness enfolded him.

The boy stood quietly, waiting until he should be needed again. Sa'id watched him; he took no notice whatever of the Arab. Inside the sanctum, Yen Hui's voice rose and fell, now in guttural Hebrew, now in singsong Chinese.

Suddenly the rabbi spoke a sharp command. Sa'id sat up and exclaimed in awe, for pearly light streamed from the doorway of the Holy of Holies and an odor beside which the savor of incense was as dross filled his nostrils. The boy's calm smile said he had expected no less.

Yen Hui called out in Chinese. The boy hurried to the altar. He stooped behind it again, came back to Sa'id carrying a small square silver plate in his left hand. Inscribed on the lamen, Sa'id saw, was the same sign the boy and Yen Hui wore on their veils.

The boy spoke. Sa'id shrugged. Seeing he did not understand Chinese, the boy grabbed his left hand and pressed it down onto the silver plate. For an instant, the magic sign was cold as ice against his skin. Then the chill vanished.

Smiling, the boy carried the lamen to Yen Hui. The rabbi emerged from the sanctum to take it, disappeared inside once more. With that strange light blazing forth, Sa'id should have been able to see him in there. He could not.

The rabbi was chanting again, now in Hebrew alone, his voice strong and sonorous. He cried out. The supernal radiance he had summoned shone even brighter. The sign Sa'id had seen on the veils and on the lamen glowed for a moment in midair before his eyes. "There is no God but Allah!" the merchant exclaimed, and threw an arm up in front of his face. He saw the symbol anyhow.

It slowly faded. As it did, Sa'id felt his fever fade with it. "There *is* no God but Allah," he said softly. He felt very tired, but otherwise as well as he ever had in his life.

The pearly radiance inside the Holy of Holies faded as well. The doorway became just a dark doorway again. Yen Hui came out through it. The rabbi also looked tired. His eyes flicked to Sa'id. "Are you well?" he asked.

"I am well, holy sir, thanks to you." Sa'id rose. He was amazed at how easy, how painless, motion could be. He prostrated himself before Yen Hui, as if he were inside a mosque.

"Up, my friend, up," the rabbi said. As Sa'id got back to his feet, Yen Hui went on, "Thanks to God and His holy angels, no necromantic or magical operations will take effect on you, and the sorcerer who created these wicked enchantments will be sorely hindered from operating thus henceforward."

"Will he?" As he imagined Bagadan's dismay, Sa'id's smile grew beatific.

"One thing more." Yen Hui drew a sheet of paper from the sleeve of his robe, handed it to the merchant. Sa'id looked at it curiously. On it was drawn a square, which internal vertical and horizontal lines broke up into twenty-five smaller squares. Most of these had letters—Hebrew letters, the merchant saw, not Chinese characters—inside; some were blank. "When next you see Bagadan," the rabbi said, "touch this paper with your right hand and, God willing, your debt will be repaid."

"Inshallah," Sa'id echoed. "God willing."

This time, the Chinese aides who ushered Sa'id into the presence of the governor of Kaifeng treated him with wary politeness, not the barely veiled amusement they had shown when Bagadan was about to rob the Arab. He took that as a good sign.

Bagadan scowled as Sa'id bowed to him. "You are well," the governor said. It sounded like an accusation.

Pretending not to hear Bagadan's tone, Sa'id politely relied, "Very well, thank you, esteemed sir."

"Get out," Bagadan growled to the functionaries who had led the merchant to his chamber. They fled. When they were gone, the governor rounded on Sa'id. *"Why* are you well?"

"Because of the power of the one God, of course." Sa'id chose not to mention that the folk who had come to his aid were Jews, not Muslims. He tried not to think about what that might mean: *dhimmi*s did, after all, possess part of the truth. And surely, had one been in Kaifeng, a Muslim holy man could have done as well as rabbi Yen Hui. Surely...

"I spit on your one god," Bagadan snarled.

"Esteemed sir, I am sorry for you," Sa'id said aloud. What he thought, however, was that Sa'id was spitting on Bagadan as well, by preventing him from harming others as he had Sa'id.

"Sorry, are you?" the governor grunted. "Ha. I know better than that. Came here to gloat, didn't you?"

"No, esteemed sir." Again Sa'id's thoughts did not match his words: his mental answer was *No, just to get my money back, you thief.* He touched the magic square.

Nothing seemed to happen. Bagadan kept right on glaring at him. The governor said, "Not only are you well, but all my sorcery has gone awry lately—the spirits will not answer me." Bagadan was not a good man, but he was not a stupid one, either. "Do you have something to do with that?" he demanded.

"Esteemed sir, I know nothing of magic. As I said before, I am sorry for you." What a liar I'm getting to be, Sa'id thought. He touched the paper Yen Hui had given him again.

It still did not seem to be doing anything. "A likely story," Bagadan snorted. He slammed a fist down hard on the desk. His expression turned calculating. "What would it take, trader, to get myself free of your spell?"

Sa'id began to cough. It kept him from blurting out something stupid, like *"My* spell?" Instead, he cocked an eyebrow and sat silent. He surreptitiously touched the paper one more time—maybe there was something to it after all.

Bagadan grumbled, "I suppose I could pay you in gold." He sounded about as happy at the prospect as a man who was going to lose a tooth.

"The price has gone up two ounces," Sa'id said flatly. "Call it requital for the suffering you inflicted on me."

Bagadan's face went dark with rage. For a moment, Sa'id thought he had gone beyond the power of the magic square, even though he did not intend to keep the two extra ounces of gold himself. Then the Mongol governor slumped in his seat. Being unable to control his spirits had to be torment for him. He shouted until one of his servitors came rushing into the chamber. "Fetch me paper equivalent to four and five-sixths ounces of gold," Bagadan told him without preamble. "Now."

The aide dashed away. He was back in seconds, his hands full of sheets of paper. *Big* sheets of paper, Sa'id saw.

Bagadan counted them out himself. ". . . Four and a sixth, four and a third, four and a half, four and two-thirds, four and five-sixths." He thrust the pile at Sa'id. "Are you satisfied?"

The merchant nodded.

"Then never let me see you again," Bagadan said.

Nodding once more, Sa'id rose and left. As long as he was still in the governor's palace, he kept his pace dignified. As soon as he got outside, he started to trot. He had never promised to do anything for Bagadan. Maybe the governor would not realize that until he tried to work magic again. Maybe he would think of it in the next minute, or the next second. Sa'id did not want to be around when that happened.

One stop the merchant did have to make. Panting, he walked into the synagogue. The door guard was dozing in the outer hall when Sa'id came in; the sound of footsteps brought him awake at once. He reached for the club beside him, then relaxed as he saw who it was.

Sa'id handed him papers worth two ounces of gold. "Give these to your rabbi, with my thanks. I would present them personally, but—"

The door guard grinned at him. "You have urgent business elsewhere. I understand. The one God watch you and keep you."

"And you." Sa'id hurried out, headed for the caravanserai to gather up his goods. *The one God,* he thought. Here in this pagan land full of pagan magic, all who followed the one God—Muslims, Jews, even, he supposed, Christians who divided Him into Three—saw how small their differences truly were, and so could work together. Might things ever be like that in Damascus?

The Arab doubted it. Thanks to the Jews of Kaifeng, though, he would have the chance to go home one day and find out.

He ran on.

The Tale of the Four Accused

Gene Wolfe

In the name of Allah, the Compassionating, the Compassionate! Praise be to Allah, the Beneficent King, the Creator of the Universe, the Lord of the Three Worlds! Then know, O Prince, that following the adventures already related, the Caliph Harun al-Rashid summoned his wazir Ja'afar one night and said to him, "I desire to go down into the city and question the common folk concerning the conduct of those charged with governance; and those of whom they complain we will depose, and those whom they commend we will promote. Do thou, Ja'afar, procure the rags of fishermen and such nets as fishermen use."

Quoth Ja'afar, "Hearkening and obedience!" So the Caliph went Baghdad-ward with Ja'afar and the eunuch Masrur, all habited as fisherfolk.

Now as they wended near the riverbank, Allah willed that they should meet the Cadi, and the Caliph, fearing that his face might be seen and he known (though it was after the fifth prayer) hung his head down, and Ja'afar and Masrur did likewise. Then said the Cadi, seeing them to walk so, "What ails you, fishermen, that you walk with your eyes cast to the ground?"

And Ja'afar, stepping forward to be spokesman, answered, "Protector of the Poor, all this day have my companions and I cast our nets, but not one fish hath come in."

The Cadi was a man of generosity and ruth, and thinking upon this answer and the downcast visages of the Caliph and Masrur he said, "Hark then to what I propose. Each of you go once to the river with me and cast the net,

75

and whatsoever you draw forth I shall buy for a gold dinar."

Masrur the eunuch cast first, but he drew forth nothing save mud and water.

Ja'afar cast after him, and brought forth from the river the head of an ass long dead, and the Cadi cursed him and gave him nothing.

Last cast the Caliph, twirling his net as the fishers do, and Ja'afar feared for the life of the Cadi, for he knew that if he should kick or curse him he should die in the morning. But the Caliph's net held fast, and the meshes were strained, and the strength of all three scarcely sufficient to draw it to the bank. Then the Cadi, looking within, saw there a wooden chest fairly made, of great size, and bound with brass; and he rejoiced. To the Caliph he gave as promised a dinar; then Ja'afar and Masrur bore the chest to his house.

When they were within the courtyard, the Cadi bade a servant bring a lamp and addressed the three thus: "Now will you go, or is it your will to remain and behold what it may be you have sold me?"

"By Allah," quoth the Caliph, "as I am a true man I shall not stir foot until I have seen what my net brought up."

Then the servants of the Cadi broke open the chest, and behold! there was within a great sack, white, and of fine Damascus cloth, and under it another, black. These were sewn at the tops with fine stitching, but the Cadi cut it with the jambiya from his sash; and when this was done, there tumbled forth from the white sack the head, limbs and trunk of a maid who had been bright as a silver bar, like her of whom the poet saith:

> *She rose like the morn as she shone through the night,*
> *And she gilded the grove with her gracious sight:*
> *From her radiance the sun taketh increase when*
> *She unveileth and shameth the moonshine so bright.*

But all her limbs had been cloven at one stroke through the bone, and when the second sack was emptied in its turn, there spilt forth just such another, save that the girl was black.

Thus the night; but when morn came bright to delight men's sight, the Caliph held court in great splendor, and to him he summoned the Cadi and described all that had occurred with such detail and correctness that the Cadi shook to live beneath the all-seeing gaze of such a monarch. "Not," swore the Caliph, "while I breathe shall any man dare to deal thus with the daughters of the Moslems. How dost thou propose to bring to the seat of my justice he who hath done this?" And the Cadi feared with exceeding fear, for he knew not how the Caliph's will might be accomplished, though he and his officers had already sought all the night.

Then came forward Ja'afar, and kissing the ground between his hands seven times spoke thusly: "O Wonder of the Age, give me this Cadi to aid me, and leave to absent myself a time from thy court; and with the help of Allah this shall be unraveled." And the Caliph said, "Bismillah!"

Then Ja'afar had the heads of the girls, black and white, displayed in the market, with the Cadi's officers standing by to ask what was known of them of all who passed. This they continued to do from morn to evening for two days, but in that time no one came forth, not even one, who would say the maids were known to him. So upon the eve of the second day, Ja'afar took council with himself, saying, "If none in Baghdad, or very few, know these maids, then it must be that they are strangers newly come hither; I will ask at the khan."

Thither he went, taking with him two of the Cadi's officers and an executioner. Now the master of the khan was a graybeard Shaykh like him of whom the poet saith:

> Time gars me tremble. Ah, how sore the baulk!
> While Time in pride of strength doth ever stalk:
> Time was I walked nor ever felt I tired,
> Now am I tired albeit I never walk!

To him Ja'afar said without preamble, "In thy khan a little time ago dwelt two maids—a black and a white. Whither are they gone?"

At this the master of the khan trembled exceedingly and said, "O my Master, I know not. They were here even as you say, and are now gone hence, but whither none but Allah—his name is Glorious and Great—knoweth."

"If thou wittest not of their going," quoth Ja'afar, "what of their coming?"

"O my Master," said the master of the khan, "two months past they came, having ten she-mules richly caparisoned and a black slave, Sa'ad hight. Whilst here they did visit various of the merchants, but most often that tailor whose shop is just without this khan. Ten days past I woke and they were gone, and the day following their mules and slave also, and that is all I know."

At this Ja'afar stroked his beard. "O Shaykh," quoth he at length, "thou has said, 'They having a black slave.' And not, 'She having two slaves, man and maid.' Why is this?"

"O my Master," said the Shaykh, "black and white were dressed alike, in fine stuffs, with their trouser bands sewn with seed pearls, and once I overheard the white say to the black, 'We are in the north now, and I am the mistress. Wend we south again I'll be thy she-mamluke.' Then the black, laughing, did some little task she had been bid. But the slave Sa'ad seemed a slave indeed, to hew and draw, and cleanse the feet of the mules."

Then said Ja'afar to the executioner and the Cadi's officers, "Now shall we speak to the tailor," and they to him, "Hearing and obedience."

This tailor had his shop at the very entrance to the khan, and a small and crook-legged man was he. To him Ja'afar said, "What of the two maids from the khan who oft visited you. Where are they now?" And the tailor trembled and said, "I know not."

"Then," said Ja'afar, "thou shalt tell us why two maids had such frequent business with a tailor."

"Prince of Wazirs," said the tailor, "each morning they brought me raiment ripped and torn. This I mended and returned to them when they brought more, and that is all I know." But Ja'afar saw he shook with fear.

"Each day they did this?" asked Ja'afar. "Would they not rather say, 'Each morn do thou come to us with what thou has mended and receive what is torn'?"

"Thy wisdom knows all," admitted the tailor, trembling more than ever. "It was at first as I said, but afterward as you said."

"Ten days since," quoth Ja'afar, "they were gone from the khan. Went thou to them that day also?"

"Nay," said the tailor. "Upon that day, the son of my sister, the best of nephews, died. I and mine mourned in my house, and I went not out."

Then Ja'afar looked upon the executioner, and the executioner upon Ja'afar the Wazir, and clearing with a sweep of his arm the table where the tailor cut his cloth said to him, "Friend, do thou for a moment only lay your head upon this wood, and fret not that thy back may become cramped thus, for I shall not require it of thee long." And he raised his scimitar till the hair beneath his arms showed; and the Cadi's officers dashed the tailor's face against the top of the table and held him there with their fingers in his turban.

Then quoth the tailor, "Prince of Wazirs, on the day named I went, even as thou sayest. In the lower part of the khan I saw the mules belonging to those women, but when I came to the upper part where they lodged they were departed. The clothing they had left with me I left there, and I departed."

"How now," replied Ja'afar. "Left without your money? Would my tailor were of thy kidney," and he nodded to the executioner.

"Prince of Wazirs!" wailed the tailor. "I went to the apartment of the master of the khan, and when he opened his door I heard within a sound like the chopping of wood. The Shaykh took the clothing and paid me, and by Allah I know no more."

Then Ja'afar signed to the Cadi's officers to let the tailor go, and all four went out from the shop.

"Where now, Master?" said one when they were well away.

"Whither the maids went we know," answered Ja'afar. "Whence the slave wended will, mayhap, ever be unknown, since he came not forth when the heads of his mistresses were shown in the market; but ten mules do not—save Allah will it—sink like water into the ground. Let us go to the horse-fair."

Then know, Prince, that after much asking at the horse-fair Allah revealed to Ja'afar's sight that the ten mules and their equipages had been bought by a trader whose caravan had departed even that day for Cairo, and after a gallop the Cadi's officers retrieved them and brought them to Ja'afar's stables.

On the day following, the Caliph held court, and when this was ended, Ja'afar went to him privately and told him all that had occurred. (But in repetition there is no fruition.) Then said the Caliph, "It seems sure this slave hath slain his mistresses that he might sell their goods and flee."

But Ja'afar said, "Light of the Faithful, by no means. If he journeyed with them from the Bilad al-Sudan, the land of black men, as it seems, why should he take them safe through the desert to slay them in the midst of the khan? And why did the Shaykh, the master of the khan, pay the tailor? And what chopping sound was it that reached the tailor's ears?"

"Then," quoth the Caliph, "it was the master of the khan. Do thou send the executioner to him."

"He is an old man and feeble," replied Ja'afar. "And I think not one who could strike strongly even at women. He is a godly man and learned, and not, I think, one eager to evil."

"By Allah," quoth the Caliph, "knowest thou the coffer nearest the door of my treasury? It holds gems and cups, coins and rings and silver and gold. That coffer will I give to him who reads me this riddle aright." And so Ja'afar went away, thinking deeply.

On the day after, Ja'afar summoned the executioner to him, and together they bought a goat in the market. This the executioner led, as Ja'afar bade him, to a wasteland outside the city wall, and hewed it to bits with his scimitar while Ja'afar observed. All the remainder of that day Ja'afar spent in his own house, nor would he permit his wives nor his daughters nor his slave girls to play or sing to him, but made all walk quietly in the house, as if it were a house of death. When the moon had risen above the wall, and most folk of his house slept, he summoned to him the black cook Mas'ud. To him he said, "Know you, Mas'ud, what dishes are most grateful to the palates of the men of your country?"

"It is not true, Master," answered Mas'ud, "that we lust for men's flesh to eat, as some say. We black men savor sweet stews, melons, sugarcane, honey-bread, the confection called girl's spinning, and such like things."

"It is my will," quoth Ja'afar, "that you should leave my kitchen for a time, Mas'ud. My steward will give thee gold, and thou shalt go into the market and open there a cook's stall serving all the things beloved by thy countrymen. Thou shalt have wooden bowls for thy customers, and any who give you the smallest copper shall freely fill his bowl with what he likes. But to each who is not well known to thee, thou shall whisper as he fills, 'The white pot and the black are mended and require you.'"

And Ja'afar told him where his stall should stand and other things needful for him to know, and when he had finished, said the black cook Mas'ud, "Harkening and obedience," and went his way.

Then Ja'afar the Wazir called to him two of his mamlukes, and spoke to them thus: "Tomorrow go to the marketplace, and in such and such a spot will you find a Rawi telling his tales—and may Allah the Compassionate send blessings and gold to him and all storytellers. Sit and hear him, but let your eyes be not upon the Rawi but upon the stall of my cook Mas'ud close by. When a black man serves himself, and serving drops his bowl, bring him to me whether he will or no."

Thus upon the day following, his mamlukes brought to Ja'afar the slave Sa'ad, a black of the blacks, broad as a bench and tall as a spear, with eyes like eggs. And Ja'afar said to him, "Thou hast slain thy mistresses and hewn their corpses and sewn them in sacks and cast the sacks into a chest and the chest into the Tigris—all these things are well known to me. If you would pray before dying, pray now."

Then Sa'ad screamed with fear and spoke at length to Ja'afar, after which Ja'afar took Sa'ad, with two of the Cadi's officers and the executioner as before, and went to speak to that Shaykh the master of the khan. To him Ja'afar said, "Thou knowest for what we come. Go first with us to the tailor's, then thou must guide us to a certain tomb thou wit well of."

Trembling, the Shaykh did as the bidder bid, and after a rough walk and tiring through thicket and thorn led Wazir, executioner, tailor, and all to a ruined tomb far from the city gate. And there he spoke a word that cannot be uttered lest devils spring from the very earth, and there came from the tomb a Marid of the Marids, a most fearsome Djinni, with tushes like a boar's and a scimitar at his waist as long as an elephant's trunk and as heavy as a millstone. Then Ja'afar, who was learned in many ways, conjured him to obedience and carried them all before the Caliph.

When the Caliph saw the Djinni, and standing with him the master of the khan, the tailor, and the slave Sa'ad, he was sore amazed.

"Commander of the Faithful," quoth Ja'afar, "thou hast promised a treasure from thy treasury to him who brought before you the murderer of the two maids. Art satisfied?"

Then all four sent up a clamor of innocence, the Shaykh whining, the slave blubbering, the tailor crying like a girl, and the Marid bellowing like a bull.

"Silence!" commanded the Caliph.

Then said that old man the Shaykh, the master of the khan, "Wonder of the Age, would you know how we four accused, so dissimilar, come to stand before you? And how the clothing of those foul sorceresses you call maids was torn each morn? And how comes this Marid from the bed of the dead?"

And the Caliph said, "I would."

"Then know," quoth the Shaykh, "that those women were witches of the worst kind. They came from the Sutherland, having learnt there, by what means true men may not inquire, of the existence of this Marid, and of the word of mastery for him. This slave, who is innocent as I of any wrongdoing, they purchased in Egypt that they might have a servitor to drive their animals, and for a second purpose that thou shall hear.

"Now upon the first night of their coming, after I had

seen them settled into their apartments in my khan, they
sent him for me, feigning that they wished to thank me.
And while Sa'ad and I stood side by side they flung bridles
upon our heads as the fowler casts his net, and no sooner
had these touched us than we found ourselves deprived of
speech and unable to do aught but stand trembling before
them, gnawing our beards and rolling our eyes."

"It is true!" exclaimed Sa'ad the slave. "O Allah, does
this man not say as you saw?" And he beat his head upon
the ground before the Caliph.

"They stripped us of our garments," continued the
Shaykh, "and mounting our shoulders, the black witch
upon Sa'ad, the white upon me, they rode us as two men
might ride two wild mares from my khan to the tomb, the
thorns tearing their robes as they went. There they conjured
forth the Marid, even as I showed thy minister, O Light of
the Moslems, and sought all the night with spells, chants
and dances to compel him to their will. When the sun once
more bestriding heaven discovered them yet unsuccessful,
they permitted him to return to the tomb once more, and
mounting us as before returned to my khan. And from that
night forward, O Commander of the Faithful, such was our
fate until Allah made an end to those unholy women. Each
night were we called forth and bridled and ridden to the
tomb. And each night ridden back again to lie groaning in
our beds at dawn. But I am innocent of their blood."

"And I!" exclaimed Sa'ad the slave, beating head to
earth once more; and the tailor and the Djinni both echoed
him loud: "And I, O Commander of the Faithful!"

"By Allah," quoth the Caliph, "it is clear from what
hath passed here this hour that those women were witches
and necromancers of the worst kind. That treasure which I
reserved for him who should bring their murderer before
me, I shall now bestow as a reward to him who rid my
domain of the accursed creatures."

Then the Shaykh, the master of the khan, kissed the
ground between his hands and recited:

Pardon the sinful ways I did pursue;
Ruth from his lord to every slave is due:

Confession pays the fine that sin demands;
Where, then, is that which grace and mercy sue?

"O Commander of the Faithful," quoth the Shaykh, "it was I and none other who slew the women of whom thou speakest."

"Nay!" shouted the slave Sa'ad. "Upon the honor of black men—" Meanwhile the tailor beat his breast and rent his garments in agony of guilt and the Djinni tore up the paving stones with his fingers and ground them between his palms that he might shower their dust upon his head.

"How now?" quoth the Caliph to Ja'afar. "We had four accused. Now we have four confessed, and the knot tangled as ever."

"Sire," replied the Wazir, "I read thus the screed. The Shaykh learnt through long listening the word with which the women summoned this Marid. That is proved by his speaking it this day for me. But he has not strength to have cleaved their bones as was done, for not even your own executioner, O Commander of the Faithful, could do so with his great scimitar when he killed a goat that I might watch, thought he is a mighty man. The Djinni then did that, thus freeing himself from the nightly attempts of the women to enslave him."

"Then it was those two," quoth the Caliph.

But Ja'afar held up a hand. "The sacks within which the dismembered corpses were laid were sewn with no unskillful hand, O Commander of the Faithful and Glory of the World. The tailor did that, and I would surmise it took but a glimpse of this Marid with his great blade to compel his service and seal his tongue. There remains of this then only the riddle of the caster-away of the chest. The Shaykh and the tailor are too slight of build to carry so heavy a load. Had the Djinni done it he should have cast it into the depths of the sea, whence even thy net should never have brought it again to the shore. Sa'ad the slave then did that."

The Caliph rejoiced to have such a counselor and said, "Advise me on this, O Ja'afar the Wise. How shall I divide the reward I promised among four? For there are cups and cups, and rings and rings, and gems and gems. How shall four agree upon a just distribution?"

Quoth Ja'afar, "Commander of the Faithful, it is needful only that each have his reward. Observe—Sa'ad hath now no master and thus no roof beneath which to lay his head, or aught to eat. Give him to the tailor and thus is he rewarded and the tailor also, for the tailor has received a fine slave. As for the Marid, let him be taught the ordinances of al-Islam by the Shaykh, and thus the one shall have education and the other such a student as shall do him honor now and make a legend for him by and by."

And thus was it done, and no mystery remained but that of the coffer from the Caliph's treasury, which hath disappeared—but some say Ja'afar got that.

THE TALE OF THE SECOND DJINNA

And when the tellers of tales had finished, they sat down, as wearied as if they had fought through the storm from which the Emir of the Djinn of the deep desert had snatched them.

"It is my turn now," came a low voice, inhumanly lovely. From the cushions of a seat of honor in the center of the amphitheatre rose a djinna.

Her robes of taffeta and sendal clung to breast and hip as she walked from the amphitheatre, and she disdained the Emir's trick of materializing and dematerializing in order to allow mere mortal men to look their fill. Her gold-shot veil was the merest formality, and her eyes, outshining the threads of precious metal, betokened wisdom and passion.

Peter and his companions rose to honor her, though the tilt of her head, the pride of her carriage, told them more surely than words that there was no way that they could honor her sufficiently.

She faced the men and unveiled. The face thus revealed bore the too-perfect beauty of the djinna. Yet it was not the face of a maiden in her first youth, but rather that of a woman who is flawless in maturity; who has reached that age when beauty and wisdom form a harmony as perfect as it is dangerous for all those who run afoul of it.

"More pleasant were it," she said, smiling in a way that heated the men's blood despite the sherbets, the cool water brought by maidens, and the refreshing breezes, "if you surrendered now." She tilted her head to one side, and watched them out of eyes that were as entrancing as they were ancient.

"You are an infidel whose women walk shamelessly unveiled." The merchant prince poked at Peter's shoulder. "You speak to her."

"Lady," he said, dropping to one knee, "I am in despair at having to deny you aught; but we must refuse."

She met his eyes for a moment, promising him joys such as Suleiman surely knew with the Queen of Sheba until he lowered his head.

"Then I shall begin my tale," she said.

The Three Brides of Hamid-Dar

Tanith Lee

Now there was a beggar, the son of a beggar, who would each day take up his post under the date tree by the Well of the Wall. His name was Hamid-Dar, and he would tell a tale of himself in his youth to which, it was said, even the Caliph had once listened, although of course in disguise.

As a young man Hamid-Dar, who was lame, had yet been very comely, and for this reason now and then certain adventures had befallen him. One morning, as he was at his usual trade, leaning upon his staff by the Wall Well, a covered litter approached, borne by four slaves of a black that was almost blue. And out of the litter as it passed had slipped a fair female hand coiled with bracelets and rings, and this let drop at Hamid-Dar's two feet, the strong and the lame, a bag of that which clinked.

Can it be, thought Hamid-Dar, bending to pick up the bag, *that I am summoned again to visit the wife of the silk merchant? Surely that litter was not hers? Perhaps it is the spice merchant's widow's sister, of whom I have heard stories, but whom I have never yet met.* And with mixed feelings he took the bag and, assuring his fellow beggars that it contained only some nuts and figs (their unripe hardness causing the rattle it had made), he went away to examine it. On opening, the bag divulged several coins, and these of gold, so Hamid-Dar was amazed. Next he found a little parchment, which read as follows: "The astrologers inform us, to all men, high and low, Fate awards great chances. But they must be risked. Come then if you

89

will to the House of the Black Doors, as soon as the evening star has risen."

Now then, thought Hamid-Dar, *this is one of whom I
have* never *heard.*

And he went straight away to the bathhouse and the
barber's, and had himself prepared there like a dish for a
queen's supper.

At the proper time Hamid-Dar found for himself the
appropriate building, for he had been earnestly inquiring
for it all afternoon. The House of the Black Doors lay in an
elder quarter of the city, an area reckoned by some to be of
ill-repute. But Hamid-Dar had no fear, for all his life he
had prospered by courage and foolhardiness.

There was an ancient archway, partly ruined, and
beyond stood the house, with its three black doors instantly
visible, but not a window to be seen. And there on the roof
like a polished diamond perched the evening star.

Hamid-Dar made so bold as to go immediately to the
middle of the three doors and knock there. At once the
door flew open. Inside was a dimness and a darkness.
Hamid-Dar paused at it, and as he did, he made out the
porter who had let him in. This was a monkey in a coat and
turban of scarlet. Bowing low, the creature beckoned the
beggar youth to follow, and scampered away through the
house.

Hamid-Dar made no further delay, but went after it, and
quickly too, seeing it traveled so fast. Until, led only by
the glimmer of the red coat and turban, he came out into an
open court that had no other door, but all about on a gallery
many blind windows.

The monkey had vanished, and the sky above was laden
with night. A second time Hamid-Dar paused, and now he
wondered. But before he could decide, a voice called down
from the windows above: "If you are Hamid-Dar the beggar, then be welcome."

"I am Hamid-Dar," said Hamid-Dar, "and I am of the
profession of beggary."

"That is well," rejoined the voice, "but answer also this.
Are you ready to take your chance with Fate?"

Hamid-Dar looked up and about, but could see no one.

Nevertheless, the voice was that of a young woman, very musical and very sweet.

"I should not have come here otherwise," he declared.

"That too is well," said the musical sweet voice.

And then there came a strange rustling and scraping. And suddenly there fell down something from the sky and covered Hamid-Dar and cast him on his knees. And when he tried to do battle with this something, it rolled him up and pulled him over headlong, and presently he was trussed crown to toes in a net of metal mesh. He gave vent then to some complaints, but on this occasion no one replied. Only the monkey frolicked over him and batted him with its tail, gibbering.

Then the net was hauled up and swung off into terrible space, and Hamid-Dar tumbling and crying with it. Up into the stars it seemed to go, and as it did so, whether by desire or oversight, his brow was dashed against a corner of the house and for a while he knew no more.

In his childhood some three or four times Hamid-Dar had journeyed with his father along the roads that led out from the city gates upon the desert. Therefore the scent of the desert and the pressure of its enormous silence, which contains all sounds like seeds within a jar, were known to him. And waking from his daze in a moving darkness, yet Hamid-Dar knew instantly where he must be.

Now this is some trick and I do not care for it, thought the young man, *and though I am lame, let me remember I have one leg and two arms and my wits.* And he braced himself for what might come next, while giving no clue to his captors that he had roused.

The net was gone, and instead he lay inside a litter such as a rich woman might employ—and indeed perhaps it was that very litter from which the fair hand had let drop the fatal message, for it had a pleasing perfume. The rocking of the litter gave him to believe that the bearers advanced at a steady trot, and were those same four Nubians he had seen previously.

After perhaps an hour, the progressive motion slowed. Hamid-Dar heard, in the vast silence of the desert, the bearers begin to converse as they paced onward.

"Our mistress Zulima," said one, "has put a burden on us, setting us to carry out this troublous deed alone. Suppose we are discovered, for what we do is unlawful, to abduct this fellow and bear him to her secret home in the desert. And she has only to say, 'I know nothing of it,' and *we* shall be burned and hacked, and may be hanged, for we are only her slaves."

And another said, "Besides, the desert is large and we might mistake the way. Lions may find us, or some evil spirit that lurks here."

"And say then," said a third, "the litter is found, who will find our poor bones, picked clean by demons and jackals?"

Then the fourth Nubian spoke, and he said this: "But if we were to cast down the litter and flee, there is no one here to gainsay or prevent us, or to pursue and catch and punish us. And possibly we may come to the river and a boat, or to a camp of brigands who will succor us for our strength, and we may live then as free men do, and *spit* upon the city."

At that, all motion stopped.

There followed a long wait, during which no word was said. And then abruptly Hamid-Dar discovered himself in a falling litter that crashed him bruisingly to the earth. And as he lay among these bruises, he heard the eight blue-black feet of the Nubians loping off as fast as they might go.

When all noise of them had faded, Hamid-Dar came from the litter and looked about.

The moon had risen and bloomed high like a white lily on the lake of night. All around, beneath the moon and the sky, lay the wilderness, her changeable hills and valley of sand, and not a single other thing in sight, not a road or a rock, but only the footprints of the slaves who had run away, and even these sinking and powdering over as the little breeze of night erased them.

"Now am I lost," said Hamid-Dar.

But presently, he saw how the moon moved into the west, and that the footprints of the Nubians, when they had carried the litter, had tended to the opposite direction, the east. Hamid-Dar resolved he would continue their course, having no other, and turning his back to the moon, set off. "For do they not say, he that seeks in the desert will always find something, even be it only his own death." And since he was young, Hamid-Dar did not yet properly believe in death.

Hamid-Dar walked a long while, leaning on his staff, which had been left to him, and the moon at his back sinking. Now and then he heard a jackal singing out among the dunes, but he had no other company.

At last there began to be a lightness in the dark before him, and Hamid-Dar knew a touch of fear, for once the sun rose, his chance and risk would be great indeed. But a moment after, coming over a rounded slope in the sand, he beheld before him a rocky defile, and there, on its far side, not a mile off, an edifice that looked to be a house carved out of the cliff, with a stairway and a large black door above.

Another black door is it? thought Hamid-Dar. *Well, they were to bring me to her secret house, they said, those wretches, the desert home of Zulima.*

And just then the sky took orange fire and the edge of the sun began to slit the horizon like a sword. Plying his stick, Hamid-Dar hastened down into the defile, and into the shade of the rock, and made toward the architecture and the doorway like a man on urgent business.

The stair he climbed with difficulty and some curses, and reached the door, which was immense, in anger. For he wished very much now to confront Zulima and demand some recompense. Thus he smote the bastion with more yet than his usual bravado. It responded by giving off a terrific clanging, such as made him stagger, while from the caves about a storm of bats shot forth and whirled around in fright before they sank down again into the dark.

Thereafter Hamid-Dar waited several minutes, but even he did not knock again.

At length, a voice spoke to him, from somewhere above. It was not the voice of the city court, being masculine and greatly amplified, yet also *whispering,* so he did not like it.

"Who knocks?"

"It is I," said Hamid-Dar fiercely, although he must nerve himself to it.

"Who is *I?*"

"In that case, it is yourself," said Hamid-Dar.

"Cease stupid games," sizzled the voice. "Tell me your name, and your purpose here, for clearly you have one."

"I am arrived at the invitation of the Lady Zulima, who has treated me poorly as does not befit her, nor myself."

"Zulima, you say? For what does she want you?"

"That is not my place to guess."

Then the unnice voice gave an awful laugh.

"You shall come in, and meet with your Zulima. Only be patient."

Hamid-Dar prudently sat down, and endured the sun, which now came over the top of the cliff to gaze at him with burning curiosity.

When the better part of an hour had elapsed, and Hamid-Dar was debating deeply on cups and pots and entire caldrons of water, the voice broke out again.

"Are you yet here?"

"As you see."

"Then you shall enter."

No sooner were the words uttered than the massive door shuddered and ground slowly open. Hamid-Dar stared this time into a cavern of blackness, but it was cool and the sun had not claimed it, and he stumbled in.

He was not twenty paces inside before the door once again closed itself up, and at that a lamp began to come towards Hamid-Dar, borne by a tall and burly man dressed oddly for a steward, and carrying in his other hand a pitcher.

"I beg you," said Hamid-Dar, "for the love and compassion of God, if that is water allow me to drink."

"It is not water, but drink you may," said the steward. And he gave Hamid-Dar the pitcher with a glare for relish.

Hamid-Dar drank. The liquid was wine. But though he had seldom tasted it, now he could not refrain, so raged his thirst.

"I am required to ask of you," said the steward, fingering at his belt an enormous knife, "If you are acquainted with the Lady Zulima, and know her appearance."

Hamid-Dar perceived in this a test. He said, "As she is aware, I do not know her."

"The greater your joy then," said the steward with a loathsome snarl, "when that you look on her. Come follow." And he went off again the way he had approached, and Hamid-Dar after him, lamenting now on the night's wreck of his anointing and barbering more than on his righteous wrath.

Up many granite stairs in the dark they went, detailed only by the steward's lamp, and came at last into a smoky stone cubicle lit by half a dozen torches. This did not resemble a lady's chamber, but Hamid-Dar took heart, seeing that the space was divided off at one end by a fretted screen.

"I have brought the rogue. Here he stands," announced the steward to the screen.

Then over its top was seen a fan, beckoning Hamid-Dar nearer.

He advanced with a sudden misgiving.

When he was three steps away the screen split and parted, and there before him on a stone chair sat—

"The Lady Zulima!"

At the steward's roar, Hamid-Dar deemed it wise to abase himself. Glancing up again, his first dismay was thoroughly confirmed.

The Lady Zulima was a giantess. Though seated, she gave evidence of being more than six feet tall. Besides she was both fat and brawny. However, from her bulk, which was swathed in brindled silk, protruded two hairy and bulbous arms, wreathed with quantities of bracelets of gold and precious stones. Sapphires and carnelians blazed on uncouth fingers having nails of uneven length, but hennaed red. Her feet, mercifully, were hidden by her swathed skirts, and her face by a thick veil. Yet upon her head was a headdress sewn all over with sequins of silver and gold, from which flawless large pearls dripped like rain from a flower. All these things Hamid-Dar saw and noted. And with his dismay became mingled a doubting avarice which nevertheless quailed. Plainly, the summoner by the Well of the Wall had been only a servant of this monstrous apparition—yet even she was adorned like a princess. Such wealth in the mistress was not to be taken lightly. Yet neither was the lady's girth and hirsute complexion, when coupled to her presumably amorous intentions.

And now she spoke.

"Pray draw nearer, gentle visitor," cheeped the Lady Zulima, in a high and extraordinary tone, somewhat between the falsetto of a donkey and the twittering of a goat. "And tell me, charming youth, why it is that you have sought me."

"Madam," said Hamid-Dar, thinking the horror was perhaps bashful—as she had some cause to be—"it is your own message, and your gift, which invited me. And your own slaves who captured me in a net, and your own Nubian bearers who brought me here, or partly so, for I was abandoned in the desert by them and might well have perished. Yet Fate conducted me after all to your door."

"But tell me, pray, what can have been my wish, that I invited you?" scrape-tweeted the lady.

"That, madam, I dare not conjecture."

"Conceivably my weak and sinful sex," girlishly brayed Zulima, "have drawn you before in secret to their houses, and there tempted you to dalliance."

"This has happened," admitted Hamid-Dar, with genuine reluctance.

"For shame!" screech-chirped the fearsome lady. "But still, come closer yet. For if that is what you suspect of me, how can I escape blame? Thus perchance we may dally a little, pretending you are my lover, and I your blushing and timorous bride."

Hamid-Dar would at that instant gladly have found himself elsewhere, it is probable even upon the desert's burning-glass. But it seemed to him, without turning to be certain, that other men had come into the chamber at his back, and stood there as the steward had done, hand to knife. And meanwhile, the Lady Zulima was stretching out her hairy hands, tickling his cheek playfully with her fan, and seizing him by the shoulder in a grip of Damascus steel.

"A little dalliance, so-lovely one, let us have," she coaxed, hauling Hamid-Dar upon her bulky lap. And as he sprawled there, to his ultimate alarm, he found she had taken him by the neck. In a much-different voice now she bellowed: "What? Do you chance, you puny squit, to breach the cavern of *Hashan, the Thief of Thieves?* Who sent you? How have you dared? I will have answers to these questions of mine. Go down and view my treasure, and there you will meet those who will move your tongue to chat!"

And Hamid-Dar had scarcely the time to realize that the Lady Zulima was in fact a huge man, with a huge man's voice and a huge man's fist, than up were raised the skirts of brindle silk and there were too a huge man's two huge feet in two huge boots that stamped twice on the stone under the chair. And at once the stone opened, and below gaped a glittering pit, and into this the man's brawny, hairy arms hurtled Hamid-Dar with a final hugely booted kick for good luck.

No sooner had the unfortunate beggar landed, and that hard among spiked and jagged items, than a gang of frothing bandits leapt upon him and dragged him up.

"See, son of a she-gnat, what jewels have been amassed by Hashan, the Thief of Thieves. See, for these may be the last sights your eyes shall look on."

Hamid-Dar struggled and begged for pity, sternly reminding the robbers that God had better eyesight than he, and missed not a single deed.

"You have only to reveal your true purpose in arriving here," staunchly maintained the robbers. "Speak the truth, and our lord will be kind."

"But I have told the truth already!"

"Thus! To the wheel with him! Heat up the oil and irons."

And in this way Hamid-Dar was propelled between towering hills of rubies and emeralds, by inland seas of pearls, through forests of golden things and wastes of silver, to a deep chamber hung with hooks and pincers and lit by the flare of fire.

For several hours did Hamid-Dar suffer in the torture-vault of Hashan, the Thief of Thieves. In pure verity, none of the greater inflictions were used on him; here the robber band contented itself with promise and description. Nevertheless they did him some harm not only to the mind and spirit, and when at last they took him from his chains he was barely conscious and mostly beyond reason.

In his dinning ears then were breathed these words: "Get you hence, for we too are pious, and would not have your death charged to us by God. It seems from your mewing you are a fool that happened here by mischance and not design. Therefore we free you. Take with you those scars and hurts we have given as tokens of what worse thing will befall you should you ever return to the treasure-house of our Lord Hashan."

And after that Hamid-Dar was flung some miles away upon the cruel sands, and lay there in his pain until the lidless eye of the sun went down, and the cool of the night walked over the desert, and brushed his battered body with her dusky hand.

"What now?" inquired Hamid-Dar of the evening. "For what have I deserved this injustice?" cried Hamid-Dar to the dunes. "Here am I, who have lived only by my bravery, taken in a trap, scourged and blistered, and lost in the wilderness as before. To this the Lady Zulima, whoever she may be, has brought me, may God hear my plaint."

Soon enough though, Hamid-Dar rose to his feet and set off in an easterly direction, limping and sometimes falling down, but having no other direction.

There is in the desert, by day or night, a sweet odor that surpasses all others, even the oil of roses or the vapor of olibanum. And this odor is that of the oasis.

To Hamid-Dar the fragrance ascended, like a water-smoke, and he turned toward it in delirium. Before the dawn, yet after the moon had sailed beneath the world, he stepped upon a carpet of sand that was sown with grass, and up to a shore bladed with wild reeds. And here lay the sky in a mirror, and he plunged in his face, and when he lifted his head, he saw below the tall palms that grew with their fronds in the earth and their trunks upholding heaven, and the stars like fishes under his fingers.

There was no other present but for a slender snake that sipped from the water as daintily as a cat. But looking beyond the trees, Hamid-Dar thought he saw a dismal low building.

"Now what is that?" said Hamid-Dar, not cheered, for it looked to him mostly like a tomb. "Whatever else," he added, "it is not the sought-for secret house of Zulima, the unknown seductress. I cannot be deceived a second time."

Then he drank again, and on lifting his head started violently. For before him stood a man in clothes of fine quality, and having three gems in his turban.

"Peace," said this man, although he spoke with a strange accent, as of a foreigner. "You are wrong in what you say."

"What have I said?" asked Hamid-Dar cautiously.

"If you seek the house of Zulima," said the man, "be sure, there it lies before you."

Hamid-Dar got to his feet, the sound and the lame, and leaned on his staff which the robbers had left him, and inwardly bemoaned the wounds they had also left.

"This lady gifted me in the city and invited me to come to her," said Hamid-Dar, "but her slaves abandoned me and her service, and since then I have been set on and sorely hurt."

"Come then to the house of Zulima," said the man. "You shall be cared for. But you must enter at your own will. My mistress cannot command."

"How far is the house of which you speak?"

"Why, it is there."

Hamid-Dar looked where the servant pointed, and he saw, in the mysterious aqueous half-light before dawn, that there was a magnificent palace beyond the palms. That he had taken it for some derelict tomb a minute earlier surprised him, but he supposed his faintness and the twilight had bemused.

If that is the house of Zulima, thought Hamid-Dar, *then after all Fate has not been malign.*

The palace rested in a garden of flowering trees, where fountains played. At the door two damsels like slim pale moons came to assist the traveler. He was welcomed in and conducted to a splendid chamber where, in a bath of brass, his abrasions were soothed. He was cleansed and consoled, and presently they brought him a suit of clothing fit, so he imagined, for a caliph. And then he was served a delicious repast, to the strains of most eloquent music.

Finally the servant of the jeweled turban entered and bowed low. He inquired if everything had been to Hamid-Dar's satisfaction, and Hamid-Dar assured him that it had.

"Then, if you will, the Lady Zulima patiently awaits your presence."

Hamid-Dar, feeling not merely restored but remade into twice the man he had ever been, hurried to follow the servant to his lady's private apartment. On every side were riches beyond hope, and all set out with such charm and taste that they nearly caused the young man to weep. Soon they reached a doorway of marble into which was set a door of palm-wood ornamented with gold.

"You have only to knock upon the door," said the servant. "At her entreaty, you have only to go in." And this mentioned, he bowed himself away with a stately gliding tread.

Hamid-Dar knocked upon the door, employing customary force. At once a dulcet voice replied: "If you will, enter!"

Hamid-Dar thrust at the door, which slid wide, and he stepped over the threshold into a chamber that reduced all the other teeming glories of the palace to a shadow-show.

At the marvel's core, on a couch of crimson satin, there reclined a maiden of such beauty that Hamid-Dar, on some deep abacus of the brain, commenced to count his blessings. She was dressed in garments whose color and texture could not be divined, they were so thickly covered by work of gold and silver, and at her waist was a girdle that blossomed with tawny topaz and green jade. At her throat and wrists were rings of gold torched by rubies and cinnabar. Her lustrous hair, which was blacker than ebony, was also barely to be seen, being woven with jacinths and beryls and hung with silver pomegranates. Between her eyes, which were large and wonderful themselves as two agates, hung a yellow pearl bigger than a pigeon's egg. Her countenance was not veiled, and might have put out the moon. She had a train of golden stuff that quite hid her lower limbs and her feet, although there was a footstool under it that was a tortoise made all of one solid emerald.

Hamid-Dar threw himself upon his face.

"Rise up, bold traveler," said the Lady Zulima, in her harp-song voice, that had too its trace of foreignness—in her, most fascinating. "For you have journeyed far and endured much, to visit me."

"That I cannot deny," said Hamid-Dar, arising. "And although I take all now in equal part, I am sorry you saw fit to capture me in a net, to dash my skull against a corner of your city house, and to entrust me to four slaves who basely, at a whim, threw me down in the desert, where I next fell among thieves who tricked and almost slew me."

"And is this so?" asked the Lady Zulima, and she smiled a clandestine smile behind her jeweled fingers, and at this Hamid-Dar could truly find no fault with her. "But now you are here with me, at your own will, and have partaken of my hospitality."

"Which hospitality outshines the sun at noon," decreed Hamid-Dar.

And he noticed then that her feet under the train of gold gave a little twitch upon the tortoise footstool for whole emerald.

"Come nearer, dear traveler," said the Lady Zulima. "I am parched for your companionship. Come nearer, as the bridegroom approaches, tenderly, his bride."

And Hamid-Dar, as he went forward, saw that again the feet and limbs of his hostess twitched rather vigorously under her golden train. And he thought, "How eager she is to caress me!" and went to take another swift step. But unexpectedly something checked him, and he could not have said what it was, but he found he stared at the footstool, and at the train.

Then Zulima said, in a most enticing way that sounded like silk rippling across pieces of money, "Why do you hesitate, bold man? Will you not risk me? I am only a woman, and can command you to nothing. You must steal upon me and bend me to your wish."

These words stirred Hamid-Dar, and he took the swift step he had meant to take, which brought him almost to her couch. But in the middle of the step, Zulima smiled at him, and her exquisite teeth glittered, and something about them made him check once more, although immediately she hid her lips with her ringed hand, and he was confused, for it almost appeared to him that every stone upon her hand was *pointed*— And in this puzzling moment, being lame, Hamid-Dar stumbled and lost his footing, and his staff slewed in his grasp and with a fearful thwack it struck the footstool and sent it spinning.

As the great emerald went, so did the train of gold. It sloughed away and unveiled the lady's feet. And when it did this, Hamid-Dar perceived that she did not have, under the edge of her skirt, any feet at all, but the enormous rounded scaled yellow tail of a serpent.

"May God and his angels defend a hapless sinner!" screamed Hamid-Dar, and turned rapidly to leave.

The Lady Zulima sprang upright on her couch, and her skirts now tore right off, and there she was, a woman with the lower body of a snake, who reached after him with hungry claws, and snapped with her pointed fangs, and flickered her thin black tongue. "Foul morsel, return to me. It is my due. Have I not nurtured you? Have you not come to me of your own accord? Return, you joint, and let me feed upon your flesh, for it is many months since such a nourishing dinner entered my house."

Hamid-Dar, as he rushed toward the door, looked back once and saw that the serpent woman was clad in grave-clothes thick with dung-beetles, and at her throat and on her arms and in her hair were tangled asps with glowing eyes, and scorpions, and spiders, and human bones. While it was the grave-stone that had lain where her feet should have rested. Just in this way were also the riches of the house, which, as he sped and clamored through it, proved to be nothing other than that it had first seemed, a ruinous tomb. And as for the bath and the supper and the music, they did not bear thinking of. Nor was there space to do it, for as he plunged by, the servants of the snake woman, themselves now in their proper shape of snakes, and one of these with three eyes in its head, lunged and hissed at him and tried to throttle, trip, and bite him. But though lame, Hamid-Dar recalled he had one good leg and two arms and his staff and his wits, none of which commodities had they. And he won into the outer air alive, and burst into the oasis shrieking and reviling all the earth and all the things that God had set upon it.

Nor did he slow his limping and hopping flight, nor cease his blasphemies, until he was far off and the sun— for time had been impeded in the serpent's house—rose from the desert's rim.

Perhaps prevented by the onset of sunrise, the snake demons had not hunted Hamid-Dar, and as the day scorched on, he saw nothing of them, nor much of anything. He found, after an onerous walk, a rock, and there he stowed himself in the shade.

"What an unfortunate am I," said Hamid-Dar. "And what has brought me to this state? Why, a woman, may God heap miseries upon her."

Nevertheless, the bath and the ointments and the food given him in the serpent's house (though they did not bear thinking of) had done him an amount of good. He resolved that he would sleep until the sunset, resuming his trek at night. For although he had lost all his luck, yet he was not dead, and did not believe that death awaited him. Therefore some other thing would come his way. But he had no aim to be duped a third time.

At sunset he rose and rejected the eastern path, to walk along beside the sun, into the south. For surely, the city might lie in that direction.

His shadow went beside him, and the sand turned bloodred, and then the sun became a gilded dome, and next a band of scarlet, and eventually was gone. Then the wind, the breath of night, blew over the desert. The stars came from their doors, and on his other hand appeared the moon.

"What woman is there on the earth," said Hamid-Dar, "that can compare with the beauty of the world?" And later, as the moon stole up the sky, he said, "What cash can buy anything so fair as God's night?" And later still, he murmured, "It is to know these truths that holy men wander into the waste." But it began to be chill, and Hamid-Dar began to be weary, and then he said, "I am not happy with my lot, nor have I been dealt with justly."

Less than a minute after, Hamid-Dar came over a high

dune, and below beheld a strand of river, blue-white as lapis in the moonlight.

"God be praised," said Hamid-Dar. For now he could - find his way to the city, nor would he thirst.

It was as Hamid-Dar climbed down toward the river that he noticed a house built among gardens near the water's brink. Such was the appearance of this edifice, being dilapidated and decayed, and haunted by noisy owls, that Hamid-Dar was quickly alert.

Sure enough, no sooner had he got within a hundred paces of the spot, than out of the broken gate there raced a pair of muscular men who, bounding up, suddenly accosted him.

"So be it," said Hamid-Dar to himself. But aloud he said in a whining tone, "Can it be at last I have reached the secret home of the beauteous Zulima?"

At this the two men exchanged curious glances, then the larger of the two seemed to recollect himself, and grinning, he bowed low. "Just as you say, *Zulima's* house."

"And I," said Hamid-Dar modestly, "am Hamid-Dar, a poor beggar, upon whom the unprecedented favor of your mistress has fallen. But I have been lost in the desert and undergone there many irksome trials."

"Oh, if you are *Hamid-Dar*, proceed at once with us, to the house, where our lady has been pining for you."

"Be it so," avowed Hamid-Dar to himself, and put a firm grip upon his staff. But at the men he fawningly smiled, and declared they might lead him.

Thus he was escorted down into the garden, where the owls peered and muttered ill of him in their own tongue, and next through an unhinged door, and across some sunken passages and empty rooms into a small chamber.

Here, upon a wooden stool, sat the form of a woman, though she was heavily veiled, both face and hair, and clad with no richness, her long plain skirts covering her lower person and her feet in a manner that caused Hamid-Dar to tighten further his grim grip on the staff.

"Madam," exclaimed the escort, "here is he that you have sought. Hamid-Dar! And he has called you by name already as the Lady Zulima."

The veiled head was inclined, and in a soft voice the

lady thanked her servants and permitted them to depart.

When they were gone, she seemed to peruse the beggar carefully through her veil. At length she said, "Since you are here and name me, I am encouraged, and will allow you to step closer."

"My thanks," said Hamid-Dar. "First let me acquaint you with my adventures." And then he recited them, the netting and stunning, the throwing by Nubians, the assaulting by Hashan, the events of the serpent's house and the flight from the serpent woman here. "Therefore," finished Hamid-Dar, "I have learnt a thing or two. And now, O vile demon or felon, whichever or both you are, do not suppose I am to be made a mock of three times. No indeed, it is in this hour that I shall take revenge for all the wrongs awarded me." And that said, he pounced upon her. He ripped her veil and her skirts and would have taken his staff to her, but she, screaming, gave him such a push that being lame and weary, he toppled down. Next the two servant men rushed in and got hold of him in a savage way.

Hamid-Dar looked up from the earth in fury, and he saw standing before him, with one foot behind the other, a handsome young woman wearing a necklace of diamonds at her throat which the veiling had concealed, and some fabulous goldwork in her shining hair likewise.

"Beast of a man," cried she, "my monkey has more courtesy and sense. How am I humiliated, nor do I deserve better for my rashness." Then she added to her servants, "Take him from my view and beat the wretch. But render him too the story I have entrusted to you. For it is my correct reward that he should gossip of me, that my shame should never end."

This uttered, she turned her face from Hamid-Dar, and the servants pulled him away into a court, where they surely beat him, and very grievously, with rods. And that done, when he was barely sensible, they rendered him the story of their mistress.

Zulima had been from her birth, though fair, lame in one foot, and for this reason, having no male kindred living to protect her, she despaired of marriage with one of her own station or fortune. Having heard of the comely and clever beggar, Hamid-Dar, she bethought herself that all men are made by God, and this one might consent to matrimony, seeing he would understand her disability, and would also gain considerably thereby. She accordingly decided to test both his bravery and his integrity. She had him abducted from a deserted house, intending that he should be delivered to her, knowing nothing of her, neither her name nor her status. For the meeting she chose a dilapidated mansion in the wilderness. Here she would plead that the money she had sent him as her gift, and her few garments and jewels, were her only dowry, along with the decaying manse and two or three servants. She would then ask if he would take her for herself, unveiling her feet, her face, and her diamonds, in mathematical order only as she had judged his responses.

When Hamid-Dar did not arrive, Zulima was at a loss, and in distress, wondering what fate had overtaken her possible bridegroom. At her order her servants quartered the sands for him, but when Hamid-Dar strayed to her very walls it seemed God had attended to her prayers. Naturally her servants recognized the young man, since they had been searching for one of his description, although they had been disturbed he already had learnt their lady's name, such was her hope of secrecy.

Alas, it is a fact she would have wed him if he had behaved one part graciously before her, and given over her delightful person and her considerable wealth to his care. But this chance Hamid-Dar had now precipitately canceled. And as he crawled lamenting toward the city, from the house by the river, Hamid-Dar, striped by blows and broken of heart, could only exalt the peerless omnipotence of Fate.

This then is the tale of Hamid-Dar the beggar, which he told of his youth, by the Well of the Wall. Its meanings are many and each must sift them as he may, and act upon them or discount them as he wishes. For there are only two constant truths in all the universe: That man is a dunce of great wit, a wise and wily fool. And there is no God but God.

TESTS OF ILLUSION

And when the Lady of the Djinn had finished her tale, she stretched out her arms, as if to accept the acclaim of her fellow djinn of the deep desert. The lack of any applause, cheers, or other noises or gestures as might be proper to djinn first shocked Peter of Wraysbury, then made him fearful. For noble ladies were fearsome in disappointment; and, were this lady disappointed, who knew what vengeance she might wreak on those who had caused it? Certainly, she would not turn her wrath upon her fellows, not with humans so close at hand (or at claw) and so easy to turn and savage.

They could not even defend themselves; Peter's hand still smarted from that ill-considered moment when he had dropped it to sword hilt. Besides, the Sons of the Prophet were not the only men to have been brought up on poetry. He too had read poems, the stories of Chrétien, the *lais* of Marie; and he had heard the mad Germans—half knights, half minstrels—sing of love and service.

There was a stirring in the amphitheatre as the djinn slowly rose to their feet, nodding their approval of the djinna's tale in silence. They were old, Peter remembered, and bored. It was much that anything at all struck their fancy.

Could he and his companions? They had survived one round of the competition. Could they withstand this lady, who was as wise and therefore as dangerous as she was beautiful?

"Art silent?" The djinna turned to Peter and his companions and bowed ironically. "Shall I claim the prize?"

Then—as if, her tale told, she resumed her modesty—
she dropped her gaze and quickly veiled herself, moving
back over the sands to join her comrades.

If her presence had cast a spell, her departure freed the
tongues of the men. Alas, however, their first speech did
not concern tale-telling, but the attributes of the lady who
had stood so near to them. All had heard stories of men
who loved women of the djinn before—and usually with
disastrous results; but it seemed to the most hot-blooded in
their midst that what transpired before the disaster might
well be worth the price.

Finally the master storyteller took command.

"O friend from the West," he hailed Peter above the
sighs and most eloquent gesticulations, "have not your
imams and mullahs—or however they are called—a saying, *'In principio, mulier est hominis confusio'?*"

Peter started. He had not known that the teller of tales
numbered the knowledge of Latin among his accomplish-
ments. He bowed acknowledgment, summoned the little
Latin that the priests had cuffed into his blazing head, and
translated ineptly, "In principal, woman is a confusion to
mankind." It was not, God knows, a line favored by any
women of his acquaintance, and yet—God also knew, all
too often, it proved to be true. Look at Arthur and Guine-
vere, or Tristan and Isolde.

"Hearken!" the tale-teller cried in a voice that not even
the most love-struck of the men could withstand. "The lady
djinna told a story of a man so skilled in detecting fraud
that he could not detect truth when it was offered him: a
wise fool. Shall we be proven such, or shall we make
combat according to the rules which have been set down?"

The merchant prince wiped his brow, his earlier desires
forgotten. "Yes," he boomed hastily. "Our own wives and
handmaidens await us at home, and it is written that we
support and sustain them. Let us hasten to win this contest
so that we may do so."

Fine words, thought Peter with a grin. His partner's tale
was told; and it would take fine words to counter the
djinna's tale.

"Sometimes," ventured the seller of carpets, "the best
way to confront deception—or the conflicts that rise up

between men and women—is with laughter. I shall speak."

"And I!" called the chief among the drivers of camels. "For truly, it is said that the drivers of camels are the wisest of men."

Two men conferred briefly, as much a matter of hand-signs and nods as of words. They trained and dealt in the very finest of horses, the jewels of princes; and they were wise in the way of high-bred, intelligent, and capricious creatures.

"We were justly scolded," one acknowledged, "for loose talk of mounting. Yet we who deal with horses deal directly with such truths. I shall tell a tale of the truth of love, my thrice-honored friend here a tale of the truth of names and even the truth of a woman believed to be false."

"Then we have our number," said the teller of tales. Arrogant as the Emir of the deep desert himself, he clapped his hands to draw the attention of the djinn in the stands.

"We have their attention thus far," Peter muttered to the merchant prince. "But can we gain their approval?"

"We would have been silenced had we bored them too badly," he answered. "But their acclaim? Only Allah knows."

The Houri's Mirror

Esther M. Friesner

Woe to the poets, cries the sage! The curse of fathers and mothers be upon them, for they fill the eyes of children with the fires of foolish ambition. Ambition's unholy flame both consumes and blinds when kindled from earthly things—gold, kingdoms, glory! How much more accursed the poets, then, who strike their fires from the stars.

There was once a simple lad named Tariq who was as pious as he was handsome. His parents both being dead, he was raised by an elderly uncle, so elderly that much young Tariq did escaped the rheumy eyes of his guardian.

The world is full of well-meaning counselors, may Allah reward them as they deserve. The old man's neighbors were no exception.

"The boy consorts with poets!" they cried. "He stands in the marketplace, listening to the babble of common tale-spinners, dreaming away the time. You know where that leads! All word-jugglers love an audience. They will flatter the boy unspeakably. They will praise his taste, his intelligence, his wisdom—"

"His looks," said one neighbor wistfully.

"Let him be," Tariq's uncle replied wearily. "He has time to dream. The old dream of being young and the young dream of living forever. He will learn. He is a good boy."

"What?" cried the neighbors. "Is sloth good? Is idleness to be rewarded? Is empty-minded vanity to be encouraged in the young, who are already sufficiently rattle-skulled?"

The wistful neighbor blinked his large, moist eyes and added, "It is a very handsome skull, nonetheless."

Tariq's uncle shrugged. "He will learn," he repeated.

The neighbors went away, grumbling.

Now it happened that Tariq's uncle too died, leaving the boy utterly alone in the world. He had not been a rich man, and Tariq had to sell nearly all the household goods in order to give him a proper funeral. Being pious, as I have said, he thought nothing of this sacrifice, although it left him entirely impoverished.

The neighbors were less pious.

"See where all your dallying after poets has gotten you!" they said, with as much satisfaction as if Tariq's uncle had been murdered in his bed by a souk rhymester. "The old man said you would learn someday. Someday is this day! Now you will learn and learn well that this world has no place for dreamers."

Poor Tariq! He had nothing, not even a roof over his head. His uncle's small house had been rented, and no sooner was the old man dead than the owner appeared, uglier than any ifrit. When Tariq told him he could not pay the rent, the man called him every vile name imaginable and threw him into the street together with three objects, unsold and unsalable, that were all the patrimony Tariq had left in this world: a battered brass cup, a square of halvah, and a crumble-edged book of tales.

Tariq brushed dirt from his pantaloons and considered his fate. Truly a piece of candy, a cup, and a book were precious little to set between himself and starvation. He had no reason to hope, and yet I tell you the truth when I say that Tariq's heart was as filled with brightness as a vizier's purse with gold.

Would that his head had been similarly filled.

"This is no matter," he said aloud. He held up his little book, of the three things the one he cherished most. "This too shall pass, for so it is written. Have not the hundred heroes bound within these pages found the themselves in worse straits than this? And when things looked direst for them, was heaven-sent help not far behind? My friends the poets tell me that I am not without some pleasing looks. Is is not always the way of handsome young men to rise from the base of the dunghill to the bed of the caliph's daughter?" Here he tucked the book snugly into the bosom of his coat for safekeeping.

At this moment, Tariq heard a loud noise from on high, behind him. Someone was clearing his throat in a marked manner, though at first the young man thought some celestial minion was attempting to get his attention before spiriting him off to the glorious future awaiting him.

It was not so. It was his late uncle's moist-eyed neighbor. The man leaned out from the upper story of his house across the way and hailed the lad. None but Tariq heard him, it being that hottest hour of the day when sensible men seek indoor shade. This was a pity, for he gave a very fine speech. He expounded on the injustice of Fate. He said that it was a shame in the eyes of the Most High how niggardly other folk had treated Tariq. He vowed that the youth was deserving of better things. Modestly, Tariq demurred in a way that left no doubt that the two men were in complete agreement.

He then asked Tariq to enter his humble home, so that they might discuss the lad's glorious future more comfortably and privily.

Smiling, Tariq said that he would be up directly. The neighbor returned his smile with a good deal of relief and anticipation and left the window. As the lad crossed the deserted street, he patted his pet volume of tales for luck, thanking the Almighty for having rewarded his faith in the poets so expediently.

His hand was a hairsbreadth from the neighbor's door when a small voice said, "I would go no further were I you." Tariq whirled. No one was there. The street remained deserted. He returned to the door.

Again the small voice grated, "Some doors open in only one direction. Enter that one and you will see."

"Where are you?" Tariq cried. "Show yourself!"

"I am right here," said the voice, and in that moment a black dwarf sat cross-legged in the dust beside the moist-eyed neighbor's door. He wore no more than a plain white loincloth and a scarlet turban, neither very clean; but the turban was ornamented by an aigrette of priceless emeralds clasping a spray of feather that appeared to be all aflame, a plume of the immortal phoenix itself.

"Who are you?" Tariq repeated. This time he uttered the question in the hushed tones men reserve for beings whose favor they must curry or whose wrath they must fear.

"I am the Slave of the Book," the dwarf replied.

"The book! What book?"

"That book, of course." The dwarf pointed to the dog-eared volume tucked into Tariq's bosom. "Your book. For a youth as widely read as you flatter yourself to be, you are extraordinarily surprised to see me. I would think magic would seem as common as bread to you."

"Slaves of lamps and slaves of rings are all I know," Tariq admitted. "I have never heard of a book holding any being captive."

The black dwarf laughed, revealing a double row of fangs white and brilliant enough to frighten off a shark. "Never heard of it? You have lived it! But come, I do not care for the world outside my warm covers. I would be happiest back among my treasured tales. What are your wishes, O my master? Let me hear them, obey, and be done with you."

"How many wishes?" Tariq inquired. "I know three is usual, but—"

At this moment, the portal at which Tariq and the dwarf lingered was flung wide. The moist-eyed neighbor stood there, nostrils quivering with all the indignation his thin blood could muster.

"Ungrateful boy!" he cried. "Imp of a thousand wiles! Is this what you do while you keep me waiting? Consorting with dwarves in a public thoroughfare? Ah, if you were any less beautiful to gaze upon, I would know you for the offspring of Iblis himself!"

The dwarf made a clucking sound with his tongue. "Overdone," he opined, "and the product of the more sensational schools of expression. I shudder to imagine the contents of *his* library—if indeed he does more than borrow certain unseemly volumes from comrades who share his proclivities. There is no elegance in the man, my master. Let us leave him." The dwarf levitated from his place, unfolded his legs to meet the ground, and began to walk away.

Tariq made as if to follow the dwarf, although his fine

black eyes were fixed in horror on his erstwhile neighbor. The man's outburst led the lad to believe that perhaps his earlier offers of help were not without a tariff to be exacted in other than coin. Tariq was quite bright, when given the proper direction.

The neighbor was having none of it. He seized Tariq's sleeve and clung to the threadbare cloth with a lover's ardor, for he had read somewhere that attachment to the garment of the beloved will soften the hardest heart.

"Do not go!" he wailed. "Turn again, fair one! May Allah cause a thousand djinn to tear my foolish tongue out by the roots. Why will you leave me? What can this misshapen blot of camel dung offer you? What is his attraction? I will dress you in the silks of Samarkand! I will gird a sword of finest Damascus steel to your waist! You shall feast upon dates and the sweet wine of Mossul! You shall never lack for coin to spend, and if your fancy turns to lighter amusement I will procure for you a host of dancing girls, each one as fair as the houris who serve the Faithful in heaven!"

The moist-eyed neighbor would have said more, but at that moment Tariq's harried sleeve tore off in his clawing hands. The man held up the sorry scrap, looked most contrite, and said, "I will buy you a new coat."

"I wish you would buy yourself a helping of common sense first!" Tariq snapped.

The black dwarf tittered. "Hearkening and obedience."

Tariq's neighbor stiffened. He dropped the young man's sleeve. His eyes filmed over with the unfocused stare of the dream-walker. Looking to neither left nor right, he strode away and was soon lost to sight around a corner.

Tariq leaned back against the wall of the house and groaned as he sank down to a crouch. "What have I done?"

"Sent a mindless man on an endless errand," the dwarf replied gleefully. "And used the first of your wishes to do it. You now have but one left. Use it wisely."

"One! But in all the tales I have heard it is three wishes," Tariq objected. "Sometimes it is more."

The black dwarf shrugged. "Therefore might it not sometimes also be less? Lamps and rings are stronger prisons than books. Their slaves are the commanders of more horrific magics. Come, lighten your heart and make your other wish. At least you do have one left you! How many men would sell their honor to have that much good fortune?"

But Tariq covered his face with his hands and wept. All that filled his mind was the thought that he had possessed two wishes and had squandered one for the sake of pique and spite. He could not be satisfied with what he owned for yearning after what he might have possessed.

"Alas, was there ever such a luckless man as I? Did you not hear what the man offered me?" He gestured down the street in the direction that his whilom neighbor had vanished. "Oh, for a life such as that! For silks, sweets, treasures, perfumes, palaces! How shall I obtain so much with one miserly wish at my disposal? Oh, pity me!"

The dwarf snorted, flaring his nostrils mightily. "So I do. I always pity fools. Cease your womanish wailing."

"Womanish! Ah, I might have had women as well. Did you not hear his promises? Dancing girls, each fair as the ever-renewing virgins of Paradise!" In his anguish, Tariq clasped at his heart, but the book still hidden in his bosom interposed. He squeezed its yielding pages instead.

The black dwarf gasped and staggered. "Master, loose your hold!" The words came as a raven's croak. "Oh, the pain runs through my every octavo!"

Astonished, Tariq complied. The Slave of the Book tottered and slumped down beside his master. "Do not do that again," he admonished, his voice weak. "When I am in the outer world, my life is tied to the life of the book."

"Is it?" Tariq's eyes widened. A look of deep contemplation crosssed his face, but did not linger. "You are unwise to tell me this, slave. Another man might hold your powers to ransom with such knowledge."

"But you will not." The dwarf spoke certainly. "Yours is a kindly soul. I have seen it in your eyes as you gazed into my pages. You might pretend to ruthlessness, but it is not in you. A man may not change his soul as easily as his coat. Besides"—he added with a chuckle—"you might threaten to snap my spine in two and still I could grant you no more wishes. Two in a lifetime to each owner of the book, that is the limit of my magic, and not obliteration itself will grant you or me renewal."

Tariq was crestfallen. A show of kindness to an other-worldly creature was often the touchstone that evoked additional help for the hero, or so the tales all told. Obviously the tales did not tell all. The dwarf saw the young man's sorrow. He was not without compassion.

"Tariq, attend me." The small being spoke with much gravity. "I cannot grant you more wishes, but nothing prevents me from showing you how to use your lone remaining wish well. Tell me your heart's desire and I will set your feet on the proper path to obtain it."

It was some time later, when the midday heat had begun to abate and honest folk were again coming into the street, that Tariq finished expounding on all he wanted out of life.

"*Bismillah!*" The dwarf scratched his head, being careful not to scorch his fingers on the plume of flame in his turban. "The grave is hardly more voracious than you! Not Suleiman ibn Daoud himself aspired to more pleasures."

"A man must seize all he can if he is to be happy." Tariq was confident, for he had heard camel-drivers speak thus repeatedly, and what philosopher was so wise in the ways of the world as a camel-driver?

"Think you so?" The dwarf's bushy eyebrows went up.

Tariq could not stand the scrutiny of those piercing black eyes. Their skepticism cut to the soul, and the dwarf spoke rightly when he said that he knew Tariq's spirit well. The young man's bold front crumbled and he bowed his head.

"Friend, I am a poor man. Happiness dwells in the inmost chamber of the heart's dearest dream, but dreams elude us. Your book teems with sorry tales of men who wandered the world without finding their heart's desire. How shall I find my own if I do not acquire everything that might conceal it? Does it lie in wealth, power, the faces of beautiful women? How can I wish for one thing alone when another might contain the balm to soothe my questing soul?"

The black dwarf heard him out, arms folded across his chest. "Truly Iskandar learned the lesson of the balance, the eye of man, and the pinch of grave-dust. Master, let your wish be to meet the Daughter of the Djinn!"

"The . . . Daughter of the Djinn?" Tariq's voice and eyebrows scaled new heights. "B—but the djinn are a fearsome race whom only the most potent images may subject."

"A man must not dip his bucket into a dry well if he seeks to draw up a flood," said the dwarf. "If you seek to know your heart's desire, I have told you the one being with power enough to grant it to you."

Tariq hugged his knees close to his body. He looked up and down the humble street where he had dwelled so long and where now he had no dwelling. To face the Daughter of the Djinn was frightful, but to face poverty was worse. All deaths wear the same fleshless smile, although some are slower to be seen. He sighed. "I so wish."

"Hearkening and obedience," said the dwarf, and both he and Tariq vanished.

Tariq saw the world blink away and return in horribly altered form. Flames were all around him. He was in a palace whose walls appeared to burn. For a time he stared into the conflagration, dumbstruck. Even the floor beneath seemed ablaze, covered with a sheet of burnished, beaten gold that reflected the leaping fires. Yet in the midst of the furnace, Tariq felt no heat. Experimentally he raised his hand and touched one of the crackling walls. His fingers caressed the flame as if gliding across the coolest glass.

All at once, the fire yielded. A door swung open at his inadvertent touch and he fell through into a room whose walls emitted a soft, silvery glow. As Tariq picked himself up from the silk rugs strewing the floor he saw that this fair light came from untold myriads of inset pearls.

"May the Most High protect me," he breathed, gazing at the splendor surrounding him. He crossed the room of pearls, passing beneath a silver archway into a third chamber, one whose walls held the soft translucence of a rose petal and gave the fragrance of a thousand gardens. A deep stream pattered through a porcelain conduit in the center of this room, and turquoise fishes drifted to the surface of it to sing praise-songs. Tariq knelt beside the stream, enraptured by the fishes' rich harmonies. One and all their songs extolled the Daughter of the Djinn: her beauty, her grace, her sweetness, and her astonishing good temper.

"If a man may believe a fish," Tariq said aloud, "the lady does not sound half so horrifying as I feared." He stood and checked his leather belt-pouch. The little brass cup and the square of halvah were still there, the sweetmeat much the worse for time and wear. Snippets of thread and unnameable fluff stuck to it. Tariq made a face. He had hoped to fortify himself with this humble tidbit before seeking out the Daughter of the Djinn, but hungry as he was, this was a sight to kill all appetites save ambition. He snorted and tossed the halvah over his shoulder.

"A GIFT? FOR ME?"

A thunderous voice shook the perfumed chamber to its foundation. The floor buckled and heaved, the streambed cracked, and the singing fishes lay flopping in the air, their praise-songs turned to dying gasps. Tariq turned, his hand dropping to his sword until he recollected that he had no sword and had only reached for it because in all the tales that was what the hero was expected to do at this juncture. Unarmed, he crouched beside the ruined stream and waited on Fate.

He saw a sight that might have reduced a lesser man to the gibberings of a red ape. Arrayed in veils as white and delicate as the falling snow, flesh firm and dark as the plums of Paradise—and doubtless as sweet—a gazelle-eyed woman of surpassing loveliness stood holding Tariq's discarded square of halvah in the palm of one adorable hand.

"IT IS NOT A VERY BIG GIFT, IS IT?" Again thunder shook the room, but now Tariq saw to his amazement that the earthshaking sound emanated from the dainty mouth of the beauty before him. It was as if a sparrow had opened its tiny beak in a lion's roar.

Tariq was already on his knees, but he made the lady a quick reverence. He had wished to encounter the Daughter of the Djinn, and beyond question this must be she. "Exquisite one," he said, "size is not everything."

"TRUE." The lady's voice lost some of its overwhelming quality with use. She studied the square of confection a moment before popping it into her mouth and devouring it, fluff and all. She licked her lips. "VERY GOOD. I AM FOND OF SWEETS, THOUGH MY LORD FATHER DOES NOT SEE FIT TO PROVIDE ME WITH THEM AS MUCH AS I WOULD LIKE. I THANK YOU, WHO-EVER YOU ARE. I HOPE THAT CONSUMING YOUR FLESH WILL NOT STEAL TOO MUCH OF THIS FINE SAVOR FROM MY MOUTH."

Tariq trembled in his skin, but did his best to conceal it. The Daughter of the Djinn was no taller than an ordinary woman, but on closer scrutiny he saw that her fine, long fingernails were really curved talons of steel, and when she licked her lips she showed pointed teeth that would have set the shark-mouthed dwarf to flight. Ruefully he realized that devouring uninvited houseguests was as much a part of the djinna's expected role as swordsmanship was the hero's. In this one point he wished the tales had been less accurate.

"Princess of All Nightmares, must our association come to such a precipitous end?"

"OH, THERE IS NO HURRY FOR ME TO DEVOUR YOU," the Daughter of the Djinn replied with a shrug of her luminous shoulders.

"But is it in fact a necessity?" Tariq asked.

"MY FATHER THE LORD OF WINDS COM-MANDED ME TO KEEP WATCH AND WARD OVER HIS CAPTIVE. I AM TO DESTROY ANY WHO MIGHT COME TO FREE HER. EATING YOU IS AS GOOD A METHOD OF DESTRUCTION AS ANY. IT IS ALSO ECONOMICAL."

"Captive?" Tariq rose to his full height and drew nearer to the Daughter of the Djinn.

"YES. EVERY MAN I FIND IN THIS PALACE HAS COME TO SET HER FREE. ORDINARILY I CONSUME FIRST AND QUESTION LATER. IN FACT, I WAS ON THE POINT OF PUTTING AN END TO YOU AS YOU KNELT BESIDE THE STREAM. BUT YOU WERE THE FIRST TO BRING ME A PRESENT. THE OTHER FOOLS BROUGHT NONE. I THOUGHT IT RUDE TO EAT THE GIVER BEFORE THE GIFT."

Tariq came closer yet. He gave the Daughter of the Djinn his most ingratiating smile, which had previously been known to cause a marketplace fishwife to deal on credit. I have said how handsome young Tariq was, and though the djinn are as a rule a shortsighted race, at close quarters the Daughter of the Djinn had to acknowledge and appreciate the mortal man's perfection. She licked her lips again, though the sweet taste of halvah no longer tarried in mouth or memory.

"It was unworthy of you, yet it was the best that I might offer. You are courteous as you are radiant, Enthraller of Kings, but you are misinformed. I know nothing of your captive and I care less to learn. I came here seeking my heart's desire. I have found it in you."

The Daughter of the Djinn was taken by young Tariq's address. Fair as she was, she had never had any suitors, perhaps due to her unfortunate appetite. She saw no reason to put off the logical conclusion of courtship, and she and Tariq were wed that very day. Because he was so pious, he insisted on the rites of the True Faith, and this was good, for the Holy Word has great power to bind creatures of magic.

He found his bride to be as ravenous in bed as he might wish, but without those delicate refinements of amatory art that lend spice to the sweetest combat. Though he fell asleep sated, he was curiously discontent.

In the morning, the Daughter of the Djinn made her husband a present of a small cordovan leather purse with drawstrings of silver. It was empty, as Tariq discovered to his consternation.

"DO NOT FROWN, HUSBAND," said the Daughter of the Djinn. "IT IS A GIFT OF GREAT POWER I HAVE GIVEN YOU, IN THANKS FOR YOUR ENDURANCE, MAY IT NEVER WITHER."

Tariq thought his bride was joking. It looked like such an ordinary purse! To play along with her jest, he said, "I am undeserving such an excessive present, my dear, but I will find a use for it. I will keep all my vast inheritance safe inside such a stronghold of power." With that he leaped naked from the bed, plucked his battered brass cup from among his shabby effects, and popped it into the bag. "There! What other purse is vast enough to contain all a man's fortune?"

He would have removed the cup then, but his bride was upon him, her scented limbs entwining urgently with his as she wrested the purse from his grasp. "DO NOT PUT YOUR HAND IN IT!" she cried. "TILT IT, TURN IT UPSIDE DOWN, SPILL OUT WHAT IT HOLDS, BUT NEVER, NEVER REACH INTO IT!"

"Why not?" asked Tariq, at the same time doing as she requested. His answer came when a tiny brass thimble tumbled from the red purse and tinged as it struck the tiles.

"THIS IS THE PURSE OF DIMINUTION," the Daughter of the Djinn said. "WHATEVER ENTERS IT IS REDUCED TO MINIATURE."

Tariq whistled softly, gazing at his wedding gift with new respect. "A greater power, and a fearsome one. But . . . of what use is it to me? A man desires to expand his possessions, not to diminish them."

The Daughter of the Djinn turned sulky. "IT MAY NOT BE MUCH PRACTICAL USE, MY LORD, BUT IT IS STILL A SIGHT BETTER THAN A MOLDY PIECE OF HALVAH. AND WHO WAS IT SAID THAT SIZE IS NOT EVERYTHING?"

"I did," Tariq admitted.

"WELL, YOU WERE WRONG," his bride countered. "OR SO I DISCOVERED LAST NIGHT."

"Nor are looks," Tariq murmured. "Or so I discovered at approximately the same time."

"WHAT WAS THAT?"

"Nothing, my love, nothing."

The excesses of the wedding night soon dwindled to the commonplaces of domesticated passion, which feeds the body but does not satisfy the soul. The Daughter of the Djinn was frequently absent from her palace, her powers being popular with many far-flung mages, wizards, and adepts. When she was gone, Tariq wandered through the many glories of the palace, his every need met by unseen servants. He was robed in silks, fed on delicacies, and might have commanded the kings of the world to be brought to do him homage, if he so wished. In brief, he had everything and more than what he had requested of the black dwarf so long ago. His hands, his purse, his pockets were full.

Only his heart was empty.

Having nothing but leisure, he wandered through the palace, eyes innured to wonders. One day—he knew not how he came there—he found himself before a door that would not yield to his touch. There was nothing extraordinary about the plain wood panel, the brass nails studding it, the multiple bolts and bars across it, the lengths of chain fastened with cunning locks. It simply would not open.

For some reason, Tariq recalled his wife's mention of a captive.

Tariq summoned an unseen servant and commanded that the door be opened. The servant's disembodied voice protested that his mistress forbade it. Tariq pointed out that he was master of that mistress, whereat the servant replied that so long as the mistress was capable of tearing the master to gobbets anytime she liked, he would remain faithful to the actual head of the household and leave talk of titles and precedence to the men of law.

Tariq made a grab for the middle air. His fingers closed upon something warm, and with a mighty struggle and loud outcry he forced the unseen servant head-first, tail-first, or what-you-will-first, into the Purse of Diminution. When he tilted it out again there was nothing left but the ghost of a bat's squeak.

A second unseen servant, apprised of his brother's fate, became more cooperative. The locked door opened.

To his surprise, no walls awaited Tariq beyond the portal. He found himself within a formal garden, the clear blue sky above, the plashing of many fountains cooling the fragrant air. On the brink of a carved stone basin, her skin whiter and more translucent than the alabaster lip upon which she perched, sat a houri, one of the ever-virgin handmaids of Allah's faithful.

He knew her for what she was at once. No mortal woman could be so perfect, with her hair and eyes so black and shining, lips so red. He fell to his knees and told himself that if he might only possess this creature, his heart would be content.

The houri did not see him at first, which gave him some time to compose his thoughts and recapture a little of his dignity. She sat on the fountain's brim and gazed into a long-handled mirror which she held in one hand. Approaching, Tariq had the dizzying impression of beholding two houris at once, a sight to dazzle any man.

At last the houri looked up. *Oh! You startled me,* she said. Her voice made music weep for envy. *Who are you? Are you my executioner?*

"Pearl of Delight, rather would I cut off that which is dearest to me than deprive the world of one instant of your life!"

Oh, don't do that, the houri said, her long-lashed eyes sweeping over Tariq's body from toes to turban. Either she was possessed of the wisdom of the Forbidden Tree, or else it was simply a matter of the naturally revealing qualities of fine silk. Whatever the cause, her gaze lingered longest and most circumspectly at the most eponymous feature of Tariq's male anatomy. *I have wasted far too long in this dreary prison as the captive of the Lord of Winds, cut off from the opportunity to follow my divinely ordained calling. Do not, I pray you, cut off anything further.*

Tariq grasped her argument. Still he felt bound to question, "Luminous One, why does this fiend keep you prisoner?"

Is it not obvious? The houri stood up and laid aside her mirror, followed in rapid succession by every article of clothing and ornament upon her entrancing person. Tariq swallowed an invisible pomegranate, rind and all.

She turned around slowly, allowed Tariq's eyes full play over every soft and snowy glory of the Creator's making. *These gifts which the Divine has lavished upon me and my sisters are for the reward of the faithful only. The Lord of Winds knows little and cares less about the True Faith, wherefore I will not serve him as he desires. The word of the Most High forbids him to take what I will not give, but nothing prevents him from keeping me pent up here until monotony compels me to surrender what morality would not.*

"Allah forfend!" Tariq cried, with true passion.

Yes, well, I hope He will, too. Her raven's-wing eyebrow lifted in speculation. *You *are* one of the Faithful, aren't you?*

If the strength of Tariq's faith had ever been likely to waver, the houri's attentions soon set it on the firmest of footings. Still alive, the young man tasted in prologue all the joys awaiting the pious after death. In his gratitude for such tenderly expounded lessons of theology, he summoned a host of unseen servants to act as witnesses and took the houri for his bride after the proper usage of the Law.

When the Daughter of the Djinn came home, she did not share her husband's newly wedded joy as deeply as a loyal wife should. She even implored Shaitan to blast the happy couple out a dragon's bunghole. Tariq cringed before his first wife's imprecations, but the houri remained calm.

You are a true daughter of the Lord of Winds. Save your fetid breath to blight the crops. She waved the long-handled mirror languidly in one hand. *Touch one hair of my lord's head and I shall summon the Lord of Winds himself to arbitrate. How think you your noble father will react to learn that your own fleshly weakness has made you a mortal's bride? A mortal who through your wonderful negligence was able to free me from my cell!*

The Daughter of the Djinn wilted miserably. "A DRAGON'S BUNGHOLE WILL BE THE LEAST OF IT," she sighed. "VERY WELL. WE SHALL SHARE HIM, AND MAY HIS MORTAL FERRETINGS DISCOMFIT YOU AS MUCH AS THEY HAVE ME."

Thus it would have seemed that Tariq was fated to enjoy pleasures beyond the dreams of ordinary men. Under a single roof—often upon a single divan—he sampled the opposing epitomes of female charm: dark and fair, fire and water, the unquenchable demands of immortal experience and the titillating reluctance of eternal virginity, he had them all.

And they had him. When it wasn't one wife, it was the other. He took to hiding in the baths with a good book. It was difficult to say which of the two looked more dog-eared, Tariq or his old companion, the refuge of his boyhood, the volume of tales that housed the Slave of the Book.

It was while he was thus avoiding the obligations of

matrimony that Tariq was surprised by his second wife. The houri was in her own modest way a greater trial than the Daughter of the Djinn. While the thunder-voiced lady put Tariq through his paces with an exhausting thoroughness, she was at least forthright about what she wanted, how she wanted it, and how many times she had better get it. The houri too knew just what she wanted, but, being an eternal virgin, she had to be eternally coy about securing her wishes.

Tariq was lazing in the scented waters of the bathing pool, blissfully transported by his treasured book to realms where females were magically satisfied by a single well-placed stroke of the pen. He did not notice the houri slip into the pool, her long-handled mirror with her, as usual.

He noticed soon enough, when she used the mirror's handle for an extraordinary purpose. One strategic touch and the man, his book, and his bloodcurdling scream leaped in three separate directions. Tariq splashed back into the water unharmed, but the book sailed nearly the length of the pool before sinking beneath the wavelets with a pathetic gurgle.

"My book! My book!" Not even his wife's clinging arms seemed likely to restrain him from plunging after it. He tried to break free, to rescue the precious object, but the houri was brooking no such nonsense.

So much outcry for so little, my lord? It is a book; and so? Books are paltry things. I know; I tried to read one once. There are many in Paradise.

"So it must be," Tariq muttered, still trying to disengage himself from his lady's grasp and rescue the foundered volume. "Or it would not be Paradise."

Bah! Paradise holds greater wonders. Do you see this? She twirled the mirror before his eyes. *In this enchanted looking glass I find more entertainment than in a thousand books! It is the mirror of heart's desire. I alone possess its secret, the gift of a grateful and repeatedly pious mage. For mastery of this as much as of my person the Lord of Winds held me captive. I have but to gaze into it, and it lets me see whatever I yearn for most and love best.*

"Ah? To view the heart's desire, that *is* a wonder." Tariq

craned his neck, expecting to catch a glimpse of himself in the glass.

"I see your own reflection!" he accused her. "That, and a dish of candied ginger."

Someone must care for me. The houri pursed her delicate lips into a sulky pout. *It is obvious that you will not. You were terribly ungentle the last fifty-four first times. And now will you neglect me for a leatherbound lump of sodden paper? What can it give you that I can not?*

A hundred different answers welled up in Tariq's throat —*Adventure! Marvels! Glory! Excitement!* Even *beauty* as well, transcending all that his wives might offer, because it was the beauty of his ever-nebulous ideals; and *love*, but Tariq did not put that name to the yearning that still burned within his breast despite the most careful ministrations of the houri and the Daughter of the Djinn. Yes, this most of all the book had given him: *love*.

The confusion of his emotions overwhelmed his tongue and left him mute. The houri was impatient for an answer, and when none was forthcoming she shoved her mirror before Tariq's face. He stared into the glass and saw his book. He also saw something more. So did the houri.

Before he could discern this second object clearly, the far end of the pool began to bubble. Summoned by its image in the mirror, the book itself rose from the depths. Miraculously whole and dry, it floated back to Tariq's outstretched hand. There was no dissimulating the unabashed love with which he welcomed it home. He had never gazed upon either of his wives with so much pure delight.

The truth is a stern mistress. Like all wives, the houri did not care for mistresses. She went an unhappy shade of crimson and swung herself out of the pool. Gesturing fiercely with her mirror, she declaimed, *Unworthy man! If you prefer to embrace dreams, so be it! We shall make you a present of dreams, the Daughter of the Djinn and I! Yes, of the dream without end, the dream of death!*

She thrust her mirror toward the open alabaster dome overarching the bathing pool. Sunlight from the central aperture flashed like lightning on the silvered glass. Bare of everything save her terrible wrath, the enraged houri was a sight to strike wise men witless.

Yet Tariq was no wise man, but a consorter with poets. He was too busy paging through his recovered book to pay heed. This made a bad thing worse. The houri expected some modicum of mortal trembling, if solely for courtesy's sake. When she got none, anger blinded good sense and she smashed her mirror down on Tariq's head before flinging herself off in search of the Daughter of the Djinn.

It was a heavy mirror with a hefty load of pique behind that downswing. Tariq's sight exploded into a dazzle of shattered glass and scarlet sparkles. He plunged under the water and floated on his back just beneath the surface, too stunned to do more than admire the pretty way the sunlight flecked the ripples. Breathing was an afterthought. He drifted equally in water and unconsciousness, though as the light dimmed and his lungs grew heavy, he thought he saw a school of silver minnows swimming down to meet his eyes.

He came to his senses with the tiled floor of the baths pressing into his bare back and the black dwarf bending over him. All this was strange enough, but stranger still was the second figure Tariq saw standing at the dwarf's back. It was a woman, unveiled and dressed in simple garb that bespoke cleanliness above luxury. Her face was passable almost to the point of prettiness, but as serviceable and unspectacular as her clothes. Only her eyes were remarkable. They darted back and forth merrily, bright and lively as courting butterflies, and all their attention was fixed upon Tariq's splendid nakedness.

Tariq gasped, surprised by the dwarf's unheralded return but more taken aback by this strange woman's cool scrutiny of his Adamite inheritance. He flailed about him for a wrap. The lady continued to regard him silently, eyes dancing. The black dwarf laughed.

"Is it so, then? Do the slivers let you see her as she sees you?"

"Who is she? What does she do here?" Tariq exclaimed. He got to his knees and, failing a handy towel, shielded himself with his hands. The lady acted as if all this were commonplace. Only her eyes moved a bit more quickly.

"Her name is Zhela. She is a rug merchant's daughter and she dwells in her father's house in Sayda. Right now"

—the dwarf chuckled—"she is reading an *excellent* book."

"What book?" Water from his soaking-wet hair ran into Tariq's eyes, but even when he wiped them dry he could see nothing in the lady's hands. She did, however, hold them out before in a way that suggested the absent tome.

Again the black dwarf vented his amusement. He squatted on the tiles beside Tariq and threw a friendly arm about the young man's shoulders. "Why, your book, my master! Yours!"

"But my book— How could she have—?" Tariq cast his eyes around the poolside until they lit upon the magically rescued volume of tales. It lay beneath the nearby rose marble bench whereon Tariq's silken robes and other possessions reposed. He pounced upon it and held it up for the dwarf's scrutiny. "Here it is. And here are you! Wherefore? I have had my wishes. You are no longer the Slave of the Book as far as I am concerned." This last he said with more than tolerable petulance in a man his age.

"Ah! But *you* are slave enough for us both." The dwarf answered Tariq's astonished gape with further merriment, then shook his head slowly. "No, my master, I do not lie. You are as truly the Slave of the Book as I, but a different book withal—the book wherein the merchant's daughter Zhela now reads of your fabulous exploits in the palace of the Daughter of the Djinn, your encounter with the houri, your present predicament."

"My fabulous exploits?" Tariq brightened. He regarded the rug merchant's child with new respect. "She finds my doings so fascinating? Clearly a woman of wisdom!"

The dwarf looked at Zhela with less appreciation and more pity. "By your adventures, the girl escapes for a time the prison of her mortal life: a strict father, a weak mother, a face and form not likely to make kingdoms burn, a dowry that will guarantee her but a middling marriage to a man who will not understand the time she wastes in mooning over the words of poets. You have rescued her from all this for but a little while, in the tale you live and she reads."

Tariq looked upon Zhela with renewed interest as he heard the dwarf's words. There was a wrenching feeling in his bosom, the painful metamorphosis of a heart long used to pursuing solely its own satisfaction. A new desire swept over it, an alien sensation, miraculous and terrifying.

"How is it that I now see her?" Tariq asked softly.

"Ha! You may thank your second wife for that. Slivers of her mirror have lodged in your eyes, young Tariq! You behold the vision of your heart's most true desire." The dwarf cocked his head to one side and regarded Zhela. "Not much to look at, though, is she?"

"She is beautiful," Tariq breathed. He recognized her now, although he had never seen her before this moment. She was another such as he, a seeker after dreams, a wanderer among the stars, a pilgrim to the shrine of words' enchantment. Could he but touch her, their joining would be more than rude combat of skin and skin. Dreams would attend her more loyally than all the unseen servants of this palace, and their love be more eternally new than the redundant virginity of a host of houris. His heart confirmed the mirror-touched vision of his eyes and leaped toward her. He stood and stretched out his arms to call her in.

She kept on reading, oblivious. A tiny line of perplexity showed itself between her brows, but that was all. Tariq came nearer, laid his hands on her shoulders, ran them down her arms, and still got no response beyond the frown-line deepening.

In anguish, Tariq turned to the dwarf. "I thought she could see me!"

"As words, my master. Only as words."

"But this is monstrous! Can I never touch her?"

"Only her heart."

"She must see me! I must speak to her, tell her that I love—"

Zhela sighed. A tear slipped from her eye.

"Very nice touch, master," the dwarf said, "Her heart is breaking for the plight of the hero who has fallen in love with a phantom lady. Indeed, she admires your romantic obsession all the more because she knows that at this very moment your doom is hastening to meet you."

"My doom?"

"Your wives."

A groan of hopelessness tore from Tariq's throat. "To find the true desire of my heart, only to lose it! To learn I love the dearest soul in all the world, and to die unable to tell her so!"

More tears flowed from the girl's dark eyes. She sniffled a little, then sobbed delicately.

Tariq heard, and his lady's grief made him forget all self-pity. He tried to brush away her tears, but this hands could no easier touch yesterday.

"Do not weep for me, angelic one," he said tenderly. "Do not sorrow. The tale will end as all tales must. If I perish, you will still hold my memory in the pages that went before. Do not forget me when the story is told. Touch the pages past, from time to time, and I will be there for you."

"Oh dear!" In her lonely room in Sayda, Zhela sighed, raising her eyes to heaven. "So noble, so handsome, so brave and fine a man! How I wish I might be with him, to lend him what poor help I could out of his adversity."

"Well?" said the dwarf, arching a brow at Tariq. "What are you waiting for?"

"Me—? I—? What—?"

"Slave."

The shameful name smashed into Tariq's brain in a thunderclap of gleeful realization. "Yes! Of course! I— *Hearkening and obedience!*" He shouted the words full in Zhela's face. A cloud of purple smoke burst from the bath tiles and the rug merchant's daughter stood before them just as the houri and the Daughter of the Djinn came screeching into the vast room.

"Overdone," said the dwarf, still coughing out purple puffs. "Melodramatic. Dated."

"Allah take all critics," Tariq growled.

You see? The houri pointed triumphantly at the mortal girl. *He collects them!*

"UNHAPPY MAN, COMMEND YOURSELF TO HEAVEN!" the Daughter of the Djinn roared. "AND MAKE IT SHORT. I GENERALLY DO NOT SAY A LONG THANKSGIVING PRAYER BEFORE MEALS."

Zhela stood as a block of salt, but only for an instant. Her eyes, once used to sweeping over no greater panorama than a written page, now took in her surroundings, her allies, and her adversaries at a glance.

"Hurry, my love!" Tariq was at her back, grasping her arms with both reverence and ferocity. "I am the Slave of your Book."

"I know. I read—"

"Then you also know that I may grant you only one wish more. For the love of the Most High, wish us far from this palace!"

"And how far is far enough? Where may these immortal creatures not follow us? I waste no wishes, my lord."

Zhela broke from his hold and went quickly toward the rose marble bench. Her hands were nimble, and before Tariq or his wives knew what she was about, she had an unpretentious little drawstring purse firmly between her fingers.

"Flower of Fairness, I see your plan, but it is useless! How can you hope to force them into that?" Tariq exclaimed, recognizing his wedding present from the Daughter of the Djinni. "You have not the strength to compel them, and who would go willingly into the Purse of Di—"

Eschewing all maiden modesty, Zhela moved swiftly as a shadow and clapped the drawstring bag over that most cherished portion of Tariq's person.

"—minution." Only the young man's voice rose when she whisked the enchanted purse away.

"FOOL! WHAT HAVE YOU DONE?" the Daughter of the Djinn bellowed, tearing out her own hair in dismay.

Oh, the wicked wasteful ways of mortal creatures! the houri sobbed. Then she turned to her co-wife and added, *Just for that, eat her up, too.*

"Halt!" Zhela raised both palms in a warding gesture. "One step nearer, either of you, and I shall wish for the presence of the Lord of Winds! I have that power."

"Believe her." The black dwarf grinned and cast an oblique glance over Tariq's newest mishap. "She does not seem to care for exaggeration."

"AND SO? CALL UPON MY FATHER! WHY SHOULD I FEAR THAT?"

"For the punishments he will deal you." Zhela ticked off reasons on her fingers. "You have failed to ward his captive—"

"WHAT IF SHE HAS LEFT HER CELL? SHE IS

STILL SPELLBOUND TO REMAIN IN THIS PLACE. THAT IS ALL HE CARES ABOUT."

"You have permitted her to lie with another man—"

"A HOURI MAY LIE WITH A LEGION AND THE RESULTS WILL BE THE SAME!"

"You"—here she turned toward the houri—"have broken the enchanted mirror which the Lord of Winds coveted."

The houri primped her curling hair as though nothing were amiss. *One hour with me and the Lord of Winds will not care if I broke a thousand mirrors. One learns a thing or two about male priorities in my profession.*

Undaunted, the merchant's daughter said, "And finally, you have both defied the Lord of Winds's desires and risked his wrath for the sake of a merely mortal mate."

Laughter of iron and pearls blended beneath the alabaster dome. Tariq's wives collapsed against each other in mutual hilarity. "AND IF WE HAVE?" the Daughter of the Djinn replied, dabbing at her eyes as her mirth subsided. "MY FATHER KNOWS WELL THE IMPORTUNITIES OF THE FLESH! OF ALL OUR TRESPASSES, THIS IS THE ONE HE WILL BE MOST READY TO UNDERSTAND AND DISMISS."

"Will he?" Zhela touched her steepled fingers to her lips. "When he sees *that?*" She pointed to the paltry results of the Purse of Diminution.

All laughter ceased. There was a moment of silence, a portion of it in respect for the departed.

"Importunities of the flesh, hm?" The black dwarf winked at the Daughter of the Djinn. "What flesh?"

"BUT TARIQ WAS—HE USED TO HAVE—WHEN I FIRST KNEW HIM HE WAS SO INCREDIBLY—" The Daughter of the Djinn folded her legs beneath her and covered her face with her hands. "FATHER IS NEVER GOING TO BELIEVE WE BETRAYED HIM FOR *THAT!*"

"Were I you," the black dwarf said, "I would not experiment with the limits of your sire's belief."

"I doubt not that the master of simoon and samiel will be able to come up with a suitably inventive and memorable punishment for his domestic traitors." Zhela smiled too sweetly at both her enemies.

"Ah, lovely ladies"—the black dwarf rolled his eyes at Tariq's bewildered brides—"at one go this mortal wench has deprived you of both the reason for keeping this young man here and the rationale for having succumbed to his charms in the first place. I suggest you do as she wishes before she deprives you of more."

So it was that Zhela made as shrewd a bargain as ever her father had negotiated in the bazaar. With the full consent of the ladies concerned, Tariq divorced himself of them in exchange for the Daughter of the Djinn using her powers to transport him and Zhela back to the cities of men. The merchant's daughter further prevailed upon Tariq's former bride to include a modest house and an immodest sum of gold as tokens of good faith.

"ONLY IF YOU WILL WED HIM FIRST, HERE AND NOW!" the seething lady replied. "AYE, AND TAKE A HOLY VOW THAT YOU WILL NEVER PART FROM HIM."

Zhela took Tariq's hand. "Never, while I live. May Allah so witness."

"GOOD." The Daughter of the Djinn had a nasty chuckle. "YOU MAY HAVE GOLD APLENTY, BUT YOU WILL LIVE IN ETERNAL WANT NONETHE-LESS." She called up a magical cloud that enveloped the young couple and bore them away.

The black dwarf elected to remain behind and see if he might not cultivate the houri's taste for literature. "I am only a slim volume of unpretentious tales," he called after the departing cloud, "but size is not everything!"

Tariq was of a different opinion, and said so to his wife when the cloud deposited them in their new home, in a prosperous quarter of Damascus. "A fine ending to the score of my adventures!" he cheeped, tearing aside his robes and gesturing expansively at that part of him no longer so expansive.

Zhela seemed unconcerned. She allowed her own robes to fall in a heap at her feet. She stepped out of them and came into her husband's dubious embrace, wreathing his neck with her arms. "My love, you seem to forget that you are still my slave, and I do have one wish left." So saying, she made it.

Automatically, Tariq squeaked, "Hearkening and o—o— *Oh, praise to the All-merciful!*" His voice plummeted at the same rate that his future expectations of joy rose. "And praise likewise to the power that has granted me so wise a wife," he said, bearing Zhela in his arms to the divan.

"Now that is truly a fine ending," she breathed. "Allah grant a sequel."

Ali Achman and
the City of Illusion

Ru Emerson

Well out in the desert, many days' journey by foot and camel from any city, there is a caravansary: it is small and dusty, with sand sifting into the few mud huts, a very tiny market and only a single well. Nonetheless, it is looked upon as a place of beauty and caravans come upon it with joy and songs and much prayer, for it is so far from the main routes, and the water is clean and good. On a day much like any other—that is to say, hot, windy, and very dry—a small caravan reached the first date trees short of sundown. Camels were unpacked and driven to water, tents set up, and while certain of the men went to bargain for dates and fruit, taking camel cheese and coffee to trade, others remained to cook an evening meal or merely to relax in the cool shade of the oasis.

Now, in this caravan were several young camels, and a great deal of trouble they were, too: fighting the packs and riders, fighting the men and each other when it came time to have those packs removed, fighting each other unless they were all ganging up on the young man—Ali, a Hindu and the newest among the caravaners—who sought to keep the young males together to and from the well and to somehow water them, while avoiding teeth and broad-toed feet.

Harrad, the master of the caravan, stood back in shade watching and now and again laughing, but he finally moved to help. The boy cast him occasional dark looks as they drove the camels back to camp, but he spoke no rude words and was indeed as deferential and polite as he had been the first time Harrad met him in Delhi many days before. Harrad for his part correctly interpreted the boy's scowls: the young camels did not spit on the caravan master, nor did they try to bite him. Ali wiped his cheeks as he tied the last of the beasts to the tethers; the shoulders of his robe were nasty with camel spit and he considered himself fortunate after today to still have a full count of fingers. So many days, and still the beasts acted so! Camels must be the spawn of demons, so they said in his country.

"You misled us, Ali," Harrad said. "You told me you had worked with camels before when you offered to trade droving for your passage and food."

"Ah, master, but I have," Ali replied unhappily. "Just —never young males."

Harrad laughed. "And what other camels should need tending on a caravan? The older ones have more sense than to fight us, or each other. I admire your spirit, however, because many others might have fled the caravan after a day or so, leaving us a man short. But you did not. And I am pleased that you keep your anger with the camels to yourself, and do not take it out on either the animals or on your fellow drovers."

Ali only smiled faintly and bowed his head as one should to an older man; what answer was there to what Harrad said?

"But I wonder why you chose my caravan at all," Harrad continued.

Ali shrugged. "To see the world and make my fortune; why does any lad leave his home?"

Harrad laughed. His tent and all his goods were still heaped beneath a tall date palm, but he had unrolled his favorite blue rug so he could stretch out upon it. At his gesture, Ali sat down nearby and leaned back against the prickly trunk of the date. The afternoon breeze had not yet become a harsh wind and after the sun of the long day, it felt cool and pleasant. "If my caravan were bound for Baghdad or Kashmir, then I would believe you! But I most carefully told you that it was not." The caravan master shook his head. "Come now, I must believe that you have a quest of some kind. Perhaps I can be of aid to you."

"I would not ask that, sir," Ali demurred.

"No, and I would not have offered in Delhi, for I knew

nothing at all of you then. I still know all too little, since you have said nothing. But I am pleased by your willingness to work hard and by your manner; surely it cannot hurt for you to tell me what you intend, and see if I am still willing to give you aid!"

Ali thought a moment, then shrugged again. "You have heard of the Wondrous Flying Wooden Horse of the Sultan Feroze Shah?"

Harrad sat up straight, his mouth an *O* of wonder. "Everyone has heard that tale! The Sultan was then but Prince Feroze Shah, and he rode that horse to Bengal, where he found himself a Princess, and she is now his Sultana and the mother of his son and heir! But"—Harrad frowned—"we go nowhere near Feroze Shah's city, and what can the Horse have to do with you?"

Ali might not have heard him; he leaned back against the tree, scarcely noticing its prickles, his eyes half-closed and a faint smile on his honest young face. "The Horse was truly a wonder, as all who ever saw it could attest: so much like a horse it appeared that it was a shock to touch its flesh and find wood there. Nor did it only walk or run as any flesh and blood horse; it also flew across the skies. Two pegs controlled its flight: one at the base of its neck just past the saddle permitted it to rise, another in the throat brought it down to earth.

"It first came to Feroze Shah from Delhi, brought by a Hindu who flew it into the Sultan's gardens and offered to trade it for the Sultan's daughter. Well! Of course, the Sultan had no intention of making such an exchange, but he permitted his son to attempt the beast and Feroze Shah mounted and vanished rapidly from sight; foolishly, he had not asked the Hindu how to ride the beast, and knew only of the peg that allowed it to rise. By the time he located the peg to let it descend, he was over the palace of the Sultan of Bengal, and the Hindu was in the Sultan's dungeons, awaiting either Feroze Shah's return or his own death."

"Every man knows the tale," Harrad said again as Ali paused. "Feroze Shah brought the Princess of Bengal away with him in secret, but before he could wed her, the Hindu took both bride and horse and stole away to Kashmir. The Prince of Kashmir killed the Hindu before he could harm the maiden, but then he proved himself a man nearly as wicked as the Hindu, for he would not return her to Feroze Shah but intended to wed her himself. They say she feigned madness to save herself from that Prince's evil intent until Feroze Shah found her and tricked the Sultan, taking back both bride and horse, and escaping to his father's city."

Ali nodded. "Just so."

"The old Sultan died a year later and Feroze Shah and his Bengal Sultana celebrate once a year, having the Horse brought from the treasuries and decorated with roses. That I know is true, for I have been in the City and seen the ceremony with my own eyes, though of course I have never been within the Sultan's walls and seen the Horse."

"Just so," Ali said again, and now he was smiling. "And you wonder why I speak of all this, no doubt? The Hindu was my father, and my mother the sorceress who made that Horse. It was part of her bride-price."

"And you wish to regain it for her?" Harrad asked. "But—that makes no sense! Feroze Shah's city is nowhere near our route, but even so, the Horse remains deep in his treasuries. He will not permit it to be brought into light save for the ceremony, lest mischief come of it!"

"With respect, sir, I do not intend to steal the Horse for my mother. She is nearly as unpleasant a person as my father, who sought to marry two Princesses while still wed to my mother. My mother, as you have no doubt guessed, is a strong sorceress in her own right, as are my brothers and my sister, while I am—well, as you see me; for some reason, I have never been able to work true magic, and this angered my mother greatly. Now, I have never spoken against my mother or my brothers, roughly though they treated me always. But one day my sister came to warn me that my mother had incited my brothers to murder me, and that they intended to do the foul deed that very night. It became necessary for me to leave Delhi at once."

"I see now why you chose my caravan."

"Because you were leaving Delhi at once also? Partially. There was another reason, however, and of greater importance to me, else I would have merely fled the city alone. You see, my sister has one particular skill among her others: she can look in her mirror and see the future. In my future, she saw my mother's murderous plan but also a vision of myself, a place called El Ashar, the City of Illusion—and then again me, in possession of jewels and gold, the Wondrous Horse and a fair Princess."

"El Ashar! Well, we go there, as you know, though it is seldom they let outsiders within the gates, and we must conduct our trading in the bazaar outside the city walls. But the Horse is in Feroze Shah's treasuries!"

"Oh, that." Ali laughed. "You say yourself, master, that Feroze Shah brings the Horse into light of day only once a year, and that no one has flown upon its back since he returned from Kashmir with his bride. Who would know if a substitution had been made?"

"The Sultan's court magicians," Harrad replied readily.

"No doubt they would know it. But to admit to the Sultan that the beast had been stolen without their catching the thief? Since they know he intends no use of it save the annual ceremony, why would they speak?"

"Why indeed?" Harrad looked around at Ali's bundles and the lump of striped fabric that was his tent and sighed. An idea came to him then. "I tell you what, young Ali, I think you have suffered enough, and so I will offer you another position, if you will have it," the caravan master said. "From today on, accompany me to the bazaars and carry my goods. Set my tent when we camp for the night, make the coffee for me, and I will release you from our previous bargain."

Ali considered this. "It seems little, compared to the camels."

"It is no little thing for a man who has traveled the deserts all his youth and most of his middle years," Harrad replied. "I have grown to like my comforts, but I dislike setting up and striking my own tents, and it would give me status in the bazaars to have a polite young man to follow with my trade goods while I walk unencumbered; if you provide those services for me, you shall eat my food, drink my coffee, and sleep in a corner of my tent from now on."

So put, it did seem a reasonable request, and Ali consented to it. Thereafter Harrad lay back on his blue carpet under the date palm while Ali set up his fine striped tent,

laid out the rest of Harrad's carpets, fluffed two fat cushions and set them within. Harrad brought his blue carpet
inside and sank onto the cushions with a contented sigh to
watch Ali measure coffee beans into the flat pan over the
small fire. The pleasant, heady smell of roasting coffee
filled the tent and wafted into the night.

Harrad tasted the final liquid with pleasure. "You have a
master's touch with coffee; that alone will be worth your
change in status. Now. Tonight there will be some trade
here, but I take no part in it; the people here are poor and
only bargain dates for coffee, things of that sort. Tomorrow
we will leave at dawn. There will be two more stops such
as this, a city where most of the trade is salt and ivory, and
then El Ashar."

"The City of Illusion." In spite of his best intentions,
Ali was becoming excited at the very thought.

Harrad saw this and smiled. He sipped more coffee.
"Now and again, merchants with special goods for the
Prince are permitted inside the city, though certain folk are
never allowed to pass the guard: beggars or the ill, magicians of any kind, thieves—the camels themselves may
not enter. They do not like outsiders, perhaps fearing that
even a common merchant might see through the illusion, if
he were near enough to it. Even a merchant permitted to
trade with the Prince can only remain one night, and only
at one of two certain inns.

"Now and again I have something special to trade, as I
have this time." He sipped his coffee, ate a few dates.
"The Prince's only daughter, the Princess Yasmina, has a
fondness for jewels, and I have brought two strands of very
fine gems indeed." He fixed Ali with a stern look. "I cannot think why I should do this, but again I cannot think of a
reason why not; you have not asked me to help you and
frankly I am not certain I believe the possibility of this
future your sister has seen. But it is an interesting tale, and
I will certainly never know how much truth there is to it if
you do not gain entry to El Ashar."

The look became even sterner. "I do not know that I
will gain entrance to the city, even with these jewels in my
possession, or that I can bring a lad with me to fetch and
carry. If these things come to pass, however, I would ask

that you cause no trouble for me. Of course, if you are the son of two sorcerers you may not be able to enter at all, for the Prince's magicians will detect you at once. Or so *they* say."

Ali laughed bitterly. "That last consideration is no consideration at all, for I am less than no magician. I have a shard of my sister's mirror and a magical scarf she gave me as a parting gift. These I would of course leave behind before entering El Ashar. You have been kind to me, Master Harrad, and I swear to you that I will do nothing which would bring you to any harm, or lose you trade with the Prince."

Harrad smiled, pleased by this polite answer. "Well, there are many ifs involved," he said. "But should they come to pass, then I will take you to see the inside of the City of Illusion."

Ali went about his tasks in the cool dawn the next day with a much lighter heart for having told Harrad the truth; and ah, how much easier was his life, now: rolling carpets, stowing the bag of coffee and rolling the striped tent, securing it with its hempen ropes! As for the city—well, as Harrad said, there was much that rode on much else, before he could be certain that he would gaze upon the Princess Yasmina or ride away with her behind him on the back of the Wondrous Wooden Horse. But he believed in the vision in his sister's mirror, for it had never lied to her.

He *must* believe it, for what else was left to him but such a menial life as this, tending the tents of some merchant or other, or fighting once more with arrogant young camels?

Ali walked beside Harrad most of the morning, so lost in thought he scarcely noticed the heat. Wicked man, his father, to attempt to wed first the Sultan's sister and then his intended bride, and he with a wife and six children at home, and the Horse stolen from that wife! He had surely brought his own fate upon him, a lesson neither his mother nor his brothers had yet seen. Surely wickedness was not worth the doing, if it cost a man his head! But men such as his father, women like his mother, they must think there was a chance that the wickedness would not be charged to them, since they continued to do it! Of the family, only he and his eldest sister did what they could to avoid black spells and evil magic, and for that, his mother had tried to have his brothers murder him!

He had escaped the very next night with Harrad's caravan, while his sister had fled northwards, searching for her own destiny there.

"A magic horse and a Princess," he whispered. Surely Harrad could take him into the city, surely he would not be discovered as a magician! After all, he could not make Harrad's carpets fly, any more than he could make Harrad's camels fly. And after all, his sister had foreseen this future for him. Surely, somehow, it would come to pass—the Princess and the Horse.

The great walls of El Ashar covered a vast expanse of sandy plain just beyond the oasis with its huge, bubbling spring that made the city possible. It glittered during the day, with its golden turrets and lacy spires reaching toward the vault of blue sky; its walls were purest white and at night it sparkled like silver and pearl. So much Ali saw at first, like everyone else. Once Harrad's tent was set up, his carpets and cushions laid out and the coffee roasted, ground, and brewed, he went past the well and stood at the edge of the line of trees, staring across sand and past the bazaar. It seemed the harder he looked, the more ordinary the city became: the turrets were neither so tall nor so infinitely slender as they appeared, nor were they clad in gold and silver, but in plain clay tiles; the walls were rough and plastered and the color of the surrounding sand. The women who came to the well were not veiled, seen straightly or otherwise, but under illusion it seemed to him that he had never seen such beauty. He did not stare too closely at the women, not wishing to be thought rude, and also he had no desire to break *that* illusion.

The bazaar on its surface was wondrous: like the city, it glittered, filled as it was with tents topped by shining golden flags. In their midst, always just beyond full sight, was a minaret of unexcelled beauty. Beneath that, all was common: tents of ordinary blue and white stripe, or plain cream or gray, undyed sheep wool. A minaret of well-shaped but quite plain stone and tile.

Why would they bother? As they walked through the narrow, crowded aisles, Ali found himself wondering that more and more. Granted that the Prince had magicians capable of creating such illusion, why would anyone care? The city was not as beauteous as it seemed but it was still fair, the bazaar was clean and neat, well stocked; the people were tall and graceful—and certainly not ugly!

Well, it was not his business, and if Harrad knew, he had not said. And there were other questions that seemed more important. "How do you judge trade goods, when you dare not trust your eyes?" he asked the caravan master finally.

Harrad laughed. "Illusion is for the eyes only, particularly here in the bazaar, else they could not convince an honest caravaner to trade with them! Any goods a man touches are as he sees them."

And so it was. Ali saw many beautiful things spread in the sun, gems of incomparable size and color that became quite ordinary when he approached them, garments fit to clothe the first wife of a Sultan became clothes that were finely made but otherwise not exceptional. "Why do they do this?" he wondered again. There seemed to be no reason save that they could; and after all, had not his mother and his father made sorcery and magic for no other cause?

Ali followed the caravan master all day, carrying his trading goods and then those Harrad traded for as the bargains were made for cloth, ivory, and wax. Now and again Harrad would cause Ali to bring forth the prizes of his trade goods: the necklace of pearl and emerald, the strand of matched rubies. Of course, no one in the bazaar could afford to purchase them but at day's end, when the merchants were beginning to roll their carpets away for the night, a message came with a safe-conduct to the city for the foreign trader and his servant. Harrad received this with a grave face, but once he and Ali were free of the bazaar, he tilted back his head and laughed. "It worked, just as I thought it would! We must hasten to take these goods back to my tents, and to find clean robes; look you upon this safe-conduct, it bears the seal of the Princess."

The Princess Yasmina! "My thanks, Master Harrad, for taking me with you," Ali finally stammered.

Harrad laughed again as they reached his pavilion. "Do not thank me yet, young Hindu! Wait until you are certain I have done you a favor! But while I am finding myself a clean robe, perhaps you might brew me a coffee?"

The caravan master and his servant stayed at the Inn of Four Moons, where Harrad had stayed before. The landlord looked upon Harrad with favor—for an Outsider—and his daughter Zenoebe waited upon them, though the landlord permitted her near no others who were not of the city. She was quiet and shy, her eyes downcast, and she spoke to neither of them. But as Ali and the merchant went to the stairs to find their room, Zenoebe was waiting in the shadows, and she whispered against Ali's ear: "Come to the kitchen at midnight, I must speak to you." Before Ali could reply, she was gone, hurrying light-footed down the stairs, and they could hear the innkeeper shouting for her.

The floors were cool at midnight, reminding him of the floors back in Delhi in his mother's home. He managed to reach the kitchen in silence, despite the lack of light in the hall. Zenoebe was stirring corn and water in a large pot. She held a finger to her lips as he came into the chamber, drawing him out into the courtyard.

He had scarcely noticed her before. Now he looked more closely. Like most of the people within the walls, she was tall and slender, her robes concealing and yet hinting at an appealing form beneath, the veils sheer and caught back to not quite hide long, thick hair and a face of surpassing beauty. Behind that, however— His eyes were perhaps growing used to piercing disguise, though perhaps it was by her choice: for he could readily see through the guise of perfection.

What he saw was a girl who would come no higher than his shoulder, and while her hair was as long and blue-black as the illusion that cloaked her, her face was not so glorious. But her eyes were kind and her smile sweet and gentle.

"Zenoebe," he whispered. "This cannot be safe, why do you wish to speak to me?"

"Several things," she whispered in reply. "My father is well asleep, and will not waken before dawn, he never does. I saw something tonight, when you and Harrad came into the house, and I would warn you. Like many city folk, since I have lived with magic all my life I see certain things or sense them. Tonight, after you and Harrad retired and I was free to return to my room, I thought I had better look into my mirror. I saw at once that you carry a portion of a mirror yourself; that is women's magic and so readily visible to another woman." Ali clapped a hand to his forehead; under it his eyes were wide and stricken. He had forgotten to leave the mirror behind!

"Since I could sense it," Zenoebe continued, "the Princess could find it even more quickly. I would suggest you leave that bit of mirror with me when you go to the palace, for they would not be pleased to find it on you." And as Ali stared at her: "I swear by all sacred things and by the Horse itself that I shall keep it safe and return it to you, when you come back for it."

"By the Horse!" Ali exclaimed. Zenoebe laid cool fingers across his lips. When she released him, he spoke in a very low whisper. "Have you see it? The Horse? Do you know where it is?"

"The Prince had his priests take it from its last master, for when his daughter heard the tale of Feroze Shah and his Bengal Princess, she greatly coveted it and Yasmina generally gets what she wants, particularly from her father." She shrugged. "It is kept in the palace, in a room near the chambers of the Princess and her ladies, so that she can look upon it whenever she wishes, though she has not looked upon it in two seasons: now she has it, it bores her. I know where it is because my brother is a palace guard, and he has seen it himself."

Ali took Zenoebe's fingers in his on sudden impulse. "I believe I can trust you."

"You can; for you know I know your secret and have kept silence."

"I shall reward you for that, somehow, though at present I am so poor I have not even two copper coins of my own and must depend upon Master Harrad for all my needs. The mirror is my sister's, and before she broke off that piece for me, she showed me a vision: I am to have the Horse and the Princess."

Zenoebe freed her fingers and smiled a little, as much to hide her own unhappiness as not. *Then which mirror lies —his sister's, or mine?* she wondered, but she did not ask it aloud. "That is a foreseeing indeed," she said gently. "If this is your right and your destiny, however, I will aid you however I can."

"You have done that already, Zenoebe, having told me where the Horse is. Though I might ask why you do these things." Ali took out the small leather pouch containing the shard of mirror wrapped in a finely woven scarf. "Keep these safe for me; I shall return for them."

"I shall. As to why—well . . ." She smiled. "Do not people often aid you? I would think they do, for you are handsome and young and well-spoken. However, everyone has reasons for doing things; perhaps someday I shall tell you mine, but not now." Zenoebe went back into the kitchen to stir the breakfast gruel and Ali went past her, down the hall. She turned and gazed into the dark after him. "I shall guard them well, my Ali." His sister had seen, had she? But foreign visions involving the city might not come out the way they appeared. And the Princess! Ali should learn a thing or two when he accompanied Harrad to the palace in the morning!

The Prince's halls were truly vast: that much of them was honest. Ali stood deferentially behind Harrad as he had the day before, holding the merchant's goods and bringing them forth as one trade was concluded and another begun. He looked all around him, and it seemed his eyes were becoming used to seeing behind the lovely fraud to find the less beauteous reality. The Prince himself was a man of very ordinary appearance and he wore only ordinary jewels in his green silk turban—not the enormous pearls and emeralds that seemed to sprout there. The rings upon his fingers were silver and tigereye, not gold and diamond, and the chamber itself—well! It was a shame, Ali thought, for the Prince's throne room was quite a nice room, and its hangings of peach and golden silk were very pretty. The appearance of it only just escaped being silly, it was so ostentatious.

He thought the peacocks were real. Who could possibly invent the horrid noise the great-tailed birds made? Indoors, it was all the worse, for it echoed through the stone chamber and hurt his ears.

The Prince was undeniably wealthy, for it was real coin he paid the merchant for the rolls of silk and brocade— Harrad was most careful about the payment coin, biting each piece of gold before he put it in his purse. That must have been accepted behavior in such a city as El Ashar, though if a merchant had bit another Prince's gold to test its virtue it would most likely have cost him his head.

The trade moved to other things—a special shipment of coffee, two small bags for which the Prince paid highly and with only the least token attempt to bargain; the tea was nearly as rare and the bags smaller, but that liquid must not have been as valued, since the bargaining took more time. Ali found his attention wandering, and he scarcely noticed as the load in his arms lessened and lessened again until there were only the two silk bags containing the jewels.

As Harrad took these and let the jewels fall into his hand, a young woman, clad in cloth of gold edged in pearls, came from behind the throne, surrounded by her maidens. Ali's senses reeled as she passed him. The delicate scent of roses and clove touched his nostrils; he inhaled deeply. The Princess came up behind her father. "Father, I have been waiting; has he not got the jewels?" Her voice, had Ali been in any condition to notice it, was high and sharp and there was a definite whine to it.

A look from the Prince silenced her, but only for a moment. "He *has* brought them, has he not? I hear they spoke of little else in the market yesterday." The Prince frowned at her, and Harrad bit back a smile, knowing as the Prince did that such eagerness on the girl's part tilted the balance in the merchant's favor.

"Yasmina, it is not seemly that you come here; leave at once!"

Yasmina stamped one delicate foot and scowled, her

dark fine eyebrows nearly becoming one. "I must *see* them, Father! You promised me emeralds before the year ended, and is the year's end not near?"

The Prince sighed, turned from his daughter, and smiled ruefully at the merchant, spreading his arms in a helpless shrug. "She rules me as did her mother; what can a man do? Let us see these jewels that had the market agog yesterday." Harrad let the Prince take them to examine.

Now Ali was still so entranced by the Princess Yasmina that illusion held him completely where she was concerned, and he had understood nothing of her speech; he could only think how low and sweet her voice. Love at its most virulent and blinding had struck him all at once and for the first time in his life, and so he was unable to see what he might have ordinarily, what even Harrad could see: the Princess was dreadfully spoiled.

Ali stood bespelled, watching Yasmina's dainty fingers clutch the jewels, glassy-eyed in the face of such dazzling radiance, while Harrad argued back and forth with the Prince and finally sold both his necklaces at very near his first-spoken price. The Princess went away with them, overjoyed, the Prince following her out almost as anxiously for he had already sent his new coffee to his chief cook and thought perhaps he could smell it brewing. Harrad roused Ali with a hard shake as soon as the Prince was gone and dragged him back to the inn.

"She is beautiful, like dawn over the desert," Ali murmured. It was the first thing he had said in hours.

"And as sweet of temper as the camels I rescued you from," Harrad snapped. This business of love made him impatient indeed. Ali cast him a reproachful look.

"That cannot be so, I would have noticed. Did I not see much of the bazaar as it is, and did I not see through the glamour that clothes the innkeeper's daughter? No, she is all my sister claimed. And I am to have her, just think!"

"I think you shall have your head presented to you in a small leather bag by the Prince's headman, and if not by him then by the Princess herself," Harrad growled. "Ali, we dare not remain within the city past sundown."

Ali blinked at him. "But, master, I cannot leave! Remember, this is a thing foreseen!"

"But this is the City of Illusion," Harrad reminded him.

Ali set his jaw stubbornly, so he looked very much like a young camel, had he known it. "I have come this far, I shall not draw back now because of possible danger. What hero of any tale won out by fleeing?" *This is not a tale,* Harrad thought sourly, but refrained from saying so.

In the end, he had to leave the boy at the inn and he walked from El Ashar alone. Ali would take no coin for wages, saying he had earned none, but he embraced the merchant like a father and Harrad embraced him in turn like a son. He was very downcast, for he did not look to see the Hindu again.

Zenoebe drew Ali into the kitchen, then, for there were no servants and her father seldom came there. "Here are your mirror and your scarf. Are you still intent upon the Horse—and Princess Yasmina?"

Ali sighed happily. "More than ever."

Zenoebe's eyes were sad, but Ali noticed none of this, any more than he had seen the true nature of the Princess. Of course, the city's spell was strongest around the palace and its Princess, as Zenoebe well knew. After all, was that not where the spell had originated so many years before— to hide that the old Prince's daughters were both ugly and willful? "Then I shall help you, as I said I would," was all she said.

"Why?" Ali asked, coming to his senses for the first time that day. "I mean—surely you would come to trouble if you were caught. Why should you help me, when you scarcely know me?"

"Why?" Zenoebe echoed. "Besides what I told you before? I am not certain. Never mind. I said I would aid you; and so I shall. Now, I am no witch, and not as clever as my mother was, but I have certain skills and a woman's art to dissemble. In this city, that art can be great indeed."

She hid Ali in the courtyard behind the jars of oil. At midnight, when she came down to prepare the morning gruel, she led him through a small hidden gate and into the streets. "My brother guards the side door tonight," she whispered. "We will be able to enter that way, and from there, they can point you toward the proper chamber." And when he would have protested, she added, "I often visit my brother at odd hours, bringing him food or simply to talk with him. No one objects, since there are hardly ever folk within the city walls save ourselves. The palace is guarded only because the Prince feels it would be improper to his status if he did not have a guard. Come."

She took his hand and led him through a maze of streets, fetching up in deep shadow next to the high walls of the Prince's palace. Down here in the dark, the odor of the surrounding town was noticeable—no longer roses and oranges but ordinary stale garbage and waste of any back street.

Ali put his small bag into Zenoebe's hands once again and followed the brother's instructions. Moments later he was on his way, his feet bare so as to make no noise on the stones.

At least the illusion in the Prince's halls was not like that of the city streets, making dead ends and openings where there were none! He came at last to the small room where the Horse was, and strange indeed it looked, a horse seeming as real as did this one among the other rare and amazing things Princess Yasmina had collected and lost interest in once they were hers.

Ali paid no heed to anything but the Horse, for he needed to find a way to move it to the broad balcony that connected with the Princess's rooms, and that in complete silence. It took time, for the Horse was heavy and his hands grew increasingly damp and shaky, while his head hurt with trying to see through both darkness and illusion and with trying to hear anyone approaching. Both Zenoebe and her brother said there were no guards, but the Princess and her maidens were all too near. At last he managed to free the carpet upon which the Horse stood and pulled that through the gauzy curtains and out under the stars.

Once in the open it took him no time at all to mount and turn the peg; Zenoebe brushed away a tear as she watched the Horse rise silently and swiftly into the night.

Ali found himself above the palace, above the walls, and soaring high in the desert. For a moment he was frightened, until he remembered the second peg that would allow the Horse to descend. Somewhere in the throat—

He rubbed along the Horse's jaw, down past the silver bridle; the jaw moved. He cried out and snatched back his hand, but a gentle voice came back to him on the wind: "Ah, master, do that again! If you knew how long it is since anyone stroked me!" Ali was startled, but the voice was so sweet and warm, he could not be afraid; he leaned forward and wrapped his arms around the Horse's throat and his left had found the peg that would allow them to descend while his right rubbed the long jawbones and the muzzle. There was another peg there, a very small one, which he must have accidentally tripped.

"My mother never said you spoke!"

"Your mother was a fool," the Horse replied, rather huffily. "She did not construct me; her father did.

"She merely stole me, as your father did later. Of course I speak! But it needs a kind person, one who would stroke even the jaw of a wooden horse, to discover that. I suggest, by the way, that you adjust the pegs carefully, as we are approaching the ground a little too quickly for my tastes."

Ali yelped in surprise and twisted the upper peg— slowly this time. The Horse leveled off at a height still well above the sand. "You feel very real, you know."

"I am supposed to, young master," the Horse said. "And your stroking feels very pleasant to me. I am quite grateful to you for rescuing me, by the way; there can be no place in this world duller than that chamber, even a treasury, particularly when one stands in it year after year. I had more fun with your father, even though his was a rather perilous journey."

There was a silence as they glided over the moonlit sand and the deserted bazaar. "I sense that I am not all the prize you wanted from the Palace." Ali started, and the Horse made a sound very like a laugh. "I *am* a magical beast, you know! Of course I sense something that simple! But I owe you a debt for rescuing me and for freeing my voice; besides, I like you despite your parentage. Tell me what you want, and we shall obtain it."

"The Princess," Ali replied readily. The Horse turned his head so he could look at his rider. Now, the Horse had seen through Yasmina at once, being a magical beast.

Clearly this youth did not. Well! He laughed again—an explosive snort.

"Well, unless you intend to steal *her,* I think we had better find you a more suitable guise. A Prince of Delhi, that is what you will be, clad in silks and bearing a pigeon's blood ruby for the Princess Yasmina."

"But I cannot afford such things!" Ali protested unhappily.

"You need afford nothing," the Horse assured him. "The Prince's magicians are not the only creators of illusion, and there are other ways to acquire wealth. But I think you had better be certain, young master, that you truly want this."

For some reason, Ali thought of Zenoebe as he had seen her last, framed by the door into the palace. He shook his head and the vision left him. "What else would I want? That was what my sister saw in her mirror, and that is what I must have."

"So be it," the Horse replied and flew on through the warm night air.

Many mornings later, as the merchants of El Ashar walked from the just opened city gates to the bazaar, they stopped and gasped in wonder. For riding up the road from the oasis came a Prince, clad all in white and sky blue, a cloak of silk fluttering from his shoulders and held in place by great sapphires, his turban of white and gold cloth draped in strands of pearl that came together above his brow in a maze of brilliant white plumes and one great pear-shaped diamond.

The face between sapphires and diamond was fair and noble, his brow lofty and unlined, his eyes dark and wise, a small smile on his lips warming an otherwise stern and strong visage. Long-fingered hands clasped reins figured in gold; the fringe that lay across his horse's face was gold, too, and gems bound the harness; the saddle and its cloths were red and gold, but the horse itself was that purest of gray-white that marks the finest of the fine, the horses that the desert lords take into their tents and call Son or Daughter.

This Prince carried no baggage save one small bag before him and a jeweled box carefully balanced upon that.

He halted at the gate, just before the guard, and dismounted with a liquid grace, and such was his bearing and his mien that the guard bowed to him though they had never done such a thing for any man before who was not their own Prince.

"I have here a gift for the Princess Yasmina," the Prince said, and his voice was as pleasing as the rest of him. He took down the jeweled box and opened it that all might see, and a cry of wonder went up as men did see: a stone as large as a man's fist lay there, glowing deeply red in the early sun. "It is, as you see, a pigeon's blood ruby," the Prince continued. "It has come to my ears that the Princess would have such a thing, and it has also come to my ears that she is a wondrous fair maiden. Now I have sought long for a bride to take to my own kingdom, and so I would speak with your Prince."

There was a hurried conference between the guard. Clearly they could not leave this honored noble to wait before the gates like a common merchant while they sought permission for him to enter—and yet, dare they simply bring him to the palace, a thing long forbidden?

Under his guise, Ali smiled to himself. In truth, there was not much illusion to that guise, certainly less of that than he thought. Ali's fine young countenance was in truth handsome and noble. The clothing and the gems were real, like the horse trappings, wangled by the Horse from a djinni he knew from his days of captivity in Feroze Shah's treasuries. The djinni had been willing enough, in spite of his grumbling, for the Horse had done him certain favors and eventually helped him escape the Shah's city. Ali had buried several bags of gold and jewels—more than enough wealth for any man—two days' ride from El Ashar. These were also gifts from the djinni, for he was properly grateful to the Horse for his freedom.

Ali called the Horse Na-Sheral, which means Light Treader. *He* was very well disguised, for unlike Ali, the Princess had looked at the Horse many times and might otherwise recognize him. Though it was unlikely she would look beyond the contents of the jeweled box.

Nor did she. Ali was still quite smitten with her, though he attempted to hide this fact while he negotiated with her father. Yasmina for her part was so pleased with the pigeon's blood ruby—and with the handsome and wealthy Prince who brought it for her—that she forgot to be rude and overbearing for some hours.

Of course, her true nature came back to the surface by dinner hour, but the Prince had sensibly insisted she remain with her women, behind the curtains—the less this suitor saw or sensed of his bride-to-be's temperament the better, her father thought. For his part, the Prince of El Ashar had never heard of Delhi, but since this Prince Ali Achman said he had never until recently heard of distant El Ashar —well, it was a vast world, the Prince thought expansively. Prince Ali was so obviously taken with Yasmina, he had accepted a much lower dowry than her father had been willing to pay to be rid of her. Better: Delhi was far enough away he would not need to see his spoiled daughter again. Suddenly, he liked the thought of that very much.

Yasmina threw a tantrum of considerable size and volume the next morning when her father told her she must prepare to leave at once, for the Prince intended to waste no time in going back and forth between the two kingdoms and wished to take her with him. "I have no new robes, Father! And what kind of thing is this, that a Princess ride across the desert perched upon the back of a horse?"

"You have your pigeon's blood ruby," her father replied coolly. "And promise of great riches in Delhi, for this Prince will never deny what you want."

Well. What Yasmina wanted, of course, was the ruby without the Prince, for she was already becoming bored with him. He was too nice, too willing to see to her every wish—what would be left for her to want, when she had everything he could give her? And Yasmina knew another thing her father carefully forgot: the illusion that bespelled this Prince would not hold far beyond the city walls. Not that she *needed* illusion, of course! But the thought of appearing less than she now appeared—if there were a way to make this Prince remain in El Ashar! Or, if not him, then another. After all, her father indulged her every want, and still would if she somehow got rid of this Prince of Delhi.

Yasmina dismissed her women and paced her chamber. What to do? She started then, and whirled about. Someone was on *her* balcony! The curtain moved and Yasmina stared at the one who entered her room. "Princess? I have a bargain to suggest—one I think you may like."

It was late afternoon of the same day when the Prince walked from the city leading Na-Sheral, with the Princess Yasmina upon his back. She wore traveling robes, but even these were beautifully wrought and the jewels she wore beneath the heavy cloak shone in the westering sun: a spill of diamonds upon her brow, strands of pearl and diamond and emerald about her throat and between her breasts the enormous pigeon's blood ruby. Two new bags hung from the Horse's withers. Ali smiled and waved at the crowd lining the streets—a handpicked guard led them, or he would never have found his way back to the gates—and even Yasmina now and again held up a hand in response to the cheers. Her face was hidden to the eyes under a dark blue veil, a sensible one designed to keep blowing sand from her delicate skin.

Once beyond the gates, Ali handed a small gold coin to each of the guards, accepted their thanks with a smile, and mounted before the Princess. She wrapped her hands about his waist as the Horse surged forward, and was quickly gone from sight.

Ali rode in a daze, letting Na-Sheral set the pace, and they rode for some time in silence. But as they came through the oasis and into the desert beyond, the Princess spoke. At first, she asked questions, simple ones about Delhi and the distances across the desert, but as Ali answered, she became more and more persistent and rude; her voice rose with each question. "How far do we ride tonight? And why must we travel like beggars, two upon this horse? A proper husband would have brought camels and a pavilion, that I might ride in comfort and in a manner fitting to my station. A *proper* husband would have permitted me to bring my own women, and to come behind him at my own pace when my wardrobe was ready, or he would have brought sufficient women to tend to me as fits my station."

"But my lamb," Ali repied kindly, "I have brought you the gem you desire. And gold and jewels, anything you wish, will be yours when we reach my palace." In truth, he wondered what the Horse intended to do about *that*, as Na-Sheral had refused to discuss it with him, and as Ali knew full well, there was no such palace awaiting him. Perhaps it was this nervousness of his, but he was beginning to sense an edge to the Princess's dulcet tones that he had not heard before.

"Gold and jewels!" she snapped. "I had those in my father's palace! It is getting late, you should not have ridden from the city this late, you know! Nor from the oasis, though *I* could scarcely have slept there! You have not even a tent, do you expect that I shall sleep in a common inn or under the stars like a peasant or a drover's wife? And what do you intend that I eat, in such a wilderness as this?"

"I do think that you should not criticize me quite so fiercely, my Princess. That is not proper behavior for a wife," Ali replied, still mildly. He cried out in surprise then as a small hand smacked his ear, quite hard.

"If you think I will crawl to you!" Yasmina snapped, and this time Ali heard the high-pitched whine. He pulled back on the reins, and the Horse stopped abruptly. Yasmina, with a little shriek of her own, tumbled to the sand where she sat cursing him most imaginatively. Ali jumped down beside her.

"I do not wish for you to crawl to me," he replied. "But I do not think I have heard one kind or nice word from you all this afternoon, and that cannot be right."

"You have done nothing to earn them," Yasmina said, and when he offered his hand to help her up, she slapped his fingers. "You have done nothing save act foolishly! I insist that we return to El Ashar until a proper escort can be arranged for me, because not even a pigeon's blood ruby is worth riding pillion from here to some kingdom so unimportant I have not heard of it!"

Ali stepped back from her: the illusion was falling from his eyes quite rapidly, and what he now saw and heard was distressing indeed: the Princess sounded as unpleasant as his mother ever had, and she had a scowl like a camel with a toothache. "I think perhaps I *shall* return with you to El Ashar—and leave you there for good! You are not worth the having, Princess Yasmina, for you are a shrew to try the patience of a holy man! I think my sister must have been wrong!" Yasmina simply stared up at him from where she still sat on the sand, and the Horse gazed at them both in what might have been amusement. "Aye, I *will* take you back to your father, and may you remain with him until you are old and wrinkled—or until you have learned manners! As for me—there is a maiden in your city, Zenoebe, daughter to an innkeeper."

Yasmina interrupted him with a little cry of horror. "Innkeeper! You have *me* and you would prefer an innkeeper's daughter? A—a *commoner?*"

"She is no Princess, save in her manner; and her smile is nobler than yours! And I am a fool. But perhaps she is also forgiving of fools. Come, let us remount."

"If you wish. But I think it is not necessary to return to El Ashar." It was Ali's turn to stare, openmouthed. That voice! It was low, sweet, and kind, and so were the merry brown eyes that watched him over the veil. Jeweled fingers pulled it aside, revealing all of Zenoebe's face. "It was a good illusion, I think," she laughed. "Nearly as good as yours and Na-Sheral's; certainly good enough to work." And as Ali continued to stare in stunned amaze, she and the Horse both laughed.

"I knew you would not want Yasmina, once you had a dose of her tongue as I so often heard it," the Horse said. "Besides, you said such nice things of this maiden, and so it seemed to me you were merely confused, as humans do become. So one night while you slept, I sought out Zenoebe, and we made a plan."

"I made Yasmina a bargain," Zenoebe said, and she was smiling wickedly now. 'I would take her place, so she need not leave the safety of the city and lose her appearance of beauty, youth, and sweetness. I am afraid she kept the dowry so her father would not be too angry with her, but one of her women filled the bags with bread."

"I would rather eat bread tonight than try to eat gold. But—what will the Prince do to her?" Ali finally managed.

Zenoebe laughed. "Do?" the Horse snorted. "What has he ever done? He wouldn't even think of punishing her; he never has. And she does still have the dowry."

"Of course, I took back the ruby," Zenoebe said. "That is not illusion, though the other jewels I wore were," and indeed, she had only the Princess's robes and the one golden chain supporting the enormous ruby. "She did not want to part with it, but I insisted upon that, if I was to replace her. That was only fair, and she wanted to leave El Ashar even less than she wanted that stone," Zenoebe added with a wide grin. "Perhaps you can have Harrad sell it to the Prince, though perhaps she will not want it now. *I* do not want such a thing dangling from my neck, for it is an invitation to robbers!"

Ali sat down in the sand next to her, rather hard; his legs had given out. He closed his eyes, and shook his head. Finally, he began to laugh. "You imitated the Princess all too well, my Zenoebe. I really hope you do not intend to use that voice upon me as yourself!"

"Ah," Zenoebe said cheerfully, "I never shall, for that is *not* me. But I thought it would not hurt for you to realize what you were losing!"

"Fair enough," Ali managed. He was still laughing. "You have solved my worst problem, of how I would explain to Yasmina that I am not a Prince and I have no palace in Delhi—though thanks to my friend here I am nearly as wealthy as one." He took her hand. "I am not a Prince, you know."

"Of course not," Zenoebe replied happily. "And what would I do with a Prince? And I would have taken you poor. But if you are so wealthy as that, I do not mind at all. We can find ourselves a fine house in the city—"

"One that is *not* Delhi or Kashmir or the City of Feroze Shah," the Horse put in. "I have seen enough of them!"

"There are other cities. Think! A fine house for us and our children." She threw her arms about his neck. "Ah, Ali, we shall be very happy!"

"Just as I was promised," he said, and knew it for truth. Wealth, the Wondrous Flying Horse, a Princess. He had more wealth than any man needed for a lifetime: Na-Sheral was both mount and friend. And—well, for a little while he *had* had a Princess. But as he looked down at Zenoebe's sweet, smiling face, he suddenly realized he still did.

Al-Ghazalah

Judith Tarr

In the Name of Allah, the Merciful, the Compassionate!
It is related in the annals of the wise—but Allah knows all!—that once in the city of Cairo dwelt a mare of remarkable lineage. For her dam was *kehailan* and queenly, daughter through many mothers of the queen of the *Khamsa,* most blessed of the mares of the Prophet, on whose name be blessing and peace; yet through her sire she traced her line to the Prophet himself. Born and bred a man and a prince, for a space and for his sins he wore the body of a horse. And being a horse, and quite untroubled by the eunuch's malady, he had done as any horse would choose to do, until love and an ifrit princess returned him to his former dignity.

The get of his stallionhood were numerous and of exceptional beauty, but most beautiful of all was the last of them. Al-Ghazalah, they called her, so like the gazelle was she: great of eye, slender of limb, swifter than the wind across the sand. Her color was the best of all colors, the bay that sprang first from the mind of Allah, Who made all things that are. Her mane was night and silk; her coat was silk and fire; a star shone on her brow.

Her existence, and that of her sisters, was a difficulty. The imams had settled it by fiat. What Hasan Sharif al-Kehailan had done in stallion's shape was only what stallions were made to do. The issue were a stallion's get, and *kehailan:* of the pure blood of the horses of Arabia. They did not partake of their sire's humanity.

None of them knew what she was, and none would have cared if she had known. They lived out their lives in peace,

160

treasured like queens, mated to kings, mothers of royal houses.

All but Ghazalah. She did not know when she first knew that she was different. She was the youngest, the last and fairest. On the day when she was foaled, her father's wife brought forth a son: the first and, by the will of Allah Who is ever merciful, the last of the children of his human form. It was inevitable that they be brought together, the sister and the brother; it was written that there be love between them, and that al-Ghazalah be the sole and cherished mount of Shams al-Din. His beauty was the sun to the moon of hers; in spirit, in temper, in fire, each had no equal but the other.

Yet even he did not know her secret. For a long while she was not aware that she had one. It came first upon her all unlooked for, in the deep night, as she drowsed by her mother's side. She yawned and stretched and thought of hunger, and there was strangeness in her. She looked at herself, and she was not she. She was something other. Something frail and soft and hairless, with toes where hoofs should be. And hands. Humans had hands, clever for opening gates, skillful in stroking one's tender places. She had hands. *She* was human.

But she was not. She reached toward the warm drowsing horseness of her mother, and something shifted. It was like pain. It was like pleasure. She was herself again, slender-legged, drowning her bafflement in her mother's milk.

The strangeness kept coming back. In the night, always: she would wake from a dream, and she would have hands. She taught herself to walk, tottering two-legged. She listened to the humans; she learned to talk, if only to her mother. She learned that she could will herself to change. She discovered the advantages of hands on latches and bolts, and the wideness of the world beyond her stable yard.

She never shifted where anyone but her mother could see her. It was not secrecy. It was a sort of delicacy. Everyone could do this, surely; no one did it in front of everyone else; therefore it was a private thing. She wondered whether all the humans were horses in the night, or whether some were hunting dogs, or cats, or even—she knew which those would be—braying asses. Her father had been a stallion. Everyone said it, though it seemed that he was one no longer. Perhaps this was only a pleasure for one's youth.

She would be sorry, if that was so. She liked the suppleness of human shape. She liked to talk; she loved to sing. She learned to read, from being tethered close by Shams as he endured his tutors. She heard the disputations of philosophers. She became, had she known it, most widely and deeply learned, while her brother and master yawned and groaned and took flight whenever he could. He would only hear his lessons at all when she was near, because it inconvenienced his teachers, and because she provided swift escape. They learned to ride well and swiftly, those masters of the arts, or they did not linger long in his service.

He would happily have dismissed them all. But his father was adamant. "I was a knave and a fool," said Kehailan. "My son will learn to be wise."

His son did not want to be wise. His son wanted to ride a-hunting, or a-drinking, or a-whoring. Shams al-Din, as his father's mamluk observed, was in all respects his father's child.

When both al-Ghazalah and Shams al-Din had attained their seventeenth year, Ghazalah knew that she was like no other creature in the face of God's creation. Mares, except for Ghazalah, remained mares from birth to death. Maidens, except for Ghazalah, held that form by day as by night. It was noted that the four-footed line of Kehailan seemed to partake somewhat of the longevity of their human forebear. It was also noted that Ghazalah seemed most fully to have held to human youth: slow to reach the fullness of her growth, and slow to settle to the placidity of age. That she remained a maiden, however, she owed to Shams al-Din. She was his. No other, be he beast or man, might have her.

She was, as she thought, content. Her secret was hers to cherish. Her brother was the fairest youth in Egypt, the best horseman, the surest shot with the Turkish bow, though he was no Turk but Arab of the holy line of Mecca.

If he was not also the wisest, if he lacked perhaps some
essence of intelligence, that was little enough to sully her
peace. She had sufficient for them both.

It is the way of mares and of educated maidens, as all
the wise know, to have no patience to spare for the follies
of love. Likewise, it is the way of young men, and most
especially of ruinously spoiled young princes, to have patience for nothing else. Shams fell in and out of love a
dozen times in a day. The swiftness of his falling out, Ghazalah observed, was directly proportioned to the swiftness
of his gaining his desire.

Therefore she was neither surprised nor unduly troubled
when, in riding through the city of a morning, he halted
abruptly and drew a long sigh. "There," he said. "There is
the love of my life."

They had come to the fringes of the bazaar; the streets
were full to bursting. But Shams had eyes for one alone.
Ghazalah discerned her easily enough by the yearning of
her brother's body on her back; and she was, admittedly,
noticeable. In that city of small, dark, slender people, she
towered like a young tree. Her hands and the oval of her
face were white as milk. Her hair under its drift of veil was
the color of gold in the forge. Her eyes were as blue as the
sky in winter, and bold, knowing nothing of modesty. They
met Shams's with most unmaidenly directness, measuring
him as if he had been the slave and she the lord of Islam.
They gave him due credit for his beauty, but reckoned his
youth and his callowness and his disinclination to use what
wits he had, and discarded him.

He, of course, was smitten to the heart. "I will have
her," he said. "I must have her. I will die if I do not have
her."

She had turned her back on him. Bravely he battled the
currents of the city, following her as best he might through
the rounds of the market: the bakers, the sweetsellers, the
cloth merchants, the sellers of spices, and, at length, the
butcher who tended the needs of Cairo's Christians. Not a
whit daunted, Shams clung to her track. It led him out of
the bazaar at last, through many windings of the city,
thronged always, never open to him when he would press
closer, armed to speak, to touch, even, it might have been,

to seize her and bear her away. Shams in love was no more to be reasoned with than a leaf in a whirlwind. It mattered nothing to him that his beloved led him ever deeper into the Christians' quarter, or that his turban and his Arab face were far from welcome there.

The woman, turning without warning, led her company of porters through a gate in a blind wall. He spurred Ghazalah so suddenly, and with such unwonted force, that she leaped like the beast of her name. The gate was swinging shut. She hurtled through it.

Shams was out of the saddle before she had plunged to a halt, prostrate before the Frankish beauty, babbling passionate nonsense.

Ghazalah snorted at the sunlit courtyard, the astonished porters, the servants arrested in mid-stride. Shams had lost his turban; his hair, of which he was girlishly vain, was tumbled in the dust. Yet even so dimmed, it shone like jet and raven.

The Frank seemed both amused and fascinated. When he began to kiss her foot, she did not at once pull away. "What," she inquired in passable Arabic, "is the meaning of this?"

He raised his head. His face shone. He had never been more beautiful, and for once he was not aware of it. "Love," he said. "It is love."

The Frank blinked once. "Just like that?"

"Like an arrow in my heart," cried Shams al-Din. "Like light in the darkness. Like fire, like lightning, like—"

"You are mad," said the Frank. She clapped her hands. The porters came, big men and burly, unmoved by young ardor. They lifted Shams, one to his head and one to his feet, and tossed him lightly through the gate.

Ghazalah did not wait to be assisted. She bolted in his wake. The gate boomed shut. Bolts slid, sharp and final.

Shams picked himself up, and he was smiling like a man in bliss. "Did you see? Did you see, sister? She looked at me; she loves me." He dusted himself off, still smiling, but sighing a little. "Of course she had to cast me out. Too many people were watching; she had no choice. Had she but been alone . . ."

Ghazalah wanted to shake him. A slave was bad

enough, but a Christian slave was unconscionable.

"So beautiful," he murmured, lost in his madness. "Lapis and gold; ivory; the merest shimmer of rose. Her feet, her hands, her perfect fingertips... her lips, like flowers..."

The wench was as tall as he was, and nigh as broad in the shoulder. Ghazalah bucked and twisted, to distract him. He barely noticed. He was lost. Utterly. Again.

She did not know why it mattered. It was not his first slave, nor even his first Christian. He had been smitten thus powerfully before, and for less cause. And yet Ghazalah was uneasy. The woman's eyes when they had rested on Shams—yes, for a breath's span they had softened. It was a strong woman indeed who could resist such beauty in a man. Yet there was more. Something strange; something awry.

Ghazalah was waiting when Shams came creeping through the night, robed in black but with splendor gleaming beneath, and on him a scent of musk and sandalwood. She suffered him to saddle and bridle her; she let him smuggle her out through the garden gate. It was not the first time they had gone so, nor the tenth. Tonight, however, she had a plot of her own, and that was not to linger docilely in the lady's garden, nibbling grass and rose petals while her brother wooed his latest love.

He was not astonished to find that the Christian's garden, like his own, like half the gardens in Cairo, had a hidden gate. Still less was he amazed to find it unlatched. Shams was nothing if not certain of his own attractions.

He did not see that the mare whom he had tethered to a hanging bough was gone, nor take note of the slender human shadow that flitted in his wake. With the ease of one who had done the same through many a moonlight garden, he found his cat-soft way to the center of his desire. Another gate, unlatched; a lamplit stair; a chamber bare of any heathen softness.

The Frank sat in it, alone, reading by the light of clustered lamps. She was not startled to be invaded by the madman of the morning, but she was not arrayed for any seduction Ghazalah had ever heard of. She was covered from head to foot in heavy Frankish swathings, her hair drawn back severely from a face innocent of paint or kohl. She shone amid that starkness like a diamond set in stone.

Ghazalah was hard put to conceal herself in the shadows of the passage. Shams, oblivious, had flung himself at the woman's feet.

"You are persistent," said the Frank.

"I am in love," said Shams.

The woman's lips twitched, vanishingly faint. "How can you know that? You know me not at all."

"My heart has known you from the moment of its creation."

"Pretty," said the Frank. "Do you do this every day?"

"Oh no," said Shams. "Never like this. Never so completely."

"Not since yesterday." Her amusement was fleeting, her eyes upon him stern. "I suffered you to come to me, only to give you warning. I am no prize for a young fool's taking. Go now, cast your eye on gentler prey; forget that you have ever seen me."

Ghazalah could have told her what that would avail her with Shams al-Din. He rose, he clasped her knees, he turned on her the full force of his eyes. They were beautiful eyes, and they were more than beautiful. They were his mother's eyes, and his mother was the daughter of the Sultan of the Afarit. No woman born of man was proof against them.

The Frank was strong: she had will to resist. But her hand had moved of itself, to touch one of his perfumed curls. Only one. The one that fell, just so, athwart his brow. That guided her down round the curve of his temple, into the first new bloom of his beard.

He smiled. Her fingers tightened; her hand leaped back as if it burned. "You are mad," she said, as she had said before.

"Mad with love."

"I know what you are. Beautiful; fickle. Light of heart, light of mind, light of love."

"Not for you," said Shams al-Din. He set a kiss upon her upraised palm. "For you, I am constancy incarnate."

The blue eyes sharpened, narrowed. "Will you swear to that? Will you swear it by your very soul?"

Ghazalah would have cried out, leaped, given her life to stop him. But she was rooted in the shadows. She could not even breathe.

"By my very soul," said Shams, "I swear to you, I shall love you and no other while yet there is breath in this body."

The Frank's head bowed. For the first time, faintly, she smiled. "How passionate you are! and how beautiful. And how very much in danger. I am a prisoner here. If my jailer discovers you, he will destroy you."

"Nothing can harm me while I have my love for you."

She touched his cheek again, lightly. He closed his eyes and shivered in delight. "Go now. Come tomorrow, as you came tonight. Remember what you have sworn."

"In Allah's name, I shall never forget."

She shuddered at that most holy of names, but she did not gainsay it. "Tomorrow," she said.

And tomorrow, and tomorrow. Ghazalah had never seen Shams so faithful, or so wondrous content. "There is no one like her in the world," he said. "She *reads*, Ghazalah. She thinks; she questions everything. She wants to know all I know of the Faith; she tells me of her own. She is a princess in her own country. Because she would not wed the man her kinsmen chose for her, and dared to run away, she was taken prisoner. When she strove to escape, they bound and trammeled her in the guise of a slave, spirited her away, entrusted her to the cruel mercies of a sorcerer. He guards her, but he fears her. He is but a master of magic. She is Melisende."

Melisende, Melisende. He wandered off, singing her name. Ghazalah's heart had gone cold. A magician. And Shams, lovely, fickle Shams, had sworn an oath on his soul. Oh, indeed, she knew how this would end.

And what could she do? She was only his mare. She had no magic to match a Christian master's, only her twofold shape and a cantrip or two.

Time passed as it must in this world which Allah has made, and Shams passed it as he must, since he was Shams. After the first intoxicating night or six, he sang his lady's name somewhat less often. There came a night, in-

evitably, when he could not escape a duty before the time
allotted for his tryst. He made up for it with redoubled
passion. And thus again a second night, and a third. He
began to notice women in the bazaar. He began to pause
when a singular beauty passed him by; then to smile; then
to essay a word or two. One bright afternoon, he lost the
whole of himself in a pair of kohl-dark eyes. They were
only eyes, and their bearer was only an hour's dalliance; he
knew no guilt that Ghazalah could perceive.

He went that night as he had promised, lightly enough if
without his former eagerness. He left Ghazalah in her accustomed place in the garden: a little sward, a fountain, a
bower of roses in full and scarlet bloom. She had not followed him since that first night, but now she waited only
until he had passed beneath the arbor, to put on her second
shape.

The chamber was the same, but the lady had altered
immeasurably. Her hair was like a fall of gold; her body
bloomed in the sheerest of silk. She smiled as he came,
and stretched out her arms. Shams fell into them with as
good a will as he had ever had.

Ghazalah saw enough and more than enough to prove
her misgivings all unfounded. She retreated with burning
cheeks, taking refuge in the cool of the night, the sweetness of the roses, the solace of her native form. Of course
her brother had nothing to fear. His eyes had conquered yet
again. The lady was his beyond any dread of treachery.

Ghazalah had known, as a mare will, that this house had
a stable, and that there were horses in it: a mare or two, a
gelding, a stallion. The stallion was given to bursts of
clamorous temper, and to beating down the walls of his
prison.

Tonight, for a wonder, the stable was silent. Perhaps at
last they had sold or slain the stallion. Ghazalah was most
pleased that she need not suffer again that nightly uproar,
and yet she found herself hoping that he was not dead: that
he was alive, and free at last of his hated captivity. She
knew what madness a locked stall could be, for a creature
born to run under the open sky.

She drank a little from the fountain, nibbled a bit of

grass. All was well with Shams and his lady. She had seen how very well it was. Yet she could not hold still. She found herself slipping from mare to woman, and back to mare again. She circled the fountain; she ate a rose. She pawed a furrow in the grass.

He was on her before she knew it: a crushing weight, a battering of hoofs, the closing of great stallion teeth in her tender nape. She screamed in rage and pain. His forelegs pinned her; his teeth clamped tighter.

The worst of it—the very worst—was that her body yielded. It opened itself. It bowed to his power.

With the last remnant of her will, she twisted. Hands clutched the great neck, knotted in the waterfall of mane. The stallion crashed down in shock and startlement. She fell with him, scrambling, straddling his neck.

He lay half-stunned. He was thunder-dark, but his eye was gray as glass. It rolled back, white-rimmed. She cursed him with every curse she knew, and a few that she had only then conceived of. They were not idle curses. She wove them into his forelock, binding him to her will.

"Lady." It was not a man's voice, and it was weak with the weight of her on his windpipe, but it was Arabic. "Lady, I beg you—"

She was beyond astonishment. She was in the white realm of wrath, where anything could be, even a stallion who spoke pure Arabic. "What right have you to beg anything?"

A stallion could shrug, after a fashion. Even if his speech had not been proof enough, something in that shrug hinted that his native shape was not the one he wore. Something in the way his eye rested on her nakedness, proved it beyond doubting. "You are very beautiful, lady. In both your semblances."

"That does not excuse rape."

"It does not," he said, which was more than a human man would have done. "It is only . . . I saw you under the moon, and your beauty smote my heart. When you changed, you startled me. I lost all good sense; I thought only of your beauty, that I must have it, and you, and any love which you could spare for me."

She snorted. The lust, at least, she could believe.

It was not comfortable, crouching there on his neck. He was bound by her spell in his forelock; she was safe enough to rise, to let him scramble to his feet. Small wonder that her back ached with the remembered weight of him. He was huge beside her, huge as a Frankish charger, deep-chested, great-necked, heavier of head than a stallion of Arabia, but fine for all of that, and spirited. If he yielded to her sorcery, she suspected that he did so as much because he chose, as because she had any power over him.

His words proved it. "I would make amends, O moon of beauty. Only free me from your spell, and I will serve you as I may."

She narrowed her eyes. His own were a little too bright for her comfort, a little too careful in fixing on her face and not on the body below it. "This is not the shape you were born in."

He bowed before her. "O percipient! Indeed it is not. Al-Barak am I, djinni of the line of Iblis. My father is a great lord of the Djinn; my mother is a spirit of ice, a daughter of the north wind, whose essence embodies itself in a white mare. The master of this house found me grazing among mortal mares, for this semblance comes easily to me, with all that accompanies it, and I have been most fond of it. He seized me, bound me with magics, brought me here to serve his will." The lean ears flattened; the strong teeth bared. "Such service as I would give, even bespelled. Had he not caught me in the act of mounting a mare, he would never have touched me. He is but mortal. I am a prince of the Djinn."

"You are a captive," she reminded him. "Or you were. Has he deigned to grant you the freedom of his house? Or were you escaping?"

His head tossed; he stamped. "I had won free. I was seeking a gate."

"You found me." Her glance was heavy with irony. "It is written, it would seem. that mares shall ever be your downfall."

He looked as abashed as a stallion could. "But you are so beautiful."

There was no accounting for the idiocy of males. Ghazalah snatched his forelock, tugged it free of the spell, pointed. "There is the gate. Now, go, before the hunt comes after you."

He did not move. "Come with me. Be my love. All the sky shall be our marriage bed."

"How public," she said. She set hands to his shoulder and pushed. "*Go*. Or do you want to be a slave again?"

He nuzzled the warm space between her breasts. "We have time. The sorcerer is occupied. Very well, when I looked, and very thoroughly."

She slapped him away. "He'll not be distracted long, once he knows that you've escaped."

He nibbled her hair. "Ah, no. He has another toy tonight. A prettier one than I. I, after all, was only mounting his mare. This one had mounted his princess."

She froze. He babbled on oblivious. "She was to be kept untainted for the one whom he calls his master. How he raged when he found that she had been taking her nightly pleasure with a silken witling of a boy!"

Ghazalah's feet had mastered her numbed intelligence. She bolted toward the shadow of the house.

She had wits enough to bolt in silence, from darkness to darkness. She passed the door and the stair. She hid herself in her accustomed shadow.

The lady stood against the wall, a robe clutched about her. Shams was cast down on his back. A man stood over him, a very large man in mail that glittered in the lamplight's flicker, with a bone-white cross upon his breast. His sword was naked in his hand; the point rested with utmost delicacy on Shams's most precious jewels.

"Shall I cut?" the man inquired. He did not sound angry. If anything, he seemed amused.

The lady drew a sharp breath. She was neither fearful nor defiant, but whitely furious. When she spoke, it was not to the man with the sword. "Oh, you lying fool! To swear as you swore, and to come to me as you came, reeking still from another's embrace."

"It was *nothing*, I tell you!" Shams's breath caught as the blade pricked, but he persisted. "It's you I love."

"What did you call the other? A gallop in the grass?"

He nodded eagerly. "That's all it was. That's all it

would ever be. I came straight to you after. She was nothing to what you are."

She spat at him. "You are vile. I should let him cut you
to the bone. I should do it with my own hands."

Shams blanched. The man smiled. "So, my lady. Was
he worth the price you must pay?"

"*Yes!*" She had startled them all, even Ghazalah
crouched beyond the door. "He is a liar and a simpleton,
but for a little while he loved me."

"Delusion," said the sorcerer.

"Better that than the one which you prepared for me."
She held out her hands. "Take me now. Do your will. I
knew what I did, and I knew how I would pay. I regret
only that this child's stupidity ended it so soon."

Now at last Ghazalah saw anger in the sorcerer's eyes.
"A fool and a fool are well matched. See, now, for what
you squandered your honor and your purity." He wound his
fingers in Shams's hair, dragging him struggling to his
feet. A poor creature the boy looked, slender as he was,
fair-skinned as a girl, with a girl's tumbled curls. But he
was man enough to fling himself at his captor, snarling in
rage.

The man held him off with contemptuous ease. "A vicious little cur. Has he teeth?" Shams snapped; the sorcerer
laughed. "So, then! You choose your destiny. By the angels
of hell, so mote it be." He smote his hands together. Shams
dwindled between them, darkened, and shrank. His snarling never abated. He sank his teeth in the sorcerer's foot.

The sorcerer cursed and kicked him loose. He lunged.
Melisende caught him before he could impale himself on
the sorcerer's sword, and held him wriggling and struggling, half mad still with rage. His snarling rose to a cre-
scendo and died. He stilled, panting, lips wrinkled over
sharp white teeth.

He was a very pretty dog, for all of that. A pup, still,
but well grown. His coat was glossy black, long and curling. His eyes were large and brown and growing frightened
as the truth sank through his temper.

"A definite improvement," said the sorcerer, "and, I
think, an acceptable compromise. You may keep him if

you choose. He should be rather more faithful in this shape than in the other."

Melisende's face wore no expression at all. She set the pup down with care, and drew back from him. "This is unspeakable," she said.

"It is just."

"Not to a Muslim."

The sorcerer shrugged. "He chose it, not I. Do you want him? Or shall I turn him out?"

Ghazalah poised to spring. Melisende struck the sorcerer with all her force. While he reeled, astonished, she knelt in front of Shams. "I refuse to pity you," she said. "You earned it too well. But I would not see you torn to pieces by the dogs of Cairo." She gathered him up and rose. "Take us," she bade the sorcerer.

Ghazalah stumbled into the chamber. It was empty of aught but air, and that air acrid with the stench of brimstone. Of her brother, of his ladylove, of the Christian sorcerer, not even a shadow remained.

She circled slowly. Feet hardened to hoofs. She stamped; the floor rang. She cried her rage in a mare's piercing scream.

"Lady," said a voice. "Lady, what—"

She wheeled, half rearing.

The stranger bowed before her, as a prince would, with grace that touched her even in her madness. He was young, and he was larger by far than men were wont to be in Egypt. His hair was dark but his skin was fair; his face was more strong than delicate, and yet in its way it was very good to look at. He looked the very image of a Frank.

He leaped from the path of her lunge. She veered, skidding, and toppled down the stair.

Bruised, winded, and unwillingly human, she lay at the bottom and struggled to gather her wits. The young man bent over her, deeply concerned and not at all surprised. He did not mar his manly beauty as most Franks did, by shaving his beard; it was cut becomingly short. His eyes were gray as glass. "Lady," he said, and his voice was a man's, and yet she knew it. "You frightened me."

Painfully she sat up. His hands aided her; she suffered

them. "I thought you were one of them," she said.

His head came up; his nostrils flared. Still, he laughed, if not altogether in mirth. "My mother's face is my blessing and my curse. Yet surely I do not smell like a Frank."

"You smell like a stallion." With him to lean on, she could rise. She had harmed nothing of consequence.

She knew of modesty; she had learned the uses of garments in nocturnal wanderings. Now she began to understand what it was that made women strive so endlessly to cover their bodies. His eyes made her think of Ramadan. A bitter fast, a purging of the soul. And after it, all the sweeter for the month's denial, a feast.

Stallions never had enough of what they were created for. Even stallions who were born to princedoms of the Djinn. She snatched the cloak from about his shoulders and wrapped herself in it, and set foot again upon the stair.

His hand stopped her. "Where are you going?"

"Back," she said.

"To what? The sorcerer is gone. In his absence I am free to wear my native shape. And you, O pearl of beauty. . ."

Had she been a mare, she would have kicked him. "You are a fool. Where is the freedom which you so yearned for?"

"All about me," he answered her. "The Seal of Suleiman ibn Daoud—may he rest in peace eternal and far from any of the Djinn—is broken above my stall, as clever as I was in tricking the stableboy to knock down the bat's nest behind it. There remains a little matter of revenge upon a sorcerer, but that is nothing; he will wait until I please to take him. You, however, O light of my heart—"

She seized him with force enough to stagger him. "You know? *You know where he is?*"

His arms were delighted to find themselves about her. "How not?" He bent his head to steal a kiss.

She bit him. "Where? Where is he?"

He licked the bright ichor from his lip and smiled. "O spirited! What does he matter to you? He is but a dog of an infidel."

She laid him flat. While he sprawled, astonished, she sat on him and seized his beard. *"Where is the sorcerer?"*

"Such fire," he sighed. Her fingers tightened; he

winced. "Lady, have pity on a poor lover! He is nowhere that can matter to you." A twist won a yelp, and taught him the beginning of wisdom. "He is in Syria, in the fortress called Krak."

She frowned. "Krak?"

"Krak des Chevaliers, they call it: Krak of the Knights of the Hospital of Jerusalem. Did you not know? He wore the eight-pointed cross often enough within these walls. He is a master of the darker arts, but he has a master of his own; it was to that one that he went. He seemed most pleased, despite the failure of his guardianship." Barak did his best to look engaging, even with her fist in his beard. "Can it be that you had a hand in it? Or, perhaps, a hoof?"

She glared at him. "*I* am not an idiot. My brother, on the other hand..." It smote her with the fullness of its force. "O Allah, our father will die of the shame!"

"Your—" He seemed, for once, surprised. "That poppet was your brother?"

He howled. She hauled him up by his wounded chin and backed him to the wall. "That poppet," she spat at him, "is the creature I love best in the world. Go, mount your mares, futter your doxies. I have battles to fight."

"Against every mage in Krak?"

"Against every mage who ever was, if so God wills it." She dropped his cloak and her humanity, and left him to his foolishness.

Hoofs thundered behind her. She lashed out with heels and teeth, but al-Barak had set himself well out of reach of either. "Lady!" he cried. "Lady, will you wait?" She had no time, and being a mortal mare and no Djinniyah, no voice to speak. She eyed the garden wall. High, even for her desperation. Perhaps, after all, the gate...

He was there, barring it, dark in the dawn. "O beautiful," he said, "do you forget what I am? I have magics beyond the measure of men. I lay them at your feet."

Feet, indeed, since she needed human speech to curse him.

He shook her curses from his mane. "O pearl of my desire, I mean no less than I say. My magics are yours. Only speak, and I shall serve you."

"At what price?"

"Price?" Even as a stallion, he could look exactly like a merchant in the bazaar: the image of innocence impugned. "Did I speak of prices? I love you. I desire only to give you joy."

And to get his teeth into her nape, and another portion of his anatomy into another part of her altogether. Her shoulders twitched at the thought. "Only that, my lord?"

"With all my heart," he said.

"All males are idiots," she observed. He regarded her, unoffended, all perfectly besotted. "A bargain, then, O prince of fools. Help me to win back my brother. In return—" His ears pricked; his body yearned toward her. "In return, you have your vengeance on the sorcerer, and my leave to seek my favor."

He snorted; his ears flicked back. "Only to seek your favor? Lady, you are cruel."

"I do not haggle," she said. "There is the bargain. Take it or leave me. Time is passing."

Slowly he bowed his head. "I will aid you, if through it I may woo you, O heart of stone and fire."

The voice that spoke the last was a man's. He cast his robe about her; he spoke a word of power. The world whirled away.

Even in dreams Ghazalah could not have conceived of Krak. There had never been another fortress like it, nor would ever be again. It reared from its bleak and barren crag, a mountain of stone raised up as by the hands of giants, vast beyond imagining. She looked up at its sheer walls and despaired.

She turned on Barak. "Why are we here? Why are we not within?"

He looked, when she paused to notice, rather paler than his wont. He lay back against the rock of their concealment, and essayed a smile. Her glare quelled him. His eyes lowered; he bit his lip. For all his size and his palpable power, he seemed suddenly very young.

"Well?" she snapped. "Out with it!"

He looked almost abashed. "It seems . . . I am strong, my lady, have no doubt of that. It seems that these of the Hospital, taken together, are stronger than I. There are walls of magic as well as of stone; they rise to keep out any stroke of sorcery."

She looked up again. The walls stared down, impregnable. "Of course," she said to them, "you would be guarded." She considered herself, with ample help from a pair of cloud-gray eyes. "You can, I hope," she said to their owner, "clothe me as befits a guest in a sorcerer's hall."

He stared at her, for once without desire. "In— Lady! Are you mad?"

"I have to get in," she said. "What better way than direct?"

"They will kill you."

"Allah will defend me." She rose, shaking out her tangled hair. "Clothe me," she commanded him.

His lips set. He rose unsteadily, drew a breath, stretched out his hands. She tensed to slap them away, but paused. A breath of wind caressed her, distant kin to the whirlwind that had brought them here. Warmth followed it, the caress of silk, the touch of unseen hands upon her hair. She looked down in wonder. He had clothed her like a queen, in robes of sublimest splendor, sunset-colored, broidered with gold, sparked with pearls and the fire of opal. She touched the pearl-woven coils of her hair; she turned her wrist to marvel at the many bracelets of gold. She essayed a step, and started. Bells tinkled as she moved. She spun. The bells sang; silk billowed, whispering. She laughed for pure delight.

Barak looked like a man smitten with a mace. His wits, however, had not abandoned him entirely: the dark robes with which his magic clothed him had melted into air. He wore the livery of a mamluk, a soldier-slave in mail and sunset silk, and on his breast a stallion rampant.

He would do, if he could keep his eyes to himself. She tossed her head, imperious. "Come," she said.

She gave her heart no time to falter. She set foot upon the steep and stone-paved road; she walked up it with all the pride of a queen and all the lightness of an Arab mare. The walls loomed above her, poised as if to fall. The sky was pitiless. Only her courage sustained her; her courage, and the silent presence at her back.

There were guards at the gate, men as large as Barak, larger yet in mail and helms, blazoned with the cross of the infidels. The power that breathed forth from them was cold and strange, like a wind from a tomb.

Ghazalah stumbled. Barak was there, catching her, lingering even here, before the faceless helms. She withered him with a glance and strode forward anew. The air seemed to cling, to drag her back, to tangle in her laboring feet. She set her teeth and persevered. Barak's breath was loud behind her. He felt it more than she, or bore it with less fortitude, but he uttered no complaint, clinging grimly to his place.

The gate was open, the portcullis raised. She knew a trap when it gaped to swallow her: a trap of her own choosing. She faced that maw with its fangs of iron, and raised her voice. It was high, but it carried, ringing in the cavern of the gate. "Peace be upon this house and all who dwell in it!"

The guards did not move. The portcullis did not come crashing down. Bravely, but with a twitching in the center of her back, Ghazalah entered into Krak.

When mailed men closed in about her, she was almost glad. They did not touch her, nor did they compel. They simply guided. Through court and hall and court again, deeper and ever deeper into the stronghold's heart. No gardens grew here, no green, no hint of softness. It was all stone, all silent but for the ring of mail-shod feet, and the sweet song of the bells about her ankles, and far away a deep-voiced chanting.

Ghazalah was not afraid. She had gone beyond it. The sun had set on a creature of sublime simplicity, a mare who on occasion could walk as a woman. In one night all that simplicity was shattered. And here was she, in the heart of the unbelievers' magic, and at her back a Djinni prince.

Shams al-Din had a great deal to answer for. When she found him again; if she could win him back to human form.

Fired with both love and temper, she pierced the heart of Krak. There, perforce, she halted. A long cold hall, all stone. Rank on rank of mailed men with crosses on their breasts. A weight of power and of enmity that bore her down and down, crushing her to the earth.

She straightened her back; she faced the one who sat in a chair of stone unmarred by any ornament. No splendor marked him, no seal of power distinguished him from his fellows. He was older than many, gaunt with the rigors of his office, yet mighty in his power. His eyes were dark and cold and still.

She bowed to him as if she had been a queen. No flicker acknowledged her, and yet she knew that she was noticed. "Master," she said directly, as Franks were said to do, as came most easily to her nature, "you hold captive what belongs to me."

The Grand Master of the Hospitallers looked down from his eminence. His nostrils flared the merest fraction; his brows raised by a hair's height, as if he deigned at last to credit that what he saw was no delusion. A woman, and a woman of Islam, addressing him in Arabic, in his own hall, before the gathering of his knights.

His cold eyes passed from the unspeakable to the merely unbearable. A mamluk, but a mamluk with a Frankish face, and Frankish bulk, and Frankish arrogance. He spoke in his own tongue, cold words, meant to chill Ghazalah into silence.

"He says," said Barak with the ease of one who is either royal or a fool, "that I might prefer conversion to the death reserved for defilers of his sanctuary."

"Would you?" asked Ghazalah, not looking back, not taking her eyes from the Grand Master's face.

She could sense Barak's smile, warm as sunlight on her back. "There is no god but God, and Muhammad is the Prophet of God."

The air shuddered and shrank. The massed knights rocked at the Truth that to them was blasphemy, and signed themselves with their false god's cross. Swords leaped from sheaths; men growled in their throats.

The Grand Master raised a hand. His servants subsided into wary stillness. This time he spoke in Arabic, if not to Ghazalah. "Do not speak those words again under my roof."

"Certainly," she said, "if you will give me back my brother."

"We hold no infidels hostage here."

She had won a victory: she had pricked him into addressing her. "You hold a woman of your own people. She has a companion. Surely you can scent the sorcery in him."

Her scorn did not touch him. "The dog? It is an infidel? That is apt."

"He is my brother. I will have him back. Will you give him freely, or shall I take him?"

"Can you take him?"

"I love him."

"Indeed," said the Grand Master. "But does he love you?"

"Does that matter?"

"To his freedom," said the Hospitaller, "yes."

She stood with her head up, striving valiantly not to tremble. Barak was no help to her. He was not human; he did not know this folly that was human love. No more did she. She was only half a woman.

"If he loves you," the Hospitaller said, "loves you truly, as a brother should love his dearest sister, then I will give him to you, and set you free."

"And if he does not?" she asked with admirable steadiness.

"Then we keep him."

"And I?"

"You may go where you will, if only it be out of Krak. Your mamluk," the Hospitaller added, "we keep. It was not wise of him to enter here where Djinn and demons are not welcome save as slaves. In whatever form they come to us."

Barak started. If he would have spoken, he never began. He stood again in stallion's shape; even as he gathered himself to rear, a man leaped, flinging a bridle over his head. Its headstall was wrought of jewels set in iron, and every gem carved with the Seal of Suleiman. Barak bowed under it, though his ears had flattened to his head, though his lips had drawn back from his teeth. He could not speak: the bit forbade, carved all about with signs of silence.

that he had a beauty mark on the point of his hip:
ly where she bore its twin.

u look like me," said Shams. He seemed surprised,
easurably so. Until he frowned. "You've always
. ?"

nodded.

lips thinned. "You never told me. Never once. I
everything with you. And you—you kept a secret."
was never time."

tossed his head. "Oh, indeed! I was closer to you
—than—"

was hurt, and angry, and as oblivious as she to use-
nodesty. She looked at him and knew her heart would
. Lovely, shallow, light-witted Shams. He could not
care that he was here. He knew only that his posses-
ad kept a secret to herself.

erhaps," said the Grand Master, "I should have deed that *you* love *him*."

ams was startled. "What—" He seemed at last to be-
aware of the hall, the knights, the weight of eyes on
ender frame. Some of them were avid.

barely paused. He set himself before Ghazalah, and
at them all. "If you touch her—if you even think of

vould have been ridiculous, if she had not wanted to

sh," said Shams, turning to hold her, patting her
emarkable competence. "Hush. I'm here. I won't let
urt you."

u had better not."

allion speaking had no power to startle Shams. They
at each other with fine fierce rivalry, until she struck
oth. "Just exactly who is it who needs protecting?"
pped from between them to face the Grand Master.
t my bargain won."

not." The Hospitaller met her wrath with icy calm.
not love; this is merely ownership. Bid the young
ose."

at is there to choose?" demanded Shams. "I'll be no
apdog."

ld you be her lover?"

Ghazalah had not known that she could be so angry.
"That was unwarranted!"

"What, do your people mete no punishment to a slave
who has escaped his master's vigilance?"

She would not answer that. In a moment, she could not.
Mailed guards had come, leading within their circle a familiar figure, and in her arms the creature that was Shams
al-Din.

The Lady Melisende regarded the stallion with recognition and the woman with interest, stroking Shams's long
black-curled ears. He seemed content, as a beast is, without will to alter what is done to it.

The Grand Master spoke to the lady, and his voice was
shocking, for it was almost gentle. "Come here, sister-
daughter."

She obeyed him without undue reluctance. She seemed
to bear him no rancor, although he held her prisoner.

"My niece," said the Grand Master, and again he was
haughty and cold, "owes this pup of yours a debt. He has
taught her what she would hear from none of us, that fidel-
ity is more to be prized than passion, and that a woman
may master a man if she keeps her wits about her. She has
agreed to the alliance which once she spurned, for the man
is royal, and gentle, and constant in his affections; and if
he cannot equal her intelligence, at least he will value it for
the treasure that it is."

"He sounds a paragon," Ghazalah said.

"He has a face like a frog," said Melisende. "But I have
seen what beauty is. In the end, since I must choose, I
know which I prefer."

Shams huddled in her arms. At her words, he whined,
barely to be heard. His eyes were huge with hurt.

Ghazalah knew wisdom when she heard it, but Shams
was her brother. "Are you any better than he? He loved
you for as long as it was in him to do. You but used him for
your pleasure."

"*I* never swore an oath," said Melisende.

Ghazalah met that cold blue gaze until it dropped. "I
pity your husband," she said. "Still more do I pity you.
Shams is young, and inclined to foolishness, but his heart
is steel beneath the fire. Yours in naught but ice and air."

"Ah," said the Grand Master, "but does he love you, woman of Islam?"

At her uncle's bidding, Melisende set Shams upon the floor. He gazed up at her, bewildered. His tail wagged timidly; he licked her foot. She pushed him away, not ungently. "Why do you fawn on me? There is your sister. Go to her, if you would set yourself free."

He turned to look, and Ghazalah's heart sank. Of course he did not know her. He had never seen her as a woman.

She gathered her will, shaping the shift from maiden to mare. And nothing came. Where her true self had been was only emptiness.

She met the Hospitaller's eye and knew. He had trapped her as he had trapped Barak, though far less openly. "Brother," she said as strongly as she could. "Brother, it is I, Ghazalah."

He did not believe her. He knew what Ghazalah was: his long-maned beauty with the star on her brow. He turned his back on her and sought refuge in Melisende's skirts.

Ghazalah rounded on the Grand Master. "This proves nothing! Love is more than a dog's acknowledgment of his mistress."

The Grand Master bowed his head a fraction. "So it is. Puppy!"

Shams came at that call, though he came trembling, snarling, snapping at air.

"Puppy," said the Hospitaller, "I offer you a choice. There is the woman whom you loved, however fleetingly. There behind you is your sister. Your lover will suffer your presence if you desire it, and cherish you more deeply, it may be, than any who walks in the shape of a man. Your sister will take you back to your kin, away forever from the Lady Melisende."

Shams stiffened at the mention of his kin, his body a cry of startled joy. But it did not endure. He sank down shivering.

"In your own form," said Ghazalah, soothing him.

"That was not in the bargain," the Hospitaller said.

Ghazalah could not even rage. Shams for once had seen more than she was willing to see, and comprehended it. All of it. There was the test. Life here, enchanted, but in his

lady's company, more intimate than a[n] Cairo, enchanted, bound in the shape o[f] all in Islam despised as unclean: a shame[ful] mockery of his father's name. Al-Kehail[a?] fool. Shams al-Din had been a fool and a[?]

"O Allah!" cried Ghazalah, though the[?] at the Name. "What does it matter if h[e] pays for it in pain?"

She never heard the answer, if answer [there was.] Barak had broken free. The bridle was on[?] reins hung loose and frayed. She caug[ht] thinking, braced as he twisted against her[?] He reared up, trumpeting his freedom, and[?]

Shams was there beneath his feet, mo[?] those merciless hoofs. Death was in them, [?] He waited for it to take him.

She leaped too late, struck too late, cu[?] Even through the stallion's cry, she hea[rd] bone. The great hoofs battered her brother [?]

She had gone mad. She knew it; she [?] she watched Barak. He stood still, u[?] flogged him with the tatters of his bridle. [?] even when the blood sprang, immortal [?] brilliant for any creature born of earth. [?] color of rain.

"Ghazalah. *Ghazalah!*"

Her arm sank down of its own accor[d] when she deigned to notice it. That voice[?]

She had lost even the little wits she[?] she heard her brother calling her, saw h[?] gray stone, real and solid and desperate[?] "Ghazalah!"

She could not fling herself into the a[?] more could she tear her eyes from hi[?] giveness of the one who had freed him[?]

Shams's fine dark brows had knotte[d] lah? Whose spell did you run afoul of[?]

"Our father's," her voice answere[d] stretched out. He was real. Alive[?] wound. And quite as bare as he was[?]

known[?]
precise[?]
"Y[?]
but pl[?]
been . [?]
She[?]
His[?]
shared[?]
"It[?]
He[?]
than—[?]
He[?]
less r[?]
break[?]
even [?]
sion [?]
"P[?]
mand[?]
Sh[?]
come[?]
her sl[?]
He[?]
glared[?]
it—"[?]
It [?]
weep.[?]
"H[?]
with r[?]
them [?]
"Y[?]
A s[?]
glared[?]
them b[?]
She st[?]
"I coun[?]
"I d[?]
"This i[?]
pup ch[?]
"Wh[?]
lady's l[?]
"Wo[?]

Shams stilled to stone, but stone that breathed. His eyes had found Melisende all of their own accord. Light had dawned in them; he whispered her name.

Cold she might be, but she was a woman, and he was Shams al-Din. She half raised a hand.

Ghazalah would not cling or beg. Shams was Shams again; the rest did not matter. Much. Would it kill her father to lose his son to a Christian?

He shivered. It was cold here for a naked man. He turned away from Melisende. "Ghazalah," he said. He sounded angry, or impatient, or ready to weep. "Will you bear me away from here, or must I walk?"

"But—" she said. She had never felt so blankly stupid. "But you—she—"

"She is not my sister." He set his fists on his hips. "Well?"

She could have cried aloud. It was haughty, and it was Shams, but it was most indubitably a choice.

The whole of her was there, full and rounded for her shaping. Shams's wonder was sweet, his gladness sweeter yet, though he masked it with temper. In mounting he managed, for an instant, to embrace her. His weight made her complete. She danced: she could not help it. No more could he help his gust of laughter.

She wheeled at the touch of hand and heel, and sprang into flight. No one moved to stop them. One thing only of all that was there, would linger, and come back to her after in memory or in dreams: the Grand Master's face. It had not warmed nor softened, and yet it bore no anger. It had lost no more than it was willing to lose, and gained more perhaps than any Muslim knew.

An honorable enemy, an honorable battle; and a victory well won.

The gate was open. Two sets of hoofs woke the echoes beneath it. They burst into sunlight and clean air and stones that bore no taint of Christian magic.

But of Muslim magic, enough and more than enough. Ghazalah had half expected the rising of the whirlwind. Shams shouted his astonishment.

Cairo embraced them with a mother's arms. They

breathed its blessed air; they turned their faces to its blessed, brazen sky.

Not so blessed the place in which they found themselves. Sunlight altered it. The grass was searingly green, the roses red as blood.

Shams spoke for his sister as for himself. "Why have you brought us here?"

"Convenience." Barak's tail switched a fly from his flank. His eye on Ghazalah was wickedly bright. "You need not fear a new captivity. The house is empty; the servants have departed. No one here can be appalled at our spectacle."

Shams glanced down at himself and blushed. Ghazalah's garments had followed her through her transformations; she gave him her mantle to wrap himself in. There were advantages, it seemed, in Djinn magic. "O prince of enchanters," she said, "you have our profoundest gratitude. And, now that by your working we are free, our leave to go where you will."

The Djinni smiled, as human in shape now as she, but no less wicked of eye. "Why, lady, I have done exactly that. Here is where I will to be. Have you forgotten the whole of your bargaining?"

She had not. She had hoped that he would.

Males were never idiots when one wanted them to be.

"Bargaining?" growled Shams.

"Bargaining," said Barak, smiling sweetly. "I agreed to aid her in her freeing of you. Surely you will grant that I have fulfilled my side of the bargain. In return . . ."

"I never said that he could have me. I only said that he could court me."

Why was she talking to Shams? Barak was laughing. Shams was struck dumb.

Barak did not remind Shams that he stood here, on feet and not on paws, because Barak had known the sole and single remedy for his enchantment. And more than known it: administered it. And thereby spared Ghazalah the anguish of slaying her brother that he might live again.

"But," said Shams, "she is mine."

Mares and women were made to be bought and sold.

Ghazalah knew that. Her temper, unfortunately, did not. "I am my own. I choose for myself."

If she had startled Shams, Shams startled both of them. His eyes lowered. "You are," he said, subdued. "You're all new to me. I keep forgetting." He paused. "What the Hospitaller said . . . Do you hate me, Ghazalah? Was it for that, that you never showed me all that you were?"

She snorted. "Hate you? Idiot. For hatred I would never have faced the Master of Krak. Nor," she added, eyes sliding sidewise, "made a bargain with that nape-nipper yonder."

"Do you want to be free of it?"

She glanced at Barak, who had the grace not to speak. "No," she said, and she had said it before she thought. When she did think, she knew that she meant it. "No, I don't want to be free of it. It was a fair bargain. He was only to court me, after all."

"You know where courting leads," Shams said darkly.

"Only where the lady wishes," said Barak.

He meant to guide her if he could. She showed him her teeth, lest he forget who rules where mares and stallions met.

He bowed to memory. The flash of his eyes was for what he hoped would be. "If Allah wills," he said, "and you, O light of my desire."

She tensed to shake her head, found that she shrugged instead. "Maybe," said Ghazalah.

Of what followed thereafter, Allah knows best, and Ghazalah who was a mare before she was a woman. She chose as she willed to choose, and found thereby both delight and joy, and of peace, little enough. Yet that was as she willed it. Al-Barak, after all, was a spirit of wind and sky, and a stallion of his will and choosing, and peace is not a stallion's virtue. No more is it a mare's. They had light and fire, and many a fine battle, and children that were the wonder of mortals and of Djinn.

As for Shams, whose folly had brought about their meeting, he had learned to swear no oaths he could not keep. Constancy in love would never be his nature. Yet good faith he could manage, and did, and when in time he took wives of beauty and of lineage, he pleased them as well as any man can please a woman. With that, in the end, even his sister professed herself content.

Such is the tale that is told in the annals of the wise, of al-Ghazalah the beautiful, and Shams al-Din, and al-Barak the prince of the Djinn who dwell under the earth. Praise be to Allah, the Merciful, the Compassionate, to Whom are known all things that were, and all that are, and all that are to be!

The Scorpion

Nancy Springer

There was once in the city of Damascus a sweetmeat seller who made himself rich and doomed by the naming of horses. He owned a small stall at the edge of a bazaar near the khalif's barracks, and the khalif's mounted mamluks and arms-bearers and cavalrymen brought their horses before him where he sold peppermint and marzipan, and also the young lords and courtiers brought their favorite mounts, and he would give the steeds names. The warriors came seriously, for they were men often enough in the company of death to sense a serious business when they came close to one, but the young lords and courtiers came to amuse themselves. For the sweetmeat vender was a man of passion, a simple man who thought every horse a son or daughter of the wind, and he spoke with fervor always. "Ah, my sweet gazelle of a filly no stallion has mounted," he would say, "you are Zircon, the golden one." Or he would say, "Ah, my handsome silver stallion, my fleet runner, you are like a fair stream between green banks; you are Saril, the flowing water." Or, "This warrior horse you bring before me is Aswald, the black jewel." And the young nobles laughed and were flattered and amused—though the sweetmeat vender, whose name was Kasbar ab Harith, did not have a flatterer's heart. It was the beauty of the steeds that moved him, not any regard for the owners. But the courtiers and princes did not perceive this, and were pleased and sometimes gave Kasbar gold coins, though when they went away they seldom used the names he had bestowed upon their horses.

Whether by reason of the gold coins, or the quality of

189

his marzipan (which was made always of the most choice almonds, and shaped to resemble songbirds) or by reason of his own good heart favored by Allah, Kasbar ab Harith prospered and took a wife.

This was the daughter of a neighboring vender, a dark, intense yet silent man reputed to be of tainted blood. One of his ancestors was said to have wandered up with the people of Romany from India, and he was shunned by many, even though he prostrated himself daily as a faithful believer. But Kasbar thought none the less of this man for his supposed Gypsy blood, for the nomadic tribes of Romany bred wonderful horses.

Therefore he took this man's daughter to wife, and did not chaffer over the dowry. And when he had led her to his home he pulled away the veil from her face and looked at her in wonder, for excepting his mother she was the first woman he had ever seen unveiled.

He saw a fine-boned, tawny face with something about it of the look of the east wind out of India, the wind out of which Allah had created the creatures Kasbar most loved. If she had been a horse he would have named her Zerdali, the wild apricot, but her name, he knew, was Lillim. She stared back at him with neither interest nor fear, though something flickered at the back of her dark eyes like the blue fire behind the eyes of a well-bred colt being ridden for the first time. It suddenly mattered to Kasbar, as it ought not to matter to a proper man and husband, whether she liked him or not.

He said softly to her, "You are like a flowered garden for beauty. You are like a pearl that has never been pierced."

And she replied in the murmuring tones proper to a woman, "The garden awaits your pleasure. You are my husband; whatever you wish of me I will do."

But not then, or for many years to follow, was he to know truly of her whether she liked him.

Those first wedded months he lay warm by Lillim's side in the nights and dreamed of horses. Never in his life had he sat on a horse, or even so much as touched one; he lived in awe of the steeds as of women. The way the Bedouins draped their horses in tassels and fringes seemed fitting to him. Horses, like women, were holy and should walk veiled. Yet, in his dreams, the horses wore not so much as a red thread to slow their speed.

His wife said to him suddenly one morning, as she served him the early meal, "My father has told me many of the Gypsy names for horses."

He looked up at her with interest, not only on account of the horse names but because perhaps she offered them out of some feeling for him . . . What feeling? Her glance on him was indifferent, her eyes a dark veil to what lay behind.

Kasbar said, "I would be pleased to hear them."

"Whatever you, my husband, desire of me I will do."

She told him the names over the next several mornings and evenings, and very beautiful names they were: Camlo, the beloved. Beval, like the wind. Orlenda, for a mare like an eagle. Lashi, lovely. And many more, for starfire, topaz, falconwing . . . Kasbar remembered them all, and some of them he used, those days, when he named horses.

He was a simple, guileless man; it took him some small time to notice the change, that the young lords came to him no longer ready to be amused but with still mouths and intent eyes, and that all the horses he had named of late kept the names he had given them. And that much gold passed his palm, and that so many horses were brought to him to be named that there was scarcely any time, any longer, for the selling of almond paste, even if the folk shopping the bazaar could have reached his booth through the press of riders and horses, which they could not. For warriors and mamluks who had ridden the same mounts for years, content with the name some farmer had given the beast at birth, were suddenly bringing the steeds to Kasbar to be renamed.

There was a young banner-bearer in the khalif's service, a frequent indulger in marzipan, whom Kasbar had served for some few years, and who had a kind face; his name was Akil ab Zal. This man Kasbar touched on the arm, whispering to him, "What is happening, that I must name all these horses?"

"You do not know?" Akil kept his voice down. Kasbar had judged him rightly; he would not mock or betray him.

"When you named Prince Nimril's new stallion a few days ago, he kept the name, for it pleased him, and the stallion ran the long race in such time as has never been seen, and pranced and pawed afterward. That alone would have been wonder enough, but the red mare you named for Serif has turned fearless in battle practice as any panther, and Kareef's lame gelding has gone sound since you changed the name. And . . ."

And many more, their numbers doubling and redoubling since the news had spread and more horsemen tried Kasbar's names. But all the names Akil named to him were those Lillim had told him. Sef, the lion of India. Harit, the fiery red mare who draws the chariot of dawn. Jal, the wanderer, for the gelding no longer lame.

Kasbar went home that night with much gold in his pouch, yet not happy. He found his tawny-faced young wife in her chamber and knocked her down on her couch, and pinned her wrists above her head with his hands before she could catch her breath and struggle with him.

"You have slept beside me," he stated. "You have watched my dreams."

She stared back at him, unmoving, and did not deny it.

"You are an afrite," he charged, for he feared he understood the blue fire behind the dark veil of her eyes.

"Call it that if you like," she said, not loudly, not softly, and his heart hurt with a fierce burning like a scorpion's sting because she had not denied it, for an afrite is a demon without a soul. Without feelings or loyalties, without conscience. Small wonder she seemed neither to like him nor hate him. He could never hope for her to like him now.

"What have I done," she inquired as blandly as if asking after his day's affairs, "but see to my husband's welfare?"

She would never like him or—or love him. Her love; that was what he truly wanted, in his heart of hearts, where the pain stung. He admitted it, though only to himself.

He eased the pressure on her wrists, admitting it. "The names you gave me," he said. "They were magical."

She said, "Because I am what I am, yes." And he felt no longer entirely sure what she was, or what burned in her eyes. An afrite, or some Gypsy witch, or some damned specter out of the east, what did it matter? He judged he would never be able to feel sure of her, never trust her. Yet . . .

She said, as if sensing his thoughts, "You are my husband. You wish me to name you no more names? Whatever you want of me, I will do."

He took away his hands from her wrists and let her sit up. And the pain huddled like a stinging scorpion in his heart, and he thought, *If I cannot have what I want, then I will have what I can from her.*

He ordered her, "I want my names for horses, the ones I think of myself, to be magical, as magical as the ones you tell me."

She nodded at once but said, "It will be so if you tell them to me and I tell them back again to you."

And with this arrangement he had to be satisfied, for she was what she was, and the magic came from her. But though he continued to bed her in order to make himself sons, he no longer slept by her side.

Every evening thereafter he told her horse names and she told them back, so that he began to name horses with cunning rather than with passion, trying to use the names he had told her. Perhaps one time out of ten the old ardor overcame him, so that he gave a horse a name he had not told to Lillim but created on the spot: for a magnificent colt the color of dappled saffron, the name Vartan, the golden rose. For a sweet-faced mouse-dun mare, the name Yunus, the dove. And others. So it was that there were always a few of the horses Kasbar had named in which no magical transformation took place, and these followed the ordinary ways of horses everywhere: they balked at obstacles, or ran away with their riders, or kicked when the saddle cinch was tightened, or stepped on their handler's feet or shied from a drawn sword. But it did not matter; the rest of the horses Kasbar named performed in a manner worthy of the horses of heroes, the horses of legend and the old epic tales. And Kasbar's fame as a namer of horses grew like fire feeding on lamp oil.

He grew rich, and not from the vending of marzipan; he sold his sweetmeat stall, and made those who wished to consult him on the naming of horses come to the street in front of his house. Then within a few years he sold his house and bought a finer one, with a room apart for his wife and a courtyard into which the horses he named could be led while he sat, taking his ease and keeping his distance, in a balcony. Then he sold that house and bought a yet finer one, nearly a palace, with a seraglio, and he bade his wife stay there, and bedded her no longer, for she had given him sons. As for the horses, he looked down on them through a many-paned window of glass, and sent out the names by servants.

To Lillim he never spoke except for those times, seldom more than once a day, when he needed to name names to her. She was a woman, and therefore of no account; she was merely the power's vessel, while he manifested it. Even as he faced her he thought of her as little as he could; she was the veiled and hidden presence in his house, nothing more, and he seldom looked on her face. In this way and by means of his wealth and importance, he kept quiet the stinging thing that lived in his heart.

It was not only the horsemen of the barracks and racecourse and polo field who noticed the marvelous strength and wind and courage of certain ever-more-numerous horses in the environs of Damascus. The khalif noticed, and made his preparations, and in due time went to war against the rebellious sultan of Tarqus, and conquered magnificently because of the matchless valor of his warriors' horses.

Kasbar smiled with pride when he heard the news, for he considered that the Commander of the Faithful's victory was due in large part to him, Kasbar the Namer of Horses.

Therefore, on the day when the khalif returned in triumph to parade the streets of Damascus with his bodyguard and his banner-bearers on their prancing mounts and his hundred of proud captured horses loaded with spoils, Kasbar left his palatial dwelling and went down to the main avenue from the city gates to take part in the city's joy.

The Commander of the Faithful was a personage both holy and remote; like most of those lining the great avenue of Damascus that day, Kasbar had never seen his ruler's face.

The shrill rejoicing of pipes and zithers filled the street; the chime of metal-shod hooves on glazed brick cobbles only added to the music, making it sweeter to Kasbar's ears. The banner-bearers came first on pure black steeds of the Caspian breed, their necks arched and their foreheads plumed and their magnificent mouths well on the bit. Then followed the mamluks, the khalif's bodyguard, on the hardy yet beautiful horses of the Bedouin breed, whose manes and tails flowed always like the east wind. Kasbar hardly noted the golden maces and silver battle-axes of the mamluks, he was so taken up with the beauty of the horses, most of which he had named. And then—

Then came the khalif, on a blood-bay charger the likes of which Kasbar had never seen, at which he gasped like a child, gawking.

Great-necked, great-chested, like a lion for power and presence and thick black mane, yet with a straight, wide-browed, wise head bowed meekly to the bit; silky of hide, so that every vein showed, hotly pulsing; round of barrel, mighty of foreleg, yet straight and clean of limb; full seventeen hands high the stallion strode, striking out with hard black hooves, yet treading as neatly as a kitten. This was a horse worthy of a khalif, no, an emperor, no, Muhammed himself.

And it was not a horse Kasbar had ever named. But if it was a horse worthy of legend unnamed by him, what then would it be if—if he gave it a name? A gift. His gift to his ruler the khalif. He would accept no gold or any favor; it would be his gift of love for such a magnificent steed and such a victorious ruler. The music yearned around his head, and his heart pulsed warm in his chest; he felt warm and lithe and young as he had not felt in years with the passion, the fervor, the ardor of his adoration.

He darted forward. His gasp of awe and his resolution had taken but a moment; the khalif's noble blood-bay destrier had not yet carried that ruler abreast of him. He dodged the mamluks, heedless of their warning shouts, hearing nothing, seeing nothing but that incomparable horse before him. "Ah! Mighty Majesty," he panted as he drew near, "ah, most puissant and holy one, let me gift you with a name worthy of him, allow me—"

For the first time he raised his eyes from the peerless horse to the rider. He looked into the khalif's face, the lean, hard face of a war leader, and it was gloating and taut and cruel.

"Prostrate yourself," the Commander of the Faithful instructed coolly, "or you die."

Kasbar flung himself to the hard roadway, hid his face against the cobbles.

"Get him hence." The chill voice had ridden onward. Kasbar did not open his eyes. He felt a few perfunctory blows from the mamluks, felt himself lifted and flung to the roadside like so much human rubbish, but he did not open his eyes until the procession of victory had passed him by. And in those darkened moments he knew himself for what he was: Kasbar the Fool. An aging, pudgy, self-important, insignificant, humiliated man.

He had been lucky. The khalif, on this day of triumphal entry, had been in a mellow mood. He could have ordered Kasbar imprisoned, tortured, ordered his thumbs cut off or worse. The thought did not comfort Kasbar. When he opened his eyes, straightened his turban and stood to go home, his heart burned with hatred as a few moments before it had blazed with—with a sort of love.

Once home, he went straight to Lillim.

She had not gained weight as he had with the passing of the years. She had not become pudgy and slow and soft like him, but only, it seemed to him when he allowed himself to think of her, more fine, or refined, the blue fire flickering ever hotter in her. He strode into her chamber, and she lifted her delicate, shrouded head in surprise when she saw him, for it was not his customary time of day to require her services.

"I want something of you."

"Whatever my husband wishes, it is my duty to perform." Her great, dark eyes regarded him without expression. Their gaze told him nothing.

He did not trust her. "Take off your veil so that I may see you more clearly."

She did so. Her mouth did not smile. It never had. If he had known other women, to make comparisons, he would have seen how her mouth refused the tight line of the matron, how it retained the sweetness and wildness of a virginal girl's full lips, even though she had given him sons. But he did not know, and did not see.

His pride made it impossible for him to explain to her fully what he wanted: revenge. Instead, he burst out, "We have named the horses well, all these years. Is it possible now to name them ill?"

She did not answer him at once. Nor did he urge her answer, for his gaze was on her mouth. It moved, fleetingly stirring the flesh over her exquisite cheekbones. A—an understanding, a twitch of mischief, then gone— she had smiled, he had seen it, but was her smile evil? Was it the smile of an afrite? He could not tell.

She said, "Whatever my husband requires of me, I will do." Yet he had sensed surely that she was more than merely obedient. The turn of events, for some reason, pleased her.

"As for the manner of the thing," she said, "it is easy. The lion wears claws. The oasis can drown. The sword bears a double edge."

Heavily he sat near her and let her instruct him.

The next day he named a young emir's horse Ensil, the sword. And within the week the animal turned on its master, cutting him down with deadly hooves. Yet no blame was laid on Kasbar, for it is in the nature of horses, as of women, to be dangerous and undependable, and there had always been some few horses on which the magic of his names had taken no effect.

All the horses that had been taken as spoil from the Sultan of Tarqus were brought to Kasbar to be named, and all of them he gave the names Lillim had told him: Saquir, the falcon, which could claw out the eyes of its handler. Al Nimor Cemal, the sleek and dangerous panther. Van Acayib, the red dragon, than which no thing is more perilous. Those who heard the names were well pleased, presuming that the peril was for the enemy; but it was not. Because of the thoughts Lillim had held in mind while she named the names to her husband, the peril was for the horses' riders, and all the khalif's servants in war.

That potentate, having succeeded swiftly in one war, contemplated another. A war of conquest; he would be more than khalif. He would make himself an empire, and rule it, and glorify Allah. The barracks and stables boiled over with drills and preparations, of which Kasbar heard. His heart turned to hot lead in his chest, for the horses he had named well—for years and years he had named them well—were still many more by far in the khalif's service than those he had named ill.

He went to Lillim. There was a new bond, a special agreement, between them since he had turned bitter against the khalif. It was as if he had put himself in a woman's place; almost he could understand how a woman might hate the one who commanded and oppressed and protected her. He slept at Lillim's side again in the nights, because he had seen her smile, and knew that smile now; it was evil. It was the same smile he sometimes smiled himself, those days. And he no longer minded if she watched his dreams. They were full of the sounds of trampling hooves and thunder; they were dark and smoldering, like her eyes.

He said to her, "It is too slow, this naming of double-edged names. I have named too many horses well; the khalif will have his way until I am too old to enjoy his downfall."

She said, "If he becomes aware of you, he will enjoy yours."

"Nevertheless: can it be done, that the names of the horses I named well can be turned to ill?"

He watched her face. She customarily unveiled herself before him, those days, for he liked to see her face. It was beautiful to him, as beautiful as the most beautiful of horses. And he was watching for the smile.

It did not come. Instead, she sighed, and her eyes looked shadowed; had he not known she was a demon creature of no feelings, he would have thought she was worried. But she merely said, "Regarding some of them it can be done. The wildfire and whirlwind can kill; even the jewels, the topaz and zircon, can cut. Those you have named after flowers, however, can in no wise be made evil." And she smiled, but it was a tender smile.

It did not displease him, the smile, though he felt the scorpion sting in his heart. He said, "It should be enough, if you do what you have proposed."

"Whatever my husband wishes of me, I will do."

Thus it came about that the khalif suffered utter humiliation and severe damage of death during his first battle of conquest. For many of his horses that had once been magnificent steeds of war fought their masters instead of the enemy, and some ran away, and some turned their long teeth and sharp hooves on their comrades. The battle was a disaster, a catastrophe, a rout in which the forces of the faithful were decimated and the Commander of the Faithful himself escaped only because of the size and strength and valor of his blood-bay charger, Al Marid—which he himself had named.

Shortly after the khalif had returned in defeat to Damascus, his servant Akil came to Kasbar's dwelling furtively, by night. Akil, like Kasbar, had grown fat; he had long since ceased to be the khalif's banner-bearer and had longtime been that mighty tyrant's sweetmeat-taster instead. It had been years since Kasbar had seen him. Yet the two men knew themselves without question to be friends.

"The Commander of the Faithful is no fool," said Akil in a low voice to Kasbar. "He is asking questions, though —Allah be praised—not of me. Soon he will have his answers. And he is raging."

Kasbar nodded; this was no more than he had expected. "I have set my affairs in order."

"You think I have come here so that you could set your affairs in order? Old fool. Make haste, flee! I have brought you a good horse; it waits below."

Kasbar ab Harith felt his breath taken away so that he could not speak. In all his life, even after he became rich, it had not occurred to him that he, Kasbar the lowly born, sweetmeat vender, son of a ploughman, that he could mount one of the noble steeds who were sons and daughters of the wind.

"Go to Baghdad, or Caspia," Akil advised, as if it were nothing to ride a horse, fleeing for one's life. "Go where you like. Your talents should make you welcome anywhere."

"A horse?" Kasbar muttered, still blinking and struggling for breath. "Thank you." And Akil nodded and took his leave.

The horse turned out to be an ordinary brown creature,

tall, sturdy, docile and willing, already saddled and bridled and provisioned. It looked on Kasbar with a large soft eye, and he gulped and turned away to run to the seraglio, where Lillim was preparing for sleep. She unveiled himself when she saw him.

"Wife, come!" And heedless of the holy law, he hurried her by the hand out of her chamber and out of the house, to where the night air blew sweet and cool on her bare face and her unmantled body, as she had never felt it before. And all the time, in haste, he was talking.

"I must go if I am to live. I had not thought I wished to live, but now—I must go. I will send for you. Here is gold." He passed her a pouch. "Here are the keys to the doors." He gave them into her hand. "You watch my dreams; you know where my treasure is hidden?"

She nodded and said softly, "The khalif will wish to take it away."

"You will prevent him. You have your wiles, and I know it. Send our sons to your father's house."

She said, "It is already done."

He nodded at her, unsurprised. "It is well. You will be able to fend for yourself? The khalif will seize the house. Let him have it. You will see to it that he does not take more?"

"You are my husband. What you wish of me, I will do."

He had been fussing with his belt, his knife, his purse, his saddlebags, but when she said that he turned and faced her, feeling the sudden need to say something true to her, something honest, before he left her. "I have been a bad husband to you," he said. "I thought I was right and good, but I was a bad husband and lacking as a man. I wanted you to love me." Her dark eyes widened, and he saw it; he drew breath to say more. "I judged it could not happen, and grew bitter. But I should not have done so." He lowered his voice. "Instead, I should have loved you."

She could see him in reflected lamplight: nothing more than a plump and aging man, pompous, moon-faced, absurdly turbaned. She murmured, "I think you do." The words drifted smooth in the night, unconcerned, without inflection. He heard, but did not try to kiss her.

Instead he said, "Name this horse for me."

"I?" She raised startled, dark eyes. "My lord and master, you should name it yourself."

"I am your husband," he reminded gently. "What I wish, you should do for me. Name the horse."

She faced the horse, the look of the frightened gazelle in her gaze. But after a moment she spoke, firmly.

"His name is Rakush. The lightning."

Kasbar nodded; the name was much as he expected. He touched his wife's hand briefly and gazed into her fine-boned face. Then he turned and with an effort worthy of a hero scrambled up onto the tall steed. Atop it he sat, feeling far too round and fragile, balanced like a glass ball on that high, narrow place.

"Go with God." Lillim's voice sounded remote.

"Until we meet again, then," he muttered, "whether in this world or another." He gave a flounce, and the horse started forward. Within moments Kasbar ab Harith had bribed the gatekeeper of Damascus and was out of the city, bound toward Baghdad on the brown horse Rakush.

Excitement drove out his fear. The night, the smooth and eager gait of the horse, were full of wonder to him. He was not unhappy.

Rakush. The lightning. Lillim had chosen the name well. The beautiful one with the blue fire yet burning behind her dark eyes, the demon woman or Gypsy seeress or spirit out of the east wind, whatever she was, she could have had either of two things in mind: that the horse should carry her husband swiftly as the lightning to safety—or that the horse should strike like the thunderbolt, and destroy him.

Either way, he would know the answer to his life's enigma. He would be at rest. The scorpion would no longer sting in his heart.

When next Kasbar lay down, he would dream of his wife.

TESTS OF TRUST

The storytellers stood before the amphitheatre filled with djinn, telling their tales of deceptions revealed, deceivers punished, and the escape from snares by good men and women. Peter of Wraysbury found himself staring at the djinn, who were listening courteously, intelligently to the stories. Intent on draining whatever novelty they might from the tales, they had ceased even to change forms.

Now they resembled nothing so much as reasonably healthy, oddly compelling men and women of great prosperity. All seemed to be of an age, that time in the middle of life when old amusements pall, but the pleasures of age have not yet taken hold. Age, he knew, and boredom were the signs that meant that he and the other captives snatched by the djinn would remain imprisoned forever in... wherever this was.

An elbow caught him shrewdly in the ribs.

"If you doze off, my friend, how can you expect the djinn to remain awake?" asked the master storyteller.

"I beg forgiveness," Peter whispered back. "Tales are not meat and drink to me as they are to you, it seems, or to the djinn."

"You were studying the sky," came the merchant's deep rumble. "If sky it be."

"Think you too that we are trapped in an immeasurable bottle?" asked the master storyteller.

It was Peter's worst fear, of being shut away forever from light, wind, and rain. He nodded curtly.

"Then consider this: bottles may be smashed, or their stoppers found and pushed open. Quick now and quietly, while the djinn are held as captive by the tales as we are by the djinn; quick, oh my comrade, leave this place and seek out the limits of our prison."

If I find this bottle's wall, how shall I let you know? How shall I return here? Peter wanted to ask. He would not have gone into battle on such a flimsy strategy; the merchant and the master storyteller must know that.

"Do not question, but go now, while their attention is held! Whether you shall find our freedom or not lies in the will of Allah, Who knows all things; but you must assist Him."

Muffling his too-conspicuous hair, Peter crouched low, creeping behind the massed bodies of his fellows until the amphitheatre receded from view and he hoped that it was safe to walk upright once again. He walked for what seemed like hours, fear cold at his heart until it wore away into a kind of habit, like the rhythm of his stride across the sand.

Was his reflection in the "sky" growing larger? Did it seem to curve as if smoothing down to form a wall? He could not tell. Time, distance, and light appeared all to be one thing in this place; he could well believe that he would walk for days, until the pouches of water and meal at his belt were gone; but could a man starve or die of thirst in this place either?

Before that, he suspected, he might go mad of the solitude. That thought made him mutter prayers to himself as he walked. He was so intent on building a barrier between himself and his fears of madness that he did not see the change in the light; did not hear the voice that hailed him.

"Stranger!" came a voice in accented Arabic. Then, in another tongue that, Peter noted with astonishment, was Latin, "I told you that I heard footsteps. Stiff-necked, unbelieving fool!"

Laughter met the insult. "Save such terms for when we argue theology. Perhaps this stranger brings hope of escape."

Peter strode toward the voices, and the light about him brightened until he could see two men, who had leapt to their feet to greet him.

He stopped short. Never in a wandering life had he seen a pair so strangely assorted as were these two men. The younger was clearly a European, tall, upright with an open, pleasant face that clashed strangely with his garb—the padded, quilted silk of the well-to-do Mongol. The other—he who had been called stiff-necked—was shorter and older, with the indefinable stamp of the scholar about him. He wore the garb of Iberia, in dark, rich fabrics. Stained though they were with travel, his robes nevertheless bore the mark that set him apart from the rest of his land: he was a Jew. Somber eyes and beard, he hung back, behind his companion, as if a long life had taught him to suspect the worst of everyone.

"Greetings, strangers!" Peter said. "Who are you, and how are you called?"

"The peace of the Great Khan be upon you, stranger!" called the man in Mongol garb. *"Per San Marco! Inglese!"* he cried, astonished.

Peter stopped dead. Only Venetians swore by Saint Mark as regularly as they breathed. What was a Venetian doing in this place?

"We are far from the Adriatic, messer," he said, using his best Latin.

"Far in years as well as leagues, sir," the Venetian said. "It has been more than half my life since I saw the Queen of Cities."

The Spanish Jew edged forward. "Are you in truth English?" he asked.

"I am Peter of Wraysbury, knight," Peter declared, "on quest for Prester John, and for freedom for myself and my companions."

"Freedom is a noble goal," said the Venetian. "Wealth is fine, but what is it without freedom to enjoy it? A trifle. As for this Prester John whom you seek, it may be that he is at the Great Khan's summer palace at Karakorum, to which men of good will of all faiths are welcome. I sought to return there, when I was taken. Here I met up with old Elazar . . ."

"Elazar?" Peter prompted.

"Names have power here," said the Spaniard, "so I shall not speak my father's or grandfather's name here. Though you and they were countrymen. We are from York, Englishman." There was an edge to Elazar's voice now. "My grandfather sent my mother out before . . ." His voice husked. "And she alone escaped to tell . . . she bore me in

Spain. Though we are banned from England now, we can never forget. Our blood stains the very earth."

The blood ran to Peter's face. York! It ws one of the places where a community of Jews had perished: self-slain, yet, in his travels, Peter had seen enough not to damn them for it. Already damned, some folk claimed they were. They would damn him too; somehow, he doubted, prideful as it was to try to fathom the ways of God, that God would agree. York: he, of course, had not yet been born. Would he have noted such carnage had he lived then? To his shame, he doubted it.

"Rest their souls," he said.

Elazar murmured something, then nodded.

"Then I shall count you as a countryman too, sir," Peter said in Arabic. "You have made quite a journey—from the Pillars of Hercules to . . ."

"To the ends of the Earth," agreed the other.

"For what purpose? You are obviously not a merchant, as is this Venetian."

The Venetian was on his feet, clearly eager to move on. Peter, however, was weary and sank to the sand.

"I deal in another kind of wares," said Elazar. "In wisdom. 'But where shall wisdom be found? And where is the place of understanding? Man knoweth not the price thereof; neither is it found in the land of the living.' Therefore, it seems to me that wisdom must be found right here. For surely, this is no place where mankind may live.

"I seek wisdom; my friend here seeks knowledge of new wares and new places that he may bring to his master; and you seek escape. Neither of you will find what you seek when you are tired and overwatched. Let us sit and share wisdom until we are all rested, and then go on together."

They could speak for hours or days or weeks—assuming that time could be reckoned here—while the djinn and his companions gamed, with freedom as the stakes. Perhaps these men could help. There was no way in which he might act, to convince them of his truth; in this place, words would have to speak louder than actions.

"Let the stranger speak first, that is, if you will, sir knight," said the Venetian. "Then you shall speak, Elazar; and finally, I myself." Drawing well-worn tablets from the breast of his garment, he disposed himself to listen and to write.

Wouldn't you know that the Venetian would get the best of the bargain? Peter thought ruefully. To his surprise, he saw irony in Elazar's eyes.

"And they call *my* people crafty," he observed.

Peter shrugged. *"Ma'alesh,"* he said, the universally useful Arabic that was a shrug, amusement, and resignation all at once. He had a tale to tell, all right; a companion to that tale of the Emperor imprisoned in Persia that had won him, in what seemed like a distant past, freedom and wealth in one Ramadan night. Perhaps this tale would win him equal fortune.

Drawing himself up in the manner of the storytellers in the bazaar at Kashgar, he summoned his wits, and began.

The Peri, the Roc, and the Undergrooms

M. J. Engh

Now, when the Emperor Valerian (to give him the title he still claimed) realized that his son was not immediately mounting an expedition to rescue him from the Persians, he began to consider how he might help himself. In many ways, life as an undergroom in the royal stables of King Shapur was easier than being Emperor of the Romans. The smell of the stables was no hardship to him, nor was the work he did there, for he had spent most of his life riding from one battlefield to the next, and he got on well with horses. But he did not like offering his back as a step stool when the King mounted a horse. (This, you understand, was in the days before stirrups, when mounting a horse was not so graceful a procedure as it is now.) He liked it least of all on the days when he had been punished for some mistake in following orders—a thing that happened often, since he was not accustomed to following orders and did not understand Persian. And though he was still as strong as a young man, and considerably shrewder, he had noticed that he was not so quick as he used to be, and his wounds did not heal as swiftly. These things made him think seriously about his future.

It did not look promising. What had remained of his army after the battle of Edessa, as he knew from personal observation, had been either slaughtered on the spot, traded for Persian prisoners, disarmed and herded off to be settled as farmers somewhere in the East, or—and this included the best fighting units—incorporated into the Persian army with handsome bonuses and more colorful insignia. He had no one to talk to, for the only person here who knew his language was one of the other undergrooms,

208

a young Manichaean who spoke incessantly of the transitory nature of human glory, the evil of this material world, and the bliss to be attained through privation and death. Valerian resented this kind of talk, and had several times expressed his resentment with his fists; but the Manichaean, though he was a sturdy youngster, never fought back, only turning the other cheek as if to invite another blow, which he generally received.

All in all, it was a bleak future that Valerian saw for himself, and a short one. He was skilled at estimating chances (a trait that had helped him to outlive many enemies) and he judged now that the chances were very poor of his surviving even a year in Persian punishment and Persian food. His back was a puffy cushion of raw flesh, his feet were bloodied and swollen, and his teeth, which had lasted all these years, were beginning to fall out. In his desperation, and seeing no other recourse, he resorted to prayer.

All this, of course, was many centuries ago—before the birth of Mohammed, but after the death of Jesus and long after the days of Abraham, so that already there had been a quantity of revelation (some would say too much) to guide humans in their blundering. In Persia, however, Abraham and Jesus did not count for much, since the Persians had prophets and saviors of their own: Zarathustra the Wise, whose teachings were doubly upheld by the learning of the Magi and the armies of the King; and Mani of Babylon, who had traveled so far and studied so well that in the West his teachings were considered a perversion of Christianity, in the East a travesty of Buddhism, and in Persia itself a very parody of the religion of Zarathustra, so that in all parts of the civilized world the Manichaeans won many converts and were much persecuted.

The Emperor Valerian, in the course of a long civil and military career, had performed countless sacrifices and intoned countless invocations; but it is doubtful if he had ever uttered anything that you or I would call a prayer. In this extremity, however, he had received no help from the gods of Rome, and when one evening he found himself alone in the stableyard, burning a pile of rubbish, he sank painfully to his knees and grumbled out a bitter and heartfelt prayer to the gods of Persia.

At this, a flame of the fire leaped up, stepped toward him, and became a beautiful woman dressed in soft garments of orange and red.

Valerian, remembering that he was an emperor, got hastily to his feet again. "Who are you?" he blurted.

"I am a peri," said the person of the flame, and she gazed searchingly at Valerian, and went on gazing for so long that in the end he asked her, with an impatient laugh, "Well? What do you see?"

"I see a lean and grizzled man," answered the peri, "who is clearly well past his prime. To put it plainly, an old man."

"I'm as fit as ever," Valerian said brusquely, and he rubbed his beard, which was gray and wiry and badly needed trimming.

"An old man," the peri continued, "in the garments of a stablehand and, as another sense tells me, reeking of sweat and horse manure. That must be particularly distressing to you, since I understand that Romans are addicted to bathing."

"You know I am a Roman," said Valerian, "because I addressed you in Latin. But perhaps you do not know that I am an Emperor. As for bathing, I consider it effeminate to spend as much time sweating and soaking and splashing about and being rubbed as my son Gallienus does. But you are right in supposing that I find my present situation distasteful. Are you a goddess?"

"I've told you," the peri said impatiently. "I am a peri. That defines me quite as well as *human* defines you—far better than *emperor* does. If I understood you correctly, you are a slave and you want your freedom. But you are not chained. What prevents you from leaving this place?"

"The walls, the guards, and hundreds of miles of Persian territory," said Valerian, "which might as well be hundreds of miles of quicksand. I do not know the language, I have no friends to hide me or soldiers to rally to my cause; and though I am as fit as ever, my feet are not in good condition for a long walk. Can you carry me through the air, bright goddess?"

The peri's expression became disdainful. "I am not an aerial packhorse," she said, "to carry such baggage as you. And if I could do it, why should I?"

Valerian's face darkened with anger, but he only said reasonably, "Why did you come to me, if not to help me?"

The peri laughed, like a flicker of little flames in the wind. But before she could give any other answer (if indeed she intended to do so) someone came running from the stable and threw himself facedown on the paving stones at her feet.

Valerian stepped back, lifting the stick he had been given to poke the fire with. But the peri addressed the newcomer very sweetly, saying, "Stand up, pretty boy. Show yourself."

It was the Manichaean undergroom who had entered the scene so abruptly. He stood up, trembling with excitement and so pale that he looked like a young and very handsome corpse. Valerian glanced from one to the other of them and lowered his stick with a snort of disgust. "No doubt it would take something more important than the affairs of an Emperor," he said, "to interrupt the assignation of a fire nymph and a stableboy. Enjoy yourselves. But I intend to finish burning this rubbish."

"Do you imagine that your prayers are unheard?" said the peri; while the undergroom turned to him, exclaiming, "This is an angel of light!—a messenger sent through the holy fire to instruct us!"

"You may call it a holy fire," said Valerian, poking at it with his stick, "but I call it a burning rubbish heap. Get on with your affairs and leave me to mine."

"Confess," said the peri, looking hard at Valerian and lifting one graceful hand. "You envy this young person his beautiful, unbroken body and his sweet face and the youth to which he chiefly owes these advantages, and it makes you sour and disagreeable to think that I would rather lie down with him than with you."

"It's true that I am always puzzled," said Valerian, "when a woman prefers a boy to a man."

"I am an immortal peri," said the peri, "and it amuses though it does not puzzle me that you in your dilapidated state think so highly of the flesh, while this well-built and charmingly adorned young creature thinks he must believe that all flesh is contemptible. The Manichaeans hold that human bodies are at best like those wax tablets you

Romans use to write on—worthless in themselves and only to be valued for whatever wisdom they may incorporate. But even wax may be very prettily molded."

"Frankly," said Valerian, "my life is more important to me than either your amours or his doctrines. If you cannot transport me to Roman territory, I am not interested in what you do, nor with whom."

"What I do," said the peri, "should interest you very keenly. With this young man's help, I propose to supply you with that transportation you crave." She turned her lovely face to the Manichaean. "Tomorrow King Shapur will announce his intention of making a journey to the East. You must be on that journey."

"To the East!" cried the Manichaean, whose face had become appropriately radiant. "It is a journey into the light, symbolically speaking."

"What interests me," said Valerian, leaning on his stick, "is that you can so confidently predict the behavior of a king. Is that because you control it?"

Now the peri's eyes grew even wider and more lustrous as she gave Valerian a look that made him step backward in discomfiture, bumping his feet together like an awkward boy. "How many times must I tell you," she said gently, "that I am a peri? Whatever lies between me and King Shapur is no business of yours. Would you want me to discuss with the King my dealings with his undergrooms? Remember that not five minutes ago you were on your knees to me."

The Manichaean, unable to endure this brilliance, had fallen on his face again. The peri looked down at him kindly, and moved a little so that the edge of her garment brushed his fingers on the paving. "Stand up, pretty boy," she said. "When the King comes for his royal ride tomorrow, you must lead out his favorite horse."

The Manichaean had scrambled up and stood staring, now at the peri's face, now at his own fingers. "But—but that is the job of the head groom," he stammered. "I am not permitted—"

The peri rolled her eyes, and a gust of wind went through the stableyard, so that for a moment the fire crackled and leaped in wild lunges. Valerian limped hastily to poke back some of the burning litter. "When I tell you,

'you must,'" said the peri, "do not answer, 'I am not permitted.' You can snatch the bridle from the groom—or, if you are too incompetent for that, at least run beside the horse where the King can see you. He will take a fancy to you—no, do not argue with me—and choose you as one of his grooms for the journey."

Valerian leaned again on his stick and regarded her acutely. "You taunted me just now," he said, "with going on my knees. I did so only because it is my understanding that the deities of Persia prefer to be addressed from that position. I will do it again if you want, because I suspect that my life is in your hands, and I would be a fool not to try to please you—just as you would be a fool to read too much into my deference. I honor your power and your knowledge, wherever they come from, and I ask you respectfully how this boy's traveling east with the King can get me back to Rome."

"Old emperor, beaten emperor," said the peri, "—beaten in more ways than one—I accept your honor for what it is worth, and answer that this boy's journey can take you wherever you wish, if only he proves himself a good undergroom." Now she stretched out her hand to the Manichaean, opening her fingers to show the jewel that lay glowing on her palm. "I will give you a useful gift," she told the boy, "if you can keep from dropping it. Hold out your hand. No, your left hand, which is the hand of secret power."

By this time the young man's face was troubled, but he held out his left hand as she instructed him. The peri took the jewel between her pointed fingertips. It was somewhat like a pink-tinged pearl and somewhat like an opal, but most like a frozen drop of rosewater with a fire in its heart. She laid it on the Manichaean's palm.

He gasped and started back, so that the stone almost fell from his hand; but at the last instant he clutched it. The peri laughed.

Now the Manichaean stood before her with drawn face and breathing hard, his left fist clenched tight. "Is a peri's gift so uncomfortable?" Valerian asked with interest.

"It is like a burning fire in my hand," said the Manichaean. "But I will not drop it."

"Better say only that you have not dropped it yet," said

Valerian. "I learned long ago that it is easy to be brave for a minute and boast about it for decades."

"He speaks with perfect accuracy," said the peri. "If he has not dropped it yet, he will never drop it. Open your hand, pretty boy."

The Manichaean lifted his knotted fist and straightened his fingers painfully. A hiss of dismay slid through his teeth.

Valerian limped closer. "I see," he said, "that a peri's gift is not to be accepted lightly. It seems to be burning its way into your flesh."

"I did not accept it lightly," said the Manichaean, but his voice was choked.

"In a little while," said the peri, "it will have burned itself in so well that no one can see it to steal it from you. But still it will lie just beneath the skin, where you can use it."

The Manichaean looked at her with anxious eyes, and again at his left hand. Valerian chuckled. "Since this stripling does not dare to question you," he said, "I will do it for him. Use it for what?"

The peri smiled very sweetly. "What burns you, pretty boy," she said, "can burn others. With a touch of your left hand you can control the fieriest steed."

Valerian laughed. "Certainly that is a valuable gift for a groom. You are lucky, boy, to buy your career at so small a price as a burned hand."

"Tend to your rubbish pile, old emperor," said the peri. "This boy and I have business together." And she said to the Manichaean, "The King's journey will take him along the shore of the sea. At one place, where you can make out the hills of a great island in the distance, the shore is rocky, and huge boulders lie scattered on the sand. Some are black, some gray, some ruddy; but here and there you will find a solitary boulder, very smoothly rounded, that is colored like ivory. You must slip away—do not tell me, 'I am not permitted'—you must slip away from the King's company and climb onto one of these. Somewhere near the top you will find a flat spot no larger than your hand. Press your left palm against it and hold it there. You may feel strange quivers and stirrings beneath you; for these boulders are not stone. They are the eggs of the rocs that nest along that coast."

"What are rocs?" Valerian asked.

But it seemed that the Manichaean already knew the answer to this question. He stared in horror at the peri. "The roc!" he cried. "It is the great bird of darkness. It is a creature of evil, earthly and fleshly and full of ugliness."

Valerian laughed harshly and poked at his fire, which was burning low. "There may have been a time," he said (addressing himself to the flames, since the peri had rejected all his interruptions), "when I was so young as to imagine some connection between ugliness and evil; but I cannot remember that time."

"There is certainly a good deal of flesh to a roc," said the peri. "They are very large birds. But most of their size is wingspan and neck, and the body is not much larger than an elephant, and almost as easily ridden. That is why you will hold the jewel in your palm against the egg until it hatches—"

"Hatches!" cried the Manichaean, falling to his knees in his distress, and holding out his left hand as if begging the peri to unburden him.

"Hatches," the peri continued inexorably, "and the chick comes out. Now, it is not well known to humans in this part of the world that a roc chick, though it cannot yet fly, is well able to run, hop, eat deer and livestock, and strike down an armored cavalryman with a stroke of its beak. As you will have hatched it by the heat of the jewel in your hand, it will look to you as its parent and follow your bidding as well as its simple brain allows. The plumage of young rocs, if they are well fed, develops rapidly, and by the time you have ridden it back to this palace it will be fledged and ready to fly."

The Manichaean, in great confusion, covered his eyes with his right hand and groaned. But Valerian threw down his stick and faced the peri again. "Why send the boy on such an errand?" he demanded. "Give me the jewel and let me ride the roc straight from the egg."

The peri laughed. "So already, old emperor, you see yourself flying through the air to Rome? You are right, of course, in supposing that this is the transportation I promised you. But you must be patient. You prize the flesh, while this young zealot condemns it; nevertheless, it is the beauty of his flesh that will win him a place in the King's expedition. Surely neither of you imagines that his only duties will be to care for horses?"

"What!" exclaimed the Manchaean, uncovering his eyes.

"Besides," said the peri, "there is a certain rhythm and measure in these things. Both the young undergroom and the elderly must serve an appropriate apprenticeship."

"Meaning, I take it," said Valerian, "that I must shovel manure and be flogged top and bottom while he is burned by a jewel and tupped by a king. Well, I don't quarrel with the process if the outcome is sufficiently good. How soon can I expect this fledgling roc?"

"Never!" said the Manichaean. "I will not be a tool to bring you this horrible thing."

"You have preached to me a good deal about winged angels and winged souls and the birds of heaven," said Valerian. "What can be so horrible about a bird, however large?"

"The roc is a power of evil, a bird of darkness," said the Manichaean; "not of heaven but of earth, and therefore filthy and ugly."

"Yes, yes," the peri said gently. "We have heard all that. And is it not an honor to be chosen to master this power of evil, if you wish to think of it as such? It will hatch out in any case; and is it not better for the hatchling to be under your control—you who are devoted to light and goodness —and used for an errand of mercy? Would I have come to you, if not to help you?"

The Manichaean looked doubtfully at his hand. "Can I truly control a roc with this jewel?" he asked. "The great bird of darkness?"

"Certainly," said the peri. "You can control any steed. Of course, you must bring it here as I have told you to do, or the jewel will lose its power forever."

The Manichaean looked thoughtful. After a moment a shudder passed through him and he lifted his eyes again to the peri's bright face. "And what you said about the King," he said waveringly, as if he were not sure which were more fearsome, to ask his question or not to ask it. "The Lord Mani has taught us that nothing is more precious than chastity, which keeps up pure even in the filth of flesh."

"But is not the chief purpose of that chastity to prevent the snaring of souls into the prison of the body?" said the peri. "In other words, to avoid the conception of children? Now, in this case there is not the least danger of such carnal incarceration."

"In fact," put in Valerian, "whatever the King pleasurably but fruitlessly expends on you, might otherwise have gone to the making of children. From the standpoint of your theology, you will be performing a meritorious service."

"I never thought of that," said the Manichaean, a little uncertainly.

"Now that these things have been explained to you," said the peri, "are you willing to do your part without faltering? Or will you be forever the stableboy who was given a jewel by a peri and made no use of it?"

"I am ready," the Manichaean said stoutly, and he stood up once again, though this time he did not spring to his feet so eagerly.

"Show me your hand," said the peri.

The Manichaean held out his left hand, and a look of surprise opened on his face.

"Yes," said the peri, "the jewel has sunk into your flesh, and left no sign but a pretty pinkness in your palm. You are ready for your work."

"The pain is gone," said the Manichaean. "God is good." He smiled gratefully at the peri.

"I have often noticed," the peri said, "that humans can adapt to almost any discomfort. And to answer your question, old man," she added, turning to Valerian so suddenly that her gauzy garments fluttered about her limbs, "you will see the bird in a few weeks, if you live that long and if the boy does his work well." And with that, she stepped backward into the smoldering embers of the fire. The flames blazed up for an instant and sank again.

Valerian prodded at the ashes with his stick. But he found nothing except the remnants of burnt rubbish.

The Emperor Valerian had long been accustomed to wake before sunrise, a habit that had helped to keep him Emperor so long; and as undergroom he found it still useful. But his hearing was not as keen as it had once been, and when something roused him from the depth of his sleep he thrashed about for a few moments in great confusion, knowing only that he was in danger either of assassination or of whipping. But a soft hand was laid across his mouth, and a soft voice said close to his ear, "Hush, old emperor. Do you want to wake the horses?"

At this, Valerian ceased his snorting and thrashing, and lay still as a log. When he had blinked his eyes a few times he could see the peri perfectly, though all else was pitch dark in the stable. She was still more beautiful than he had thought, and at her gentle touch he remembered that he was not only an emperor but a man.

"There is no time now for dallying," the peri said severely. "You must be ready to ride the roc."

Valerian raised himself on one elbow in the straw of the stable floor. "I have been ready for weeks," he said. "I have waited for news of this bird of yours, but no news has come."

The peri's mouth curved like a tendril of fire-lit smoke. "Do you think any courier could outrun the roc?" she said. "The bird itself will be here before the news of it. It is running through the dark as you lie here, and very soon you will hear the beat of its talons on the earth. Are you afraid to ride it?"

Valerian lay back again, looked up at the peri, and laughed shortly. "Goddess you may be, or peri, or whatever you choose to call yourself; but I doubt if even you can imagine how much and how little I fear to ride that bird, if it exists. If it comes here, I tell you flatly I will ride it. But I am not at all certain I will ride it back to Rome."

The peri's look grew scornful, a terrible thing to see in one so lovely. "Are you so broken, old emperor, by a few floggings and a little humiliation, the things that any slave knows how to bear without loss of pride? You will find your fellow undergroom, when he arrives, not nearly so humbled."

Valerian stared back at her. "I have heard news," he said, "though not of your fabled roc. You, who know all, or at least more than undergrooms and emperors, may know that last week a string of Roman prisoners were sold in Ctesiphon, and I have spoken with three or four who were bought for the King's household. I know that my son Gallienus, now that he is sole Emperor, is undoing most of what he and I worked together to achieve. He has already repealed some of my most wholesome laws, such as the banning of Christianity — and mark my words, that vicious superstition is more likely to bring down the Empire than any invader. He has alienated my friends in the Senate, which must always be the source of an emperor's legitimacy. And with the war in Gaul not yet finished, and King Shapur planning new incursions from the East, Gallienus and that insufferable daughter-in-law of mine are wasting time and money on a city of philosophers to be built in Egypt." Valerian passed his hand across his eyes and looked again at the peri. "No, I am not so soft or so foolish as to imagine that an emperor can ever rest easy, though I confess it daunts me a little to see my work set back a dozen years by the son I was so proud of. But there is another thing." He sighed wearily, and his mouth set in a stubborn line.

Now the peri, kneeling beside him, burst into peal after peal of laughter, that chimed like bells around his ears. "Lie still, then," she said, "if a stable floor is the proper bed for you. No doubt you know that better than I. But you are mistaken about many things, not least about Christianity. No throne is so secure as one supported by an absolute and intolerant deity. The gods of Rome will perish because of their easygoing ways. Lie here and think of that, while I go out to meet another undergroom, one who has a better opinion of himself." And she rose lightly and passed out of sight into the darkness.

Valerian struggled to his feet, cursing softly, for his joints were always stiff in the nighttime. He more than half expected to be stopped by one of the other stablehands who slept in the straw around him, or by one of the sentries who patrolled the grounds, or by one of the great watchdogs chained at every entrance; but all these seemed to be sound asleep. Indeed, he stepped over a sleeping sentry in the outer yard, and took advantage of the occasion to arm himself with the sentry's spear. He did not see the peri. But now he felt a thudding in the ground, and knew it for the thumping of the roc's feet.

Here under the starry sky he could make out the dim shape of the outer wall that surrounded the King's palace and stables. As he stood for a moment considering it, he became aware of the peri beside him, warm in the chill darkness. "You spoke of another thing," she said, "that holds you back from returning to Rome. What is it?"

"Never mind that now," said Valerian. "I need to get over this wall to meet that heavy-footed bird of yours."

"That bird will cross far higher hurdles than this," said the peri. "Stand back!"

Now a huge shape loomed suddenly above the wall, rose and spread, and descended heavily into the yard. There was no time to stand back. The wind of the roc's wings tumbled Valerian like a dry stick caught in a whirlwind. Nevertheless he held on to his spear, clasping it upright against his body to avoid damage to either of them, and he was on his feet again and brandishing the spear before the windblown rubbish in the yard had settled.

"Well done, old emperor!" said the peri. "It would not do to be timid of your new steed." She stood beside him, her garments still fluttering like flame-tips.

"I said I would ride the thing," Valerian answered, breathing a little heavily. "I do not intend to die in the straw of King Shapur's stable. But I do not much care where it takes me."

The peri raised her arm, and a strange light, that seemed only a clear darkness, illuminated the yard where they stood. The young roc towered above them, its head higher than the palace roof. Tufts of sooty down showed between its shining black feathers. It beat its wings like a new-fledged chick eager to fly, so that they were shaken again by the wind it made, then cocked its head and stared down at them with an eye like a boulder of black glass. On its neck perched the Manichaean.

"Come down, pretty boy," called the peri.

The Manichaean touched the back of the roc's neck with his left hand, and the great bird bowed like a courtier, laying its tremendous beak on the ground. The Manichaean leaped down and stood before them. His face was pale, but he carried himself more like a great satrap than a stableboy.

"Well done, young rider!" said the peri. She looked at Valerian and laughed a glittering laugh. "Why so sour, old emperor? Does it wound your pride to hear yourself and this boy commended in the same words?"

"I have survived worse wounds than that," said Valerian, and he stepped forward to mount the roc's neck while it lay low.

The Manichaean moved quickly, stretching out his arms to bar Valerian's way. "By my permission," he said, "you may ride the bird of darkness. But be it understood that the reins of power are in my hand, and when we come to your dominions you will follow my guidance. I would not raise my hand against King Shapur, for he is the child of light and the King of Kings, even though he clings to the outmoded teachings of Zarathustra and has not yet understood Lord Mani's truth. But Romans are the slaves of evil. I have mastered this creature of the dark, and I will do the same with you, and use you both to spread the light westward to Rome and across the world. Kneel down!"

As he said this, he shot out his left hand and touched Valerian's shoulder. The old man was not quick enough to dodge or parry that swift stroke; but in the next instant he swung round his spear and knocked the Manichaean sprawling.

The peri bent over the fallen young man, touching him with her warm hands and comforting him. "Your jewel," she said, "gives you no power over humans, only over beasts. It is lucky for you that you did not raise your hand against King Shapur, who would have had you crucified on the spot. Now get up and behave yourself like a good groom. I have given you the means to become an excellent one, and the Emperor Valerian has furthered your career by merely thumping you a little when he might have run you through."

Meanwhile Valerian had swung his leg over the roc's neck and prodded it experimentally with his spear. At this, it reared its head aloft, carrying him dizzily upward. He gripped with his legs, as he might have gripped a horse's sides, and after a little shifting and sliding among feathers the size of palm fronds, he settled into what seemed a natural saddle where the creature's neck dipped to join its shoulders.

The Manichaean got up slowly, pausing for some time on his hands and knees. He looked a little reproachfully at his left palm. "Nevertheless," he said, gazing up at Valerian on the roc's neck, "this bird comes to my whistle, and will go nowhere without my command."

"If that proves to be true," said Valerian, "you will regret it, because in that case I must kill you. But I hope you are wrong." He shifted his spear, lifting it to whack the roc's neck.

"Wait!" the peri commanded. Valerian stopped his motion quickly enough so that the spear shaft barely tapped the glistening feathers. The roc danced a little on its huge clawed feet. "Where will you go?" the peri asked.

"You are more likely to know that than I," said Valerian. "Over the wall is as far as I have planned. After than, out of Persia, if I can—to Africa, or India, or Scythia, or for that matter the Hesperides or the Elysian Fields."

"Not back to your own empire?" said the peri, smiling.

"It is no longer mine," said Valerian. "My friends and my lovers are dead or changed into enemies—or, still worse, into people I no longer care about one way or another. My son is intent on remaking my world into his own. If I went back now I would be an ugly anachronism, able to muddy the stream of time for a few years but not to turn it back to the channel it has left. No, I would rather go anywhere else."

"And there was another thing you meant to tell me," said the peri.

Valerian looked down at her, and at the Manichaean standing beside her. "I expected to be tired if I lived long enough to reach this age," he said; "tired of battles and backbiting and political coalitions, economic crises and incompetent bureaucrats, rebellions and invasions and epidemics and mutinous troops and taxes in arrears and the occasional assassination attempt. None of this surprises me. But I had not fully realized until I looked on you, and on this stupid, beautiful, dangerous boy whose youth glows from him like the light of a golden lamp in a shabby room—I had not realized how tired I would be of myself. My body creaks when I move it. My skin is like a worn-out garment, wrinkled and stained and patched with scars, that no longer fits me very well. My memory seems to be failing—chiefly, I suspect, from a lack of interest on my part. My eyes are clouded, my ears are stopped up, and every sense blunted or fogged, so that I cannot quite feel even the reality of these stiff feathers against my buttocks or the wood of this spear shaft in my hand; and if I lay with you, fiery goddess, it would be less real to me than lying with a dream, and I would feel nothing keenly but the mockery of your laughter. So I do not want to go back to the places where I was young; and I will not be greatly sorry if this dark bird carries me high above the mountain peaks and there throws me off. But I will not die here in the straw."

Now the peri laughed very brilliantly, like cut glass sparkling in firelight. "Old emperor, old fool!" she said. "Don't you know that a snake's eyes grow clouded before it sheds its skin? It is the same with humans, though few of them ever understand that. You can cast off your scars and your weariness. You need only to shed your skin."

"It is what the Lord Mani teaches," the Manichaean put in eagerly. "We must shed this dirty and demeaning envelope of flesh and rise into the light."

"Be still," said the peri, "until you learn to use words for something else than displaying your ignorance." And she said to Valerian, "Suppose I show you how to shed your skin. Will you still ask no more of your steed than to carry you high and toss you to destruction?"

Valerian laughed a choking laugh. "There are almost three legions of my soldiers settled somewhere far to the east of here. If I can turn this chick to my will—and it is only a chick, after all—I would like to show King Shapur that I can set up a kingdom of my own within his very boundaries."

"You would not go back to Rome, even then?" asked the peri.

"No!" said Valerian. "I have told you why. Those reasons still hold good, whatever skin I stand in. But show me how to shed this ugly hide, and I will show you what I can do without an empire."

The peri turned to the Manichaean. "And you," she said, "can show your skill as a groom. Call down the bird to me."

The Manichaean whistled. The roc, with a throaty cluck that shook Valerian on his perch, bent its neck and stooped, laying its beaked head once more on the ground. The peri sprang lightly up and sat sidewise just in front of Valerian, swinging her legs. "Take off your clothes, old man," she said briskly.

The Manichaean, whose religion did not allow him to approve of bodies, made a disparaging noise. But Valerian tucked his spear among the stiff feathers and pulled off his garments without hesitation until he sat naked on the roc's neck.

The peri's mouth curved in a slow smile. She touched her fingertips to his chest, just below the dint of his throat, so that he swallowed loudly; then she drew them straight downward. The skin cracked open like a splitting seed pod.

Valerian dug his fingers under the edges of the old skin and peeled it back as if it were a garment indeed. It came away with a crisp sound, sticking a little around his eyes and at the ends of his toes and fingers. But he worked vigorously and got it all off in one piece. The roc was disturbed by the violent movements on the back of its neck, and the Manichaean was kept busy soothing and quieting it, which he did very skillfully.

When it was finished, Valerian stood upright, balancing on the roc's neck, with his skin in his hands. His face shone, and he breathed with deep breaths. The peri looked at him appraisingly. "The air smells sweet at dawn," Valerian said. "I had forgotten that."

The peri held out his garments, which she had picked up to save them from falling. "Dress yourself," she said, "old snake. It would not do to enter your new kingdom naked."

Valerian looked at his old skin for a moment, and tossed it to the ground. He ran his empty hands over his body, and his face changed. He began to examine himself closely. After a little, he barked a laugh.

"You cheated me, peri," he said.

"No more than you did me," she answered, "when you knelt to me only for form's sake. Come now, we are neither of us such fools as to trust with our whole hearts; for I am a peri, and you are old. Nevertheless, we can please each other very well. What made you suppose that an immortal, to whom lifetimes are seasonal phenomena, would prefer a boy to a man?"

"I thought you meant to give me back my youth," said Valerian. "But though my new skin is unscarred, it is still wrinkled; and though my senses are keener than they have been for years, they show me, among other things, that I am still an old man."

"But as fit as ever," said the peri, smiling more sweetly. "Body is the wax on which mind is written. If I had scraped away the old wax to lay down new, I would have destroyed you, old emperor—and I did not want to do that. To give you back your youth would be to give you back your stupidity and your ignorance and all the resounding betrayals that youth is capable of suffering and inflicting. You would have been a prettier person, but a less interesting one. Put on your clothes."

"I cannot quiet remember," said Valerian, looking at the Manichaean, "what it was like to trust with a whole heart. But I think I can remember that it was not entirely bad." He took the clothing that the peri held out to him, and chuckled dryly. "I see you have done better by my clothes than by my flesh. These are royal garments."

"Not better at all," said the peri. "These are only trinkets to please your future subjects, who will want their king to be grandly dressed. But do not scorn the body under your new skin. It is old, but it is sound. And whenever it becomes irksome to you, you can shed your skin again."

"How can I do that," asked Valerian, watching her very steadily, "without your help?"

"You cannot," said the peri, swinging her legs. "Hurry, old snake. Dawn is lightening, and our steed is restless."

Curious sounds came from the long throat of the roc. Its shoulders twitched, and it rubbed its head uneasily along the ground. Valerian finished his dressing and settled himself again into his seat, taking up his spear. He said nothing more, but clucked as he might have done to a horse, and rapped the roc's neck sharply with the spear shaft.

Instantly it reared its head and straightened its legs, so that they were carried high above the yard. But as it moved, the Manichaean moved faster, grasping a feather shaft and swinging himself up onto its neck.

The peri laughed. "So you will not wait to see whether King Shapur can be persuaded to forgive his runaway undergroom? Do not imagine, pretty boy, that you can turn this bird anywhere that I do not want it to go."

"I would not if I could," said the Manichaean. "You are

one who makes your own light, and I would rather die than do anything to displease you." He loosed his hold on the small feathers at the back of the roc's head and slid down its neck till he was close to the peri.

"Well," said Valerian, "we can take the boy over the wall, at least, and set him down wherever he wants to continue his career."

"Your Majesty will need grooms," the Manichaean said eagerly. "And I will be the best groom in the world."

"A few minutes ago," Valerian pointed out, "you tried to make me your slave. Well, we can discuss the matter." He reached backward with his spear and tapped the roc's shoulder.

The great bird beat its wings, making a thunderous noise, and lunged at the wall. Valerian gripped tightly with his legs and leaned forward, grinning. The roc cleared the wall in a soaring leap and raced off, flapping its wings faster and faster, so that a violent wind buffeted the countryside; and with a squawk of triumph it left the earth and rose eastward into the lightening air.

When people awoke in King Shapur's palace, they found the discarded skin in the outer yard, and recognized it as Valerian's by the scars. From the talon marks on the earth, and the effects of the wind, they understood something of what had happened. So they tanned the skin by way of evidence; and when King Shapur came home from his expedition, he gave out that Valerian had died of old age and debility, and had the skin hung up as a trophy in the great temple of Ctesiphon.

But some say that Valerian reigned for many lifetimes in a kingdom in the East, and perhaps reigns there still, though not under that name. For some say that he became a Manichaean at last, and others say a Christian, and that he is known to Christians as Prester John. But no one knows the end of this story.

The Merchant

Melissa Scott

"Do you know what he's done?"

Mahomet Ben Ferran blinked at the little man sitting opposite him, bald head thrust forward like an angry hawk's. The resemblance was strengthened by the fringe of white hair, cut close as feathers, and the hot hazel eyes. Ben Ferran blinked again, and lifted a hand in protest. "Is this a fit greeting, considering the gold I've brought to your coffers today?"

"Allah be thanked for your safe return and the health of your people and your beasts," the little man recited, this time in expressionless, unaccented Turkish. "May he smile on your further ventures." He returned to the Spanish that was his native tongue, and habitual between the two men. "Have you heard what's happened to Minale?"

"I suspect you are going to tell me," Ben Ferran answered.

"Hah." Simon Lainez checked abruptly, the coffeepot suspended in midair, its scoured copper gleaming in a stray shaft of sunlight. After an instant, he finished filling the two cups, and handed one to his guest, saying, in a calmer tone, "I thought you would want to know."

Ben Ferran nodded, absently admiring the interlaced pattern of cups and tray, and took a cautious sip of the thick liquid. "I do."

"He's made a proper fool of himself," Lainez said grimly. He set his cup aside, and pushed himself up off the cushions. Ben Ferran watched him pace the length of the room, the dark red silk of his coat swirling around his legs. Outside the fretted windows, in the oven-hot garden, a bird called plaintively; in the cool shadows beyond the arch of the inner door, a child laughed, and a woman answered, a startling sound. Lainez did not seem to hear, a dark silhouette against the latticework of the window, the sunlight behind him brighter than the coals of the little brazier. His face was in shadow, but Ben Ferran knew from his voice that he was scowling.

"Alessio Minale is in love," Lainez said at last, and stalked back toward the cushions. "A fair youth—honey-fair, he calls it—some twenty years his junior."

"Venetian?" Ben Ferran asked.

Lainez's long mouth twisted into an expression that might have been the beginning of a smile had the eyes not still been hot and angry. "Of course. And well born, too."

"Of course," Ben Ferran murmured, his own eyes wary.

"But I would do him wrong to say he doesn't love Alessio," Lainez went on, with heavy irony. "He loves him as the Sultan loves us Jews: give me money, we'll call it a loan, and I'll let you admire from afar—but don't expect a return on the investment."

"Have a care, Samein," Ben Ferran said, but smiled at the wry truth of the words.

Lainez lifted an eyebrow, and continued more quietly, "It's not my affair, I know, but to borrow—the boy borrowed money for his marriage, for his courtship, from Alessio, of all men, and Alessio borrowed money to give to him. From Halil."

Ben Ferran's head lifted. "Why not from you? And why Halil, of all men? Has he lost his mind?"

Lainez shrugged. "I don't know. Can I read his thoughts—if indeed he thinks—in such a state? If he'd come to me, he could have had his money—"

"And a lecture on his follies, too," Ben Ferran murmured, with a faint smile.

Lainez ignored him. "—without any hazard. But no, he goes to Halil, and then what must he do but sign the bond, with a pound of his flesh the price of a forfeit."

"And he forfeited," Ben Ferran said. The coffee was cold in his cup; he set it aside with a grimace. "It's that time of year, I know—all his capital was abroad, and nothing had returned?"

Lainez nodded, the same grim almost-smile playing on his long mouth. "Just so."

"And is Alessio well?" Ben Ferran asked, when the other did not continue.

"Hah." Lainez turned away again. "The bond was revoked: there was no blood mentioned in the agreement—typical Christian sophistry, which I did not expect in Alessio, even to save his life. And Halil renounced payment in open court." He was silent for a moment, the harsh line of his profile stark against the brilliance of the latticed window. "But Alessio is ill. He wastes away, eaten up by something the doctors cannot recognize, much less cure. And I can't stand by and see it happen."

"You think this is Halil's revenge?" Ben Ferran asked.

"What else?"

"Have you any proof?"

Lainez glared at the taller man, still sitting cross-legged on his cushions. "If I had proof, Mahomet, would I just be standing here?"

Ben Ferran grinned up at him. "Not you, Samein."

"Simon," Lainez growled.

They were both silent then, the grin slowly fading from Ben Ferran's face. "You're certain?"

Lainez spread his hands. "I would swear it in open court, today, if the judge would take my oath. But I can't prove it."

"Halil has always been a blot, a pimple on the fair face of Aleppo," Ben Ferran said pensively at last, and pushed himself to his feet. He was tall, almost a head taller than Lainez, and a year on the long caravan-road to the East had reduced a thin body to bone and whipcord muscle. "It's past time he was burst."

"A charming metaphor," Lainez said.

"But indisputable." Ben Ferran ran his hands through his coarse, gray-streaked hair, dislodging his elaborate turban. He straightened it automatically, adjusting it to the angle that most flattered his lined, engagingly ugly face. "I think we'd best go see Alessio."

"If he'll see us," Lainez said, but clapped his hands for a servant to clear away the brazier.

Ben Ferran smiled sweetly. "He'll see me."

Alessio Minale had leased the same house for the fifteen years he had managed the affairs of his cousins' trading house, a modest, comfortable building in the Frankish quarter, almost in the shadow of the low-spired church and its fortress-thick walls. His steward, a perpetually mournful man a few years older than his master, favored the visitors with a rather dubious stare, but escorted them through the heat and heavy scent of the inner garden to Minale's private chamber. It was cooler there, the windows shuttered against the fierce sun, and the flower-smell of the garden was only a little stronger than a memory. Minale himself leaned back against the pillows of a low divan, one arm in its black silk sleeve thrown across his eyes. A blond young man was sitting on a stool at the foot of the divan, reading from the large book in his lap.

"—four quintals salt at the same price, with tax paid to the Emir, bringing the total—"

"Sir," the steward said. "Simon Lainez and Mahomet Ben Ferran." He bowed deeply, and withdrew.

Minale waved the reader to silence and slowly lowered the arm from across his face. He had always been a slender, fine-boned man, one of those elegant men whose strength is implicit in their very grace, but there was a new and disturbing fragility about him now, shadows like bruises beneath his brown eyes, and a frightening transparence to his ivory skin, as though the bones were wearing through it from within. Ben Ferran winced, and Lainez, who had seen it before, looked away.

"Send your catamite away, I want to talk to you," he said roughly, in Spanish.

"Manners, Samein," Ben Ferran murmured.

Minale's eyebrows rose. "And why, Señor Lainez, do you assume my servants speak no Spanish? You're welcome to my house, Mahomet. I didn't know you were back in Aleppo."

"I returned yesterday," Ben Ferran answered.

Lainez grimaced. "We must talk, Alessio. In private."

The reader closed the account book and bowed, then slipped away, closing the door behind him.

"Serafino?" Lainez said.

"Perhaps I should rename my household to please you?"

Minale asked. "Please, sit down, Mahomet. As he came with you, I won't waste time apologizing for his behavior."

Ben Ferran grinned, and seated himself cross-legged on the waiting pile of cushions. "One grows used to it," he murmured.

"Bah." Lainez rounded on them. "Nothing has changed, has it?"

"Sit down, Simon," Minale said. "No, nothing's changed."

Lainez kicked the stool away from the foot of the divan, spinning it expertly into a place from which he could watch both of the others, and settled himself on its padded top. "Well, then. Will you let me make inquiries?"

"I've made inquiries." Minale pushed himself almost upright against the cushions, drawing his gown closed around him. "I found nothing."

"What do you mean, nothing?" Lainez demanded.

Minale smiled. "I thought the word had a common meaning."

Ben Ferran cleared his throat. "Pray excuse my ignorance, but I'm coming somewhat late into this sink of confusion. Inquiries?"

"Halil's no wizard," Minale said. "If this is his doing—and no, Simon, I'm not convinced it necessarily is—he must have hired someone, either to perform the spell or to teach it to him." He glanced at Lainez. "But the only thing of remote interest my people found was that the vegetable seller who casts horoscopes is dead—"

"There," Lainez said. "You see?"

"He fell down the stairs from his roof while drunk," Minale said, "in full view of his two sons and the district constable. I don't think it was anything but natural."

Lainez glared. Ben Ferran said, "Alessio. This does seem to be more than coincidence, this—illness of yours."

Minale sighed. "No. No, I don't think it's coincidence. But I can't find any evidence that it isn't."

"There is always the bond itself," Lainez said, after a moment. The others looked at him, and he shrugged. "It's the only contact you've ever had with Halil. It's a place to start, I thought—so I bought it."

"He sold it?" Minale said.

Lainez nodded, grim-faced. "Which ends that as a line of inquiry."

"Not necessarily," Ben Ferran said. He glanced at Minale. "Forgive me for mentioning one further, admittedly degrading possibility, but—have you thought of paying the money owed?"

Minale said reluctantly. "I would rather see him in hell, at this point, even now that I have the money. But it's worth a try."

"I bought the bond at the usual discount, fifty percent of the value less the exchange fee," Lainez said. "I won't make a profit off it."

"No," Ben Ferran said. "You will pay the full amount, Alessio, and you, Samein, will accept it—all of it. Otherwise the spell will not be broken."

"If there is a spell, and if it's so constructed," Minale murmured. "Oh, I know, Simon, I have nothing to lose. Very well. Do you have the bond?"

"Yes." Lainez fumbled in the purse he wore at his belt beneath the scarlet gown, and produced a much folded packet, which he held out to the Venetian.

Minale eyed it with distaste. "I remember the terms," he said, and pushed himself to his feet.

"And well you ought," Lainez retorted. Minale ignored him, stooping over the lock of an ironbound coffer that stood against the room's inner wall.

"May I?" Ben Ferran asked, and held out his hand. Lainez handed him the packet, and the caravan leader unfolded it carefully, scanning the neat letters.

"Linen," he said, after a moment.

"I noticed it at the time," Minale said. "For durability, I'd thought." He straightened slowly, holding a small leather purse. The worn sides bulged, and there was a soft familiar noise of coins. "This is the full amount, no more, no less, in sequins, as accounted in the bond."

Ben Ferran looked up from the creased linen. "I don't see anything out of the ordinary," he said, and handed the paper back to Lainez.

Minale held out the purse. Lainez accepted it, saying, "I take this as full payment of the debt written herein. The debt is discharged."

Minale took the bond, glancing unhappily at the writing.

"Burn it," Lainez said, and looped the purse strings through his belt.

"This—" Minale stopped abruptly. "You know my hand, both of you. I did not sign this." The hand he extended with the paper was trembling.

Ben Ferran took it from him before Lainez could reach it. "No," he said, after what seemed an interminable time. "It's very like, but not quite perfect. This is evidence that would stand in court, my friend."

"Evidence of what?" Lainez asked, with another of his angry smiles, and took the bond from Ben Ferran's hand, staring intently at the lettering.

"If he sold a forged bond—if he went to the trouble of forging the bond, then we were right," Minale said, "and the bond is the key."

"But why sell?" Ben Ferran said, almost to himself, and shook his head. "A foolish question: to keep business as usual, of course."

"We have to get the true bond," Minale said.

"We could go to court—I could go to court," Lainez said, still with that angry smile on his face, "plead forgery and demand Halil produce the real paper. And by the time we had a judgment, you, Alessio, would be dead."

Minale looked away. "What other choice do we have?"

Ben Ferran smiled. "Ah," he said gently, "and well you asked. Leave that small thing to me."

The other two exchanged unhappy glances.

"But, Mahomet," Minale began, and Lainez waved angrily at him.

"Do we have a choice?"

The two men sat silent in the flickering lamplight, not quite looking at each other. In the central recess of the massive standing cabinet, the clock ticked steadily. Its single hand stood midway between midnight and the first hour of the day; Minale glanced at it, crossed himself in perfunctory acknowledgment, and looked away.

"More wine?"

Lainez shook his head. "Where the hell is he?"

"I wish I knew." Minale refilled his own glass yet again, and set the bottle aside, running a square-tipped finger around the gold-chased rim: Venetian glass, very fine. The wine was good, too, smelling faintly of summer. He drank, seemed almost surprised when he set the glass down empty, and reached for the bottle again.

"Alessio. Is that wise?"

Minale smiled slowly, and set the new glass down untasted. "Perhaps not. But I'm running out of alternatives, at least of good ones."

"Oh, he'll be here," Lainez said. "With half the town constabulary at his heels probably, and expecting us to come up with some explanation that'll save his skin—but he will be here."

Minale laughed soundlessly. "And men wonder why I didn't come to you for the money."

Lainez lifted an eyebrow at him. "I'm here, aren't I?"

There was a little silence, and then Minale nodded. "You're here."

The silence resumed, broken at last by a faint sound from the street below the window. Lainez's head lifted, and Minale waved for him to be silent. The sound was repeated, a soft clatter of pebbles against the stone below the shutters. Minale hurriedly undid the latch and leaned out into the night. Lainez heard him swear softly then, and saw his shoulders move convulsively as though he'd caught something flung up from the street.

"Let me." Lainez stood quickly, came forward to take the rope from the Venetian's hands. Minale released it with a grimace, and Lainez braced himself to take Ben Ferran's weight as the caravan leader pulled himself up, hand over hand, to the window. He crouched in the embrasure for a moment, grinning, then jumped down lightly onto the scrubbed floor.

"You could have gone to the door," Minale observed.

"Not him," Lainez growled, and nursed his skinned palms.

Ben Ferran laughed softly, and sketched an elaborate obeisance. "Rejoice, my friends. I have it." With a flourish, he produced a much folded paper, and tossed it onto the divan. Minale stared at it, his eyes very black in the lamplight, but made no move to pick it up.

Lainez made a derisive noise, and unfolded the sheet of linen, then scanned the lines of clerk's writing. "Well, Alessio?"

Minale leaned over his shoulder. "Yes," he said at last. "That's my hand."

"I don't see anything out of the ordinary," Lainez said.

"That, Samein, is because you're not looking properly." Ben Ferran twitched the sheet out of Lainez's grasp, and held it gingerly above the flame of the lamp. For a long moment, nothing happened, but then, quite suddenly, shadowy pale-brown letters appeared, half obscured by the words of the bond.

"A child's trick," Minale said. "My Christ."

"Not so childish as all that," Ben Ferran answered.

"Turkish," Lainez said, and looked at Ben Ferran. "And no symbols."

The caravan leader nodded. "Yes, precisely."

"I don't understand," Minale said.

"It is a spell," Ben Ferran said, "as you guessed, Samein—but written in Turkish, not one of the esoteric tongues. A sort of penalty clause, triggered by your being unable to pay. And by the court's decision, of course."

"I see," Minale said softly.

"Can you break it?" Lainez asked.

"I think so," Ben Ferran said. "But not now. Not until dawn."

Lainez nodded. "For once, you're taking the wiser course."

"The demons of the night would hardly aid our efforts," Ben Ferran said.

"Then we'll wait," Minale said, in a voice as rigidly controlled as the hand he extended to the bottle. "Will you take wine, Mahomet, and tell us how you—obtained—the paper?"

"Ah." Ben Ferran accepted the Venetian goblet, and raised it to his lips, the lines of laughter tightening at the corners of his eyes. For an instant, he looked almost young again. The illusion vanished as he set the glass at his feet beside the pillows. "As you know, Halil lives at the very end of the street of the Silversmiths, some distance from the clamor of the bazaar—"

"We know that," Lainez said, and seated himself on a padded stool.

"Let him speak, Simon," Minale said from the divan.

"Thank you," Ben Ferran said. "—some distance from the clamor of the bazaar, in a house that some might call more like a fortress than the dwelling of a mere merchant. It is a grim place, and its grimness is unrelieved by the presence of those flowers of humanity that some call women—did you say something, Samein?"

"No."

"I thought— But no matter." Ben Ferran smiled. "As I was saying, Halil has neither wife nor concubine to share his house—nor boy neither, Alessio!"

"I didn't say a word."

"Malicious tongues say," Ben Ferran resumed, "that there is no wife because no woman would have him for a master, and no concubine because such creatures are expensive. Others whisper that there was once a woman there, but that she was a Christian slave, and hanged herself, loving her God better than her mortal owner.

"But though there are no women there, the household is far from empty. Halil loves his gold, and he fears robbers more than demons. Four black eunuchs guard his gates— fearsome creatures, trained to kill silently and skillfully, and question the intruder later. And a hunting cat prowls the lower floors at night, half starved and ready to devour the unwary.

"All this I knew, Alessio, when I left your house this afternoon. To speak truth, I was somewhat daunted by the thought of these defenses, and cast about in my mind for some way that I might honorably decline to make the attempt—"

"Bah," Lainez said. "You delight in looking for trouble."

"—but the Prophet speaks often of the obligations of true friendship. So I turned my steps toward the bazaar itself, and went in search of my cousin Bedir. Now Bedir —who is not properly speaking my cousin; I call him so after a small affair in Damascus some years ago, when he incurred an obligation—but no matter. Bedir, not to put too fine a point on it, is a thief, and an excellent one. I have often consulted him on the finer points of his trade, particularly in the art of entering locked and well-guarded buildings. After all, one must not disappoint a lady—but that is not to the point."

"No," Minale agreed, smiling.

"Bedir is never an easy man to find, as indeed one might expect. I walked the length of the bazaar, and saw no one I knew might know him; I walked back again, and this time, I stopped in the shade of a rug merchant's awning, to catch my breath in the heat. And as I stood there, I heard a familiar voice behind me.

"'Cousin Mahomet,' it said, 'I think you're looking for me.'

"'Cousin Bedir,' I answered. 'I was indeed. I have some business for you.'

"'Come inside out of the sun,' my as-good-as-cousin said, 'and we'll talk.'

"So I went inside, into the darkest and coolest room of the rug merchant's shop, and we sat down together on a pile of the merchant's stock, and I explained to my almost-cousin just what it was I wanted. 'I need your help,' I said, 'to find this bond.'

"'And why should I help you to help a dog of a Christian?'—I beg your pardon, Alessio, but that was what he said—'Especially when the house in question is the house of Halil, and all Aleppo knows how well guarded it is.'

"'Very well,' I said. 'I will not ask you to come with me, not even for the sake of the good turn I did you in Damascus, but only this one small thing. I know there is a drug your kind uses, to tame watchdogs and such. Prepare a dose for me, in such meat as a leopard would eat, so that I may search freely inside the house. The rest,' I said, 'you may leave to me.'

"Bedir did his best to dissuade me from my plan, but, when he found me adamant, sighed deeply and beat his chest in mourning, saying he would never see me again. But, since it was my wish and I was his friend who had always been good for him, he would prepare the meat for the cat, and wait with it for me at the coffee shop at the head of the street of the Silversmiths. So I went away, and bathed, and changed my clothes, so that I was dressed as you see me now, all in black and the darkest of blues, with a dark veil to wrap across my face.

"Bedir was waiting as he'd promised, with the packet of meat beside him. It was not yet dark; I waited there, drinking coffee, and we talked of many things. At last the light faded, twilight deepening to night and black shadows. The moon was at its last quarter, and there were clouds in the sky.

"'A good night,' said Bedir, and I nodded. 'I wish you luck,' my almost-cousin said, and slipped away into the shadows. I was left alone.

"I paid my bill, and gathered my package, adjusted my sword at my side, and took my heavy traveler's stick in my left hand. With Allah's mercy, I told myself, I would not need to shed blood. And so I made my way down the street of the Silversmiths toward Halil's house.

"If it seems a grim building in the daylight, it is doubly so at night, bleak and cold. The moonlight flashed once on the cold stone of its facade, perfect and forbidding as an Egyptian temple, and then the clouds drowned the light. I told myself I was grateful for the darkness, but my heart sank within me. Still, I told myself, this is for a friend— and I wrapped my scarf across my face, and slunk down the street in the shadow of the houses.

"Two black eunuchs stood within the shadow of the doorway. They looked lazy enough, one leaning on his staff, the other sitting half-asleep, his back against the door itself, but I knew well enough that those looks were deceptive. One wrong move, and their scimitars would be out, and I—for all that I am a master swordsman—I would find myself hard-pressed to deal with both of them. More than that, the noise would surely rouse the entire street, and then how could I succeed in entering the house?

"I pondered the matter for a little while, and then an inspiration came to me. I made my way by inches to the doorway of the last house before Halil's, and waited there, searching the doorsill for some stone or pebble or some small thing that would make a noise. At last I found a stone, and threw it into the alley between the houses opposite. It fell with a clatter into—by the sound of it—a heap of broken pottery. The eunuchs sprang to attention, the one who had been asleep scrambling to his feet and the other drawing his scimitar. The blade gleamed in the darkness, and I was very grateful for the clouds that hid the moon, and me.

"They paused, listening, and I threw my second stone. This time, the first eunuch took a step forward, out of his doorway—and I leaped forward, swinging my staff. I struck him behind the neck and brought him down, and flung myself around to face the other. He cried out, once, but I was too quick for him. I struck again, and he slumped back against the door.

"But he had cried out. Hastily, I seized the other's body and dragged him back into the doorway, hiding him with my own body. I drew the scarf closer about my face and waited, leaning on my staff as though it were a spear. Further up the street, a door opened, and a man leaned out.

" 'Is all well?' he cried. 'I heard something—'

" 'All's well,' I answered, through the disguising scarf. 'A dog startled him—' and I nodded to the eunuch at my feet. The man nodded, and closed his door again. Still I waited, until I was certain no one else would come to investigate. Then I set my staff aside, and rummaged in the eunuch's clothes until I found the great bunch of keys. Slowly, so slowly, I drew them out, and fitted them one by one into the lock, until at last I found the one that fit. I turned it, wincing as the lock groaned a little, and then I was inside.

"Almost at once, I heard the cat cough in the next room. Hastily, I unwrapped my package, and flung it ahead of me, then froze still as a statue. The hall was very dark; I could barely see my own hand as it threw the meat. I heard a snuffling then, and the soft sound of pads on the marble floor. I could feel my heart hammering in my chest, and feared the cat would hear it, too. I stood there for what seemed an eternity, and then, quite distinctly, I heard a different noise. The beast was eating.

"I held my breath, listening to the tearing noises, and the crunching as its great jaws snapped the bones. And then I heard it stand and walk toward me. There was something different in its walk; it stumbled, staggered as it went. I prayed Bedir's drug would take effect before it reached me. It came closer, so that I could hear its breathing. Its hot breath was on my feet—and then it fell, so close that its head grazed my shoe. I stood frozen for a long moment, and then made myself step over its inert body. There was tinder in my purse, and a dark lantern, also the gift of Bedir. I struck sparks and lit the lantern with an unsteady hand. The cat was asleep on the tiles of the entrance hall, and would not harm me.

"The rest was simple. Halil's strongbox was in a little room to one side. I picked its lock—a simple thing—and lifted the lid. The box was filled with coin, and papers; I rummaged through the latter until I found the one I wanted. I held it close to the lamp to be sure it was indeed the original, and the hidden letters appeared. 'Allah be praised,' I whispered then. 'I have what I came for.' The cat was still asleep; I stepped across his body, and eased open the great door. The eunuchs lay still unconscious—or dead; I neither knew nor cared—and the street was empty before me. I slipped from the house, and came here to you."

There was a moment's silence, and then Minale applauded softly.

"Very nice," Lainez said. "Now let's hear the real story."

"I am offended," Ben Ferran said, but he was smiling.

"Does it matter?" Minale asked. "He has—we have the bond. That's enough, surely."

"Just once I'd like to hear him tell the truth," Lainez said.

Ben Ferran's smile was fading. "There is one thing I will say—and it is the exact and absolute truth, Samein. I have never been in a place that seemed so empty, in spite of all the things and all the people that were in that house. It was all not quite—real."

"Unreal?" Minale said, after a moment.

Ben Ferran nodded. "As though everything was present only because Halil had thought about them for a long time, and now he was forgetting."

There was a little silence, and then Lainez said explosively, "Nonsense!"

Ben Ferran shrugged. "As you please."

"Halil is not a wizard, has never been a wizard, will never be a wizard," Lainez continued. "It's ridiculous."

"It's what I felt," Ben Ferran said. "Hate's a powerful force, Samein."

"Are you trying to tell me," Lainez began, "that Halil brooded and brooded, there in his house, until all that brooding overflowed and he became a wizard?" His voice, which had been angrily skeptical, trailed off into a sort of question.

Ben Ferran shrugged again. "Why not?"

"Why?" Lainez retorted, but without conviction.

"He has no cause to hate me so much," Minale said.

"Oh?" Ben Ferran looked at him and, after a moment, the Venetian looked away.

"Yes, I've bested him more than once, but that was business. My God, I've gotten the better of you before now. It's a game, not a war."

"Halil," Ben Ferran said lightly, "was never a sportsman." He saw Minale's face, and said in a different voice, "Alessio. You are a Christian dog, an infidel, a lover of boys and a drinker of wine—and all Aleppo, Turk, Christian, and Jew, calls you an honest man. He, the sound businessman, the true believer, they vilify. Were I Halil, I would hate you, too."

"God help me," Minale murmured. "So what do we do now?"

"Burn the bond," Lainez suggested.

"No." Ben Ferran glanced at the window, the darkness still showing absolute through the cracks in the shutters. "No, we do nothing until dawn."

"And then what?" Minale asked. "Forgive me for pressing the matter, Mahomet, but . . ."

Ben Ferran held the bond above the lamp flame until the hidden letters reappeared.

"Let me see," Lainez said. "Why is it written in Turkish, of all languages?"

"Does it matter?" Minale asked, still softly.

"Turkish is not an esoteric tongue," Ben Ferran answered, still staring at the pale letters. "Were Halil a wizard—were he a wizard, Samein, he would not have written this in this way, and you were right all along."

"Of course, but I don't see how that helps us," Lainez snapped.

"And I was right, too," Ben Ferran continued, as though the others had not spoken. "And therein lies our solution. This is no spell: Read it, Samein, do you see any sign that law or logic were obeyed? It's a wish, an ill-wishing—I'd say a curse, but it lacks the proper forms of that as well— written out by a man who hates one thing more than all others, and put that hatred down onto paper. I wonder if he even hoped it would work, or if he simply had to do something, having hated so long and so deeply."

Lainez shook his head. "It couldn't work, not the way you've said."

"But it has," Ben Ferran answered. "And therein—"

"How?" Minale said.

Ben Ferran looked at him, an odd, predatory smile curving his full lips. "You will pay the bond, Alessio. That is all."

"I have paid it." Minale shook his head.

"You paid me," Lainez said. His eyes were fixed on Ben Ferran. "Is that it?"

Ben Ferran nodded.

"For God's sake—" Minale bit back the rest of the sentence. "Explain this to me, Mahomet, in a way I can understand, or I shall surely murder you."

"It's thus." Ben Ferran looked down at the bond, his mobile face suddenly very still. The letters were fading again, almost invisible, but he made to move to recall them. "This is neither curse nor spell; it has no power but Halil's hatred, and no structure but his wish. If you fulfill the terms of the contract, return him his money, this ill-wish will no longer have an existence, and you will be free."

"And if he refuses to take the money?" Minale asked.

Ben Ferran shook his head again. "He cannot."

"Then we'll go to him, first thing in the morning," Lainez said.

"I doubt that will be necessary," Ben Ferran said, and smiled. "I doubt that very much indeed."

The sun had been up for some hours when Minale's steward tapped gingerly on the door of his master's chamber. Lainez roused instantly, coming bolt upright in his chair, the hot eyes roving once around the room as he remembered where he was. Ben Ferran uncoiled from his pillows, one hand reaching beneath his coat for the long dagger he wore tucked into his belt. He came to his feet in a single continuous movement, and moved quickly to the door, setting a finger against his lips. Minale woke more slowly, the bone shadows very prominent beneath his skin.

"Yes?"

"Messer, the merchant Halil is below, and demands to speak with you."

"Demands?" Minale's eyebrows rose. "I will see him," he said, after a moment, "but not here."

"In the garden, messer?"

Minale nodded, the heels of his hands pressed against his eyes. "Yes, that will do." He glanced then at Ben Ferran. "Will it?"

The caravan leader nodded.

"Very good, messer," the steward said. A moment later, they heard his footsteps fading down the narrow staircase.

Minale jammed his fingers into his hair, thick still, but faded to a sort of cloudy brown. "I must dress," he said, after a moment.

"You're fine as you are," Lainez said impatiently, and held out his hand. Minale took it, and pulled himself slowly to his feet. Lainez steadied him until he caught his balance. "A bad morning?"

"Not a good one." Minale managed a rueful smile. "Would you bring the money, Mahomet? And my stick?"

Ben Ferran complied in silence. Minale leaned heavily on the ebony staff until he reached the top of the stairs, but then, with an effort, straightened to his full height and made his way down into the garden almost without its support. The others followed him, Lainez swearing under his breath.

"Be quiet, Samein," Ben Ferran murmured, and was obeyed.

The garden was still thick with morning dew, though the sunlight pouring down out of the cloudless sky would soon drive away that dampness. The air smelled cool, green, the heavy scents of the flowers still sleeping, not yet released by the afternoon sun. Halil was waiting in the center of that freshness, a thickset, vigorous man who paced angrily from side to side, only just restraining himself from striking at the unfolding flowers. Hearing footsteps, he swung to face the stairs, his plain linen robes swirling about him. His turban was set askew, and strands of coarse white hair emerged from under the brownish folds.

"You have something of mine, Minale," he said. His heavy jowls were unshaven, his pale eyes fixed on the Venetian.

"The bond is mine," Lainez said, and stepped forward to stand at Minale's side. "You sold it to me, Halil. It's mine by law and custom."

Halil ignored him. "Thief, Christian pig, return what you took from me."

"I am prepared," Minale said very slowly, matching the Turk stare for stare, "to pay the bond."

Halil jerked as though struck, his head rocking back on his thick neck. "What?"

"I am prepared to pay the bond," Minale said again. He held out his hand, not looking to either side, and Ben Ferran placed the purse in it. Still slowly, Minale extended his hand toward Halil, his fingers curled around the bulging leather as though around a weapon.

The Turk did not move, his eyes suddenly wary in his immobile face. "The bond was disallowed. I have no rights in it."

"I will pay it," Minale said.

"There is nothing in the law that prevents you from accepting," Ben Ferran said, "and nothing in the judgment of the court, either."

"I have sold the bond." Halil did not move, but it

seemed briefly as though he took a single step backward, away from the extended purse. "Pay him."

"You sold me a forgery," Lainez said with contempt. "And that is actionable, too."

"Accept the payment," Minale said, "or refuse me."

"I—" Halil licked his lips. "I will do neither."

"You have no choice," Lainez said.

Ben Ferran said, almost in the same instant, "The law of the land and the law of the Prophet, Halil. One or the other, you must choose."

"Do you accept my payment?" Minale asked, and took a single step forward. Halil lifted his chin, his eyes fixed now on the purse in Minale's hand, but said nothing.

"Give me your answer," Minale said, and stepped forward again.

"No!" Halil slapped at the purse, striking it out of Minale's grasp. "I will not take it, and be damned to you."

"And be damned to you, Halil," Ben Ferran said quietly, "for that's what you've done."

The coins lay spilled on the packed earth, a bright fan of gold in the sunlight. Halil stared at them, blinking a little, as though his sight had suddenly clouded. Minale drew a deep breath, his eyes opening wide in startled pleasure, and straightened, taking his weight off the supporting cane.

"You've killed me," Halil said quite softly, and looked at Minale. "Dog, infidel, boy-loving drunkard, you've killed me!"

"As you would have killed me," Minale answered.

Halil stood silent for a long moment, staring at Minale, an ancient anger etched on his heavy face. Then he spat deliberately on the spilled coins, turned, and walked away with labored steps. The others watched him go in silence, not moving until they heard the distant sound of the main door closing behind him.

Minale shivered. "He will die."

"Yes," Lainez answered fiercely, "and it's right."

"When he refused," Minale said, as though the other had not spoken, "the spell turned back on him. I felt it lift from me, from my very bones, and turn on him, and he will die." He looked at Ben Ferran. "Mahomet, what if he had taken the money?"

There was a little pause before Ben Ferran answered. "I don't know," he said at last. "He was no wizard. Perhaps he might have lived, the spell ended, not broken; perhaps it would have been the same, and he would have died just as surely. The words he used were ambiguous; I can't say."

Minale nodded.

"What do you want to do with this?" Lainez asked, and kicked at the scattered gold.

"Bury them," Minale said. "Bury them deep and far away from my house. I want nothing to do with them, and I wouldn't dare give them to anyone, not after all that's happened."

"I think that's wisest," Ben Ferran agreed.

"As you wish," Lainez said, and stooped to gather the coins back into their purse. "I'll take care of it, if you like."

"Thank you," Minale said. "I'm very much in your debt, both of you."

"Sign no more bonds," Lainez said, with a grim smile.

"Friendship is a sacred duty," Ben Ferran murmured. "And I always disliked Halil."

There was another little silence, and then Minale nodded. "But nonetheless, I thank you." He clapped his hands then, summoning his steward from the shadows of the house. "You will stay to dine? I haven't heard your latest adventures, Mahomet, and I doubt you even had time to tell Simon."

"I would be delighted," Ben Ferran answered.

"Can you top the last set of lies?" Lainez asked. "That I'd like to hear."

"I've never lied to you," Ben Ferran protested, smiling, and Minale laughed. They moved together into the house, the bond forgotten in Minale's private chamber. After a while, the young man Serafino came to fetch an account book, and found the scrap of linen lying beside the door. The letters were too old and faded to be legible, and therefore the thing could not be important. Whistling between his teeth, he twisted the scrap into a long spill and jammed it among the coals of the brazier, then turned away before he saw it burn. The linen smoldered for a while, and finally took fire, and was consumed. That evening, a rumor swept Aleppo, and was confirmed the next morning: the merchant Halil, residing at the end of the street of the Silversmiths, had died at his desk, perhaps of an apoplexy. He had no heirs, and his fortune was scattered to the winds.

Beyond the Golden Road

Charles Sheffield

The wise men in the court of the Great Khan say that Life and Death are the two great arcs of the world. Close to each other at birth, they move apart in middle life, and in old age they converge again and finally meet.

I am too young to be a sage, and I do not question the words of wise men and great philosophers. But when we finally stumbled across the merchant caravan in the wastes of the Tarim Desert, I knew that the arcs of Life and Death for me, a young man, stood no more than a fingernail apart.

We had been walking for six days, the last two without water. According to the soldier Ahmes, the desert should have been no more than four days' travel wide. Long since we ought to have emerged from its eastern margin and found the Ghadi oasis. Instead we were dying under a late-October sun.

Ahmes was not a man to understand guilt. He strode on, still strong and erect, still carrying his curved damascene sword and leather shield. A gray-black layer of dust covered his cheeks and caked around his lips, but his face was as cheerful as ever. He was sucking on a smooth pebble, and now and again he would turn to us and smile his mysterious crinkle-eyed grin of white teeth.

I had carried most of our baggage, and all of the water for as long as we had water. Now I was staggering, close to collapse. Johannes, who *does* feel guilt—much too acutely—knew how near I was to giving up. He had an arm around me, half carrying me forward, while he whispered encouraging words. "A little farther, Dari," he said, "it cannot be more than another hour or two. We have come too far, you and I, to be stopped now." And then, when I was near weeping with pain and thirst and weariness, "I am sorry I brought you here. But courage, little Dari. This too shall pass."

He liked Ahmes. He had trusted him since we first met in the freezing heights of the Hindu Kush, winding our way east through the high snowy passes and glittering glaciers. Ahmes had led us then on a supposed shortcut, one that left us lost and shivering on a mountainside, in air so thin and clear and cold that the midday sky looked purple-black, and the leaves of the flowering plants were as brittle as dried tea. We had been lucky to survive that day, and had done it only by taking a hair-raising slide down three thousand feet of a blind snow-slope. It could have ended in a precipice. The luck of Ahmes, it ended in soft snow and, just below, a pleasant valley.

Johannes believed him even now, when we had been led so far astray that our lives were again in terrible danger. He could not see past that bluff, cheerful exterior to the bloody, reckless warrior inside. But I knew Ahmes. I had seen men like him all my life, ever since I was a mewling baby.

And now Ahmes was going to be the death of us all.

I leaned my head against Johannes's shoulder. He would always be kind to me, but he would not listen, would not think of me as a man. I was still "little Dari," even though I had grown half a head since we set out from Acre more than a year ago. He had never taken me seriously, and now there could never be a chance for such a thing.

"Eh-hey!" The shout broke into my thoughts. Ahmes had been walking twenty paces ahead, and now he turned to grin at us in triumph. "There we are. Straight ahead."

And there it was. The luck of Ahmes. A rising streak of dust on the next sandy ridge. Within that dust as we topped our own dune I could see the line of camels and ponies, walking nose-to-tail along the high line of the hard sand. Five minutes later I had my face buried in a juicy section of *hendevane*—watermelon. Nothing had ever tasted so good.

I swallowed cool red pulp, ran the cold, sticky rind across my forehead, and looked up. Ahmes was chattering with half a dozen of the merchants while Johannes, less fluent, did his best to follow the babble. I had been coaching him for a year, but his ear was blind and he did not have my gift for languages. As Ahmes talked now of the desert crossing, just as though we had planned everything this way, Johannes was nodding. Was it worth pointing out to him, one more time, that the advice of Ahmes had been hopelessly wrong, that we had found no oasis where he promised, and that the encounter with this caravan was nothing but the act of a kind Fate?

Useless. Johannes thought and spoke nothing but good of anyone. Except himself.

I did not want to hear the lies and boasting of Ahmes. I finished the slice of melon and began to wander back along the broken line of the halted caravan. And there, in the middle of a group of soldiers who each looked even bigger and stronger than Ahmes, I had my first sight of her.

The witch-woman.

At the time she seemed no more than a girl, sitting on the most beautiful little pony that I had ever seen. Can I confess it, that my interest was drawn first to that darling horse, dappled dark-brown and black, with a flowing white mane? I coveted that pony.

She sat upright on its back, muffled in a dark blue cloak from feet to eyes. Those eyes were wide, with irises the color of honey, and eyebrows thick and black above them. From her bearing I took her for a fully mature woman, perhaps the senior wife of one of the merchants. Only when I looked closer could I see that she was not so old. Fifteen or so, and my senior by only two years.

She urged her pony forward along the line toward the head of the caravan. When she arrived there she stood staring at Johannes, and ignoring Ahmes. That was unusual. Ahmes was tall and broad and loud, the dominant figure in most groups.

"Who is that?" I spoke to one of the foot soldiers, a man wearing fronded leather leggings, and pointed to the woman. I had spoken in Turkic, but I was ready to try with Pushtu and Persian and Arabic if that did not work.

He understood me all right, and so did his companions. They all roared with laughter.

"Eyes off her, little warrior," the man said. "She is forbidden fruit. Kings-meat, reserved for the Emperor himself. Anyone who touches her will find he's two balls short. You don't want to lose 'em, do you, before you've had a chance to use 'em?"

He was burly and bearded, but his eyes were good-humored and they took the roughness from his words. And he had told me something of supreme importance. If the woman were intended as a bride or concubine of the Emperor, then the caravan must be bound for Karakoram itself and the court of the Great Khan. That was many days' travel away, but by staying with them, we would reach our own destination. We were luckier than we had realized.

It was late afternoon, and our arrival had provided a sufficient reason for the traveling merchants to stop for the day. The girl came riding slowly back along the line, and the soldier next to me saw my look.

"All right, little warrior, go and talk to her if you want to. Talk is certainly permitted." He laughed, but he was not laughing at me. "We are here to protect her, but not from talk. And we will protect you too, if you need it. Go."

I did not need to approach her. She was heading straight for me. When the pony and I were nose-to-nose, she stopped and pulled the veil of the *chador* from the lower half of her face. I saw a straight nose with flared nostrils, a lower lip full enough to be new-stung by a honeybee from the thyme fields of the Alborz Mountains, and a skin as pale and clear as their first-fallen snow. Kings-meat, indeed.

"Dar-i," she said, and it was the first sign that she was a witch-woman. How did she know my name? "Dari, the caravan is stopping now. When we eat the evening meal, I want to talk to you."

Her accent was strange, her voice deep, and I could only just understand her. She was not from this part of the world, but we had enough common language to talk freely. Before I did more than nod she had swung around and was heading down the line. I was left looking at the pony's swaying haunches. And then Johannes was calling me from the head of the line, needing help to converse with the merchants.

I sighed. How would he have managed without me, if I had died out there in the desert? How *had* he managed, in his many years before we ever met?

Nataree, her name was. She came from the mountains north of Kabul, far to the west of this eastern desert, and because of her great beauty she had been picked out by the local khan from all the girls of his region, and sent to be a bride for the Great Khan; or to be whatever the Great Khan, in his wisdom, wanted her to be.

She smiled when she said that last piece, as though it were a joke. I nodded, just as though I understood, and wondered why we were talking at all. I wanted to get back to Johannes; he was not safe without me.

"Your own journey," she said at last. "It is also to visit the court of the Great Khan?"

"That is correct."

She was silent for a long time, those honey eyes staring into the distant firelight. We were sitting apart from the other groups, off in the cold and dark that fills the world twenty paces or more from the fires. She ate daintily and little, as though food were nothing to her. At last: "But you have no gifts for the Khan, no wives, no jewels, no new inventions?"

And now it was my turn to be silent. Our mission was certainly no secret, but it was perhaps better explained to people by Johannes, not by me. But he could not explain to her!—not until he learned to speak her language. And even then, there were things that he might not want said, about his own reasons for being here. On the other hand, what harm could there be in my telling Nataree of the questions we sought to answer? We would look for information from anyone.

"We are here to learn certain things of the court of the Great Khan," I said at last. "And we do bring gifts. Gifts of learning."

Her eyes glowed with interest. I began to speak, and as I did so I reflected that this at least was not misleading. We brought learning, and no one could doubt Johannes's fittingness as an ambassador of knowledge and wisdom. I had known it the first time we met, at the house of my master, di Piacenza, the papal legate in Acre.

I had been there for two years as a house servant, sold from Bactria via Bokhara. When Johannes appeared at the house he was ushered in at once to see the legate. I was there, as usual, to run errands or to bring tea and sweetmeats. I sat at my master's feet. As Johannes came in I saw this ancient, bent-shouldered man. Then he lifted his head, and something strange and wonderful was revealed. A young man and an old man were living together in one face, with wisdom, knowledge, and love shining from pale blue eyes. I had never seen such abstract intelligence in a human countenance, coupled with such naivete for worldly affairs.

"Welcome, Johannes of Magdeburg," said my master. He spoke of course in Latin, and I had reached the point in my knowledge of that language where I could understand everything that was said. But I had not revealed my progress to M. di Piacenza, not mainly in truth because I sought to deceive him, but because I was thus allowed to be present in many cases where I would otherwise have been excluded. "A good journey from Venice, I trust?" added my master.

Johannes nodded. So far as he and my master the papal legate were concerned, the proprieties had now been observed and they could get down to business. I never ceased to marvel at the abruptness—the crudity—of the leaders of the Church of Jesus. In my homeland, even relative strangers would chat for a few minutes and drink tea or wine together before they began any work of negotiation. Here, it was hello, hello, now let's talk business.

"We have made a list," said my master, "in cooperation with his Holiness and the advisors in Rome. We have seven reports—rumors, let us call them, pending some confirmation—of strange inventions and discoveries in the regions ruled by the Great Khan, Kublai. We would like to know more about them." He held out a roll of paper, tied with bright blue ribbon. "Study these at your leisure as you travel, but let me offer you my own opinions in a few words. First, the Philosophers' Stone, which can transmute base metal to noble metals."

Johannes smiled at once and shook his head.

My master nodded. "I know. We have seen it on a hundred lists, and it never reveals anything but fraud and deceit. But it was reported by Father de Plano Carpini, the Franciscan, on his travels for his Holiness among the Mongols, and he is an honest man. It should be checked. Let us move on to others of more interest. The Auromancers, the little worms that spin golden thread, they sound at first impossible. Except that silk cloth is surely no myth, and there is good evidence that it is made by a little worm or caterpillar, far off in Cathay. You must check the Auromancers. Myself, I believe they exist. Possession of that secret would be a path to great wealth, but we do not ask that you seek to buy or steal an Auromancer. Only seek the knowledge of truth or falsehood of the story.

"Now, I am more skeptical of the Templars, next on our list. I might perhaps believe a centipede three feet long, with a sting fatal to humans—though all such wondrous beasts have a habit of shrinking, you know, the closer you get to their home territory. I find it harder to accept such a centipede as a Templar, a temple guardian intelligent enough to know the difference between worshipers and robbers. And when we are told that such creatures are *themselves* worshipers in the temple, we tread on strange ground indeed: the notion of a soul in the body of a beast. That is a clear heresy. But you, Johannes, will separate truth from falsehood."

(I sat quiet at the feet of M. de Piacenza and hugged myself with excitement. Johannes of Magdeburg was heading off beyond the rising sun, to Cathay or farther, on a journey of magical discovery, and I would give my right hand to go with him. How could I persuade my master to give me permission?)

"I will group together and pass over the questions of birds as big as elephants, or of two-headed fire-breathing lizards, or of peacocks that eat only rocks and shit pure opals," went on my master. "You will surely ask about them. But whether they exist or whether they are no more than myth and legend will make little difference to the Holy Church. Neither property nor belief is at issue, merely human curiosity. However, this last item is another matter." He tapped the yellow paper. "Ants, says Father

Carpini. He heard of ants the size of men, Quarry Ants who operate the diamond mines of the Great Khan. Ants that speak in human tongues, ants who have learned the use of fire, ants who worship a divine creator. You know what that would do to the roots of our beliefs."

Johannes nodded. He knew, but of course I did not—not then. Later, he explained to me that they were concerned because in his religion God made Man in his own image, and so creatures other than those in the shape of Man could not worship or have souls. They would have to be Satanic creations, inventions of the Devil.

"Now," concluded my master. "Here is the letter from his Holiness, for delivery to the Great Khan Kublai. According to Father Carpini, the Great Khan lives in such splendor that material gifts are useless, although almost everyone offers them. We hope that your own scientific and mathematical powers will interest the Khan more than anything else. Do you have any new suggestions for this?"

While my master was still speaking, Johannes reached into his battered brown bag of calf's leather and pulled out a little book, bound in red. "This is not new, but I think it may be new to the court of the Great Khan. It is the *Liber Abaci* of Leonardo of Pisa, known as Fibonacci. I have studied it closely, and I believe it to be of overwhelming importance for science."

"Indeed." My master looked at the book, and to tell the truth there was a skepticism in his voice that only someone who knew him well would recognize. "This little volume here?"

"Yes. It introduces a quantity, the *sifr*, or *cifra*, and a new way of writing numbers based upon it. I agree with Fibonacci, this will transform every aspect of calculation, from astronomy to the sale of goods. With your permission, and the permission of his Holiness, I propose to instruct the philosophers at the court of the Great Khan in the mathematical techniques of the *Liber Abaci*."

"Oh certainly, certainly, do that if you wish."

But it was clear that my master thought this of little consequence compared with Auromancers and Templars and Quarry Ants.

By contrast, Nataree seemed indifferent when I spoke of

animals with near-magical powers, and flamed with curiosity when I mentioned the little book that Johannes carried with him everywhere.

She had huddled inside her cloak as she listened to me talk of Johannes and our mission, with only her eyes showing. Now she suddenly stirred and said, "Tell me more about the book. Tell me what it allows you to do."

I tried to explain; and of course, I could not. I had heard Johannes talk a hundred times of the new methods, and seen him do calculations so fast that some scholars swore he must be in league with the Devil; but nothing of Johannes's technique had ever made sense to me.

Nataree listened to me for a while, then pushed back her cowl and stood up. "Dari, you do not make sense. It is not your fault. I will talk about this to Johannes myself."

And then she was moving, heading for the line of camp fires. As she walked away, I was tempted to shout after her, "Talk all you want, you silly girl. Johannes does not speak your language, and you do not speak his." Then I shivered, and remained silent. I realized that in the hour or less that we had been talking together, Nataree had somehow caught much of my vocabulary and accent, and was already speaking closer to my own choice of tongue. I am quick with languages; most people would say, incredibly quick. Could anyone, ever, learn another's language in a few hours or a few days? Only, I would say it again, if she were a witch-woman.

I was cold, not fully recovered from our ordeal in the desert, and again feeling hungry; but I did not go back at once to the cooking pots and the warmth of the fires. I felt strongly disloyal and ashamed. In thinking to acquire information, I had learned nothing, and perhaps I had told too much.

It was good that Nataree had left when she did. Otherwise the force of those pale, piercing eyes might have sucked out of me the rest of the story of my first meeting with Johannes; and that was something that he surely wanted no one to know about—not even me.

My master, when the official business was over, had drawn a chair up close to Johannes, and his voice changed to a solemn tone I had never heard him use before. I froze at his feet.

"My son," he said, and Johannes bowed his head. "Do not look on this journey as a punishment, or even as a penance."

"Father di Piacenza, your holiness, I try not to not think of it that way. I try to see it as an opportunity."

"It is, indeed. An opportunity to give service to God, and a chance to renew your faith. If you would like to tell me what happened to you . . ."

Johannes had sighed like an old, old man. "That is part of the problem. Nothing happened. There was no event, no moment of temptation, no sight of Satan high on a church spire trumpeting at me like a thousand elephants to bring me to sin. But the more I studied, the more I asked questions, the more I tried to understand—the less became my certainty. I waited and prayed and hoped. Six months ago I at last went to Monsignor Alienti and asked for advice. He suggested some kind of pilgrimage, and thought that with my interests and background in the sciences, one of an unusual type might better serve both me and the Holy Church. And so here I am."

There was a great simplicity and honesty to Johannes, no one could mistake that. And although what he said made no sense at all to me, apparently it did to my master. "If the result of this mission is that you are helped," he said, "then even if nothing else is accomplished, it will not be a failure. A soul is quite beyond price. Nothing is more important than your return to full conviction."

Johannes's eyes were turned down, but I could see them from where I was sitting. Instead of the clear certainty they held when he spoke about mathematics and the *Liber Abaci*, now they were tormented and filled with misery.

"You have questions," my master went on. "The Church has no objection to questions. It welcomes debate and logical thought; it even thrives on paradox. But logic must ultimately be subordinated to Faith. We begin with Faith, and end with Faith, and Faith conquers all. If in your studies there was a failure to understand God's plans for the world down to the level of the smallest logical detail, that is proof only of human fallibility. It adds to the glory of

God, if understanding Him is not simple. You are making a grave error, if you say, 'Because I cannot understand everything, God is lacking'! Remember again, the soul of a human is priceless."

I listened closely—and still I had little idea what he was talking about! It was more of the cold tangle of Christ that I heard so often in the palace. All words and no warmth. But this time I felt something new: the pain in Johannes. I was so drawn to him, so taken with him, I could not dismiss this dialogue as unimportant.

"Perhaps," Johannes said after a few moments of silence, "I will convert the Great Khan himself, to make him become a follower of Christ."

His voice was wistful. My master blew that sorrow away with a great gust of laughter.

"Ah, my Johannes, would that you could! But no, we are not so ambitious as that. Go east, and bring back a little new knowledge, and your faith made whole, and that will be all we can ask." He finally noticed me, staring up at him, and switched at once to speak in Persian. "Now then, Dari, why are you still here? Off, and bring *chai* for our honored guest."

I would never have a better chance.

"Master," I said, and bowed low. "The honored guest has come a great distance, and I think he must travel farther. I heard you talk of the court of the Great Khan. That is far, far away. If the guest does not know the language you are using now, or those of the tribes still farther to the east, he will find travel very difficult. I have some gift for languages. I would be honored to serve him, and speak to others on his behalf."

My master stared at me as though he had never seen me before in his whole life. I shivered, and waited. At last he smiled. "This desire to serve does you credit, Dari. But there is one problem. How can you help the holy Johannes, when you cannot even speak *his* language. What would you be able to say to him, or on his behalf, if you cannot understand him?"

"I would say"—and now I turned to face Johannes himself, and changed to Latin; not very good Latin, on purpose, since I did not want to upset my master with my earlier eavesdropping—*"Domine,* I want to serve you. My Lord, I will go with you wherever you go, and speak on your behalf, and make your goals my only goals."

M. di Piacenza's mouth hung open. "Such cheek! You'll do no such thing. Be off with you, little Dari, get out of here and bring hot tea. Johannes and I have much to talk about."

I went, and my feet bore me along the carpeted corridor like the wings of eagles. My master might fool Johannes with the severity of his manner, but he did not fool me. When he was angry he called me 'Daryush,' when he was pleased with me, it was 'Dari'; when he was *really* pleased, it was 'little Dari.'

I was going, I was going, I was going, I was going.

Johannes of Magdeburg and I, we would travel east and east and farther east. We would walk the shining world, go together beyond the eye of the rising sun, to travel the Great Silk Road—the Dragon Road, the Smoke Road, the Snowy Road, the Golden Road, the magic road that would lead to the court of the Great Khan himself.

I hugged myself. I was going!

When I lived in Bactria, before I was sold to M. di Piacenza, I slept always with the horses and the camels. My master told me at once when I reached Acre that he did not want me stinking of animals in his house, and he made me bathe often and sleep in an inside chamber; but I have never lost my fondness for the warmth and comforting smell of the great beasts.

In desert country, now, where there is no hope of forage, all the animals of the caravan are herded together for the night in the middle of the circle of camp fires. It is smelly and intimate there, and the finest place in the world in freezing weather. When I at last came in from the darkness, chilled to the bone, I headed inside the circle for old time's sake, and also for a late-night look at Nataree's beautiful dappled pony.

To my surprise, Johannes was at the first camp fire I came to—and he was sitting with Ahmes and Nataree.

I watched for a few moments before I joined them. Johannes had his beloved *Liber Abaci* held out in front of him, and he was doing most of the talking. Nataree was listening very closely, and asking occasional questions in a slow and correct Persian. My teaching for the past year had been enough to allow Johannes to follow her, and to reply to her.

"So this mark," she was saying. "The *sifr*. It does not mean that *hichi*—nothing—is there. It says that there is something specific there; that in this space there are no tens in this particular number. So it serves to mark the place where numbers of tens are written. This number, 308, has none of the tens. Three tens of tens in this place, here. No tens, in this place here. And eight units, here."

"Exactly right!" Johannes leaned forward and gripped the hand that touched the book, something which he definitely should not have done. I looked around at once to see if her guards had seen, but they were arguing and dozing by the next fire. "And the *sifr* can mark the position of any sort of number—it could show, for instance, that there are no hundreds in a number which has some thousands and some tens. It makes calculation easy, almost trivial."

Nataree was nodding, while Ahmes was yawning. I can't say that I blame him. I'd heard Johannes and his "sifr position notation" far too often myself. But Ahmes was by no means asleep. His eyes were on Nataree, and the expression they held was one that I had seen a hundred times. I am perhaps a little skinny, but I am fair-skinned and graceful in movement, and many men have found me attractive. I have never given myself to one, but I recognize that red-eyed glaze of blind lust easily enough; and Ahmes had it now. If he was not careful, he would get himself into worse trouble than any he had seen so far.

"Teach me more!" said Nataree suddenly. "Let us do another calculation!"

"Give me a problem!" Johannes was as excited as she, like a child showing off a toy. "Any numbers that you choose."

"My age, added to your age, added to his age, added to his age." She pointed at me and Ahmes.

"Too simple—once I know the ages." Johannes made a column of numbers. "Twenty-eight, that is me. Thirteen, that is Dari. Ahmes, how old are you?"

"Twenty-three years." The soldier shrugged. "And what good will your answer be when you get it?"

"And I am fifteen," said Nataree. But as Johannes made his column of numbers, and did odd things with it, I saw through her game. She wanted to know how old Johannes was. And she found out, without asking.

But why did she want to know? To cast horoscopes, perhaps? To set a spell on him? Nothing made sense. She was destined to be a bride of the Great Khan, that was her future, and the future of Johannes was irrelevant to her.

I was suspicious. I disliked Nataree anyway, without needing more reason. She was a witch-woman, and I had already given her too much information about me and about Johannes.

The whole desert was wider than Ahmes had said—far wider. If we had not met the caravan, the three of us would have ended as sun-dried corpses, days short of any supply of water and we had been only in the Little Desert, the western end of the Great Desert.

Even with the experienced merchants of the caravan to guide us, the journey across that Great Desert was not easy. The most foolhardy traveler would not plunge on into the heart of the *Takla Makan Shamo* itself, the place that we had been heading for, in our sublime ignorance. The caravan turned north on the Great Desert's western margin, to find and follow the southern edge of the *Tien Shan*, the Celestial Mountains, where we could take our water from their snow-melt.

It was four weeks before we reached the plain that we would follow northeast toward Karakoram itself. The weather turned colder and colder. We would find Karakoram, home of the Great Khan, a snow-girt city with (according to false legend) walls of gold and towers of diamond.

Not that at all, said the merchants, many of whom had made this journey before. But a place of incredible wealth, nonetheless. And what, pray, did we hope to trade there?

They were polite, but it was a politeness reserved for madmen. I could tell what they thought of us, but Johannes could not. He did not speak Turkic. He knew what he knew only through my translations, and I was not about to translate the "Ah!"s and "Oh, yes?"s and "Indeed?"s that greeted discussions of new science and strange mathematics.

After the first week with the caravan I began to be aware of other things. The caravan itself was by no means a single unit, as it had seemed when we first encountered it. It comprised three groups in addition to us. First, the true merchants, devoted only to the acquisition and sale of trade goods. They were easy to understand, because the nature of a trader is the same in Samarkand or Karakoram as it is in Acre or Persepolis. Unless they were dead, they would haggle endlessly and price everything they saw. If they could have done it, they would have set a value for my master on Johannes's immortal soul, something he had said was impossible!

Then there was the party from Kabul, including Nataree and her guardian soldiers. She would arrive at Karakoram a virgin, they told me, or they would all die. According to Khosro, my soldier friend in the leather leggings, a girl-gift for the Great Khan had once arrived in Karakoram from the local khan not only seduced, but visibly pregnant! The local khan's ambassador in Karakoram had ordered that the whole group of guards be flayed alive. The Great Khan, in his compassion, had given instructions that the men be strangled first, before their skins were removed and sent back to Kabul. There was no love, according to my friend, between the Great Khan and the lesser khan of Kabul. The homage offered to Karakoram was a grudging and reluctant one, provided only because of fear of the Great Khan's long arm of power.

With that threat of slow death hanging over them, it was amazing to me that the guards of Nataree took their duties so lightly. That they would allow me to talk to her freely and even wander outside the camp with her was not perhaps so surprising, since my voice was not yet a man's voice. But she wandered the whole caravan, with apparently control or even surveillance of her actions. I understood that better after a few days. The man who could seduce or rape Nataree would be an unusual one. The fire and ice in her eye frightened most people away (though not

Ahmes—he still had that look). She spent her time as she chose, almost all of it talking endlessly to Johannes about things that no sensible person was interested in. He was delighted! For the first time, someone cared about science and mathematics and understood his precious *Liber Abaci* as fully as he did.

And beyond that, Nataree learned Persian—and Latin from long sessions with Johannes—so fast it surprised even me. However, not even the guards were worried about Johannes. They saw him as a holy man, a man whose life was consumed with learning, one whose pure soul shone from his clear eyes.

What fools we were, all of us! We could not see Johannes as she saw him.

Well, with Johannes talking and talking to Nataree and not wanting an interpreter at the moment, I had plenty of time on my own hands. The third group in the caravan was the drovers, the men who looked after the horses and the camels. Since I had been raised among drovers, it was natural for me to seek them out. Within a few days I was a dungboy, an honorary member of the group. We trailed last in the caravan, and carefully collected all the dung and dried it. Each morning we did the same thing within the camp. In the desert it was our main fuel, the difference between raw, unpleasant food and delicious cooked food.

A dungboy is like a fly, present everywhere and totally invisible. No one noticed me with my flat pan and shovel. And as we were emerging from the foothills of the Celestial Mountains I saw something I was not supposed to see.

One of the soldiers sent to guard Nataree was an odd man out. His name was Maseed, and he was a skeletal, long-limbed man with a huge nose and a walleye. But it was his actions, not his appearance, that made him noteworthy. While the others sat around the fires, drinking or dozing, he sneaked off by himself, outside the perimeter. With nothing better to do, I went after him; and since he took pains to make sure he would not be followed, why, I took even more pains to avoid being seen. Once he was convinced that he was alone, he set a cup on top of a rock, moved three or four paces away, and threw a small round pellet toward it. I say he threw, but actually the pellet was

propelled with an almost imperceptible flick of the middle
fingertip from the thumb, and flew so fast and so invisibly
that I knew of its motion only by the rattle of its arrival in
the cup. His accuracy was astonishing. I counted, and he
missed only one or two times in a hundred. Even when I
looked for it, I could not follow the pellet's flight.

He did the same thing over and over, day after day;
flicked and flicked, while I watched and wondered. What
was he doing? I was tempted to ask Nataree about it, to see
if it was a game or custom of her country, but I never did. I
would not accept the idea of her doing me any favors.

No less odd, late one night I crept out to watch Maseed
. . . and found Ahmes with him. They were away from the
others by their own little camp fire, heads close together.

"One simple act," Maseed was saying, "and that one
with no risk. A moment's diversion. After that, wealth will
be yours."

"And the other?" asked Ahmes. "The fair one was
promised."

"The promise will be kept. Her body will be yours, to
do as you like with. But you must make the move exactly
when I tell you, precisely as I direct. Then there will be no
danger at all."

I had often wondered what Ahmes was doing on this
journey. I had suspected the oldest motives in the world:
blood and gold. Now I had proof of that, and I was ready
to add lust to the list. Ahmes was a mercenary, pure and
simple, and he could be bought by anyone who could afford him. But as to *what* he and Maseed were doing . . .

I waited and watched, a lesson I had learned almost
before I could walk.

Meanwhile, we steadily drew nearer to the city of Karakoram, the home of the Great Khan. From twenty miles
away it was finally visible across the snowy plain, a great
rising tower of blue smoke above the horizon. When we
camped for the last night, we sent our runners on ahead to
make sure that the Great Khan knew we were arriving. An
unnecessary gesture, the merchants said, since Kublai
Khan's own intelligence service had made him aware of
our approach for at least the past five days; however, noti-
fication of arrival was diplomatically necessary.

On that final cold evening, I sat close to the camp fire and listened while Johannes and Nataree talked together. Not on the speculation of any sane person, as to the sights and sounds to be found in the court of the Great Khan. By no means. It was as bad as being back in Acre, listening to Johannes and my master.

"You do not understand," he was saying. "Faith is the most important thing in the whole world, since it leads not only to happiness on earth but to life eternal. And faith is what I lost. I have lost it still."

"No," she said. "It is you, Johannes, who understand nothing." She was speaking Latin, and it jolted me to realize that her knowledge of that language now seemed to match my own. "You say you have lost faith. All that you lost is simpleminded certainty. There are many faiths in this world, dozens of them, hundreds of them. Who is to say that your church's Trinity is truer than this man's demons, or that man's different beliefs? Your prophet, Christ, you say he is the son of God, and he was taken to the top of a high mountain and tempted with all the treasures of the world. Very well. I am the daughter of God, or at least one of God's daughters. If you would allow me, I could take you to another peak, just as real, and tempt you with a whole other world, just as sacred."

It sounded as though she were offering her body—and yet just as clearly that was not what she meant at all, for she went on, "You tell me yourself, your geometry and your calculations are eternal, pure logic that will exist forever. The proof of the parabola theorem that you showed me today, what could ever be more beautiful than that? Surely *these,* and not some fixed group of worldly ideas, are your *veritates aeternae,* your eternal verities."

"You don't understand me," said Johannes. He sounded anguished, and yet at the same time enthralled. He loved this sort of pointless talk. "What I mean is this . . ."

And off he went, on another camel ride across a desert of theories and proofs. He was the most handsome and wonderful man I had ever known, and he was never anything but patient and thoughtful. But he was also the world's most obstinate and persistent man when it came to his ideas, and the hardest man to understand when he talked about them. But perhaps she did understand him, very well. For although they had talked like this many times, endlessly, hour after hour, neither ever seemed to tire of it.

I left, and became a dungboy again. No one saw me, wandering along with my flat pan and shovel. And near the end of the camp, where few people went because the food and water was far off at the front, I again saw Ahmes and Maseed. They were saying little, but Ahmes was holding a beautiful little shield of polished brass. Maseed had placed a metal cup on a rock, and was standing four paces from it. In the twilight, I saw him lift his left hand to touch his ear, and at that moment Ahmes dropped the shield. It fell clanging to the ground, and a second later Maseed flicked his finger. There was a rattle of a round pellet into the cup.

"Very good," he said, and he laughed, but there was no humor in his voice. "One more time, and that will be the last time."

It was something bad. Maseed was a bad man. I knew that, as surely as I knew that Johannes of Magdeburg was a good man. But what were they doing? I sought Johannes, to ask his advice, but he was no longer by the fire, nor was he with Nataree. She was with her guards, settled in for the night.

I wandered around the whole camp, and finally went into the beasts' circle and lay down for comfort next to the dappled pony. Tomorrow that pony would carry Nataree into Karakoram itself. And then perhaps Johannes would stop talking and begin his search for the knowledge that we came for. It would be nice to know we had succeeded, and could begin to think whenever we chose about the journey home.

Karakoram certainly had walls, but they were not of gold, nor were its towers of diamond. According to Johannes, it was less of a city than other places he had been, Paris and Rome and Athens. However, it was a wonderland by my standards, and it was undeniably the home of the Great Khan, ruler over an empire that stretched across more than half the world.

We came to it across a long, cleared plain, and from

miles away we could see the great palace within the walls. It was huge, a hundred paces long and seventy wide, towering up on its sixty-four wooden columns on their granite bases. Inside the city itself most of the buildings were of brick, including Shamanist shrines, mosques, and temples of Buddha.

"And perhaps one day," said Johannes, "a Church of Christ." But he did not sound very confident.

I had finally found out where he went the previous evening. He had wandered off by himself, alone into the night, something he was apt to do when he wanted to work hard on his beloved calculations. No one else in the world had his power of concentration on a single problem. I had known him to stay in one place for twenty-four hours, totally lost in thought.

Today he was pale and moody, rubbing the palm of his hand along his forehead and his unshaven chin. I told him what had happened last night with Ahmes and Maseed, and asked him what he thought was going on. He heard me all right, I know he did, but instead of replying he stared at me as though I were a passing cloud. Then he reached out, and touched me gently on the shoulder.

I said he was never anything but loving and patient, and that is true. But when the philosophical fit was on him, he could be unreachable.

We were entering Karakoram, the whole unwieldy procession of us, and soon we learned that our audience with Kublai Khan would not happen for another day. Fortunately, most people in the caravan were not seeking to pay their respects to the Great Khan. The merchants went their way, the drovers another, and a group of about a dozen of us, including Nataree and her guards, were left to hang around near the entrance to the palace, and haggle with the local merchants for an evening meal at inflated prices. I did our haggling. Johannes was not good at that sort of thing; he would believe whatever the storekeepers told him.

After dinner I once more sought him out. As always, he was talking to Nataree, their incomprehensible babble of circles and lines and squares. I interrupted them. I told Johannes again what I had seen with Maseed, and at last I asked Nataree if she, as Maseed's countrywoman, knew the meaning of his ritual. She listened closely, and so did Johannes, but then they both shook their heads. They did not disbelieve me, but the mystery remained.

Our audience with the Great Khan had been set for early the next day. Soon after dawn Nataree's soldiers were up and busy polishing their brass. They all wore new tunics and their best headgear.

I wished I could have done the same. I was supposed to be the interpreter for Johannes, and although in the desert a little dirt didn't show, now I was aware of the whiff of horse and camel dung that came from my clothes. Brushing at the dirt just made it worse.

All the groups who would be presented to the Khan entered the palace at the same time. Naturally, all weapons, and anything that might conceivably be used as a weapon, were left outside with the palace guards. It would hardly be a necessary precaution, since the person of the Great Khan was always surrounded by his trained guards.

First into the palace was a group of rich merchant princes from India. They were seeking trade agreements, and to increase their chances they brought lavish gifts of ivory, jade, and sapphires. Next was the Nataree party, with smarmy Maseed in front and Ahmes, bearing the little ornamental shield on a velvet cushion, just behind. It was clear that it was to be a gift for Kublai Khan. Nataree, beautifully dressed in a long gown of purple and white, walked demurely after them. She looked no more impressed by the court of the Great Khan than she did by anything else.

We came last, after Nataree, with Johannes clutching his copy of the *Liber Abaci*. It seemed pathetic, and I wondered what sort of reception we were likely to get. Ivory and jewels as gifts, then a beautiful new wife, and then us, a dung-smelling servant and a man carrying one battered book with the world's most boring information inside it.

The greeting hall itself was enough to unnerve me. It was over forty paces long, and the floor and walls were covered with the most beautiful tapestries and carpets I ever saw. Each one depicted some aspect of the life of the Great Khan—hunting, hawking, receiving royal guests, bestowing honors, or sitting in judgment on cases of noble wrongdoing. The rugs of the greeting hall were so thick that our advance across them was almost silent.

At the far end of the hall the Great Khan was already present. He was sitting on a carved wood and ivory throne, painted in gold and brown, and as we all came in he did a surprising thing. He stood up, and then to my amazement he walked past the Indian merchant princes, past Ahmes and Maseed and Nataree, and right up to Johannes. He stared at us without speaking. His robes were fine gold cloth, woven perhaps from the thread of the Auromancers that we had come so far to study, and he carried a long golden staff.

"Great Emperor," I said, and my voice cracked on the first word. "It is an honor to be here at this great court. We bring no material gifts, but our respect is not less for that. We hope we bring something more precious than rubies or gold. We bring knowledge."

His face was stern and terrible, with a long, straggly mustache across a thin upper lip. But then he smiled, just a little. "A king can have enough gems and jewels," he said. "But no man can ever have enough knowledge. And I receive wives on many days, but strangers from so far away are a rarity. Welcome."

Johannes was smiling also, not understanding a word. My knees were wobbling. All I could say—croak, that's a better word, for my voice had chosen the worst possible moment to begin breaking to a man's tones—the one word I could utter was "Thankyou."

Fortunately it did not matter, because the Great Khan had taken the *Liber Abaci* from Johannes's hands and was already turning to the other groups. Our audience was not over, but to avoid a slight to anyone, all would be greeted formally before longer discussions began.

The group accompanying Nataree presented to the Great Khan a set of gorgeous goblets of finely chased gold, and equally fine plates on which they were seated. He took them, made a little speech of formal thanks, and called at once for wine. A servant hurried forward with a glass flask and filled the cups, passing one each to half a dozen of the surrounding nobles.

One of Nataree's party offered a toast, to the long life

and prosperity of the Great Khan, and lifted his cup. Kublai smiled, but instead of drinking he passed his own goblet to a dark-skinned servant standing next to him. The black man sniffed cautiously at the wine and poured a few drops into a little beaker that he held. We waited. When nothing happened after a few seconds, the man sipped a little wine and finally nodded. He handed the goblet back to Kublai Khan.

While this had been happening, the whole assembly was frozen—until the Great Khan moved, no one could move. When he finally took the goblet, and lifted it in front of him, everyone relaxed and lifted his own glass.

Out of the corner of my eye, I saw Maseed reach up to scratch his left ear. Inevitably, I looked across at Ahmes, and at that very moment he dropped the brass shield from its velvet cushion. It made a hollow, brazen boom as it hit the thick carpet. Everyone turned to see what was causing the noise.

Everyone except me. I knew what would happen next, and already I had turned to look at Maseed. The flick of the finger against the thumb was a tiny movement in the direction of the Great Khan. I waited for the familiar rattle that signified the arrival of a pellet within a cup. When it did not come I thought for a moment that he must have missed his target; and then I realized that a full goblet of wine would silence the sound completely.

One of Nataree's guards had bent over to pick up the dropped ornamental shield, while another was giving Ahmes a vicious cut across the shoulders with a whip.

The Great Khan, after the few moments of distraction, ignored what was happening to Ahmes. He offered a brief and formal statement of thanks and a welcome to Karakoram, and again raised the goblet to his lips. As he did so, I leaned close to Johannes and whispered, "He did it, same as I told you. Threw something—into the Great Khan's cup."

I spoke in Latin, probably with some brainless idea that my insolence in speaking in front of the Great Khan would somehow be less in a foreign language.

Johannes had no such inhibitions, and for once he was not off in his clouds of calculation. He looked at me for one split second. Then he jumped forward, pointed at the Khan's goblet, and cried out what I knew but dared not think: "Don't drink that cup! It's poisoned."

He was lucky he wasn't run through on the spot. Not knowing the language, he had shouted in Persian. Half the Khan's guards had no idea what he was saying. But then Nataree took an instant cue from Johannes, and she shouted out, too, in Turkic: "Don't drink. Poison!"

There was a tremendous hubbub. The Khan had the gold goblet at his lips. Now he jerked it away. The soldiers around him drew their swords, but of course they didn't know what to do next. They had seen nothing, and had no idea who to attack.

Maseed, standing four paces away, tried to look innocent, but I recovered my voice, pointed at him, and cried, "That one! He threw a pellet into the cup, when you were all looking at the dropped shield."

Well, Maseed was too wily to run, but it did him no good. After five minutes questioning of me and, through me, Johannes, Kublai Khan had learned all that we knew and surmised. He ordered that Maseed and Ahmes be taken away and forced to drink from the same goblet. Maseed began to scream and beg for mercy. But as the Great Khan said, if the goblet were not poisoned, then no harm would come to them.

It showed us that he was a merciful Khan. Whatever happened to Maseed and Ahmes, it would be better than a death by slow torture.

They were dragged away. Kublai Khan turned again to me and Johannes.

"Tell your master this," he said to me, as calmly as though assassination attempts happened every day. "I owe him my life. Tell him to ask any favor, and if it is in my power I swear that it will be granted."

Well, this was the moment when I knew that Johannes and I would succeed brilliantly in our mission. The Great Khan was promising it. Auromancers, Templars, Quarry Ants, we would learn all there was to know about every one of them.

Johannes was silent for a long time when I told him the Great Khan's promise. The whole court waited. At last he turned away and looked at Nataree. She nodded, with one slow movement of her head, and closed her eyes as though in prayer.

Johannes looked back at the Great Khan. "I would like . . ." He paused, and his voice strengthened. "I would like to take this woman, Nataree. I ask that you allow us to travel freely, she and I, through your territories, toward the rising sun and beyond, on to the end of the world to seek true knowledge."

Everyone was silent, waiting for a translation. My heart was a lump of stone. I had to pass on those words, but it was too much for me. I stood, tongue-tied, until at last one of the merchants chimed in to translate what Johannes had said.

Then the Great Khan frowned. "Nataree?" he said. He looked at Johannes in incomprehension.

An old advisor came forward and whispered something in his ear. Kublai Khan nodded, but he looked no less astonished. He stepped closer to Johannes.

"Honored guest, you have saved my life. For far less than you have done, a hundred women would be yours. That gift is not sufficient. The woman Nataree is nothing to me—why should she be, when I never saw her before today? Ask again, and ask more, much more, or you will shame me as the Great Khan of the Tartars."

Again the merchant translated for Johannes, and at last he nodded. This was it, surely, the moment when he would ask for the answers to all our questions. But he did not. Instead, he moved to Nataree's side, put his arm around her—and turned to point at me!

"That young man" (a man at last! But how bitter the feeling) "is Dari. He is as dear to me as my own life. He has no parents, no family. Would you take him, Great Khan, and give him a home and an education here, in Karakoram?"

The Great Khan stared at me while the request was translated, and I felt a shiver from top to toe.

"Come here," he said at last. "Come close."

I walked forward, and began to kneel before him. He caught my arm in a grip that could have broken it, and would not allow me to sink to the floor. Before I knew what was happening, he pulled me close and kissed me on the forehead, then on both cheeks. He looked around him.

"Dari belongs here," he said. "From this day he is not Dari, he is *Dari Mangu,* and he is a member of my own family." And then he went on—the thing that made the whole court gasp aloud: "Dari Mangu is my son, as much as any of my sons. Like them, he is in the line of succession to become the Emperor, next ruler of Karakoram, the Great Khan of the Tartars. Come, all of you, and offer loyalty and obeisance."

Man after man came forward.

I stood there quaking, the smell of dung still strong upon me, while promises of love and servitude poured into my ears. After half a minute, I began to weep.

That was one year ago. The snows have come again to Karakoram, but Johannes and Nataree have not returned. They went off to the east, to the great sea and beyond.

I think about them always. Did Johannes find a faith, I wonder, somewhere in the breathing world, to replace what he lost long ago in Magdeburg? Did Nataree show him, as she promised, all the kingdoms of the earth?

I do not know.

I thought that Nataree was a witch-woman when first I met her, and I think she is a witch-woman still. But now I suspect that every woman is a witch-woman, casting her spells on men.

I do not hate Nataree, but I resent her greater freedom. Even as a gift-girl to the Great Khan, she could do what I could not. When she held those long, intense conversations with Johannes as we traveled from the Great Desert to Karakoram, she surely fell in love with him. That was easy to do. But having fallen, she could then speak her love. Whereas I . . .

I could not, because he would not allow it. The Holy Church of Johannes told him that love from me was anathema, a mortal sin, a love so forbidden that it was wrong even to say its name.

I was trapped. I loved, as much as she, perhaps more than she, but I could not speak without making him feel revulsion.

And so I live on, in the court of the Great Khan. I have power, I have luxury, I have influence. Perhaps one day I will in truth become the Great Khan, Emperor, Lord of the Tartars, ruler of Karakoram and half of the known world.

Power, glory, honor, possessions: those are all mine. They feel like nothing. Nothing but waiting, waiting, until the convergence of the Great Arcs at last brings its own peace.

It was right for Johannes to leave his old Church, with its cold Christ, its stern laws, its bleak Heaven. There was nothing there for him, nothing for anyone who loves.

But if he had to leave that church, why could he not have left it for me?

THE RUSE THAT
FAILED

And when the Venetian finished his tale, all three men sat silent and thoughtful.

Finally, Peter looked up and smiled at the other two. "Have we all somehow insulted one another? Or have we, instead, each insulted ourselves lest anyone else do so? Yet, I think that only friendship has been meant. Do you agree?"

He glanced over at the Jew, who had said that he sought wisdom. Apparently, wisdom included the nature of the men with whom he must deal; and he took some fairly drastic ways of acquiring it. Elazar met his eyes and shrugged.

Laughter, when it came, was irresistible and long-needed. "Gentlemen, brothers," Peter said between chuckles, "oh, how I like your ways with words!" He clapped the shorter, older Jewish sage on the shoulder.

Elazar managed—just—not to flinch away from that overly hearty accolade. The Venetian shrugged.

Embarrassed, Peter sought a distraction to break the mood.

As if his wish were father to the deed (which in this place it might well be), he saw a flicker of opalescent light. "Look! Is that a djinni?"

"The light is much like what we saw when you first approached," said the Venetian.

"Not so! This is brighter and more varied, but not, I think, the aura of a djinni. Perhaps it is some other poor prisoner," said Elazar. "Let us wait and see."

The light brightened, reaching a rainbow frenzy then

275

moderating and expanding. Now it was a cloud.

Finally it resolved into a nimbus of light that illumined the figure of a youth who, clearly, had not yet his full man's height, muscle, or beard. He was garbed in the dress of a noble Hindu, and he carried himself with the unconscious grace of a prince.

"Of Rajasthan," said the Venetian. "Such men are warriors."

"There is no battle here," called the approaching Hindu, "for here there is no battlefield, no, nor cause for war, save against our captors."

"Well spoken!" Peter said. "Do you know aught of this place?"

Without replying to that question, the Hindu stopped in his tracks. "Never have I seen one such as you, save in carvings of Iskandar, who, it is said, had eyes like the sky. But you, with your hair like a rakshasa; surely you are not of Iskandar's race . . ."

"A rakshasa is a fire demon," supplied Elazar.

"A salamander?" Peter whispered, revolted both by that idea and by the Hindu's too-obvious admiration. How far had the precious tales carried, anyhow? What made it worse was that this too-perfect young stranger moved with the grace of the statues of Krishna he had seen and admired in Khotan. He did not want to admire this princeling, not at all. He did not even want to meet his eyes.

"I am a man of the West," he answered curtly. "I came with a caravan for which I seek freedom. Know you aught of this place?"

The Hindu advanced, standing too close to him. That in itself was no overture or insult; to an Englishman, no one in the East ever stood at a sufficient distance. You were forever inhaling another's breath, treading on his toes—not to mention what you might do to his honor should you grow angry at the constant press, the too-close faces surrounding you. A circle of clear space about one was not a thing that men of the East required; and Peter had had years to accustom himself to that, and not to flinch aside, as now he did. The Hindu smiled and stepped back, flicking his eyes to his feet for a moment.

"I have some small power of foreknowledge," he said.

"And I have found a place where, I think, such may be applied."

"Can you find it again?" asked Elazar.

"Aye," said the Hindu. "Magic, like a beast to be hunted, leaves its own spoor. Come; let us track it."

Having no choice, they followed. The sky, had Peter glanced upward, could have shown no stranger assortment of men. Under pretext of guarding their flank, he took care to stay well away from the Hindu.

Abruptly, their reflection confronted them, slanting down until they faced themselves, distorted, elongated.

"The wall of the bottle!" Peter approached and ran a hand down it. It was cool, pleasant to the touch, without the slight bumps and irregularities of ordinary ware. The Venetian rapped it with his knuckles and nodded approvingly.

"Can it be shattered, do you think?" Peter wondered. His hand dropped to his sword, then flinched away. Taking his headcloth, he wrapped his hand in it and grasped the scabbarded sword and detached it from his belt. The stink of singed cloth rose; God grant he did not smell singed flesh as well.

"No!" cried Elazar.

"What other choice do we have?" asked the Venetian. The Hindu folded his arms and murmured something about karma.

With all Peter's strength, he swung the hilt of his sword against the glass of their prison.

It rang like the Ch'in gong that had been the prize of his partner's last caravan.

"The blessings of Allah be upon you and upon your newfound friends," intoned the Emir of the Djinn of the deep desert. Did he look darker of hair, less wearied than he had before, or was that a trick of the light?

"Oh, fool, fool," said the Emir. "Did you think that we have not tried to shatter our prison? How should mere Sons of Adam succeed where the djinn have failed?"

"A trick," Peter snarled at the Hindu. "You tricked me, you rotten . . ."

"Hold!" The Emir of the Djinn held up clawed fingers. "Your companions did not betray you. Things will go as

they are, not as you would have them. But if you are looking for a scapegoat"—Elazar eyed knight and djinni warily
—"look to your own rashness, your own temper, which
burns as hot as your hair."

Did everyone have to comment on his hair now? Peter
flung down the scorched headcloth in mute frustration, and
the djinni shook his head.

"And is it also not truly written in your own Book, man
of the West, that anger is a deadly sin?"

Peter forced out the admission: "Aye. One of the dead-
liest."

"Then you should thank me for preventing you from
falling further into sin. Or into discourtesy; for my thrice-
honored father, he who resigned the rule of the djinn of the
deep desert, is about to tell his tale, and you must be
present to hear him."

Then it was hopeless, all hopeless. All of Peter's
travels, all of his care had come to this: the companionship
of strangers, the contempt of a djinni, and a hand that
began to ache abominably where his sword and scorched it.
His eyes began to sting almost as badly as his hand.

"I have salve for burns," Elazar started to say, but the
djinni forestalled him.

"No need. The journey back in time will heal him, for it
will undo the action that cost him that pain. Now, my
guests, if you will prepare yourselves . . ."

They were falling upward again; the wind was rushing
by as the djinni raced back toward the amphitheatre, wherever it was; and, worst of all, the djinni was laughing at his
hopelessness.

THE TALE OF THE THIRD DJINNI

The Emir of the Djinn of the deep desert eased Peter of Wraysbury, the Venetian, the Spanish Jew, and the Hindu prince down beside the master merchant and the remnants of his once-great caravan.

"Did you find the way out?" asked the merchant.

"This"—he could not say the words, not before the wide eyes and knowing smile of the Hindu prince —"brought us to the wall of that which confines us, and I sought to batter through. I succeeded only in summoning conveyance back here, however. Escape, unless we achieve it here, is hopeless."

The merchant nodded and pointed to the amphitheatre. "They still listen. They even laugh, at times, but nothing changes. Even when you and two of your newfound companions were overheard telling your tales, the djinn changed not even by as little as one gray hair."

"I shall tell a tale, if you like," volunteered the Hindu.

"With a voice like that, I should hope so!" the master storyteller agreed. "Otherwise, I fear that we are losing them. We need all the help, and all the hope, that we can get."

"Hope?" a deep voice mocked them. "A delusion and a snare of mortals. Long ago, I forsook hope, as I forsook power, releasing hope to the winds; releasing power into my son's hands. He was eager for it—a flaw of youth. It will pass. All will pass."

In the amphitheatre, all the djinn were rising, were flicking hands and claws in salutes to the ancient djinni who now approached. He had been tall once, splendid once; now his hair and beard were totally white; his back was stooped, his body almost skeletal; and even the powerful voice that had compelled their attention had an ashen quality. But he had only to whisper to compel immediate attention.

What a ruler he must have been in his prime! Peter thought. But what had he said? He had resigned power as not worth the having? In the name of God, what was?

As the eldest of djinni approached his son, the Emir performed a profound bow, almost abasing himself before him.

"You are right to listen to me," said the eldest of djinn. "For I remember Suleiman and his father Daoud before him, when we yet flew unfettered through the vain world. And I remember the terrible day that Solomon shut us into this . . . this pleasure dome in which now we live, and marked it with the seal we could not break. One thing more I remember: the words of he who conquered us. 'Vanity of vanities, and all is vanity.' I have had many ages in which to meditate on that.

"Share my meditations, my children. For now I shall speak."

The Tale of Sindbad and the Mid-day Demon

Marvin Kaye

> Thou hast nor youth nor age,
> But, as it were, an after-dinner's sleep,
> Dreaming on both—
> > *Measure for Measure*,
> > William Shakespeare

In the reign of Caliph Haroun Al-Raschid, there dwelt in Baghdad in opulent splendor an aged mariner named Sindbad. Once his enormous wealth had been the envy of all his merchant neighbors, but when he revealed that long durance of pain, privation and harrowing danger attended the attainment of his riches, these same barterers and tradesmen determined to rest content with their safe and homely lot, and thanked Allah for it.

But one morning when the sun glared sharp and merciless in the blanched unending skies, a dusky-complexioned youth caparisoned in the flowing milky robes of the desert tribes sought out Sindbad and, smiling with seeming sincerity, begged the particulars of the sailor's colorful history, which rumor had carried even to the distant oasis from which the stranger claimed to hail.

Now Sindbad had so often told his tale that it no longer held novelty for those who knew him, therefore his parched spirit was whetted by the stranger's demand; so for many an afternoon the mariner told of travail and travel amongst rocs and giant eagles, great fish huge as islands, ferocious apes, ogres and dragons; and as his thin voice piped endless wonders, he paused betimes to quaff smooth soothing draughts of wildflower-honey wine.

At length he depicted his last and darkest predicament: wedding a noble bride only to learn upon her untimely demise that the custom of her land dictated that the living husband be interred with his dead wife. Sindbad thanked the will of Allah for permitting him to escape the cavernous burial vault, upon which felicitous circumstance once and for all the sailor renounced high adventure and fled to Baghdad, there to ensconce himself in grace, peace, and the comfort provided by an estimable fortune; upon which summatory declaration Sindbad at last fell silent.

Now all the old man's friends agreed that he had never told his story better, but the dusky stranger rose to his feet, haughtily whipped his pale robes about him, fixed the company with a harsh accusatory glare and thus berated them:

"Shame upon thee, merchantmen of Baghdad, O shame! Is there not sufficient commerce in this populous and bustling city? Repent the cupidity which bruits abroad this crafty fabulist's fabrications to entice gullible lackwits to undertake arduous journeying in hopes of hearing marvels; whereupon this wizened prevaricator spendthrifts time that his auditors perforce must dawdle in the vicinity donating hard-earned coin to the capacious coffers of Baghdad!"

On hearing the stranger's inflamatory remarks, the citizens, venting dire maledictions, rose in a mutinous body and would have flung themselves pell-mell upon the youth and torn his raiment and savaged his person, but that Sindbad, silencing them with an imperious gesture, bade all be seated, which command they reluctantly obeyed. Then with stern and dignified mien, the aged sailor rose and made the dusky foreigner this reply:

"Rash archer who practiceth thy bow not upon true targets but looseth wayward shafts that chancely injure the innocent, if thou perceivest grievance with that which I have told thee, then it is with Sindbad alone that thou must hold quarrel and not these gentle trading-folk, whose artiface extendeth not beyond that shrewd business sense that all who speculate in goods hopefully doth possess."

"I am amazed," said the stranger, "that your countrymen have been taken in by that ridiculous picaresque which you have rehearsed for my sake, but let that go: at your word I take you, Sindbad, though it is at your word I gag; yet I'll proffer apologies to thy comrades, since you assure me that your hyperbolic asseverances are unaccompliced. In which circumstance, I, as representative of the frank-speaking desert peoples, do urge and exhort the citizens of Baghdad to cast from its municipal bosom this unprincipled tale-teller."

Upon pronouncement of this strange harsh sentiment, knots of merchant heads bent together and a buzz of guarded discussion arose severally amongst the tradesmen; and though some glanced at Sindbad with friendly compassion, others regarded him uneasily, and these were those whose commerce was dependent upon maintaining the custom of the desert chieftains. Wisely perceiving their predicament, Sindbad again gestured with the easy authority of one long used to possessing wealth and its attendant respect; when he did, all abridged debate and listened. Thus spake he:

"O desert-dweller, sheerly to slake thy curiosity did I recount the saga of those voyages which I undertook in my heyday. I asked no token for my trouble, and these my countrymen must aver that though I've dwelt with them some twoscore years, not once in all that time did Sindbad solicit monies from friend or stranger."

This rejoinder provoked a spate of head-waggling concurrence amongst the Baghdadians, but the dusky other swiftly retorted:

"Though I own no coin hath passed between us, yet thou hast filched from me a commodity of inestimable worth that never can be restored: I mean those precious life-moments fruitlessly expended listening to thee."

Saith Sindbad, "Each man valuates his life at a rate none else may properly assess; therefore, stranger, setting aside that noncalculable grievance, what possible grounds canst thou advance to prove that I, an innocent graybeard, must suffer exile?"

"That very innocence is what I severely question, sailor. What is the true source of thy vast wealth? Shall we foolishly believe you plucked diamonds from valley floors and mountain caves? O, ye simple merchantmen, is't not far likelier that Sindbad's riches be the massed booty of a pirate who conceals his misdeeds with preposterous prattle?"

Uttering a universal aspiration of shock and fear, the assemblage gazed with astonishment at the mariner, who, with a mighty effort of self-control, drew not the dagger which his hand flew to grasp, but his countenance whitened as if it had been cut from the chalk-cliffs of distant Donburraiah; and in the hush successive to the stranger's accusation, some who tented Sindbad believed it must be guilt that made the sailor wax pale. But the old man had not survived the tusks of the savage beast nor the flesh-eating tribe's terrible teeth to quail in the jaws of calumny. Drawing himself erect, he coldly and sternly addressed his enemy in this fashion:

"Were I and thee of an age, presumptuous youth, short shrift I'd make of the slander thou hast pronounced and the slanderer who pronounced it, but since time hath dimmed mine eye and unsteadied my hand, I must seek otherwise to restore my good name and reputation to these, my suddenly confounded countrymen. Therefore I do propose that you and I set sail upon the salty circuit of those same exploits whose truth thou hast denied."

A sinister smile twitched the corners of the youth's mouth as he retorted:

"You think I fear to chance your fictive perils, Sindbad, but you are mistaken; you shall repent this rash challenge."

"Nay," the sailor demurred, "thought I do not delude myself that in my decline I will survive dangers that taxed my uttermost resources when I was young and virile. But when shall we depart?"

"This very moment," saith the stranger, waving his hand, whereupon street, merchants, yea, Baghdad itself and its teeming populace all disappeared like an insubstantial dream-pageant; whereupon the mariner perceived he was in the presence of some formidable entity.

The sailor and his adversary stood upon the afterdeck of a sea-girt vessel lacquered all in black. Sindbad regarded his companion with new interest. The stranger no more affected a youthful guise but now appeared cosmically ancient to the aged mortal, who ventured this remark:

"Whosoever ye may be, at least I take comfort in knowing that thy plan to disgrace me hath miscarried, since my doubtlessly dumbfounded compatriots witnessed our miraculous passage."

"Despair thy consolation," the other sneered. "I planted the illusion in their minds that they saw the two of us embark seaward in this barque. Despair altogether, Sindbad, for I am the Demon whom the Frankish infidels call Accidia, the only fiend sufficiently puissant to venture forth in daylight; I am master of that spiritual discontent which one day shall be accounted most potent of all the deadly sins. But in this age of simple belief, my powers are comparatively untried. Therefore I mean to test thee. Prepare, sailor, for the most terrible trial thou hast e'er endured."

So saying, Hell's emissary waved his taloned claw, whereupon an enormous waterspout seized the vessel, whirled it aloft, spun it swiftly in reverse and dropped it with a colossal smack in a choppy sector of sea where the mariner espied two points abaft the port beam a familiar islet, small in size, looming green with shrubbery, seemingly a corner of Paradise mislaid. But Sindbad, staring bleakly upon it, proclaimed:

"This vile spot must be shunned. Its promise of safe harbor is illusory. My shipmates and I were despatched thitherto with orders to seek out fresh water; as we wandered o'er the surface we were unharmed, but when we lit a fire to cook our frugal meal, the smoke awoke that awesome monster-fish which yond accursèd isle is in truth; shaking off the sands and greens which rooted on its back whilst it slept, the creature dove into the sea and drowned every man jack but me."

Saith Accidia, "It is remarkable, Sindbad, that an experienced mariner like you could never hath wondered how that a creature of the depths could drowse so long upon the sea-top . . ."

The demon's question startled the old man; in truth, it had not occurred to him before, but now that he considered it, the thing appeared utterly impossible; still, it *had* happened as he remembered it, so, dismissing the problem, Sindbad uttered repeated warnings to the fiend not to harbor the ebon vessel, but ignoring him, Accidia steered the ship close in, set cloven hooves upon the beach and ordered the mortal to follow, which command Sindbad was powerless to resist.

Hours passed; the pair trudged the circuit of the island's edge, crisscrossed the interior, surmounted the loftiest peak; but where'er they tramped, Sindbad saw nothing more than turf and slate-gray rock which Accidia prodded with a sharp stick to no effect. At length the fiend kindled a fire; Sindbad waited trepidatiously for disaster to engulf them, but all that came to pass was the eventual guttering of the dying flames.

"My memory, it seems, is fallible," the sailor murmured uneasily. "After all, this must be another place."

"Nay, Sindbad, my magic is attuned to your brain-patterns. This is the very isle you visited. But the mortal mind's a fallible mechanism. I do not doubt that you believe that once you saw a large fish hereabouts."

"Nay, not hereabouts!" Sindbad shrilled. "I say this island itself was the great fish!"

"They why didn't it wake up when I set fire to it?"

"It can only be because the monster is dead!"

"That assumption cannot be proven, Sindbad, except you swim down deep into this murky water and seek out I know not what evidence." With that, Accidia feinted as if to tumble the sailor backwards o'er the ship's rail, but Sindbad hastily skittered aft, saying:

"Though I were equipped with gills to breathe beneath the ocean's roof, I still should not do this thing, fiend, lest thine evil nature prompt thee to move the ship in my absence, marooning me here; therefore let us leave this place. By Allah, I do aver that we shall find not far from here that true isle whereon the colossal roc doth build its nest."

Accidia gestured cynically; he and the sailor returned to the black-lacquered ship; the demon gestured again; another waterspout catapulted them o'er the ocean. Before Sindbad could catch his breath, they reached the beach of the very spot he had bespoken. They disembarked; and now the mariner searched long and diligently, but no trace could he discover of that predatory bird so big (according to legend) that it is capable of snatching up full-grown elephants in its talons to feed unto its ravenous progeny.

At length, Sinbad sat with aching back abutting a palm-bole and murmured dispiritedly that, after all, perhaps it was not the mating season of the roc; with that, the weary sailor closed his eyes and drowsed. The fiend took pity on the old man and let him sleep; but lest this action compromise the reader's credibility, be it remembered that Hell's officers once roved the sylvan fields of praise, and even Lucifer himself, it hath been rumored, yet carries slumbering deep within his sinful breast the unregenerate seeds of nobility.

The next morning, Sindbad sprang up early, eager to expunge the preceding day's disappointments; so from sunup to late afternoon, he guided his diabolic doubter from one exotic spot to another, but nowhere did they find those giant snakes and mammoth apes that the sailor promised.

"I am sure," Accidia allowed, "that with the proper diet and a dearth of natural enemies, certain reptiles and simians well might grow to generous size; why, there are boa constrictors that easily measure twenty feet."

Sindbad's choked reply empurpled his countenance. "Suggesteth that in my arduous journeying I lacked the wit to distinguish between awesome monsters of staggering proportion and mundane beasts of the wild? Go to; I *know* I witnessed marvels!"

"Certainly you did, old man," the fiend solicitously crooned, "but modify your passion lest you overtax your superannuated constitution."

Accidia's ironic tone did not escape the sailor, but neither did the soundness of his counsel; therefore, quelling his wrath, Sindbad quietly determined to prove to the skeptic the accuracy of his memory. So they proceeded to pursue the thread of the mariner's past, alas, to no especial end: the ogre's bone-littered grotto was long untenanted; the lineage of dragonry had expired and that valley which Sindbad claimed was carpeted with gems now bore a rich blanket of briar-moss whose carbon content, Accidia conceded, might well convert to diamonds in a few million years.

That evening, the sailor prowled the devil-ship's black deck, musing on the morrow's ordeal, when he must enter the cavernous burial-place of his long-deceased spouse, there where once upon a time he had been immured alive. When young Sindbad escaped that dreadful spot, he vowed never to revisit that land, lest its wrathful gods punish his affront to native tradition, but now the prospect of a supernatural manifestation seemed infinitely preferable to his present state, bereft as he was of certitude.

Sindbad leaned over the taffrail and stared morosely into the calm depths of the phosphorescent sea. The scene brought to mind the haunting words of the barbarian poet Djal Dubralz:

> *The barque did seem to float above a bottom of dry sand*
> *Until a darting form disturbed the placid element;*
> *Stooping to peer, I beheld a school of tiny fish*
> *Scavenging among the spiny shells and rocks.*
> *Admiring the beating purpose of their blood,*
> *I yearned to bless their life-sustaining dance—*
> *And then the distant stars and I shed bitter tears.*

Midnight. Though Sindbad closed his eyes, he could not sleep; over and over again in the theater of his mind the mariner replayed the fearsome voyages of his youth, but now they seemed no more substantial than Oriental shadow-puppetry; that past which had so long defined him left behind no trace save that which lingered in his thought; and as Accidia well might have pointed out, who can trust the reliability of an old man's wits?

"Fie!" Sindbad proclaimed, bolstering his own courage. "Verily, this mode of thinking is the devil's handiwork; value it not, for see: the very presence of this sorcerous ship, nay, the existence of the demon himself *is sufficient assurance that the world is full of marvels!*"

The sudden easy logic of Sindbad's idea so startled and delighted him that he chortled with glee; he knew it signified victory over the subtle fiend's diabolical system of despair. But at that moment, the bright sparkling stars sputtered and died. Vessel, ocean, sky, Accidia, all were no more.

Blackness; beneath bare feet, uncut stone. When Sindbad's eyes grew accustomed to the dark, he discerned a few feeble sun rays straggling into the gloom from narrow rock-chinks. Now he knew where he was; in that vast subterranean death-vault where, for the past double decade, his late wife's bones reposed. At first, Sindbad presumed his sudden presence in the cavern was but the latest of Accidia's unnervingly precipitate scene-changes, but as time crept by without any further significant event coming to pass, the sailor began to ponder his position with growing unease.

"After all," he murmured fearfully, "what if I never left this place? Here there is no food nor drink; the stifling air is unhealthy. Perchance all my elder days, my wealthy retirement in Baghdad have been but the aberrations of a dying mind." His dilemma was cynically cruel: with the demon's disappearance, the sailor's brave new proof was also gone; perhaps Accidia was nothing more than hallucination, each perilous exploit of his youth the effluence of a disordered brain.

But Sindbad still did not give way to despair. Casting about for some viable solution to his problem, he conceived that if his memories were true ones and he had indeed left his dead bride's side more than twenty years before, thus violating the sacred custom of her people, his reappearance in the tomb well might prompt the offended deities to visit fell revenge upon him . . . and yet, the mariner bitterly reflected, what fate more terrible than this present wretched torment could they possibly devise?

Frenzy seized him; in the desperate hope that the commission of some new act of sacrilege might court divine retribution, Sindbad caught up in his arms his wife's rotted carcass; flesh he had once found pleasurable to clasp now crumbled in his grasp; his hands held bone-shards; he dropped them in disgust.

A long silent time passed. The light began to fail; the sailor, unharmed, unpunished, waited in semidarkness, pondering questions that fallible mortality can never begin to resolve. But then the grandest of revelations struck him: there *was* a test so sweetly uncomplex that Accidia could not frustrate it, and being accomplished, it must finally set at naught all the insidious labors of the mid-day demon!

Thus reasoned Sindbad: if indeed he were a delirious middle-aged man recently buried alive, when he picked up his dead wife's body, it should have better maintained its integrity; yet inasmuch as the forensic science was not much advanced, the mariner, though no stranger to death, was not confident as to the advancement of his mate's morbidity; still, the dissolution of her earthly relict suggested his ultimate triumph, for since the cavern contained nothing in the way of sustenance, he soon must expire; but if, as he believed, he was an old man, a condition wonderfully simple to verify, then his escape to Baghdad must be fact and if that were true, why not also countenance the perilous adventures of his youth?

His first impulse was to gaze upon his own face in a mirror, but Sindbad had no reflective surface secreted upon his person, and instruments of vanity were not permitted in the crypt. Then he reminded himself that the texture, coloration, and puckerings of age would also be evident upon the flesh of his extremities. But by then, the moted daylight had faded and evening entered the tomb. Sighing wearily, Sindbad composed himself for slumber; as his eyes closed, he wondered idly whether with the dying of the sun the mid-day demon's powers—if that the twain truly existed—also waned. Thus, steeped in strange new thought, darkness enfolded him, spirit and flesh, and when at last the long night elapsed and came to an end, so did Sindbad.

And this is the single that Scheherazade reserved and did not tell her husband-king Shahriyar, lest he repent his charity and destroy her utterly.

TESTS OF LOVE

Having finished his tale, the eldest of the djinn stood silent for a moment. A great sigh of weariness and disappointment came from the djinn in the amphitheatre, and he savored it the way a lady might inhale the fragrance of attar of roses. Then, he turned toward the humans who watched him with the dulling eyes of wanhope. For the first time, he smiled.

Then he faded away, leaving but a flurry of ashes that spun upward for a moment on a gust of wind, then died into stillness. All about the amphitheatre, the light was waning, as if the contest were already over, the victory already announced. Even the merchant prince sat with his head in his hands.

Accidia, Peter thought. He had told the Emir of the Djinn that Ira, or wrath, was a deadly sin. But of the deadly sins against which his faith warned him, Accidia was worst, offspring as it was of pride, a pride that forbids even the weakest of hope. It was not, an old priest had once told him, Judas's treachery that had condemned him to the pit, though that in itself were sufficient; it was that he had, in his pride, considered himself to be beyond repentance, beyond the Mercy. He had despaired, and despairing, had fallen.

Did Peter really want to imitate Judas?

"We can't let him win!" he cried at his comrades. "Wake up!" he ordered, shaking first one man, then another back to alertness.

Was it illusion, or did the light in the amphitheatre ap-

291

pear to flicker a little more brightly? The men looked up at him, as if hoping—and thank God for that—that he might be able, somehow, to help them.

"Think!" he commanded. "I'll set you a riddle; let's see if you can solve it."

"Riddles," said the Emir, materializing beside him, "were not in our bargain."

"Our *bargain,*" retorted Peter, "is not yet complete."

"Then in the name of Allah, tell your stories and make an end of this. I am excessively wearied of this game, and wish it had never begun," the Emir said, with a bit too much emotion.

"My riddle, friends," Peter said, wishing he had the training of a singer or storyteller, or even of a general, to instill hope and courage with his voice alone. "What is it that can conquer despair?"

His companions were silent, though the Hindu's head came up.

"In the name of God, answer me!"

"What can conquer despair?" To his amazement, a young silk merchant rose. "Kindness."

"Hope," said another man, with whom Peter had never before spoken, though he knew that he drove camels and wrote verse when he had a chance.

The Hindu spoke last: "Love," he said.

"You have all solved my riddle," Peter said.

One by one they rose and filed to the center of the amphitheatre, there to play out the last throw of the game.

Feather of the Phoenix

Katharine Eliska Kimbriel

Know, O reader, that when the children of Almighty Allah tell *their* children of ancient heroes and heroines, often their memories are selective. Stories of Sindbad the Seaman, greatest of travelers, are always told, as well as the tales of Aladdin and Ali Baba. The Wazir's clever daughter Scheherazade and the slave-girl Morgiana are held up as models of duty and loyalty, so that all modest young women will strive to emulate them. But have you heard, O reader, of the youngest daughter of Sindbad the Seaman?

It was the sons of Sindbad who suppressed the tale. At this date we cannot know whether it was because they feared for their sister's reputation, or merely because they did not wish to be held up to her example. Let it be a lesson to all who would hide the light of Allah's justice— history has forgotten the names of Sindbad's four sons and elder daughter, but the name of his youngest child Laylah belongs next to her sisters-in-spirit Morgiana and Scheherazade.

Know, then, that in the city of Baghdad during the reign of the Commander of the Faithful, Harun al-Rashid, there lived the greatest of travelers and merchants, one Sindbad the Seaman. He had returned from his seventh voyage wealthy beyond measuring, both in gold and in honor, and ready to settle down and enjoy the rewards of his labor. With him was his only wife, the daughter of that Sheikh whom you have read of elsewhere, may the mercy of Allah Almighty be upon his soul. They were very happy together, and they were blessed both in gold and in honor;

for Sindbad's maturity was like a sunlit river rippling in the wake of a tall ship.

In due course Sindbad found himself the father of first a beautiful daughter and then four healthy sons after her, such as must delight any father's eye. Last, and unlooked-for, came his second daughter, black of eye and curly locks, golden as a harvest moon. She had a knowing look for one so young, and so Sindbad named her Laylah, for the nighttime, and for all that stirs in its mysteries.

How could he not adore her? Bright of wit and lovely of form, a healthy and happy child, Laylah grew up to be the household favorite, and this brought her not only indulgence but watchfulness. No spoiled brat, she, for her elders expected her to be dutiful and loving, and treated her in a like manner. In this atmosphere, Laylah grew up an exceptional maiden.

Her mother privately worried about her; how could one as wild as she, her father's favorite, become the sort of wife and mother expected by every servant of Allah? Between Laylah and her sister, more than a dozen years her elder, there was little comparison. Alike in looks, perhaps, but while the eldest would sit sedately under the date palms of the gardens and work fine silk pieces, Laylah was more likely to be climbing the trees! Instead of absorbing the lessons of the household, Laylah studied algebra and astronomy and geography. Clothing was something to protect the body from the sun, and yes, Laylah understood about keeping household, but who cared for such things? There was plenty of time for that—now she wanted to hear her father tell again about the great rukh bird, whose egg was as large as the dome of a mosque.

Remonstrating privately to her husband was of no avail —Sindbad merely laughed and hugged his wife.

"Why are you so worried? Does Laylah not know her lessons from the Koran? Does she not know her duty to her parents? You feared we would never marry off her sister, and yet the son of the Wazir himself asked for her to wife!"

"But when she goes to the market without a servant—" his wife protested.

"I have taken care of that. My faithful Harun will be by her side whenever she desires to stretch her legs. Do not fight it, love of my life," Sindbad encouraged her. "It is from God!" By this he meant that Laylah's fate was already decided, and that no amount of meddling would change it.

The path which led to the Phoenix began one evening in Baghdad when the sun was slowly setting. After resting through the heat of the day, Laylah had wandered into the garden, her geometry book clasped to her bosom. It was a ruse—she was not in the mood for geometry (which, unlike algebra, she found frustrating). In truth she was a bit melancholy, and had no one with whom to unburden her heart. Setting her book on a stone bench, Laylah walked to the back of the garden, embracing the roses climbing up the brick walls of the enclosure. The aroma of beeswax, honey, and tea filled her nostrils, as well as the delicate china rose scent. Cascading blooms of cream, pink, yellow, and white covered the walls, a display envied by most of the wealthy of Baghdad. Only three homes boasted of such beauty—Sindbad's garden, his eldest daughter's own courtyard (for cuttings had traveled with the new bride) and the gardens of the Caliph himself.

Twilight descended upon her; a servant brought her a lamp of sweet oil burning brightly enough to read by. Still Laylah remained among the roses, heedless of stray insects drawn to the heady fragrance. Only after darkness was wrapped around her did Laylah leave the climbing shrubs and settle herself with her book. It was a magnificent night, warm yet not sticky, and the stars covered the sky like the white roses tumbling down the bricks. A sigh escaped unnoticed . . . her father was displeased with her, and Laylah was sad.

A crash startled her; jumping slightly, she lifted her head, looking wildly around the courtyard. Another crash, and some scraping noises . . . oh, of course—next door. Even the recurring mystery of their noisy neighbors did not stir her this night.

Curling a silk scarf around her neck to shield it from a stray breeze, Laylah was soon absorbed in the geometry. She muttered to herself as she worked—math always brought out this response in her—and pulled leaves off a nearby flower in frustration. A Greek had discovered the properties of geometry, although an Arab had connected the science to algebra and arithmetic. Laylah suspected the Greek of purposely trying to torture his Semitic neighbors with this "gift." Tonight frustration reached impressive proportions.

"Can no one explain the reasoning behind this infernal theorem?" she cried aloud, slamming her fist onto the book. Instantly contrite, she bent to see if she had damaged the precious pages.

"I probably can," came a voice.

Straightening, Laylah's eyes searched the darkness. "Who is there?"

"Do not be alarmed, daughter of Sindbad!" came the soft voice once again. "I was sitting in contemplation upon the words of our Lord Mohammed when I heard your plea. My teachers have been skilled, and if I can assist your studies, I would be honored to do so."

At this Laylah stood and circled the brick path, listening. Alarmed she was not; curious was a much better word. "Where are you?" she asked, since the voice had not answered her first question. "And what makes you think I am the daughter of the great Sindbad?"

Gentle laughter reached her ears. "I am the only place I could be, Dark Rose! On the other side of the wall, of course. I am your neighbor." There was a pause, and then the sound of rustling papers falling from a height. "As to how I knew you, my tutor has told me of the scholarship of your household. You are the only daughter under your father's roof—who else could you be?"

"You are the son!" Delighted, she sat down again on the bench. "The old scholar who came to dine with my father said he was instructing the only son of his master. But he was foreign, very foreign—your Arabic is flawless!"

"Thank you," the tenor voice said modestly. "Languages are my gift. But I have lived most of my life in Baghdad, you see, so of course I speak Arabic."

"Why do you call me 'Dark Rose'?" Laylah asked.

"I saw you recently, leaving for the market. A wisp of black curl, as delicate as your wall of blooms! And so you are the dark rose."

"Your tongue is gilded, kind sir," Laylah said quickly, for surely such words were not proper—they had not even been introduced. "But you said you are a scholar of geometry?"

The voice admitted to special knowledge, so Laylah described the theorem she was studying. After advising her to get a stick so she could draw in the dirt, the voice patiently and by memory went over each step of the proof, explaining how each step was reached.

"But why start with this angle and not the second?" she said plaintively at one point.

"Because you must start from what is known and move into the unknown," the voice told her. "Can you understand why?"

"I suppose," she murmured. "The unknown is more interesting, though."

Rich laughter roused her from her thoughts. "Only the daughter of Sindbad would prefer the unknown!"

Although Laylah was glad her assistant was pleased with her company, she had not thought the comment amusing, and said so.

A few chuckles still escaped, though the voice was tranquil. "It does not surprise me that you fail to see the humor of it. You are used to wonders, seek them, even, for your father faced marvels and lived to tell the tale. Young woman, do you not know that most people would make the sign of the evil eye, and call on Allah to avert such a fate?"

"I must admit it had not occurred to me." His words reminded her of the scene earlier with her father, and she sighed.

"Why so sad, Dark Rose?"

"Sad?" she said quickly, giving her voice a bright edge.

"When you come to the garden at night, and your mind is not on the stars, it is usually because you are sad. Do you wish to speak of it?"

They had already talked for too long—Laylah knew it. He was easy to talk with, and it seemed the most natural thing in the world to want to confide in him. That he could be so perceptive through a wall of brick!

"You may think it foolishness, but I have hurt my father's feelings, and that grieves me."

"So should it. This shows your love for your father."

Laylah moved to a bench arched over by roses and

leaned against the cooling brick wall. "You see, two years ago, I was betrothed to the brother of my eldest brother's wife—do you follow that?" The voice assured her that it did. "He was part of the merchant family my brother married into, and it was deemed a good thing for me to marry the brother. He was a kind man, and was proud of my scholarship, so I saw no reason to weep."

"Why should this be a problem?" The voice was both puzzled and concerned.

"Because the man died of fever before we could be wed. I am sixteen years, and should be married now, but who will want such an old bride?" In this Laylah voiced a real concern, for at sixteen a woman should be well on her way to presenting her husband with his first heir. "Now, whether it is my father's wealth and good name, or something else . . ."

"Yes?"

"I have had two offers. One is from a cousin of the Caliph, which would be flattering except that he made the mistake of asking if he could dine with us. He is an ox! A handsome man, skilled with sword and bow, a leader of the Caliph's troops . . . and I doubt he has ever had an original thought. The second offer is from a man my father's age! To be a second wife, of course. He is quite wealthy, and I think he would be kind to me . . . but his first wife is not happy he wishes a young bride, and I think it would be hard on me, in that household." She sighed again.

"Surely your father, who dotes on your footsteps, would not marry you to such men?"

Wryly, Laylah said: "Men do not look at it the same way. Certainly the Caliph's cousin is a true believer, as well educated as my brothers . . . but I do not think it had occurred to my father that I would be stuck with no one to talk intelligently with for the rest of my life!"

"The other offer?"

"Mother knew the first wife was unhappy about it, and told him. He was in a rage, which rarely happens, shouting about what he would do to anyone who made my lot a hard one—oh, it was silliness! I told him I did not mind marrying a man my father's age, if he could only find one with a kind first wife, who had borne her sons, and was not jealous." Laylah ran her fingers across a satin rosebud. "Father was *very* angry after I said this, and sent me from his presence."

The voice chuckled.

"It is not funny!" Laylah cried, jumping to her feet.

"No, not the way you think, Dark Rose. Do you not see? Your father had made a good match for you, to kin who would respect your talents and try to make you happy. Fate decreed otherwise, and now he must begin anew." The voice chuckled again. "I think you *have* hurt him, Dark Rose, for it hurts his pride, and perhaps his heart, that you would think he would take an offer you feared or disliked."

"And I am called clever!" Laylah groaned, throwing a limp rose into the depths of the garden. "I must think of how to apologize to him. Thank you. I was convinced it was because I was unmarriageable." Suddenly something occurred to her. "I have told you the pain of my heart and I do not even know your name!"

"I am called Kaliad," the voice said gravely.

Now, for all her distraction that day, Laylah *was* clever, and she immediately noticed that the young man (he sounded young, at least) did not give his father's name as well. This was indeed a mystery, right up there with why no one had ever seen other than servants and the old scholar leave that house. But it would be rude to ask, and so she curbed her ready tongue.

"I am Laylah, daughter of Sindbad the Seaman," she responded, her tone as formal as his own. Even as she spoke, she noticed that the evening star had fallen below the rim of the wall. "It is late! Thank you again for your help."

"Will you come and speak again to me?" Kaliad asked quickly, and his youth was revealed in his anxious words.

"Of course," Laylah said warmly. Her thoughts were busy as she gathered up her book and started back into the house. If Kaliad called a farewell, she did not hear it.

So the wheel of fate was set in motion.

Now, a pampered daughter of such a wealthy family is rarely alone, and in due course Laylah's many conversations with Kaliad were reported to Harun, her father's manager of household. A slightly portly man in his prime, named for their great Caliph, Harun was not one to rush into decisions. He knew that Kaliad was by rumor an invalid, unable to leave his home. He was no doubt lonely. Still . . .

Before long Harun was sitting in the garden, seemingly reviewing the household accounts but actually eavesdropping upon Laylah and Kaliad. For his excessive chaperonage (for this was excessive during the Abbasid period) Harun was given quite a fright.

It was early one morning near the end of August, and Laylah had just settled herself in the rose garden when a tremendous crash reached her ears. Clasping a hand over her mouth to control her giggling, Laylah waited through a long period of silence. Finally: "Kaliad?"

"I am here." He sounded a bit out of breath.

Her giggles bubbled over. "I came to tell you the continuing story of my unwedded state—I think I must be cursed! But I hear you are surely even more cursed, by the clumsiest servants in Baghdad!"

There was a pause, and Kaliad's reply was very formal. "You do not begin to know what you speak of, to call your current plight a curse!"

At this, Laylah's weeks of musing clarified into a single thought. A young man who never left his house . . . "Kaliad," she said softly, "are you accursed?"

After several minutes she feared she had offended him. Just as she was about to apologize, Kaliad said heavily: "Yes, Dark Rose, I am accursed."

"My poor friend! How did this happen?"

"You are not afraid?" He sounded surprised.

Laylah considered. "Well, it is not . . . contagious, is it?"

Kaliad's merry laugh ran through the gardens. "Only the daughter of Sindbad could show such courage! No, Dark Rose, it is not contagious. The curse was set upon my father's head, but I and I alone am its victim."

"Can you speak of it, or does the subject pain you?" Naturally Laylah was curious, but she was sensitive enough to know he might not wish to discuss it.

"There is not much to tell. My father, Dark Rose, is . . . he is a powerful man, a leader among men. I think . . . I suspect he was too proud, especially of his skills at war, for are they not Allah's gift, and little of his own doing? At any rate, one day a stranger appeared at his door and said to him: 'Pride ever stumbles upon the path to God! You must do penance for this arrogance, this overwhelming joy you take in your skill at arms.' Well, my father made a serious error—he laughed." Kaliad's voice was gloomy.

"Laughed!" Laylah was stunned. "At a total stranger? He could have been a sorcerer, or a djinni, or an angel—" She broke off.

"Indeed, an angel in disguise. That stranger drew himself up, and responded to my father's amusement. 'It seems you are a fool. Very well—I tell you that the sons of your body shall be as graceless and inept as you are practiced!' And then he vanished."

"Without . . . that was it?" Now the crashing and banging in the garden next door made all too much sense.

"Oh, he told my father how the curse could be broken —and then said that anyone who knew the secret could not undo the curse! Even I do not know it, although I think my tutor knows." Kaliad sighed. "At first father did not believe in the curse. But when I was born, it is said the skies darkened over the mosque in our city, and lightning struck the tower of our house. By the time I was walking, it was apparent I was a moving disaster area, drawing inanimate objects like your roses draw bees. It did not affect my mind, praise Allah. I am acknowledged a brilliant scholar, and have special skill at understanding military tactics. I am even," he added with a shy pride unheard in his previous statements, "skilled at the art of dagger throwing. Such beautiful patterns I can make with a set of balanced blades! But that is it."

"Why do you hide? You are not . . . misshapen, are you?" This was gently asked.

"You, who know I cannot walk a straight path from house to bench without crashing into something? You ask this question? I cannot sit a horse for the length of the bazaar without falling off, and camels—" His shudder carried in his voice. "I am well formed, my tutor tells me, and as healthy as any could want . . . but I cannot be my father's heir. His . . . subordinates would not accept one who could not lead them into war at need."

"You are an only child?" Laylah could not imagine anyone continuing to have children in the face of such a future.

"I have one sister, who is about two years younger than I am. By that time, my father knew the curse was true."

"Oh, Kaliad!" What could she say? To be a disgrace in your father's eyes!

"He has worn mourning since I left home, I am told, and prays daily in the mosque, asking forgiveness for his sins." Kaliad sounded very sad. "At least this has saved my father's soul, though the years be long for me. Not all are as fearless as you—few wish to associate with a cursed man."

Faithful Harun did not wish *anyone* to associate with a cursed man—especially not the delight of his master's eyes! It was time to speak to his lord, and Harun rushed to Sindbad's chambers.

"O, my lord," Harun said, "I have allowed a great evil to occur!" Prostrating himself, the man immediately launched into the tale of the courtyard conversations.

"Cursed?" Sindbad exclaimed as Harun reached the end of his story. "The boy actually *told* her he was cursed?"

"His very words, my lord and master," Harun replied mournfully.

There was silence for several minutes. Finally Harun hazarded a peek, tilting his head so he could see the face of his lord. Sindbad was running his fingers through his beard, his expression thoughtful, his eyes alight . . . with amusement? Harun forgot to look humble and sat up. This was very odd.

"I will be dining with the tutor this evening, and I will be sure he is aware of their talks." Sindbad suddenly chuckled. "Harun . . . do not stop my daughter in anything she desires—anything. Only observe and report to me."

"My—my lord?" Harun could not believe his ears.

"Do not fear, faithful Harun! This is not the work of Iblis the daemon. Allah the Compassionate sees all and knows all; he will protect my child." With this, Sindbad dismissed his retainer and sent him back to keep an eye on the vivacious Laylah.

In the early evening Laylah returned to the garden. Anxiously she rushed to the brick wall between the two courtyards and called for Kaliad.

"He is not here, mistress, but I will fetch him," replied a sturdy voice. In a few moments Laylah heard the sound of pottery breaking, and knew that Kaliad approached.

"Laylah?" He had hurried; the word was thin and breathy.

She did not ask if he was all right. Knowing her own brothers' pride, she would not wound Kaliad's. "My father went out to dinner this evening," she announced without preamble. "Upon his return, he told me he had—stumbled —into a great lie, and had ruined my chances to ever marry!"

"But what is this?" Kaliad said in surprise.

"It—it seems the cousin of the Caliph pursued his suit, and, knowing I did not want to marry him, father made up a story. Father told the man that my mother reminded him of a promise he had once made—that he would marry his daughter only to a man who brought him the feather of a phoenix. Well, the Wazir's son certainly did not bring such a thing to my father! So . . ."— Laylah grimaced, not certain if she wanted to laugh or cry.

"You are the only daughter left, which means your suitors must bring Phoenix feathers," Kaliad finished for her. "The Phoenix! A wonder of the ages! Yet your father never saw it in his travels, did he?" Kaliad's words were almost dreamy, and no wonder. There was but one Phoenix—it was the most magnificent bird in creation, as wise as it was beautiful, and the rarest of creatures.

"I do not think he did—if he saw it, he did not tell me the story. But the problem is, surely the cousin of the Caliph will repeat this story! And if that is the case, then how can I be married, when there will be no Phoenix feather for my father to show his friends?" Laylah had remained calm up until now, but her voice had begun to quiver.

"Your father will think of something," Kaliad said soothingly. "He is a very clever man! Perhaps he can find a

rare feather which looks like it could belong to a Phoenix—"

"That is not quite honest, is it?" Laylah interrupted.

"Well . . . it is certainly a fine line. Sometimes a small
lie must be told, to prevent a greater tragedy. Of course,"
Kaliad continued, his voice thoughtful, "perhaps someone
will bring you a feather from the Phoenix!"

"Don't be ridiculous!" Laylah snapped, beginning to
pace. "No one knows where to find the Phoenix! It has
been seen in many, many places, from here to the Nile!"
The girl was thankful for her crossness—it was keeping
her from crying, which would be embarrassing.

"I . . . might be able to find it."

Kaliad's words dropped into the night like pebbles in a
pool. Laylah whirled, unable to believe she had heard correctly. "What did you say?"

"I said I know where to find the Phoenix." His voice
was patient, as always.

"How? Where?" she shrieked, and then clasped her
hands over her mouth. "Do you really know?" she said in a
penetrating whisper.

"I have a very good idea." Something brass fell off a
table and began rolling on the ground; when Kaliad spoke
again, he sounded closer to her. "I love such tales, even as
you do—and I have studied the legends of the Phoenix."

"Oh, tell me!" Laylah sat upon the bench against the
rose-covered wall.

"Well . . . it was an exercise in scholarship," he explained, sounding a bit embarrassed. "I took my great map
of the known world and marked where all the reputable
sightings took place, and when they took place. Then I
used the position of the stars and the time of year that the
great traveler Abu Sir saw the Phoenix immolate itself, and
calculated when the Phoenix last was reborn."

"And?" Laylah said, eager for the location.

"I discovered the Phoenix has a regular pattern in its
movements. It is only a matter of determining where it
would be at this point in its travels."

"Kaliad! You are brilliant! Where would the Phoenix be
in this year and season?" She snuggled against the wall, for

she did not consider the answer something to be shouted across the courtyard.

"I suspect it has returned to the northern deserts of Iraq," Kaliad told her. "It has been almost five hundred years—when the sun crosses the girth of the planet and begins its flight away from us, then the Phoenix will immolate itself in the oasis dedicated to Abu Sir."

"But where is it? Do not tell me it is uncertain, or I will scream!" she warned him.

"I do not *think* it is uncertain. There is a trade village called Wadi al Ubayyid at the edge of the desert; the oasis is supposed to be near there."

"The Wadi? The dry stream which used to run into the Euphrates River?" Laylah said softly.

"The very one." His voice grew thoughtful. "In the last few hundred years this village was born to become a place for the Bedouin to bring their wool for trade. Merchants bring things to exchange with the Bedouin, mostly fine cloth, metal, flax, and barley."

Laylah was busy planning. "How far is this village, of Wadi al Ubayyid?"

"Across both the Tigris and the Euphrates—at least six days by caravan."

"Only that? And to a trade center—the preview before goods reach Baghdad . . ." A smile started to curl across Laylah's face.

"What are you thinking, Dark Rose?" Kaliad suddenly said. "Will you wait until a suitor interests you, and then tell him the secret?" Was there a bit of sadness in his voice?

Laylah was too busy thinking to question his tone of voice. "Of course not—I must get there before the Phoenix leaves again!"

"You?" Kaliad sounded incredulous.

"Why not?" Laylah tried to control the sudden edge in her voice.

"No!" It was a shout. There was a deafening crash, and Laylah leapt to her feet in response. Banging and clattering came from the other side of the wall, and several thuds. She heard the scrape of wood against brick, a slap of leather, and then to her amazement an arm appeared above the top of the partition, thrashing frantically for purchase.

Visible in bright moonlight was the form of a clean-shaven youth.

"You cannot go! It is too dangerous!" he gasped, grabbing a protruding rose cane.

A mistake. Swallowing a cry of pain, Kaliad released the branch and disappeared. Thumps, snapping twigs, branches cracking, and finally a splash followed him to his end.

Her heart in her throat, Laylah raced to the edge of the bench. Only one rose in the garden was thornless; seizing the thick branches of the vigorous shrub, she quickly scaled the ladder of violet-scented white blooms. Reassuring sounds of splashing, as well as the tinny song of a wobbling brass container, continued to emanate from the other garden. Behind her a man's anguished croak of protest rent the night, but she did not hear it.

"Kaliad! Are you hurt?" That he should take such a risk!

The neighboring garden was rimmed with lanterns; one had survived the deluge. Slowly rising from a tangle of wooden benches, reed tables, brass dishes, and myriad pieces of vines and flowers was a tall, slender youth perhaps the age of her third brother. He was sopping wet and wringing the excess water out of his tunic. Allah was with him—at least the stone statue in the fountain had not fallen over on him. As he raised his face, she saw the smooth, sharp-boned features of an attractive Arab youth, his sleek dark hair (he had lost his kaffiyeh head-covering in the water) and slightly upturned eyes hinting at foreign blood.

Outlined in moonlight, the lantern picking up the high points of her face, Laylah was clearly visible. For a moment Kaliad seemed speechless, and then he said: "You *are* a dark rose!"

"And you know very little about roses if you grab their stems without checking for thorns!" she responded, laughing. "You *are* all right?"

"Of course. I think it is part of the curse. I never seriously injure myself—I just make myself a laughingstock." Wincing, he removed a thorn from his hand. "But, Laylah, you do not know what you are thinking! True, the Phoenix will be as close to our people as it ever comes, but others can calculate its movements as easily as I did!" His voice lowered. "And the type of people interested in such information are usually sorcerers." His arm moved quickly in the sign to avert evil, and they heard fabric rip.

Laylah giggled. "I can see your curse can be a nuisance! But, Kaliad, surely we would not have the knowledge if we were not meant to act on it?"

He did not look convinced. Moodily sucking on his wounded hand, his eyes narrowed in concentration. Laylah had four brothers; she knew that look. There followed a brief, spirited argument, conducted in heated whispers for fear of attracting attention.

"But, Dark Rose, you do not understand! I *must* be the one to go! I am an adult, and I kick my heels in this house, awaiting my father's pleasure." He was almost pleading. "Think! If *I* can return with a feather of the Phoenix, then my father must admit I—am worth *something*, even if I am worthless to him."

"That is extremely unfair! Men have all the fun!" she cried, and then his words registered. "Kaliad, I forbid you to speak of yourself in such a manner! Think what a tutor you could be—or a merchant! I bet you have spied out possible trade routes or connections that no one else has ever thought of!"

"I *have* been considering a way to transport Chinese roses," he admitted, not meeting her eyes.

"But—" She stressed her next words. "Alone on the road to Wadi? You admitted you cannot ride to save your pride! Can you even sit in a wagon or a litter! Your servants pretend not to notice the noise you make, but—"

"I had to get to Baghdad somehow," he reminded her quickly. "We both have a need of this feather. It is your freedom to marry whomever you please, and my chance to prove my worth to my father."

"Then come with me!" As he gaped at this statement, Laylah rushed on: "I have recently expressed an interest in fine fabrics, to please my mother. I will wager I can convince her to take such a trip!"

"As we have not even been properly introduced, I am not sure your father would approve," Kaliad pointed out wryly.

"Pooh! My father approves of the same type of people I

do—did I not acquire my good taste from him? Are you not a gentleman, and honorable in your intentions?" This was indignant.

"Of course I am honorable in my attentions!" His response was heated. Placing his hands on his hips, he studied her a moment. "Perhaps we can solve all our problems. You say you are not afraid of the curse?"

"No." Laylah settled herself with dignity on top of the brick wall.

"Not even to be with me daily, as we seek the Phoenix and convince it to give us a feather?" He was quite intent, his eyes on her face.

"I told you I was not. Why would I lie about such a thing?" He was so serious, she almost felt uncomfortable.

"Neither of us is a good prospect—to any but ourselves. Let us find the feather, and return it to your father. Perhaps he would consider *my* suit, if I brought him the feather he desires."

Laylah was quite stunned by this suggestion. To marry Kaliad? It had never occurred to her . . . and then she wondered why it had not occurred to her. *Because he is already such a dear friend. One never gets to marry a friend.*

"It does not bother you—that I am already sixteen, and likely to be seventeen before we could wed? Your father would not think me too old?" she blurted out.

"If the feather does not convince my father of my worth, nothing will," Kaliad said evenly. "I will throw myself upon your father's mercy as an apprentice, if necessary, but I will convince him I am the husband for you."

Suddenly smiling, Laylah told him: "We will not have to grow old alone, praise Allah! Then together we will seek the feather?"

Kaliad grinned in response. "If you can get out of your house and to Wadi, then together we will seek the feather!"

Beneath Laylah's dangling feet a soft, reproachful voice spoke. "Please, my young lady, will you get down from there?"

Startled, Laylah looked down and saw plump Harun, lantern in one hand and wooden ladder in the other, looking beseechingly up at her.

"By Allah, you have wronged me, Harun, you who

claim the title Faithful!" she cried, pointing a finger accusingly at him. "Have you so little honest work for your hands that you must follow me like the Dog Star tails The Hunter?"

Harun bowed very low, clearly aggrieved in spirit. "I am the manager of your father's household, my lady, and its safety is my first concern. You are the most precious thing in the house of Sindbad—did you not know?"

"And you have my best interests at heart?" Laylah asked him.

"I do, my lady." A cautious man, Harun remained bent over.

"And you agree that what you have heard is in my best interest?" she qualified, fixing bright black eyes upon him.

Harun unfolded himself and peeped carefully at her. "It is plain that you think this is in your best interest," he temporized.

"Indeed! You will help me plan the trip!" Leaning over the tops of the roses, Laylah whispered, "Do not worry, I can always deal with Harun."

"Of course I will, my lady," Harun said clearly, setting the ladder against the wall. "I will even accompany you."

"Unnecessary, Harun," she said airily, stepping daintily down the ladder.

"Then I must follow you" was Harun's mournful reply.

She met his anxious gaze for a long minute. "You would, would you not, my fluffy sheep?" she murmured, eyeing the paunch of his stomach.

"I am afraid so," he agreed. "No matter how many meals I need miss!"

Laughing, Laylah called good night to Kaliad and promised to return with news the next day. "Very well, Harun, we will let you join our conspiracy! Come now—bring that ladder and tell me where my mother is, for I must suggest a journey to her."

Chuckling despite his worry, Harun lifted the ladder to his shoulder and followed in her wake.

As it happened, Laylah was able to convince her mother to consider the journey. Sindbad's wife was a modest and frugal woman, but fine fabric was her weakness, and she knew the merchants who controlled the cloth trade doubled the price of what they bought from the traders. Such a trip was an irresistible temptation to the woman.

Still, she hesitated—until Harun gallantly offered to escort the women of the household upon their journey. Sindbad cinched the argument by pointing out that it was no more expensive to eat upon the road, and that she could probably buy enough cloth to array both herself and her daughter for what she usually spent on herself.

Laylah questioned Kaliad endlessly about the details of the trip. How much extra money should she bring? Did he have suggestions on what clothing they should wear, while they searched the oases near the town? Kaliad was not pleased about *that* question, but finally said that the simple clothing of one of the servants would surely serve.

This information in hand, Laylah spent much time puzzling out how to acquire certain items. Buying them in the marketplace was impossible—it would draw too much attention. Then her eye fell upon a clerk in her father's shops, a young apprentice who was near her size. She merely waited until the youth had disappeared into the public baths one day, and then made off with his clothes. It was awkward, but she consoled herself with the knowledge that she would wash and return the clothing after her little trip.

Time was running out; their departure was upon them. Many people were going on this "little trip"—numerous household servants and even porters who were totally unfamiliar to Laylah. One hunched old man was almost frightening, he was so disreputable-looking. Anxiously Laylah searched for Kaliad; the young man had refused to tell her what he would be wearing, for fear of her somehow betraying her knowledge.

To her delight she was to ride part of the way, well protected from the hot sun by veils and a robe. Once free of the bustling streets of Baghdad, the caravan halted and Laylah transferred from her mother's litter to her preferred mount, a sweet-tempered barb filly. Glancing around at the confusion of people, both walking and riding she still saw no sign of Kaliad.

The disreputable porter losing his bundles signaled the arrival of her friend; Laylah stared in astonishment at the apparition which appeared. Not only his ability to draw objects into his path (from Laylah's angle, Kaliad had seemed several steps away from the hapless porter) but his very costume astonished her. For Kaliad had chosen to dress as one of the northern Kurds.

The people of Kurdistan, in the far north of Iraq, were both followers of Mohammed and nominally under the Caliph's rule, but they were an enigma. Their loyalties were to Allah and to their own people first—all others of Iraq came afterward. Their life-style and dress were also radically different. Kaliad was dressed in the bright colors of the Kurds, white shirt and baggy trousers belted with a wide sash of red, the pants tucked into scarlet leather boots with upturned points. Most interesting were the daggers strapped to various parts of his body; Kurds wore their weapons openly and proudly. The Kurds, like the Bedouins, were to be approached with caution.

Could his ruse work? She considered it as her group joined a larger caravan heading west. Kaliad had implied knowledge of several languages; the Kurds were said to be Aryan and Mongol in history, both taller and slightly foreign in looks. Kaliad could probably pass as a Kurd, and people would avoid him, which protected his identity (and any inanimate objects in the area . . .).

At dinner Harun informed her mother that a Kurd was familiar with Wadi al Ubayyid, and for a fee would guide them there. Laylah hugged her knees to her chest and kept silent; it had begun! She had only to journey quietly and carefully—the real adventure would begin in Wadi.

The trip took ten days, not six; Laylah's mother could not stand the midday heat, and needed to rest. Silently Laylah fretted; about her mother, about their quest. Near evening on the tenth day they arrived in the town of Wadi. By then even Laylah was bone-weary. It was larger than she had expected; the marketplace was packed with both Iraqis and Bedouins, and even a few Kurds. This alarmed Laylah until she heard a shopkeeper cursing someone for clumsiness. Turning in her saddle she saw the remains of a fruit booth, ripe citrus and dates tumbling into the street. Ah, Kaliad had left the caravan! He would change back into Arab clothing and blend into the crowds.

As they reached the inn, Laylah heard the rising call to prayer, and knew that Wadi had its mosque as well. After everyone had paused for evening devotions, the group commandeered a wing of the hostel.

Dinner revived her spirits. Fortunately her mother was tired and wished to sleep; Laylah politely agreed with this plan. Soon her mother's breathing became slow and heavy, and Laylah was able to dig for her disguise. A sound outside their window, of glass crunching, caused her heart to pound.

"Who?" she whispered, hoping it was Kaliad.

"If it is not me, you are supposed to yell for help," came Kaliad's voice. It was such a sensible suggestion Laylah had to suppress a giggle.

"It will take me but a moment to dress," she told him.

"I am not sure it is worth your time," was the glum response.

"What? There is a problem?" Laylah asked, pausing in her actions.

"I am not sure," Kaliad replied, starting to move closer to the mat-covered window. Another piece of glass shattered.

"Do not move! My mother is not that heavy a sleeper!" Leaning against the outside wall, Laylah said: "Explain."

"I asked around in the marketplace, after I changed my clothes. I found the oasis of Abu Sir."

"Already? But that is wonderful!" She clamped her hand over her mouth, but her mother, exhausted, did not stir.

"Maybe not. The oasis of Abu Sir is now the courtyard of the mosque."

"What?"

"The courtyard of the mosque," he repeated.

"Then . . . Kaliad," she started in a voice that promised fury.

"It was the site of the last pyre!" he insisted. "But Laylah, that was five hundred years ago! This village was not here the last time!"

"By Allah, what do we do now?" she whispered, trying to keep the defeat from her voice.

"All is not lost. After I practically destroyed the coffee-house where I asked about the oasis, I took the food they had sold me and retreated to the courtyard. I shared my dinner with a mullah, and asked him if the Phoenix had ever been sighted in the area. He said he himself had seen the Phoenix, and only a few moons ago!" Kaliad sounded both insistent and reassuring.

Laylah struggled not to laugh at his calm recitation of the destruction left in his wake. "Do you think he is telling the truth? Or did he see something else, and think it was the Phoenix?"

"I think it was the Phoenix," Kaliad said firmly. "Why should the bird change its habits for mankind? The problem is how to search without people noticing. It is obvious few here know of the legends of this area—after all, the Phoenix only recently returned to this desert."

"Where do we start? I understand this bazaar is busy well before dawn; Mother will be ready to go looking for cloth." Now that she had reached the moment of decision, Laylah realized her mother was going to notice her absence and be frightened . . . she did not want to frighten her mother.

"I think we should start by circling the town and identifying the closest oases," Kaliad suggested. "It might be roosting there."

"Good idea. Can you fetch the horses while I get dressed?" Laylah asked.

"Horses? Not until we must! Tonight we search on foot!"

Laylah was adamant—there was no time to lose, her mother could not be kept in Wadi forever. Horses. She was dressed and braiding her hair when Kaliad finally stopped arguing. Slipping out the window, Laylah led the way to the stable, praying fervently that no one noticed Kaliad as he tripped over every bucket and stone in the yard.

Once in full moonlight, they paused to adjust Laylah's kaffiyeh, which had proved more difficult to tie on her head than it had ever looked. Once Kaliad was satisfied with her appearance, they threw blankets upon two of their horses and led them away from the inn.

The search was fruitless. Their speed was not great, for the horses were still worn from their long day traveling.

Laylah made it worse by constantly looking over her shoulder, convinced that they were being followed. Together they checked several oases in the immediate area, but there was no sign of the Phoenix—not even a stray feather.

"It does not drop feathers casually," Kaliad grumbled as they made their way back into town before dawn. He had fallen off his horse at least a dozen times, even at a walk, and both man and beast were disgusted with each other. "We must find the bird and *ask* it for a feather!"

Laylah, on her part, was struggling to stay awake. Her dual identity of dutiful maiden and nightly adventurer was going to be difficult—ten days on the trail had exhausted her. "I hope you know what language the Phoenix speaks," she muttered, glancing over her shoulder once again. No sign of pursuit, yet she was *certain* someone followed, just out of sight . . . and they had reached the mosque, which promised many hiding places . . .

"Hold!" Kaliad barely whispered the word as he reined in his mount. Halting next to him, Laylah glanced over in inquiry, her eyes scanning the great courtyard of Abu Sir. "Do you hear?"

Rustling in the palms above . . . the flapping of wings . . . silence. "What—" she began, but Kaliad lifted a hand in warning. Leaning to dismount, he once again fell off the horse, this time pulling the blanket with him. The horse swung away from his sprawled form, its manners preventing it from walking off. A rush of wings reached their ears again, and then the cracking of branches.

A sudden thought seized Laylah, and a lump rose in her throat, freezing her breath. Surely it could not be—not in the center of Wadi al Ubayyid! Strangely enough no one was yet in the courtyard, although she had seen the muezzin who would call to worship entering the mosque even as they had entered the paved court.

Sliding from her mare's back, she moved toward the huge date palm in one corner of the grove. Immediately a wave of fragrant gums and spices swept over her—frankincense, ginger, cinnamon, allspice, myrrh—and she started to walk faster. *Creator of the Universe, say we are not too late!*

A trill of unearthly music laced her eardrums, and Laylah cried aloud: "No! Wait! I beg of you—we must ask a boon!"

"Too late! Too late!" To her shock, the words were in perfect Arabic, in a voice ageless as the sun itself. Bursting into song, the powerful yet delicate sound gained in volume and glory as the first light of morning streaked the sky. For a moment she saw it; its head was covered with golden feathers, its body and wings iridescent and multicolored like the shimmer of a field of peacocks. Then a red beam of sunlight struck the abode—no, pyre—of sticks and berries, and both nest and Phoenix burst into flames.

"No!" Behind her the horses shrieked in fear, but she paid them no mind. They were too late—in a moment the Phoenix would be gone, winging its reborn body to Egypt. Kaliad was struggling to hold the horses—losing them— Laylah paid them no mind, tears streaming down her face as the beauty of the ages charred before her eyes.

As the last notes of the death song faded into the light, the musical voice of a muezzin rose from a nearby minaret, calling the faithful to worship. Hoofbeats clattered into the distance, and Laylah knew the animals had escaped from Kaliad. He was limping to her side, half-trampled by their mounts, rubbing an injury. Silence . . . Kaliad was also watching the smoking pyre.

Why did the Phoenix not rise? Eyes wide, Laylah turned to Kaliad.

His face was ecstatic. "It is true! A fragment of legend is truth!"

"What is true?"

"Have you never heard of the egg of the Phoenix?" This was a whisper; taking her elbow, he slowly led her back into the depths of the town, passing groups of men arriving for morning prayer. "There is an account which says that only the first ray of morning can immolate the Phoenix— or resurrect it. Right now in that smoldering nest is an egg of solid gold. Tomorrow morning at dawn, when the sun first strikes that palm . . . then the Phoenix will rise!"

Her eyes lit up. "There is still a chance?"

"Of course!" But he frowned as he said it.

"What is wrong?" she asked quietly, rearranging her head-covering so her beardless face was invisible.

"Do you remember I warned you that others could read the signs, even as I did?" At her nod, Kaliad continued: "I am not worried about today—the courtyard is the major meeting place for the local men, it will be crowded with dozens who saw nothing, and know nothing . . . and would call a guard if someone tried to climb that palm. But to-night . . ."

"Someone could harm the egg?" Laylah said anxiously.

"Someone could *steal* the egg—if the first rays of the sun do not strike it tomorrow, it will remain only a lump of gold, and the Phoenix will be lost forever. A powerful lump of gold . . . wizards have predicted it is the Philosophers' Stone itself!" This was spoken so softly that it was almost inaudible, but Laylah heard it.

"Then . . . surely others will be watching. At least one," she replied.

"Yes. And tonight—" He left his words dangling, his eyes on their horses, which had stopped to browse on a bale of hay.

"Tonight we must watch, and guard it," Laylah announced, seizing both bridles and dragging the animals back toward the stables. A gargled sound came from Kaliad, but Laylah ignored him. "We must watch," she repeated.

"Inshallah," Kaliad muttered: God willing.

The day was an agony for Laylah. There was no way to hide her exhaustion; her mother awoke refreshed and ready to descend upon the bazaar. Of course the good woman noticed her daughter's dragging feet, and after a time asked Harun to escort her back to the inn, so she could get some rest. It was only after he had left that Laylah realized Harun was looking a bit tired himself. Had he been the elusive visitor dogging their footsteps the last eve?

Laylah slept straight through the heat of the day, waking only when the sun was low in the sky. Her mother had returned, a porter in tow, his back piled high with several bolts of material. After displaying her acquisitions with tremendous pride, her mother ordered a meal and proceeded to tell her daughter all the gossip of the bazaar.

A snap of glass or fired clay sounded; Laylah knew Kaliad was near. She listened to her mother's story with half an ear, hoping the woman was tired enough for an early sleep.

Desert heat had turned the trick—after food and a bit of recitation from the Koran, her mother was happy to turn in, sure that the next day would be even more profitable. Laylah was cautious, waiting until the woman's breathing had slowed before changing back into her dusty boy's clothing. Sliding her one dagger into her belt, she took a long, heavy coil of rope as well. As prepared as she could ever be, Laylah slipped out the window.

Kaliad had gone ahead. Gliding swiftly and soundlessly, Laylah hurried toward the mosque. Somehow Kaliad had made it to the feet of a mullah who was about to preach, without pulling down every trading stand in the final alley. Settling next to him, she saw that they had an excellent view of the huge date palm. There was plenty of light left, between the fading streaks of sunlight and the first few lanterns—the moon was already rising in the east.

All too soon the mullah's lecture was completed; the audience began to drift away, in search of food and amusing companionship. Kaliad asked a final question of the teacher, giving them an excuse to be among the last to stand. Only then did Laylah whisper in her lowest voice: "Have you been here all day?"

"Most of the day" was the response. He definitely looked tired; she hoped he had napped occasionally.

"As soon as everyone leaves, I will make sure *it* is still there," she told him, and seated herself upon a retaining wall.

Several men loitered, loath to move along. It could be innocent . . . or not. Hoping they were merely engrossed in good conversation, Laylah ignored them and concentrated on what Kaliad was saying. Out of the corner of her eye, she saw the last group walking in the direction of the coffeehouses. Finally!

"Did the muezzin leave?" Kaliad whispered.

"Yes." Standing, Laylah stared at the date palm, gauging its angle.

"What did you mean when you said you would make sure the egg was still there?" Kaliad asked.

"Just what I said." The rope would be a good precaution . . . removing the coil over her shoulder, Laylah draped it around her waist and hurried to the palm. Quickly tying the rope around the trunk, she began climbing up the tree.

"Wait!" There was nothing between Kaliad and the date palm, so he fell over his own feet. "Wait!"

Already halfway up the enormous palm, Laylah glanced down at him. "I do not think pausing here is a good idea," she told him. Making short work of the climb, Laylah tested the fronds of the palm with one hand. They were remarkably strong, still fresh and unscathed from the fire of that morning—surely capable of supporting her weight. Burrowing like some small predator, Laylah concealed herself in the head of the tree, leaving her climbing belt as security.

Parting the fronds, she peeked into the charred nest. Gold—magic gold, glowing in the moonlight! Later it struck her as odd that the sheer value of the egg had not tempted her. Now, she could think only of the Phoenix —how large would it be? Born with its previous lives remembered, with no need of parents to teach it the way of Allah . . . she wondered if it was lonely, and reached a trembling hand to gently pat the shell. To her wonderment, the egg was soft! So, a Phoenix still lived within . . .

"It is safe," she whispered loudly to Kaliad.

"Then come down!"

"But how can anything happen to it if I am here?" she pointed out reasonably.

Kaliad was losing his temper. "Laylah, we are talking about sorcerers! They do not need to touch the egg to remove it!"

"Then we are already lost, unless . . . if I recite the Koran, do you think that might keep any magic from harming the egg?" she suggested.

"Do you know enough of it by heart to do such a thing?" Kaliad asked, considering the question.

"I am a *hafiz!*" she replied, shocked. [A *hafiz* is an honorific given to any youth or maiden who memorizes a

sizable portion of the most holy book.] In the failing light
Laylah could see Kaliad shaking his head in a resigned
manner. "Do you think it is a good idea?"

"Are you certain you will not fall down?"

"Well, not positive, but fairly certain," she responded.
"I have my climbing belt, just like the date harvesters."

A long sigh drifted up to her. "I will hide in the courtyard. If you sense any presence—any presence at all other
than my own, call down, and I shall join my voice to
yours."

Pleased that he chose not to argue the point, Laylah
agreed, and rearranged herself on the fronds to begin her
vigil. She knew she could recite the Koran for at least four
hours. Some passages would therefore require repeating,
until the pale light before dawn told her to vacate her perch
or risk the flames of the Phoenix. Obediently she began to
recite her lessons, keeping her voice low and warm to
avoid undue strain on her throat.

The first intrusion was a mere tickle, a testing of the
area. Only one watching for magic would have noticed it.
Shivering, and not from cold, Laylah raised her voice, the
pure words of the Koran ringing through the darkness.
Sensation passed her by—whatever it was, it had retreated.

The second time was more obvious; vapor drifted
toward the nest, tinged with luminous, venomous green.
Even Kaliad had seen it—recognizing the passage she was
reciting, he joined his voice to hers, warding away the
poison.

Stillness was the watchword—for an hour or more,
nothing. Once Laylah had resented her long lessons spent
over the holy book. No more; submerging herself into the
words, giving the passages phrasing and meaning, Laylah
discovered new meaning in every sentence. Her devotion
to Allah rang in every syllable, and it was fortunate this
was so, for the next attack came in the form of a djinni.

Wind arose from nowhere, and a column of dust swirled
into the courtyard. Laylah increased her volume, hoping
that Kaliad could hear where she was in the recitation. As
her chanting gained strength, she saw a pale glow emanat-
ing from the nest. Was the egg capable of defending itself?

The rising moon was obscured by the funnel of dust, and Laylah was glad of it. Briefly she saw the djinni, and her throat grew dry with fright. Its size was beyond imagining, and its expression horrifying—this creature would not hesitate to swat her like a fly, if she stood in the way of its duty. Pressure grew around her, like great hands trying to crack an enormous shell. Her voice did not falter, though her entire body trembled.

Sucking began, like a dust devil, inhaling the courtyard itself, pulling fronds off the palm. The nest and its occupants did not stir . . . and finally the djinni desisted. A flicker of wind, a wordless snarl blaspheming the name of Allah, and it was gone. Somewhere down the narrow street she heard a crash of metal against wood. Several moments later, there was splashing in the courtyard pool.

"Laylah?" The whisper was anxious.

"I . . . I am fine, Kaliad," she finally replied. "And you?"

"It pulled off my kaffiyeh, but I found it in the alley," was the reply, and Laylah knew where the noise had come from. "Dark Rose, I think . . . I think there is a wizard nearby, casting spells. We have thwarted his attempts—now we must expect physical attack. Do you have a knife?"

"Yes, I do," she assured him.

"Do not pretend to be your father!" This was sharp. "For defense only!"

"Of course," she assured him, hiding deeper in the fronds and checking her safety rope.

An assault finally came when the sky to the east was beginning to pale. A man gave a yell, and suddenly the sounds of a fight reached her ears. Screaming, cursing, blows upon flesh—a fire blossomed in the booth at the end of the bazaar, and Laylah could see many moving shapes.

Unease swept over her . . . she felt, rather than heard or saw, another in the tree. Afraid to move, she hesitated before lifting a frond to peer below.

A shrouded figure was tying a safety belt. Swift as a child, he started climbing the rough bark of the palm. Laylah's heart rose in her throat as her fingers clenched the knife. *He is on the wrong side of the tree—it will be hard to get through the branches.* Drawing the curved blade, cautious of its sharp edge, she waited, as oblivious as he to the fight below.

Slip-rasp, slip-rasp . . . the climbing rope had stopped below her own. Leaning down, Laylah felt for her rope . . . and the rope below it. Purposefully she cut; once, twice, thrice. The rope began to part.

He knew! His rope was slipping; the man grabbed for a handhold, missing Laylah's arm by fractions. As the rope broke, Laylah whispered the name of Allah and poked blindly with her knife. It found a target.

Shrieking his pain, the man let go, scrabbling for something, anything—she poked his hand again, hardening her heart, remembering the sight of the Phoenix. This time he let go.

It seemed forever until he reached the ground . . . into the wading pool, although Laylah doubted it had saved him. Feeling faint, she checked the security of her rope once more as reality swept over her. The courtyard was in chaos, animals panicking, men hollering for help, flames leaping from the roof of a nearby building—

"Kaliad?" It was a fearful question. She could not stand it—moving the belt to loosen it, she started down the tree, awkwardly, haltingly, because of the knife in her hand.

Reaching the ground, she discovered she was the center of attention—unwelcome attention. Someone in long robes, screaming something at her in a language she did not understand— Green fire flew from his fingertips. That she understood! Knowing it was too late, she flung herself to the ground—

The spell vanished. The sorcerer stood against the flames, frozen—falling. As he fell, she saw the knife protruding from his chest.

Looking wildly about she saw Kaliad, on his knees, another knife at the ready. His face was grim and smudged with blood, but his hand was steady, despite a woven basket stuck on one foot and half a bolt of cloth dragging behind him. Not far behind him stood Harun, gasping his exhaustion through the hollow rim of a broken pot. The shards were scattered over the unconscious man at his feet.

Above their heads, the Phoenix burst into flame.

This time they were not the only witnesses. Crying out in amazement, the crowd moved quickly to the far side of the courtyard, away from both the burning tree and the smoldering bazaar.

"Who disturbs my sleep?" came a melodic trill.

Laylah opened her mouth to speak, but nothing came out.

Apparently the question was rhetorical. "Both thief and vile sorcerer are dead; the most high God has judged," the Phoenix announced. "The others were spellbound, and cannot be punished." Swiveling its elegant head to one side, it fixed its glowing eyes upon Laylah and Kaliad. "Ah—the young ones! As it was promised, so it is done. And what will you ask of me?"

"We . . . It all started—" Laylah began softly.

"Not your history, daughter of the Seaman!" the Phoenix said quickly, the mutter in its throat suspiciously like a chuckle. "Am I not wisdom incarnate? Even sleeping I Am and I Know—from the holy words which passed your lips to the battle which raged for my person. Now, tell me the wish of your heart!"

"The wish of my heart?" She brightened. "Can you remove the curse upon Kaliad?" Beside her, Kaliad exclaimed in surprise.

"No, maiden, I cannot," it responded. Before these words could mar her trust, it added: "But you can. To touch a feather of the Phoenix while in the coils of an evil one would be your death, young man—but she can take my feather. Its power softened by human hands, it can heal you." Ruffling its breast with a golden beak, the bird loosened one tiny, downy golden feather, which floated slowly into Laylah's hands. "Take it by the quill and touch him lightly—then drop the feather and draw away!"

Wondering, Laylah did as she was bid. As the golden plume floated to the ground it caught fire, charring like parchment. When it had burnt to fine ash, the Phoenix trilled.

"For your faithfulness, and your loyalty; for guarding my person with both blood and holy words, such is my gift."

Laylah and Kaliad could only stare at each other in astonishment . . . and sudden tragedy. "We have nothing for your father!" they said simultaneously.

"It is not necessary."

Both Laylah and Kaliad turned at these words. Two men had braved the sight before them and drawn near— one, still wheezing from the exertion, was Harun, but the other, a hunched old man wrapped in rags, was—

"Father!" Laylah threw herself at the merchant, who now straightened to his full height.

"I fooled you, child! I was among the caravan all the time, and yet you did not guess?" Laughing, oblivious to the crowd, Sindbad hugged his daughter. His long, pointed fake nose was bumped off in the exchange. "A mere household servant! In case you needed some help—" Turning to Kaliad, he added: "And you did not need much —I set the fire, you know. It rattled that sorcerer beyond recovery; his Phoenix spell fell apart! But I owe you my daughter; after all, you saved her life. I saw the feather—it was enough!"

"Not enough," cooed the great bird suddenly. "In answer to prophecy you came, an instrument to preserve the Wisdom of the World. Never before has my day of rebirth happened close to the abode of man! So we are even, you and I. But still, there is this . . ." Twisting suddenly, the bird unfurled its magnificent tail and shook it. A long, impossibly refulgent feather fell from the heights and drifted to Kaliad's feet. "For the wish of *your* heart, young man—for your dowry, maiden. Others have sought the Phoenix; some for fame, some for fortune, some merely to see the unknown. But none have ever dared pity the Phoenix, much less comfort it." Having finished speaking, the bird shifted, lifting its rainbow-hued wings.

"But, Phoenix!" Laylah cried as Kaliad bent to retrieve the feather. "Who will protect you next time?"

"Have no concern, daughter of the Seaman," it trilled, rising into the air. "In five hundred years, I shall have no need of protection! Farewell!" Larger than the greatest eagle, actually growing before their eyes, the Phoenix threw itself southwestward, racing the rising sun to Egypt.

It left behind a courtyard of mute and terrified people, uncertain whether they had seen a miracle or a devil. As the muezzin's voice rose in belated call, Sindbad and Harun pulled the two youngsters toward the streets.

"But ... but what did it mean, no need—" Laylah started to say as Kaliad thrust the feather into her hand. It softly glowed at her touch.

"Not here, child of my heart! Back, back to the inn!" Sindbad whispered.

"It means, Dark Rose," Kaliad murmured, chuckling, "that in five hundred years there will not be a village here!"

"Do you think—Kaliad! You have not tripped once! You must write your father immediately!" Laylah said delightedly.

"I have already written the King of Samarkand about your quest," Sindbad announced. "No doubt an emissary of His Majesty awaits our return to Baghdad."

"King of Samarkand?" Laylah looked at Kaliad out of the corner of her eye, and saw that he was blushing. After a long moment of silence, she thoughtfully said: "I can see how that made your condition a trifle embarrassing ... "

Kaliad started laughing.

Here ends the tale of the Feather of the Phoenix, as told by Harun the Faithful. Laylah the Dark Rose married Kaliad, heir of Samarkand, though they remained with Sindbad and his wife until Lady Death claimed those elders, may the mercy of Allah Almighty be upon their souls. The two then departed unto Samarkand, with Harun the Faithful in their train, where Kaliad in due time succeeded unto his father's throne. He proved a good and wise ruler, and a fine horseman (once a few bad habits were corrected ...). The gift of the Phoenix went with them, and remained the wonder of their kingdom, though it never glowed for any but Laylah and her descendants. In time the palace of Samarkand boasted of a rose garden that surpassed any west of China, though Laylah thought her joyful children the most beautiful blossoms of all. In great delight did Laylah and Kaliad enjoy the gifts of Allah all the days of their lives, until there took them the Destroyer of Delights and the Sunderer of Societies, the Plunderer of Palaces and the

Garnerer of Graves, and they were translated to the ruth of Almighty Allah.

And what, O reader, of Harun's other tales of the Dark Rose of Baghdad and the Feather of the Phoenix? *Wa Alla A'alam*— Only God knows the future.

The Soul of a Poet

Cherry Wilder

There was once a poor poet in the city of Baghdad and when he was more than forty years old he came, by a series of tragic accidents, into possession of a modest fortune. At once his mode of life was changed. He moved into his uncle's house in a better quarter of the great city, he dined, nay, he feasted with friends old and new. Even his name was changed from Khaleb Rak to Khaleb Qarrak, a condition of his uncle's will.

Khaleb was glad of a chance to bear all this with a good grace, to remain, as he hoped he was, a simple man with the soul of a poet. How long had he contented himself with the bare necessities of life in his hovel near the wharves? He had taken joy in simple things and in the privilege of living in the golden age of the world under the benign rule of Haroun al Raschid. He never tired of singing the praises of the great Caliph. He rejoiced, privately, when his verses came into the libraries of the rich or were sold as broadsheets. When times were hard he joined his one and only wife, Lalia, at making lampwicks.

Lalia was of an age with Khaleb and he believed that she was the most sensible woman he had ever met. She had accepted their lot cheerfully and made much out of little. Years past, their only child, a son, had died in infancy, and Lalia had borne no more children. Their sorrow bound them together. Now Lalia accepted her riches as she had done her poverty. She managed Khaleb's household well, put on finer clothes, and saw to it that her husband made a good impression.

Late at night in his bedchamber, when they were enjoy-

326

ing a last cup of nabidh together, Lalia suggested that he take a new wife. Khaleb was alarmed at the prospect.

"The nightingales are not singing so loudly as before," he said. "Spring is not on my head. Roses are not under my feet!"

"Rubbish!" said Lalia. "You are in the prime of life. You have money and room in the house. You need . . ."

She did not go on to say exactly what it was that he needed. At any rate *she* needed help in running the house and she could do with some companionship. Besides, a new wife might bear him a son.

He felt the old excitement rise in him at the thought of a son but he was still shy of the formalities. Procuring a new wife, a young wife, was a tedious business. Lalia had an answer to that too. Tomorrow they would go together to a certain slave market and see what was on offer.

"Ah, that is a terrible thought!" protested Khaleb.

"You have inherited four of your uncle's slaves," she pointed out.

"Only four!" he exclaimed. "You mean that the tall Nubian . . . ?"

"No, he is a slave," said Lalia, "but the gardener, Old Habib, is a freedman."

"All the same," said Khaleb, "to purchase a girl . . ."

"To rescue her!" said Lalia. "Some poor young things from the mountains. These girls are unspoiled, wild as birds."

"And then," said Khaleb, "if she proved . . . suitable, I might set her free and make her my wife."

"I knew," said Lalia, "that you would see it my way, husband."

Next day they dressed in their best and were carried in a litter to a market not far from the northern gate, accompanied by the tall Nubian house servant.

Khaleb did not enjoy the experience at all but he put on a brave face. The transactions were conducted very respectably and he saw that the customers were all of the better sort. There were women, veiled and unveiled, in a shelter at the end of the platform and he allowed Lalia to go amongst them. She spoke to the women, sometimes touched their hands but did not look at their teeth or pinch their flesh. At length she returned to her husband at the back of the crowd.

"Trust me, Khaleb, I beg of you," she said. "You must purchase the tall girl in the blue veil sight unseen. You must make the transaction privately with the Slavemaster. On no account must she be unveiled on the block."

"Is she so beautiful?" breathed Khaleb.

"She will do very well," said Lalia.

Khaleb went directly to the Slavemaster, who sat on a cushioned chair curling his mustachios, expressed his wish, and began to drive a bargain. This was indeed a girl from the mountains of Kurdistan, eighteen years old, guaranteed a virgin. Beautiful, one might say, but not to everyone's taste. Hearing the domestic virtues of the other slaves extolled by the Slavemaster's assistants, Khaleb grasped that this girl was *not* skilled in anything very much. Could she weave, cook, sing, dance, or play an instrument? She would soon learn, insisted the Slavemaster, moderating his demands a little. At last they agreed upon a price, sealed the bargain with a cup of sinfully strong nabidh, and once the gold had been weighed, the girl was his.

Khaleb and his wife set out in their litter again with the Nubian walking behind, leading their new slave by a halter. When they were out of sight of the market Lalia bade the bearers halt and let the girl step in through the silken curtains.

"Slip down your veil, my dear," she said. "I did not quite catch your name."

Trembling, the girl obeyed and Khaleb felt a strange thrill of compassion. She had rather pale skin, strong features, and of all things, green eyes. Her hair was luxuriant and dark red, an amazing color. She was well grown but not voluptuous. She was also shocked and terrified.

"My name is Zorima," she whispered.

"Child," said Lalia, "this is your master, Khaleb Qarrak, a poet and a man of property. I am Lalia, his wife."

Khaleb saw that Zorima hardly knew how to behave to a master. She bowed her head a little. Lalia questioned and her story came out. She was the daughter of a mountain chief; her mother, a woman of Georgia, had died some years earlier. Now none of her clan remained. She was the sole survivor of a local war, sold into slavery by her father's victorious enemies. She had been spared rape in order to bring a decent price.

"There now," said Khaleb, "your time of trial is over, Zorima. You have come to a sheltered garden."

There followed six moons of domestic felicity in their new house on Fig Tree Street. Zorima left off trembling and learned to smile and, eventually, to laugh. In fact, she learned everything they tried to teach her. She could cook and clean and even sew, after a fashion, and she could read, write, and cipher. She sang wild mountain songs in a tuneful voice. She was, moreover, an excellent listener, always ready to hear tales of wonder, of marvelous voyages and enchanged lands.

So they all lived together in great harmony and Khaleb told himself that this was a long gentle courtship of his new betrothed. He wrote several appropriate lyrics. He did not know how much Lalia had told Zorima of their plans for the future.

There was harmony within the house but outside a storm was brewing. Khaleb brought his best efforts to managing his new estate. He was on terms now with merchants and officials as well as poets and petty tradesmen. He saluted the agents and courtiers of the great Caliph as he went about the streets. He waited upon several nobles and was once seated at dinner four places away from the brother-in-law of Jaffar, the Grand Vizier. It was borne in upon him that his uncle, Abu Qarrak, had had powerful enemies. The sudden death of the old man and the hunting accidents that had taken his two sons appeared in a sinister light.

Khaleb became uncomfortably aware of faction and intrigue that he scarcely understood. Secretly he began to doubt the justice and benevolence of the golden age in which he lived. While he was planning a dissertation on this melancholy theme there was a sudden round of arrests. His uncle's friends fell from grace and as Khaleb himself was poised upon the very brink of the abyss he received a timely warning from his gardener, Old Habib.

"Young Master," whispered the old man. "You have no time left. The house of Qarrak is proscribed and you bear the name. Fly, fly before it is too late!"

"In the name of Allah!" cried Khaleb, "I have done no wrong! Whither shall I fly. . ."

"I know a distant place where you will be safe," said Old Habib, "and I will guide you there. I have already spoken to the Mistress."

Khaleb found Lalia clearing out the strongbox and Zorima tieing up their necessities in a carpet. With a last gesture he scribbled a parchment freeing the Nubian and his fellow slaves. In the dusk of the summer day the fugitives crossed the sheltered garden, where a last nightingale was singing, scrambled through a secret door in the wall, and took to the dark streets of Baghdad.

After a long and trying journey by boat, on horseback, and on foot, they came to Old Habib's home village far to the northeast of Baghdad, in the neighborhood of Samarkand. There, with the last of his gold, Khaleb was able to purchase a small farm, hidden away in a green valley. He worked his land, fished in the stream, and gave thanks for their lucky escape. What did it matter to Khaleb Rak, the poet, if his fortunes had altered so suddenly? Did not the great city of Baghdad improve with distance?

In spring, watching Zorima gallop up and down on their old sorrel mare—for riding was one thing that she did very well indeed—he knew that the time had come. When he helped her from the saddle they stood very close for a moment and Khaleb said:

"Zorima, my girl, you are set free. You are no longer my slave!"

Her smile came and went. He pressed on:

"I will use no ceremony," he said. "I am a plain man although I have the soul of a poet. Be my wife, Zorima!"

Zorima sighed deeply and smiled and gave him a kiss.

"You have been kinder to me than any man in the world," she said, "and I am honored to be your wife."

There was, indeed, no ceremony but documents were signed and Khaleb visited the local Imam. Lalia and Zorima kissed and called each other sister. Khaleb took great delight in his new bride and felt his strength renewed in her embrace. They had not been wed for more than a moon when a traveler happened along and claimed hospitality for the night.

Khaleb saw that this was a very strange old man, his skin impossibly wrinkled, his beard long and forked, his deep-set eyes black, with a red glint in them. He rode a black horse and carried a tall gerfalcon upon his gauntlet. The name upon a leather reliquary about his neck read: "Hadji Selim."

"My house is yours!" said Khaleb. "We will serve you as best we can, Hadji Selim."

Everything went so well that Khaleb was more than ever convinced that the old man was a magician. As the evening went on the stranger was very civil to Khaleb and accepted a scroll of his verses. He praised Lalia's exquisite lamb and her pastries. He discreetly complimented Khaleb on the beauty of his second wife, Zorima.

The lamps were burning low and Khaleb was about to lead Hadji Selim to the spare bedroom. Suddenly Zorima came into the room and bowed, although she had never learned a truly self-effacing manner.

"Lord," she said, addressing their guest, "I have found this amulet in the stableyard. It must be yours!"

Hadji Selim lost his serenity for a few seconds. He patted his robe then reached out most eagerly to take the amulet from Zorima's hand. It was all of thick yellow gold, a tube of gold the size of a man's thumb, set with rubies and emeralds.

"Mistress," he said, catching his breath, "I value this precious thing as I do my life. Good Khaleb, I beg you to summon the household so that I may reward you all!"

"Hadji Selim," said Khaleb, "we ask no reward."

Nevertheless he clapped his hands. Lalia came from the kitchen followed by Old Habib, their only servant.

"First let me demonstrate," said Hadji Selim.

"Old man," he said, turning to Habib, "I am sure there is some useful piece of equipment of moderate size which you need about the farm?"

"Indeed, Lord," said Old Habib. "We could do with a new rake, larger flails, a billhook . . ."

"What shall it be?" asked the guest. "Wish for one of these things."

"The billhook then," said Old Habib. "I wish for a new billhook!"

There was an instant thump and it lay before them on the carpet, its blade newly tempered and glistening. Old Habib picked it up gingerly and tested it with his thumb. He gave thanks to Allah and to Hadji Selim who had worked the miracle.

"Your servant's wish has been granted," said Hadji Selim "and he will receive a little more than he bargained for. Every wish is manifold, either in its making or in its fulfillment. Sometimes it is hard to tell where a wish begins or ends. There is, however, one sound principle to be followed. You, Khaleb Rak, you, Mistress Lalia, and you, fair Zorima, each have one wish. Think well, do not take too long and do not tell your wish until it has been fulfilled."

Khaleb felt an inner trembling and looked nervously at his wives. Lalia folded her hands, Zorima stared at Hadji Selim. Now surely, thought Khaleb, it is time to be wise and generous. He believed that he knew the principle of which the magician had spoken. He thought of his dear wives and he thought of Old Habib who had saved their lives and brought them to this place and who now received only a billhook. So he included the old man in his wish although it made the formulation somewhat cumbersome. *I wish that the members of my household . . . Lalia, Zorima, and Habib . . . will each come to his or her heart's desire.* He trusted that this would be counted as one wish.

"I have made my wish!" he said firmly.

"And I," said Lalia.

"And I," said Zorima.

Hadji Selim bowed his head and smiled. He went on his way next morning and it soon became clear that he had left a wake of magic behind him. Every dish and cup that he had used replaced itself as soon as it was broken. Silken coverings appeared upon the spare bed. A flowering almond tree sprang up in the stableyard at the very spot where Zorima had found his golden amulet. The simple billhook which Old Habib had received never needed to be sharpened and it could not be lost. The old man was able to summon it to his hand every morning.

At the place where the mysterious traveler had forded the stream, exotic plants and flowers sprang up. Strange birds were seen in the tops of the willow trees and at dusk fabulous beasts . . . a gazelle with golden hooves, an old gray unicorn . . . came to drink. Khaleb found that he could live with magic as with everything else; he put his wish out of his mind. In three moons Zorima became pregnant and in the fullness of time she bore him a son.

Khaleb was wild with joy but he knew that every child's life was precarious. He spent his days bent over the cradle of Haroun ben Khaleb or walking about in the fields half-mad with hope. This *must* be a world in which his son would survive and grow to manhood! Two moons passed, then three, then six and at last he heeded the words of Lalia when she sat the baby on his knee.

"He is the strongest child I ever saw," she said proudly. "You have a son, Khaleb Rak!"

Then Zorima, coming in with the child's teething syrup, said softly: *"My wish has been granted!"*

Khaleb left off talking nonsense to little Haroun and observed: "My dears, I am the happiest man in the world . . . but I cannot say if my wish has been granted or not."

Privately he thought that it had been granted, in part. Zorima had wished for a son. What could be more natural? Was this perhaps the heart's desire of *both* his wives? Hadn't he rather counted upon the fact that it might be? Then Lalia said unexpectedly:

"One wish has come to pass . . . but I will say no more."

Haroun was weaned early, at a year old, and he continued to thrive and grow and do remarkable things. Khaleb did not know when his life had been happier.

Only Zorima was a little strained and pale; she strode about in the river meadows. Late at night Khaleb found her alone before the house watching the night sky. He noticed for the first time that her braids had been cut. Her thick cap of hair was barely shoulder length. Had he not read or heard that long hair sapped the strength? Perhaps her hair had been cut as a health measure, because she was still weak from the birth and nursing of Haroun, that sturdy rascal. At that moment the child began to fret, inside the dark house.

"Lalia will settle him down," said Khaleb. "Come, Zorima, sit here by me on the step."

He was full of tenderness for her, for his mountain girl, who had given him his son. Zorima said: "Tell me about the stars . . ."

While he held forth, Khaleb was overcome by nostalgia for his uncle's sheltered garden in Baghdad.

"Alas," he said, "I am neglecting my poetry!"

This was at the new moon; and when the moon was full, Zorima came to her heart's desire. At the end of a long golden day in late summer Old Habib came panting into the house. Khaleb was sipping coffee.

"Master!" cried the old man. "A wonder!"

"What now?" sighed Khaleb. "Is it another peacock by the stream?"

"O come, I beg of you!" panted Habib. "The young Mistress . . . who knows what she will do?"

Mystified, Khaleb followed him out of the house and Lalia came after them with Haroun in her arms. There stood Zorima. There beside the stream, grazing quietly, was a magnificent horse, snow white. Along his back, breaking the light into shafts of iridescent fire, were his folded wings.

"Zorima!" said Khaleb.

She turned from gazing at the winged horse and he saw that she was transformed with longing.

"I must go to him!" she said. "If I can once mount upon the winged horse he is mine! He will fly with me to enchanted lands!"

"Zorima, you cannot leave us!" said Khaleb in a shocked voice. "I am your husband!"

"I have been a true wife," said Zorima, "but I can stay no longer!"

"Zorima . . . here is your son!"

"I love Haroun," she said, "but Lalia is as much his mother as I am!"

"I treated you kindly! I taught you all I could!"

"I gave you all that I had to give," said Zorima. "I even gave you my one wish. I wished that you should have a son."

"Oh, Zorima, I made you my wife! I set you free . . ."

"Free?" said Zorima.

Khaleb looked at Lalia where she stood holding the

child and he felt that she too had echoed this word. He had wished this sorrow upon himself: Zorima must have her heart's desire. He unclenched his right hand and there he found three of the candied almonds that he had been eating with his coffee. It was kismet. He sighed and said:

"So be it . . ."

He cast the almonds one by one into the grass at Zorima's feet and each time he repeated the words "I divorce thee."

"Oh, Khaleb!" said Zorima and her voice was full of love and gratitude.

"Wait!" said Lalia. "Wait, dearest sister, you will be cold!"

She planted Haroun in his father's arms, ran into the house, and came back with a jacket. Zorima gave Haroun a kiss and brushed away her tears. She scooped up the three candied almonds and walked swiftly across the meadow. Khaleb saw that in her billowing white trousers and the green velvet jacket (a piece of his old finery from Baghdad) she looked like a young prince.

She came to the charmed circle of ground near the ford and the winged horse lifted its head. Slowly Zorima came nearer, laid a hand upon its neck; it nuzzled in her palm for the sweet almonds. Then as they watched, enthralled, she grasped its silvery mane and sprang upon its back. The glorious creature made a few light steps upon the soft turf, then spread its wings and rose up prancing into the sky. The watchers all cried out. Zorima, firmly mounted, waved a hand and was carried out of sight.

Khaleb Rak was stricken to the depths of his soul. Little Haroun fretted for a few nights for the loss of one of his mothers but Khaleb remained deeply troubled. Lalia comforted him as best she could.

"Husband," she said, "I blame myself. Zorima was not meant to stay. Who can keep a wild bird in a cage?"

"Wife," said Khaleb, "I have been granted a son. What was it the magician said? No one knows where a wish begins and ends. I am partly to blame for this coil of fate."

Life went on as before and the farm prospered. There were other farmhands now and Old Habib was allowed to sit in the shade. Once he spoke to Khaleb wistfully of a group of village elders who were making the pilgrimage to Mecca.

"Good Habib," said Khaleb, "you must join them! We will buy a place for you in the caravan!"

"Oh, Master!" said Habib. "Allah be praised! Now I will have my heart's desire."

If all wishes were so easily satisfied, thought Khaleb. What of Lalia, his remaining wife? What had *she* wished for? He was teaching his son every day now and Haroun was as bright as he could have wished.

"Father," said the child, "did my other mother ride away on a horse?"

Khaleb fobbed him off sadly, foreseeing complications later. Zorima had not precisely *ridden* away, had she?

"Haroun," he said, "your mother has gone to heaven."

"Father," said Haroun, "I am tired of counting. Tell me a story."

From time to time Khaleb was visited with long vivid dreams of strange lands. He saw uncharted seas and islands and the realms of foreign princes; he walked in the market-places of great cities and in the marble palaces of kings. It seemed to him that he was carried through the upper air and walked upon the very tops of the mountains. Then he made his way through jungles, thick and green, thronged with monkeys and parrots and beasts so extreme that he must straight away note them down when he woke to pre-serve their strangeness in his mind. Now and then his dreams were peopled with men and women and with demons. He spun his dreams out himself when he woke and the heroine or hero of these adventures—for it was often more seemly to have a hero—he called Prince Zorim.

For years he worked patiently at the tales of Prince Zorim and at other verses, sad lyrics of a lost love. The few guests who came to the farm were pleased by his tales and the people of the village were asked to direct travelers to the house of the poet Khaleb. So his fame grew and the world came closer and when Haroun was twelve years old it was no longer unthinkable that the boy might be edu-cated in Baghdad. Jaffar the Grand Vizier, who had thrown down so many, including Abu Qarrak and his sons and his unworldly nephew, had been himself thrown down.

At last, when he least expected it, there came a delegation from the golden city, right to his door. As a sign of good faith it was led by an officer in the palace guard, a tall Nubian, whom he had set free as he went into exile. The poet Khaleb Rak Qarrak was invited to visit the court at Baghdad for a season. His writings had found favor in the eyes of the most high, the Caliph Haroun al Raschid.

Khaleb received the invitation with dignity and agreed to leave his retreat, though only for a season. A great feast was given in the village for the delegates and for Khaleb, who had been honored by the Caliph. When all the shouting had died he was alone with his wife Lalia and to his surprise she took his hand and wept and said:

"Husband, my wish is fulfilled. At last I have my heart's desire!"

"Then my wish is granted too," said Khaleb, "but tell me, wife, what did you wish? To return to Baghdad?"

The time was evening; Haroun came trotting home from the feast on his new pony, a tall boy with dark red hair and Khaleb's own brown eyes. Down at the stream two white peacocks walked on the enchanted ground and in the almond tree in the stableyard a nightingale was singing.

"I wished," said Lalia, "that you would become a true poet. I trust the judgment of the Caliph in this matter."

Khaleb was not unaware of the implications of this wish. Had he not been a true poet for years? Or was it not enough to have the soul of a poet? Had the loss of Zorima and the dreams that, perhaps, she sent to him, drawn out his true potential? Was there, even in Lalia, a hidden critic? Every wish was manifold and there was no end to wishing. At least, so far as he could judge, all three persons who had received the gift of a magician, Hadji Selim, had adhered to the first principle of wishing. He decided to use it one day as a moral to a tale of magic: *"Wish benefits for others, not for yourself."*

The Flower Princess

Diana L. Paxson

"Warriors of Mewar, rejoice, for Ajaisi Rana comes!"

"Behold, the heir of Khoman, the heir of Bappa, the heir of Goha, comes into his hall!"

The salutations of the *charans* rolled out in swift succession as the rana passed, and a murmur of deep-voiced greeting followed him, rolling from pillar to pillar of the great audience hall. Through the high windows came the breeze that blew always about the rock of Chitor, pungent with the scents it had captured on its progress across the plain.

"Prepare to receive him with honor!"

"Prepare to receive Ajaisi, the Lion of Chitor—"

As if he did not hear them, Ajaisi paced forward across the cold marble tiles, his eyes on the golden umbrella of state at the end of the hall, his head held high, borne on a wave of titles from bard to bard.

"Welcome the wielder of Viswakarma—"

"—lord of the Sisodias—"

"—regent of Siva—"

"—head of the Suryavanshas, child of the sun!"

For Ajaisi this litany still seemed unreal. These were his father's titles, or perhaps his older brother's. It had only been a year since the battle of Sthaneshvara. The *tikka* mark itched between his brows. To hear himself hailed in such terms still seemed like sacrilege.

"May you have abundance!"

The rana's foot was on the first step. He turned, seated himself on the great silk cushion beneath the umbrella, and tucked his legs beneath him.

338

"May the gods be gracious," said the last *charan*, old Kilparam, who had held the position of Raj-Kavi since before Ajaisi was born. He had seen four princes raised to the *gadi* of Chitor, and made verses to celebrate all of them. To Kilparam, Ajaisi was simply one more. The royal bard took his traditional position on his lord's left hand. The wailing of the horns died away.

Ajaisi sighed and looked at the chieftains ranked in precise order with their warriors behind them. Weapons clinked softly as they sat down, proudly meeting his eye. There must be many among them who felt as uneasy with their titles as he did. The best blood in Rajasthan had fed the field of Sthaneshvara when Prithvi Raja and his allies fell before the Afghan hordes. But Rajputs did not show grief for warriors who died well.

It is not my father I am grieving for, thought the rana then, *but myself.*

One by one, the Mewar chieftains came forth to do their homage. Ajaisi made himself meet their eyes calmly, but it was hard, when old Kailun Rao bowed before him, and he saw the ghost of Gayatri's proud glance in her father's face. It was harder when Rukmini's younger brother came forward, and Ajaisi thought of the child that she had been expecting when she died. At least no one would come to him wearing Setu's smile. All the men of her family had died on that bloody field.

"—Muhammad Ghori has eaten Ajmir and Delhi, but the word comes that they are making a tough meal . . . too busy digesting them to come against us in the next year— maybe the next generation . . . have time, my lord, to build back our strength . . . barbarians will get a surprise if they think to attack us again!" Jaimul Rawul's hennaed mustaches quivered with emotion.

Ajaisi blinked, realizing that he had hardly comprehended a word that Jaimul had said. He nodded gravely, hoping that the great warrior had been too caught up in his own dreams of glory to notice his lord's inattention. Not that it mattered, he had heard all this before. It was for the benefit of the chieftains that Jaimul was repeating it all. There was a growl of approval.

"We have time, then, to repair our fortresses and breed new sons to replace those who are gone!"

At Kailun's words, Ajaisi stiffened with an awful certainty that he knew what was coming now.

"But a man without wives can have no sons!" The old man exclaimed. "My lord, why do the women's quarters of your palace remain empty? It is not right for a man to be alone—still less for a sovereign! Even the gods must be married, and how can you expect to retain their favor if you flout their law?"

"From father to son the lordship of Chitor has descended for six generations, and the *charans* of my line have praised them," added Kilparam. "My son stands yonder. Where is the son who will follow you?"

"I have heard you—" said Ajaisi as Kailun drew breath to speak again. "There is no need to say more!"

"You have heard us, but what have you done?" asked Jaimul.

"You will not tell me my duty!" the rana said between his teeth. "Nor will you tell me when it is time to cease mourning those who are gone." He took a deep breath, fighting to retain his dignity.

He had done his duty to his clan and married—three times. Three women as beautiful as devas had illuminated his life, and all three of them, believing that he had perished with his father and brothers at Sthaneshvara, had fulfilled their own duty to him by dying together upon one funeral pyre.

Ajaisi shifted position on the gadi and felt the pull of partly healed scars. *It was almost true*—Jaimul had borne him, unconscious and bleeding from eighty wounds, away from that dreadful field.

If I had died we would all have been together in glory. Were my dear ones surprised, I wonder, not to find me awaiting them? Will they bar the gates of paradise against me when I finally come, because, however unwillingly, I fled the field?

"But *I* will tell you," said Jaimul. "You are *Ma-Baap*, our father and our mother, and as it goes with you, so will it go with the land. Mourn all you please, but marry!"

"Not now!"

Even the least of the warriors sitting next to the wall recoiled, and Jaimul lost a little of his ruddy color. The rana forced his voice back under control.

"I know my responsibility, but I must have more time!" He took a deep breath and looked around him. "If there is no other business for this gathering—"

Taking this as a signal the court was ending, servants started to come forward with the scented handkerchiefs. Attar of roses hung heavy on the air.

"Lord—" Mahendra, the chamberlain, gestured sharply and the servants stopped. "There is an embassy from Jaisalmir. They have gifts for you, *Bapuji*, honored father— will you receive them?"

"So long as those gifts don't include a coconut!" said Ajaisi, and was rewarded by reluctant smiles at his reference to the traditional symbol for a marriage alliance.

He sat back, feeling the atmosphere around him begin to relax again. The musicians had begun to play, and servants were moving among the columns, offering *pan* on silver trays. In a few moments, Mahendra returned with a small procession behind him, lengthened, Ajaisi realized after a few moments, by the fact that the promised gifts included a carpet of some size. He lifted one eyebrow, and Jaimul shrugged. The deputation consisted mainly of warriors, but the man who stepped forward to receive his greeting wore the sacred thread of a Brahmin and a yogin's saffron robe.

"My master congratulates you upon your accession, and regrets that it has taken so long for him to send his greetings. We—we also lost many at Sthaneshvara, and since then . . ."

Ajaisi lifted a hand. "Holy one, there is no need to say more. We have all suffered in this terrible year."

The Brahmin nodded. "But my lord wishes to win your friendship. Accept, then, these gifts as a token of his regard."

He gestured, and the Jaisalmir warriors set down before him a tray of silver covered with a silken cloth upon which rested seven emeralds that caught the light in spurts of green fire. He gestured again, and the men put down upon the step a chest of carven sandalwood inlaid in ivory which proved to be filled with pearls. They stepped aside then, and the servants who carried the carpet moved forward, lowered it carefully, and, with a swift tug, set it unrolling across the floor.

For a moment Ajaisi was confused by the blaze of colors—garnet and ivory and russet and deep blue. Then his eyes focused, and he began to follow the intricate patterning of geometric and floral forms with appreciation. Within the outer border, the carpet was divided into rectangles whose borders led one into another, drawing the eye further and further in until it reached the central medallion.

The rana's gaze moved across the maze of color, then he blinked and looked again. From the random swirl of forms a face leaped suddenly. One moment it had been a design of flowers, and now it was the face of a maiden whose face shone like the moon. He took a quick breath. The scent of roses that had been fading was suddenly overpowering. Ajaisi cast a swift glance around him, saw appreciation in the eyes of his warriors, but not wonder. And yet, when he looked again the face he had seen was still there.

The image stared back at him with Gayatri's eagle gaze, but the perfection of feature was that of Rukmini, and yet not quite, for she had Setu's mischievous smile. Ajaisi felt his eyes sting, blinked quickly, and looked again, and now he could not understand why he had thought he recognized the features of his dead wives. He had never seen this girl . . . he had never seen *anyone* so fair . . .

"What is wrong?" asked Jaimul. The others were chattering. The rana looked up, and saw that the Jaisalmir priest was watching him.

"Who is she?" His voice was hoarse and he swallowed. "Did they send you here to offer her to me?"

"What are you talking about?" Jaimul's gaze followed his rana's to the rug, then returned to Ajaisi's face again.

"You don't see her?"

"All I see in the rug is flowers!" the warrior answered him.

"She is the Flower Princess, she is Kishna Bai," the yogin spoke softly. "You are one of the few who have been able to see her. But all that we can offer you is her carpet, for her image appeared within it the day she disappeared."

Ajaisi took a deep breath and straightened. "Is it so?"

Jaimul was staring at him, and the chamberlain Mahendra, who had overheard the last of this, looked from one to the other with a frown.

"You are all so eager for me to marry!" The rana laughed a little wildly, and gestured toward the carpet. *"There* is the image of the woman who could make me forget what I have lost. That is the face of my bride!"

"What magic is this? Would you ensnare our lord with a spell?" Jaimul Rawul's mustaches bristled, but the Brahmin stared back serenely.

"Not by design. My raja sent the other gifts to seal an alliance, but the carpet comes with a father's plea, and if there is a spell in it, it is the work of gods, not men. The Princess refused to wed the man my lord had chosen for her. In his madness he cursed her," said the priest. "And in the morning, she had been taken, no man knows where. Her hand is for the warrior who can see her, and who, having seen, is willing to seek her and bring her home once more."

Ajaisi Rana reclined upon his cushions, watching the pale smoke from his hookah spiral toward the painted beams as if it were dancing to the music of the vineh that throbbed in the adjoining room. Gradually, tight nerves were easing, but he did not think the drug would bring sleep soon. Although his body was relaxing, the rana's mind remained curiously alert. The colors of the carpet spread out before him seemed to have taken on an even deeper glow, and the face of the flower princess shone ever more clearly.

Only she, of all women in the world, now has power to stir me. Is it because she is unattainable? he wondered then.

If he took more opium, he would cease to care, but he had sought that refuge too often. More than once he had wondered if he should go to Delhi and fight his way through Muhammad Ghori's guards. He was unlikely to succeed in killing the Afghan ruler, but that was not what had stopped him. It was the thought of the retribution that would inevitably descend upon a weakened land.

Or perhaps it is simply that my courage is gone . . .

The liquid in the belly of the hookah bubbled melodiously and the vineh quavered and jangled from the anteroom. The flames flickering through the pierced-work of the brass lamps began to burn low, sending shadows to chase the smoke around the room. Ajaisi lay back, letting the awareness leach out of his body limb by limb until only vision remained, following that hypnotic flicker of light—dark—light across the patterns of the beams, the carpet, the walls.

Ajaisi drifted between the worlds. When the flicker of light began to assume a form he was not particularly surprised. He watched the smoke swirl in thickening draperies around a shape that was slender yet substantial. Shadow molded curves like a temple sculpture, flowed out in waves of night-black hair. The figure swayed in rhythm to the pulsations of the vineh. The rana strove to glimpse features, but the filmy scarf was modestly drawn down.

"*Ajaisi son of Surya . . .*"

He struggled to answer, but no sound came. The figure moved closer.

"*Speak to me in thy heart, lion of Chitor, for it is thy heart that hears me.*"

"Mata!" All his fear and wonder were in the word, for surely it was Vyanmata, who watched over Chitor, or Mata Bhavani, the Great Goddess Herself, who had come to visit him here.

"*Nay, I am maiden, and doomed to remain so unless I have thy aid!*" A white hand drew the veil aside, and his heart leaped within him as he recognized the face he had first seen formed by the carpet's flowers.

"*I am Kishna of Jaisalmir, a mortal maiden, but I come of the race of Princes, and I lay it upon thee to rescue me!*"

And at those words, the blood of Goha, the blood of a thousand ancestors who had never refused a challenge, awoke within him.

"Where shall I find thee?"

"*Seek northward beyond the Passes. Journey to the Hills. My prison is near Kailas the holy mountain . . .*"

"The Hills are mighty, and their peaks beyond numbering. How shall I find the right one?"

"If thy faith does not falter, thou wilt be guided," she answered him. *"See clearly, choose wisely, and thou wilt win me. But remember, give me not what thou dost want, but what I need! Lord of my heart, I call thee—come to me—come to me—come to me!"* Light flared brilliantly around her, and then there was only darkness.

When Ajaisi came to himself again, the first light of morning was glowing through the carven screens.

"There is left one other son of the line of Goha," said Ajaisi. "I proclaim Hurba my Yuvaraj. Make my brother your king if I do not return."

"My lord, this is madness!" Jaimul's knotted fist struck his knee.

Calmly, the rana lifted his cup and sipped at the steaming tea. He could feel the minty tingle in his belly. He could feel the breath of life in his lungs, the fire in his breast. He had been dead, but he was alive once more.

"Is it?" he asked when he set the cup down again. "You yourself assured us that we have little to fear from Muhammad Ghori for a time. Even if I fail to find the princess, by the time the Afghans are able to trouble us again, Hurba will be a man. I will make you regent until then, Jaimul—will that satisfy you? Who better could guard the land?"

The old rawul's eyes burned. "Its rightful lord!"

"Don't you understand?" Ajaisi burst out finally. "After everything that you and the others have said to me? I *cannot* be true lord of this land without a queen! And I would be no true Rajput if I refused the lady's plea—now it is a question of honor, as well. I *will* seek her, Jaimul, and you will not deny me if you love me, if you love Chitor!"

There was a silence. Somewhere birds were singing. From the courtyard below came the sound of women's laughter. Ajaisi wondered if the old warrior had heard the words he could not say: that he might meet his death on this quest, but that if he refused to go, for certain his life would not be long.

"My lord . . ." Jaimul's voice was harsh when he spoke at last. "Have I deserved that of you? I will not seek to dissuade you if your fate thus draws you, but I will not let you go into danger alone! Let Mahendra rule the city—he'll enjoy it. I ride with you!"

In the end, it was easier to let Jaimul have his way. When Ajaisi set out at last he was attended by a small army, which included the Rawul, and Kilparam, chief *charan*, and Sveta-ketu, the Brahmin from Jaisalmir. Behind them, the rock of Chitor rose stark above the plain. Twelve miles around at the base, and six at the summit, the hard rock of the slopes was yet only a foundation for bastions and soaring walls crowned with a thousand fretted towers.

Ajaisi looked back as he rode, feeling a sudden pride in the fortress that had never fallen to an enemy. Surely, whatever came of his quest, the glory of Chitor would endure. Meanwhile, the sun emblazoned on his crimson banner shone as brightly as the one above, and the rains had spread a veil of green across the plain.

The blue line of the Aravuli hills rippled along the horizon, pointing the way. But they dared not take those hills for their guideline, for that way lay Ajmir and Delhi and their enemies. Instead they bore eastward, following the Chambal through the land of Bundi and Gwalior. Several times there was fighting, for not all the Islami invaders were with the hordes of Ghori. But when at last they came out into the broad, fertile plain of the Ganges they were still a goodly company.

This was flat land, fat land, thickly settled and cut up into fields; no room here for the great herds of goats and cattle of the Rajputana. It was a land rich in fruit and grain, but for all its wealth, the men of Mewar longed for broader vistas and a cleaner wind. Still they went onward, and presently they began to glimpse the dark forests of the Siwalik hills as a shadow upon the horizon, and beyond them blue ranges whose peaks scraped the sky.

"This earth is a portion of Brahman," said the yogin reverently. *"The sky and the heavens are portions of him. The oceans are a portion of him. All these form a foot of Brahman."*

Ajaisi looked around him and took a deep breath of air heavy with the scent of life. Since early that morning they had ridden through the lush vegetation of the *terai,* and if it had not been for the insects, he might have thought he rode through paradise.

"And this—whatever it is—" With conscious self-restraint he brushed away the crawling thing that had landed on his neck, instead of crushing it. "Is this a part of Brahman too?"

"Surely," said Svetaketu calmly.

Ajaisi looked at him and sighed. Holiness was worth something, apparently—if the creatures which made his own skin twitch did not avoid the Brahmin, at least their proximity did not seem to bother him. The rana ducked to avoid a swinging branch of bamboo, and looked back along the line. Men and horses were still following in good order, though the animals started nervously at the strange scents and sounds. This was the realm of the tiger, and a man or beast that strayed was in danger. They had lost one horse that way already, and another when a leopard startled it and it broke a leg stampeding down a hill.

The leopard and the tiger are beasts of prey, as we are, he told himself. *I should not be surprised. Perhaps a party of holy men could pass through these jungles unscathed, but if the gods had wanted us to be Brahmins, we would not have been born to wield the sword!*

Whatever came of it, at least this quest was serving one purpose, Ajaisi thought then. For hours, even days at a time, he forgot to mourn. Instead, he had his dreams.

Approaching the forests, he had feared to be lost in them, but as he drew physically nearer, his lady's power to reach him seemed to grow. At first there had been only vague visions that disappeared with the dawn, but gradually they became clearer, so that now he had only to close his eyes to see her face before him, only to breathe in to scent her perfume. *"You will be guided,"* she had told him, and it was true.

And still their path led upward, so gradually at first that one scarcely noticed one was climbing. But in time, bamboo and stately sal began to give way to sturdy oaks and the tall deodars whose spicy incense was fanned by every breeze. Now the road grew steeper. The horses labored up one slope only to be faced with an equally perilous descent. The rivers that carved their way through the gorges were swift and chill. When a dozen men were swept away in one crossing, even Jaimul recognized the necessity of leaving their plains-bred mounts and most of their riders at one of the villages, of hiring bearers for the baggage, and for the men, the sturdy, surefooted ponies of the hills.

Now, every turning brought them a new vista—blue ridges laid out behind them to bear witness to the distance they had come, and before them, peaks that shone like molten silver at noontide, and at sunset veiled themselves in bridal shades of coral and saffron and rose. This was the Himalaya, the Abode of the Snows. Distant indeed were the sunbaked plains and the high walls of Chitor. Now, at times, they looked into gulfs in which their fortress could have been dropped like a child's clay castle down a well. Even Kilparam's songs were silenced, though he said, when the rana asked him, that he had only ceased chanting the lesser epics in order to compose a greater one.

"This journey, my lord, is worthy to be remembered! When has a ruler of Rajasthan traveled so far? And even I can see the virtue of telling a tale with a happy ending once in a while!"

Ajaisi looked at him. "You think, then, that my quest will end happily?"

The Raj-Kavi shrugged. "It is at least a story of love to leaven the songs of war."

"Of love . . . yes . . ." He closed his eyes, and immediately the face of Kishna Bai was before him, glowing like the rhododendrons that hung in brilliant masses above the path. But the wind was cold. Ajaisi remembered the sheer drop beside the path and opened his eyes again, blinking at the dazzle of sun on snow.

That night they halted at a cluster of mud and earth huts glued to the rocks midway between earth and heaven, like the nests of the swallows that nested in the towers of Chitor. There was only sour milk and cheese and bread hard as the stone to be had for provision, but their own supplies were running low. The Brahmin, who only ate his own cooking in any case, muttered about purifications, but the rest of them accepted the hospitality of the village gratefully. Yet even Svetaketu unbent a little when the villagers begged his blessing. Buddhists they might be, and worshipers of all the devils of the Hills besides, but they knew how to honor a holy man.

For days, they said, they had watched the party approaching—tiny dots against the dark slopes that seemed to move perhaps six inches in a day.

"Yes, we know Kailas," said the headwoman. "Long ago, many pilgrims come, but no more . . ."

Svetaketu sighed. "It is the war. When the enemy is at the gates, men have little time for sacred things. Since boyhood I have longed to see the holy mountain whence the four sacred rivers run . . . *'It is the monarch of mountains . . . on its upper slopes is the assembly hall of Brahma, a hall rich with fountains out of which is forever flowing the elixir of life.'* "

The villagers widened their eyes at the flowing Sanscrit phrases, but Ajaisi frowned. Had the Brahmin lured him all this way because he desired an escort on a quest of his own? But it was the princess herself who had told him that she was imprisoned near Kailas. What could he believe in, if he doubted her?

All the next day they toiled upward, following the fellow the headwoman had sent with them as a guide. And then they passed the last stands of shivering birches and came out suddenly into brilliant sunlight, blinking at the great rainbowed swathes of anemone and gentian, saxifrage and potentilla that poked their heads through the melting snows. There were no birds here. The only sounds to trouble these great silences were the scrape of hoof on rock and the eternal sighing of the wind.

"Kishna Bai . . ." the wind whispered. *"Kishna Bai!"*

Ajaisi shook his head, but the blood pulsed in his ears. The purple and pink, the scarlet and blue and gold of the flowers that carpeted these heights were too brilliant beneath the blazing turquoise sky. Like the jewel colors of the Jaisalmir rug, they confused the senses. *This is her palace,* thought the rana. *This is the realm of the Princess of Flowers!* He slitted his eyes against the glare.

He swayed to the movement of the pony beneath him as

the animal picked a path across the stones, and the colors blurred and swirled around him until he saw hangings and carpets and cushions, the silken sway of women's veils. Then the heat on his back shifted to sudden chill as they passed into shadow.

Ajaisi's eyes blinked open. Guards and guide were disappearing around the shoulder of the mountain ahead of him. To his left gray stone sheered upward to slopes still higher, blanketed with snow. His pony pulled up, snorting, as wind gusted down in a whirl of white from above. The rana began to urge him forward, then let the rein fall. As once before from the smoke of his hookah, so now from the snow a figure was forming. Shimmering draperies revealed and concealed fair limbs; he saw eyes sparkling through a veil.

"Sun of Chitor, go back!"

Heels dug into the pony's sides. A white arm lifted in warning and the animal stopped, trembling.

"Oh my love, beware, beware!" She seemed to flow toward him and Ajaisi reached out to her. The horse shuddered beneath him, or was it the stone? His arms embraced mist, her voice filled him. A cry from ahead of him echoed it, and then all other awareness was lost in a gathering roar as the mountain began to move.

The heavens were falling. Ajaisi's pony screamed and reared and the rana flung himself out of the saddle, scrambling backwards as uncounted tons of snow loosened their hold on the slope above them and, with every second gathering more speed, slid down the mountainside. Ajaisi clung to a boulder as white immensities thundered past. A few screams, a dark figure tossed like a leaf on the flood, then only the deep demonic roar that obliterated hearing as the endless cascading whiteness overwhelmed sight . . .

"Ajaisi! My lord—Ajaisiiii . . ."

He could hear again. Still dizzied, the rana loosened fingers that fear had welded to the stone.

"Here—" A crow could have croaked more loudly. Ajaisi pulled in air and tried again. "I'm here!"

"Mata be praised! You're alive!" Kilparam slid off his pony and knelt in the snow. "Oh, what a tale! What a tale!"

In a moment, it seemed, Jaimul was beside them, mustaches bristling with emotion, gripping Ajaisi's shoulder as if he could not quite believe he was real.

"We thought you were gone, my lord!" added the bard. "The snow came down like—like—" He shook his head. "Even I have no words. But all we could see was white, and we heard cries . . ."

All three turned to look where the path had been, where now there was only a solid slope of snow.

"Who else . . ." whispered Ajaisi. "Ojah? Sangram? Bhupal?" They shook their heads, and he groaned.

"The priest is still alive," said Jaimul finally. "He's back there, rooted to the rock and calling on Shiva."

"They say that Shiva lives in these mountains." Kilparam looked around him, shivering. "Only a god *could* live here for long!"

"My lord, we must get away from here!" said Jaimul. "Men are not meant to tread these paths. The gods have showed their anger—let's not wait for them to speak to us again."

"You go . . ." Ajaisi swallowed, thinking of the men whom the mountain had taken, men who had followed him to battle, men with whom he had hunted and feasted and sung. "This is not your quest. Too many have already died for me!"

"Too many have died for a delusion!" growled Jaimul. "Bapuji, come back to the plains where you belong!"

"A delusion?" Ajaisi shook his head. "She saved me, Jaimul. I would have been swept away with the others, but my lady stood before me in the path. I have sworn to free her. I cannot return to Chitor without honor, and I will lose mine if I turn back now. But there is no reason for you to stay."

"And what of *my* honor?" Jaimul said dangerously. "How much would remain to me if I returned alone? I did not abandon you on the battlefield. Why insult me by asking me to leave you now?"

Ajaisi sighed. "Then *you* go—" He turned to the *charan.* "Go home, and tell—"

But already the bard was shaking his head. "No, my lord, not until I know the ending of the tale. But maybe the

priest will turn back—" He gestured back down the trail.
"He is only a Brahmin, not a warrior, and he has just discovered that his gods are real!"

Whether Svetaketu had more courage than the bard believed, or whether he feared the perils of going back alone,
the Brahmin also insisted on continuing the quest. They
backtracked until they came to a branching trail, and turned
onto the new path. Soon they came to a cairn of stones
crowned with a tattered prayer flag, and knew that it was
men, not demons, who had made it. And when, as evening
was falling, the trail dipped down through the birches, they
glimpsed a flicker of light like a fallen star, and came to a
monastery that looked as if it had grown out of the hill.

That night the four survivors rested under a roof, and
though the cold air was heavy with the smells of rancid yak
butter and unwashed humanity, it was better than a frozen
tomb. But for Ajaisi, sleep was long in coming. The faces
of the men they had lost appeared beneath his closing eye-
lids; the pulse that pounded in his ears echoed with their
cries. After the battle of Sthaneshvara it had been the
same.

He tried to comfort his grief with the Brahmin's preach-
ings. His men had died as warriors. They had earned a
speedy rebirth, perhaps as Brahmins, or more likely as
even greater warriors in the service of their clans. But they
had all grown so close on this journey. Though religion
forbade it, Ajaisi could not help but grieve for the particular couplings of body and spirit that he had known. When
they returned without those men, more widows would seek
the funeral pyre.

But he had to rest, he would need his strength on the
morrow. He closed his eyes resolutely, and after a time fell
into an uneasy slumber...

*Ajaisi is marching through a wasteland of ice, wind-
sculptured into fantastic filigree. The men of his guard are
ahead of him, hunched figures that appear and disappear
through veils of blowing snow. He calls to them to wait,
hurries to catch up with them. And they stop. As he
reaches the first, the man turns, and turning, reveals a*

face distorted beyond any semblance of humanity.

"Go back," says the rakasa. "We belong to you no longer. Go back, lord of men. Rudra the Destroyer is our master now!"

"I cannot go back," Ajaisi's dream-self cries. "Without my consort I cannot live. How shall I find her?"

"Follow, then, if you have the courage. But you may not like what you see!" The demon laughs. Now all of them are laughing. He takes a step forward, and the others form a guard of honor around him, but Ajaisi knows that he is their prisoner.

As they march, the landscape grows ever more fearful. Glittering pinnacles rise around them like the columns of a temple, and from the overhanging banks of snow more demon-faces grin. The cold air rings with cruel laughter, and now and again another avalanche crashes like a gong. The ice arches over them, becoming a passageway through which they enter the mountain.

Now the way leads downward to a great cavern. More rakasas are dancing there—female forms contorted into a thousand forms of terror. They cavort in a ragged circle around a still figure whose face is hidden by a veil. But by some other sense than sight Ajaisi knows her.

"Kishna!" he calls. "My lady, Kishna Bai!"

She hears and turns to him with outstretched arms. But the rakasas surround her, gibbering, and with gnashing teeth and flashing eyes the demons rush upon him. Thunder shakes the cavern. They bear him backward, and between him and the princess a man-shaped darkness gathers, a column of roiling storm clouds shot with flickers of light.

Ajaisi stares. His quaking legs will no longer uphold him and he sinks to the ground. The clouds congeal, and then, at last, the rana sees Him—the Lord of the Thunderbolt, blue-throated, though the rest of his body is blazing like fire. Three eyes glow from his forehead, and that triple glare sears Ajaisi's soul!

"Lord of Tears, have mercy—" Ajaisi knows Him now.

"I am without beginning, without middle or end . . . I am the Pervader, the life you breathe . . . I am the Fire of Destruction, and That which is Devoured, all that has been or

shall be. Dost seek liberation? Thou dost cross beyond death, knowing me."

The great voice rolls like thunder, shaking Ajaisi's bones.

"Lord of Wrath, I am in Your hand. I am a warrior of the Land of Princes, and I know that I must face You without fear." This is not wholly true. Ajaisi's mind tells him what to say, but his heart trembles with terror beyond reason.

"I can release thee from the pangs of love and fear . . . I can free thee from the Wheel." The stare of those three eyes still transfixes him.

"No." Ajaisi shakes his head, and even as he speaks he wonders at his own temerity. *"I am bound to redeem my lady. Release us or destroy us, Lord, but do not torment us by this captivity that is neither one thing—or the other. Set us free."*

"Know that the only way thou canst achieve thy lady is through Me . . ."

The demons draw away, and trembling, Ajaisi moves forward. The boiling clouds are thinning. He glimpses the figure of the princess through the body of Rudra, glimmering as though seen through a veil of pale fire. He comes closer; she turns and he sees her features grown demonic. With lolling tongue she grins and beckons to him with bloody hands. Yet still he seeks her. He enters the fire.

The world explodes in flame and thunder . . .

Ajaisi woke, shouting, with the afterimage of the lightning bright behind his eyes. He was burning—no, it was cold that made him shake so. Then Jaimul was beside him, murmuring softly as though he comforted a woman, drawing the coarse blankets over him once more.

In the morning he wondered if all of it had been a dream. But the extra blankets were still around him—Jaimul's blankets. Something in the warrior's glance kept him from thanking him.

It is my honor to suffer for her; it is his, to suffer for me, Ajaisi thought then. *We are all bound on the same wheel.*

* * *

"Yonder lies the road to the holy mountain," said the head lama, sipping buttered tea. "But we know of no garden."

Ajaisi drank from his own cup, and felt a welcome heat spreading through his bones. The monks were poor, but they had shared what they had with a generosity that would surely earn them merit. Blankets and simple fare for the road were packed into neat bundles by the door. He thought of his dream, and frowned.

"Or a cavern?" he added. "Have you any legends about a great cave under the hill?"

For the first time a ripple emotion troubled the lama's disciplined serenity.

"Not in Kailas," he answered finally. "But if you continue on this path, you will pass a great rift in the mountainside. Our legends tell us that it leads to a cavern, but it is an abode of demons. You do not want to go there."

As soon as the monastery was out of sight behind them Jaimul began arguing with him. To seek death when there was no other option was the Rajput way, or to meet it bravely in the hunt or in battle. But this deliberate meddling with the powers of darkness was pure foolishness. The gods were already angry—why stir them up further?

"But the darkness also is holy..." Ajaisi turned to the Brahmin. "Isn't that true?"

Svetaketu looked up at him, and the rana saw a face much thinner than it had been in the plains. Since the avalanche the priest had been very silent.

"The Lord of Sleep is the Being-of-Darkness..." in a low voice he answered. "That is the teaching. But I give you warning—in this place the veils that shield us from the full force of the Divine are very thin."

"What, is the great priest afraid?" Jaimul began to laugh.

"Why do you think we worship the gods through images at home?" Svetaketu went on as if he had not heard. "In that form, they can be safely seen by unenlightened men. But on the peaks the energy of earth is released into the ether. Here we have no such protection. Here they are pure powers, that may only be faced by those who are pure. I

have served the gods lifelong, but many lives remain before I will be free—Yes, I am afraid!"

When Svetaketu did look up, even Jaimul was abashed
by the pain in the Brahmin's eyes.

Ajaisi took a deep breath. Why had he even needed to
ask? If he closed his eyes he could feel his beloved calling,
he could feel the darkness drawing him. Whether he would
find death or life when he found her he could not tell, but
he was bound now by something deeper than honor to try.

"I have always written songs of battle," said Kilparam.
"Will you make me a singer of hymns?"

"Be easy," said Ajaisi. "It will take a warrior's heart to
follow me where we are going now—"

He pointed, and they saw that the lama had spoken
truly. An hour's march had brought them to the pass, and
here the rock of the higher slope was broken as if it had
been slashed open by a giant sword. The supplies they had
been given at the lamasery included torches. Silently,
Ajaisi lit one and led the way to the opening.

The passage that led downward into the mountain was
not precisely a path, or if so, it had never been made by the
feet of men. But men could follow it. Breath coming
harshly and sweating with effort, they picked their way
along. From time to time a flow of chill air cooled their
faces, but the deeper they went, the warmer they became.

We are going to Shiva, thought Ajaisi. *He is the fire . . .*
His neck ached with the strain of the climb, or perhaps it
was with expectation. But they met neither beast nor
demon, they saw only stone, and in the end, not even a
pathway, for the chasm ended in a cavern, dark as the
womb of the world.

Had they marched for a day, or less, or longer? In this
eternal night there was no telling. One after another, the
men sank down upon the stones. The torch faded to a
flicker. Kilparam's head rested upon his crossed arms and
Jaimul began to snore. Presently even the priest's head
sank upon his breast.

"Sleep, my beloved companions, sleep on, sleep well,"
Ajaisi said softly. "I think that I must find another way to
travel now . . ."

He settled himself to stare into the darkness, inbreathing

and outbreathing as long ago the Brahmins had taught him. Why had he doubted? Why had he worried? All existence had narrowed to one thought, one purpose. With every breath, his heart cried out the mantra of his quest—the name of Kishna Bai.

The torch had died. Dazzled by darkness, vision responded with dots and flashes of brilliance. Ajaisi ignored them, breathing steadily until all awareness of his body fell away. And presently, a light that was not of the world began to glow before him. He saw an opening in the stone of the cavern. The light grew, and through the passageway he glimpsed trees. They drew him. And then he was inside; the greenery closed around him. Now there was only the garden, and he was alone.

No, not entirely alone. As he walked between the fragrant deodars, he saw before him a wall of weathered stone. There was another gate here, with a warden before it, standing at attention like the jagirdar who guarded the women's quarters at home. But the sirdars of this place were demons . . .

"Who dares to walk in the garden of Rudra?" The roar of the challenge was like thunder.

"A king and the son of a king. Who are you that dare to question me?"

The great head swung toward him, bulging eyes flaming. This rakasa was red in color, man-shaped, but hideous, with bandy legs and a belly that bulged over his wrapped lunghi, and long, heavily muscled arms. Sharp teeth glistened and the long tongue curled as the demon spoke again.

"I am Dandasuka son of Pulastya, and this gate is my charge."

"I am Ajaisi the Gehelot, son of the Sun, and Rana of Chitor. What *dasturi* must I give you to let me enter here?"

"A bribe?" The rakasa looked away, and then, almost coyly, back again. "They call me a Night-Roamer, but I cannot run with my brothers, for my feet grow cold. Give me the boots thou art wearing and I will let thee in!"

Ajaisi looked down at the feet of the rakasa and then at his own, wondering how the creature thought that the felt boots he had bought to wear in the mountains could possibly cover such misshapen appendages. But this was no great sacrifice—he could buy more boots on the way home, or wrap his feet in cloth.

He pulled off first one boot, then the other, and the demon, laughing gleefully, grabbed them. But the rana did not notice by what miracle Dandasuka got them on. Through the soles of his feet he could taste the bare earth of the path—he drew up knowledge of the earth through his feet as a plant draws nourishment from the soil.

Delighting in every step, he passed the capering demon. Beyond the gate, the path wound among mango trees heavy with fruit. Bamboo rustled softly in a warm breeze; somewhere he could hear the music of running water. He moved from grass to path and back again, savoring this new awareness. Why had he ever worn shoes? For a moment he forgot why he had come.

And then, suddenly there was a barrier, a palisade of polished bamboo that curved away to either side. What was another wall doing here? With increasing anger Ajaisi moved along it, looking for the opening.

A long hiss stopped him in his tracks. It came again, and he looked upward, flinching involuntarily as he met the cold gaze of a great cobra that had draped itself along the top of the palisade. Or herself: for as he looked again, the upper part of the serpent's body flowed into a new form— a woman's smooth arms and round breasts, three heads, each with a woman's smiling face, and all of them still as blue as the scales of her nether coils.

"Whence comsssst thou?" Great silver earrings set with sapphires swung as the naga unlooped a coil and swayed downward until one head was at a level with his.

"What dossst thou ssseek here?" asked the second head as the body turned.

"I have come from the world of men to find the Flower Princess, Kishna Bai. Open the gate to the garden, that I may go in—"

"What presssent wilt thou give to meee?" Poison fangs glittered as the third head smiled.

Ajaisi felt at his neck, but his bracelets and necklaces had all been packed away when they reached the Hills, and Jaimul held the bag with their gold.

"I dessire that ssilk that bindss thy head," said the first head.

"Give it mee . . ." "Give it mee . . ." said the second and the third.

After a moment's hesitation, Ajaisi reached up to his turban, pinned with the jewel which was the only mark of kingship he still bore. Since he became a man he had never appeared in public with his head bare. Wind tugged at the cloth as he pulled it off, and blew the silk out in a fluttering crimson stream. Before he could change his mind a delicate hand plucked it from his fingers, and the naga draped the silk across her breast and shoulders, twisting so that each head in turn could admire the effect.

The naga's movement seemed to release some hidden catch, for abruptly a section of the palisade swung inward and Ajaisi darted through.

This garden was filled with roses, white and every shade of pink and heart's-blood red. Perfume swirled around him on every breeze, dizzying in its intensity. With playful fingers, the wind stroked his hair, freeing strand from sweat-matted strand. Had his turban been so heavy? He felt as if that wind could carry him away, and his bare head was blessed by rays of an invisible sun. Like the roses, he drew in light and transformed it into energy.

Swiftly he spiraled inward, following the path. Surely, his beloved was near! The roses grew more brilliant, their scent almost palpable in the warm air. Color intensified until he realized that it had become a barrier, a hedge of thorns and roses guarding the heart of the garden, itself guarded by a shining figure with the body of a man and the brightly plumaged head of a bird.

Ajaisi stopped short, head bowing in instinctive reverence, for this was a gandharva, an elemental spirit of the heavens, a ray of the sun.

"Son of Surya, why hast thou come here?" The voice of the gandharva was like music, and its vibrations stirred an answering tremor in his loins. How long had it been since anything had aroused him? Even his visions of the princess had not touched the depths of his manhood. But suddenly he ached with need.

"I was dead," he cried. "Let me live again!"

"Give me your sword . . ."

Ajaisi stepped back in instinctive denial, hand closing on the jeweled hilt of the weapon at his side. An ancient saying warned against trying to separate a Rajput from his horse, his mistress, or his sword. Could one be the price of the other? Without his weapon, was he even a man?

The shining one came closer, crooning softly, and Ajaisi felt the strength leave his limbs. A divine fragrance overwhelmed his senses, the gandharva's touch thrilled through his flesh in waves of slow fire. He scarcely noticed when the weight at his hip fell away. He knew only that within the holy lingam the power of Shiva was rising, and the hedge of roses was unfolding to reveal a glowing passageway.

The interior of the garden was a sphere of shadowless radiance where a single palm tree rose slender as a maiden from a circle of emerald grass. He stood staring. His body was shaking with passion, but where was the woman who had aroused him? He saw only the Tree and the three coconuts that hung from its cluster of foliage. Slowly he moved toward it.

"Ajaisi . . . Ajaisi . . . oh my beloved!" It was a whisper, wind rustling among fronds of green . . . Only a whisper, but he knew it from a hundred summer nights: it was the voice of Gayatri, who had been the first of his brides. He reached out to the nearest of the fruits and it fell into his hand.

"Ajaisi, thou sun of my life, oh thou king of my heart!" More strongly, more sweetly, another voice sang. And this one also he recognized, for just so had Rukmini serenaded him when the vineh played. The rana lifted his hand to the second coconut.

"Ajaisi, oh my husband, hast thou forgotten me?" There was laughter in the third voice, Setu's voice. As he picked the last of the coconuts, Ajaisi's lips curved in an answering smile.

"I thought I had lost you," he murmured, clasping them to his breast. "I thought you were dead, and I wanted to die too!"

"Set us free—" cried the voices from the three coconuts. "Beloved husband, only you can set us free!"

"But how?" He knelt and set them on the grass.

"Give me food," the answer came. He fumbled with the drawstring of his bag, surprised to find that his hand was trembling. He had a little hard bread left that he had been given in the monastery. Carefully he laid a piece on the triple mark at the top of the nut. For a moment nothing happened. And then, with a soft moan, the coconut split open.

A gray mist boiled up from within. Twisting and swirling in the wind, from a column of smoke it took the form of a woman, and then, as he reached out to clasp her, a demoness that leered at him with a rakasa's snarling mouth, but Gayatri's beautiful eyes.

"Canst thou replant the uprooted tree?" The apparition slipped through his grasp, laughing, and the wind whirled it away.

Ajaisi started after it, but in moments there was nothing, and now the voice from the second coconut was calling his name—

"Give me water! Give me water!"

Ajaisi pulled out his water bottle and worked the stopper free. "Rukmini," he whispered. "Don't betray me, too—"

Water trickled across the rough rind. He saw it darken, absorbing the moisture, absorbing more and more water until suddenly it cracked into three. And once more the ghostly form flowed upward, changing from the woman he had loved to a contorted shape that shifted from one terror to another until he hid his eyes and turned away. But he could not close his ears to the mocking cry:

"Canst thou return the fish to the sea?"

Shaking, the rana looked at the last fruit of the tree. "Setu," he whispered, "my laughing girl—what dost *thou* want of me?"

"I am cold . . . cold," came the soft plea. "Sun-lord, give me your fire!"

Ajaisi sat back on his heels. The hope that had flared so wildly when he reached the heart of the garden was ashes now. But what had he done wrong?

"The fire . . . the fire brings liberty . . ." said the voice from the coconut shell.

Slowly he took out the fire stick and punkwood from their bag, gathered together a little dry undergrowth from the grass, and began to twirl the stick between his fingers. There was a trickle of smoke and the punk began to smolder, then the glowing stuff leaped into flame. He rolled the coconut against it, half hoping it would be extinguished. But the dry husk caught instantly. For a moment he saw a globe of fire, and then a sharp crack and the spirit going up in a rush of smoke and a peal of mad laughter that made his flesh go cold.

"Canst turn the Wheel back to be free?"

Ajaisi rolled onto his knees, sank down until his forehead pressed against his crossed hands. Madness . . . he was mad . . . but he had not known it until now . . .

Had he come all this way, endangered his kingdom and killed his men, for the three shattered husks that lay there on the grass? With the voices of the dead they had spoken to him, but in this life he would never see his loved ones again. Everything that had happened to him was illusion. The sages taught that all the world was maya, and for the first time he believed them.

He crouched there, shivering, while an Age came to its ending and began once more. He huddled with no movement but his own breathing to tell him he still lived, until at last, above the sound of his breath, he heard the whisper of palm fronds rustling together in the wind . . .

"Prince, why dost thou pursue the fruit, which perishes, and ignore the Tree?"

All strength had left him. Ajaisi sank full length upon the earth, turned over so that he lay upon his back, gazing upward. It seemed to him then that slender trunk of the tree arched over him, the fringe of green hung downward like a veil. But if it had been a rakasa with sword poised to slay him he could not have moved.

"Vyan Mata, Bhavani, help me, have mercy on me, Kali Ma," he breathed. And like an echo he heard a voice speaking from memory—

"Give me not what thou dost want, but what I need . . ."

What do I want? he wondered then. He wanted his three wives—he still ached with the pain of losing them a second time. He wanted all things to be as they had been before Sthaneshvara, before the Afghans had come, before . . . before the beginning of the world! With a flicker of humor he recognized the logical conclusion of these dreams.

Finally, his choices were clear. He could sink back into Shiva's eternal sleep and die to the world, or he could embrace it. There were no other ways.

And what did she—the woman—what did she need? Ajaisi saw suddenly that this also was a thing he had never considered before. She too was imprisoned. She had summoned him to set her free . . .

He must have made a decision, for he found that he was sitting, facing the tree.

"Who are you?"

"I am the Mother Tree, I am Shakti, I am Kishna Bai."

"What do you want of me?"

"Embrace me . . ." came the rustle of leaves. "But not as a suppliant, nor as a conquerer. Arise, and join thyself to me!"

And at her word, the power of movement rose in him as sap rises in the spring, bringing him to his feet and bearing him across the grass. All awareness had focused to this one moment of life, or death, and in this moment they were the same. And he set his arms about the slender trunk of the palm tree and laid his cheek against the rough bark, and felt it grow smooth. And as that which was hard began to soften, that which was weak grew strong; and as that which had been resistant became yielding, that which had been powerless stiffened, until Shiva was joined to Shakti indeed.

"Awaken, my beloved, and let us greet the day . . ."

Ajaisi opened his eyes and blinked, startled by the brilliance of the light. He had expected the darkness of the passage, or the luminous splendor of—of what? Already that awareness was being dimmed. . . . Memory drowned in sensation as the woman in his arms turned to him. He did not know how they had come here, nor did he care. Visions of gods and demons were subsumed into a single reality.

Kishna Bai . . . Kishna Bai . . . Kishna Bai . . .

"I see the dawn in your eyes," he answered, looking down at her.

Warm blankets were wrapped closely about them, but he could feel the sweetly curving length of her pressed against him, and her face shone like the new day. It was the face he had seen in the carpet, in his visions, and yet it was not the same. This was the face of a human woman, all the more beautiful where it missed perfection. He looked down at her, trying to memorize every feature simultaneously.

"What is it?"

"Forgive me—I thought I saw the others in your face, but you are <u>not like</u> them at all—" he said stupidly.

She smiled. "I shall be all women to you, my husband, as you shall be all men to me!" Her arms tightened around him. "I shall be the mother of heroes!"

And I shall beget them! Ajaisi knew that now he had that power.

Someone coughed, and the rana realized that the humped shapes on the ground nearby were Kilparam and Jaimul. They lay at the entrance to the rift on the breast of the mountain, partially sheltered by an overhang of stone. Eastward the rising sun set the peaks ashimmer with rainbow fires. Farther down the slope someone was sitting, staring out at the stark cone of Kailas, the holy mountain. Even before the strengthening light showed him the faded saffron draperies Ajaisi knew it was Svetaketu, and understood also that the Brahmin would not be returning with them to the plains.

He has made his choice, he thought then, *as I have made mine.* The rana's gaze came back to the road that curved down around the mountain, and as he turned, his princess raised herself on one elbow beside him.

"Lion of Chitor, arise," she whispered, "and let us go home."

DAWN SONGS

The Hindu finished his tale, then steepled his palms before his face in the courtly greeting of his kind, a salute to his hearers. From the amphitheatre came sighs and the sort of tears that heal almost as surely and as deeply as do laughs and smiles. Then he extended his hands to the two men who had spoken before him, that they too might share in the silent acclaim.

Behind them rose the rest of the men of the caravan, standing united, varied though they were in race, faith, occupation, and temperament.

As they stood there, the Emir of the Djinn of the deep desert approached them. *Surely,* Peter thought, *the webbing of wrinkles in his face has diminished. Surely, the djinn have been restored to some semblance of hope. As have I.*

The Emir of the Djinn saluted the humans. "The blessings of the one God, by whatever name you bless Him, be upon you for reminding us what where life exists, love and hope are too."

The humans stood, hopeful and fearful, before him. Whatever verdict the Emir passed would seal their fates forever.

"You withstood us," he said, as if in wonderment. "We snatched you from the breath of a storm we conjured; we put on our most fearsome aspects; and even when we conjured despair and breathed it at you, you held firm. Certainly, you have satisfied the first condition of our game.

"You entertained us. You replied to our tales with tales of your own that have held our attention—and far more

365

besides. We shall have memories now that will last us for centuries.

"But"—Peter's heart was leaden in his breast—"as you see, we are not made young again."

"Then," said the master storyteller, "have we failed to divert you?"

"That, no," replied the Emir. "And for that, we owe you reward. This much is our gift and our recompense: we will free you, all but one. That one must stay to lighten our days and dreams with the fire of his humanity."

This time, it was the humans who sighed with regret.

"For our sakes," pleaded the Emir. "Be merciful and understand. One of you—just one!—we must keep to hearten us that we cannot wander where we will, when we wish."

Aye, but which one? The question hung unasked in the heavy air of that place. All of the mortals had families, obligations, did they not? Certainly, those who traveled with the caravan did.

What of myself? thought Peter. *My parents are dead. I have no wife, no children; and my brother is heir. What ties me to the world? Only my quest; and that is as much of the next world as it is of this one.*

"Greater love," he recalled to himself, "hath no man save that he lay down his life for his friend." How better to demonstrate to his friends the truth of his faith, the truth of Christ's sacrifice, than to sacrifice himself for their well-being?

He met the Emir's eye; and the djinni nodded gravely. At that moment, Peter knew that the djinni, subtle past mortal calculations, had planned that he, of all the humans, remain.

And would it be so bad? He had risked slavery once; and having faced it, he knew how few fears it held for a man whose mind was at peace. This durance would not be slavery; likelier by far that the djinn would gift him with every luxury that their ancient, fertile imaginations could conjure.

He stood forth and spoke before prudence could dry up his voice. "I shall remain," he said.

The humans sighed with relief; the djinn's sigh was assuaged, contented. They had their mortal to protect them from despair.

"Yes," said the Emir. "I think that you are the one. But,"—his voice took on a heightened tone—"bethink you, O Son of Adam, what you do. Consider that, once he is vowed to us, no man can escape. Though," he added ironically, "I know that you will enliven us with your hopes and plans."

That escape would be totally impossible, Peter had not reckoned; but he supposed that it was inevitable. "I am prepared." He bowed and made as if to stand beside the djinni.

"No!" cried the Hindu. "I offer myself in the flame-hair's place!"

"For love?" asked the djinni as Peter compelled himself not to flinch.

"Aye," said the prince. "For I am not lacking in fore-knowledge; and his is a face I have long foreseen." He looked at Peter of Wraysbury and smiled. "Man of the West, I have asked naught of you that would do you what you term dishonor, naught—but that you remember me with kindness."

"I cannot accept," said the knight; but prince and djinni shook their heads, gainsaying him.

Already, the Emir began his ritual.

"Bethink you," he intoned again, "son of Adam, that no man can escape our prison."

Abruptly the Hindu laughed. Then he tore off the wrappings of his headdress, and long, dark hair flew free, to brush slender shoulders and frame a face that had—Peter saw it now—ever been too fair to be that of even the fairest youth.

"Call me no son of Adam!" cried the princess. "Call me daughter of Eve, and expect that I shall try as long as breath remains in me!"

Peter took one step toward the princess, but she held up a hand.

"The tale I told is one of my family line. Nonetheless, though you knew me not, my name is known to you."

"What is your name, lady?" he asked.

"Karida," she said; and surely no name had ever

sounded as fair. He had dreamed of such ladies; even before he knew that they existed in aught but songs, he had
dreamed of them. And now one had offered herself to him.
He needed no reward from the djinn, not even his freedom,
if such a creature walked the earth and exalted him with
her smile.

She smiled and held out a hand to him. He was about to
fling himself down beside her, when the master storyteller
forestalled him and gestured toward the djinn.

They were smiling; and more than that. Even as Peter
watched, they chuckled, snickered, laughed, wept with
laughter, and rolled on their cushions until they could re-
cover breath; at which time they howled, roared, hooted
for glee and delight until, once again, they struggled for
breath. The assembled djinn shrieked with mirth so terrible
and so musical that the mortals flung themselves onto the
quivering sands just as it reached a pitch that shattered the
crystal which had bounded them for so long.

With a clash of such purity that surely the music of the
spheres could sound no more sweet, what had been a
prison fell in jagged shards that melted before they touched
man or djinni, melted into a dew that tenderly bathed
everyone in that place.

There was silence, and then a great, collective gasp of
wonder. Peter raised his head and looked out upon a race
transformed. Now the djinn were young and alive with
hope, flushed with life, and bright with humor.

The Emir approached Peter, still chuckling and wiping
tears from eyes that shone from a miraculously unlined
face.

"You—all of you have won your freedom," he declared. "Praise be to Allah, you have won ours as well."
Then he bent double, once again convulsed by laughter.

"That I should live to see this!" he cried between peals
of merriment. "Do you know how long we have lived, how
many tales we have listened to; and of those tales—how
many bad ones? Always, always, in the tales, some maiden
poses as a male and saves the day.

"But never did I dream that I should see the hackneyed
story come to life. More yet: I never would have believed
that I could have been startled and moved by it. And yet, I

have; and I am; and Allah bless you, Princess, and grant you strong sons and many years."

The teller of tales shrugged. "We have fallen on degenerate times," he murmured to Peter. "Even the djinn now aspire to be critics."

"Mortals, you have made us laugh, and laughter has given us new youth. Our debt to you is beyond payment, but we shall try to pay it."

"I want no payment," said the princess Karida's voice. *Not from you*, said her eyes.

"Go on, fool!" whispered the merchant to Peter, and gave him a shove.

His blood thrummed in his veins and urged him, that very minute, to seize her in his arms. Even when he had thought her a prince, he had not been insensible to the grace of her carriage, the lustrous depth of great, dark eyes, the smooth pallor of her skin. But Karida as a princess stole his breath away and returned it to him, made faster and hotter.

Speed were no proper way to woo such a lady. Slowly, he approached and sank down on one knee. She flushed, all maiden in that instant, and glanced away. Emboldened, Peter took her hand and kissed it, fingers and palm.

"If you permit, lady," he said in a voice that shook, "we will speak of this further, and in a decent quiet. I would court you by all the proprieties of your race and of mine."

The maiden nodded and withdrew her hand.

"Dawn," breathed the Emir. He breathed deeply of the wild, free air of the deep desert. The sky was pale and clear, but the first banners of dawn had begun to flutter at the horizon. "The first dawn in Allah knows how long that we may fly free with never a thought to return to our prison; which, in any case, no longer exists. We must return you to your friends."

Again came that sense of falling upward, to land softly on a huge dune. Below them lay their caravan, an orderly pattern of men, beasts, and baggage. Stationed about it were guards. One saw them and shouted a welcome.

They were about to hasten down the smooth face of the great dune when a second guard shouted a warning.

"There!" cried the Venetian. "See where my master's men come riding!"

Below them in the camp, men hastened to grasp weapons; the merchant prince hastened down the slope, Peter following, his lady's hand in his.

"Hold still!" called the Venetian, his voice carrying so far that even the approaching Mongols looked up at where he stood.

From the folds of his garments, he pulled out a piece of massy gold, stamped with the sigil of the Great Khan. He held it up, and, as the sun rose in a titanic blaze, its beams struck the gold, and light went up like a beacon of welcome to all who walked the sand that day.

About the Authors

STEPHEN R. DONALDSON is the author of the best-selling Thomas Covenant novels, for which he won the John W. Campbell Award. He is also author of the two "Mordant's Need" books *(The Mirror of Her Dreams* and *A Man Rides Through)* and of a fascinating story collection, *The Daughter of Regals.*

RU EMERSON didn't discover fantasy and science fiction until early in her twenties, when the novels of Anne McCaffrey and Andre Norton tempted her to try her luck at writing. Her first book, *The Princess of Flames,* was published in 1986, followed by her Nedao trilogy. Currently she's working on a retelling of the Cinderella legend.

M. J. ENGH, former librarian, is author of the novels *Arslan* and *Wheel of the Winds.* She has traveled in Italy, France, Yugoslavia, and Turkey, stalking the noble Roman lady Galla Placidia whose life story she is currently writing.

ESTHER M. FRIESNER is the witty and prolific author of the Twelve Kingdoms series, and the award-winning *Harlot's Ruse,* as well as the modern fantasy *New York by Knight* and its sequel *Elf Defense.* She is currently researching a novel set in both medieval Europe and in Araby.

MARVIN KAYE has written thirteen science-fantasy and mystery novels, including *The Incredible Umbrella; The Masters of Solitude* (with Parke Godwin); *Ghosts of Night and Morning;* and *A Cold Blue Light;* and has edited a number of fantasy anthologies, including *Masterpieces of Terror and the Supernatural.*

KATHARINE ELISKA KIMBRIEL has published two novels so far—*Fire Sanctuary* and *Fires of Nuala*—and several short stories. She resides in Texas with her husband and two cats.

TANITH LEE, winner of the World Fantasy Award, the August Derleth Award, and many others, is one of the most versatile writers working in the fields of fantasy and science fiction. Equally adept at writing fantasy or sf, short stories or novels, she is known for tales of werewolves, vampires, amorous robots, and the Arabian Nights–like stories of a melancholy Death and his attendant demons.

LARRY NIVEN is the multiple Hugo Award-winning author of *Ringworld* (which won both Nebula and Hugo Awards in 1971). Though he is known especially for his high-tech science fiction and for his collaborations with Jerry Pournelle—most recently *Footfall*, a Hugo nominee—he is also the author of some fine fantasies, among them *The Magic Goes Away*.

DIANA L. PAXSON is rapidly consolidating her reputation as a versatile, thoughtful, and magical writer of high fantasy, historical fantasy, and contemporary fantasy. One of her finest books to date is *The White Raven*, a retelling of the legend of Tristan and Iseult.

MELISSA SCOTT was the 1986 winner of the John Campbell Award for best new writer. Among her novels are *The Game Beyond*, *Five-Twelfths of Heaven*, and *The Kindly Ones*. Currently she is completing her dissertation on military history at Brandeis University.

CHARLES SHEFFIELD is a past president both of the Science Fiction Writers of America and of the American Astronautical Society. He has published six novels to date of fantasy and science fiction, including *The Web Between the Worlds*, *Between the Strokes of Night*, and *The Nimrod Hunt*.

SUSAN SHWARTZ is also editor of *Hecate's Cauldron*, *Habitats*, and *Moonsinger's Friends*. Her novels include the Byzantium's Heirs trilogy, and *Silk Roads and Shadows*. An Arthurian specialist who earned her Ph.D. at Harvard, she is currently working with Andre Norton on a novel of Han dynasty China.

NANCY SPRINGER is author of the Isle trilogy *(The White Hart, The Silver Swan,* and *The Sable Moon)*. Her novels *Chains of Gold* and *Wings of Flame* are set in a fantasy kingdom reminiscent of Persia. Recently she has turned to contemporary fantasy in *The Hex Witch of Seldom*.

JUDITH TARR is author of the Crawford Award-winning Hound and the Falcon trilogy, as well as of the Avaryan Rising trilogy and a handful of extremely well-received short stories. Her most recent novel is *A Wind in Cairo*.

HARRY TURTLEDOVE is the author of the four-book Videssos Cycle. He has written numerous short stories, especially for *Analog, Asimov's, F&SF,* and, yes, *Arabesques I* and *II*.

CHERRY WILDER's novels include *Cruel Designs* (currently available in Great Britain), *The Luck of Brin's Five,* and the Hylor Sequence. She wants to make it perfectly clear that, contrary to popular rumor, she was born in New Zealand, not Australia; there's a slight matter of 1,500 miles of open ocean separating the two.

GENE WOLFE is best known as the author of the Book of the New Sun. Winner of the Nebula, the World Fantasy Award, and the Campbell Award (to name only a few), he is also author of *Soldier of the Mist, The Isle of Doctor Death,* and *Free Live Free,* as well as almost a hundred short stories.